IN THE LINE OF REBELLION

L. A. TUCKER

Book Cover by Daqri Designs.

Illustrations by Waqa So.

First edition 2025.

ISBN 979-8-218-66306-3

❀ Formatted with Vellum

For those who change when they see they should.

CONTENT WARNING

This novel includes elements such as torture, serious injuries, death, and some graphic descriptions of injuries and blood.

PROLOGUE

In the distant future . . .

ALL COUNTRIES *previously residing on the planet known as Earth have established their own planet. Over the past three decades many of these planets were attacked or overthrown by an incredibly powerful dictator, Bentuari, who rules from afar. The planet of Gavriila is no exception. Bentuarian Loyalists enforce strict curfews and show no mercy to keep their fellow Gavriilans in line, aware that even a spark of dissidence can bring about a rebellion.*

CHAPTER 1
AVEDIDA CITY

AVEDIDA CITY'S POLICE CHIEF, Avyer Nikolai strode through the long dim jail corridor to the interrogation room. His footsteps rang out, echoing on the metal walls around him.

So much to do, so little time. Why couldn't Kuzmin handle this himself? He knows the ropes. He knows that I also don't like to be bothered when I'm about to eat.

While Avyer appreciated Kuzmin's enthusiasm routing out Gavriilan Spark rebels, having to mop up after his officers put a damper on his evening plans. Specifically, dinner.

As he neared the interrogation room, he eyed himself in the mirror-like walls, smoothing down a few untidy black hairs under his cap. *And that will need a trim soon.* He scrutinized his scruffy goatee.

Avyer paused at the interrogation room door. "Any information yet, Petrov?"

"I don't know, sir." Petrov stood at attention. "They've been in there for over an hour."

Avyer frowned. "Open the door."

A scream escaped as soon as the door opened. "I don't know what you're talking about!" A female voice pled.

Probably not. Avyer entered the soundproof interrogation room as Officer Kuzmin stepped back from the woman strapped to a chair in the center of the room. She doubled over in pain as she strained against the armrest straps chafing her wrists. Locks of gray hair obscured her face.

"You are wasting time," Kuzmin said.

"You're one to talk," Avyer scowled. He struck Kuzmin in the face with a resounding smack. "Did you try the stun cuffs?"

"No, sir." The officer nearly raised a hand to the red welt on his face then thought better of it.

"Bring me two, now," said Avyer.

Kuzmin straightened. "Apologies, sir."

"Just get the cuffs," Avyer snapped before whirling back to face the prisoner.

The woman slumped over. She wiped a smudge on her face, which smeared from her cheek to her chin. She shook hair out of her face. Her pupils constricted as she raised her head to peer past the glaring interrogation lamp. She blinked at the police chief. "I have nothing of value to offer." Her voice quaked. "I don't know anything about any rebels."

"I'll be the judge of that," replied Avyer. He shoved her against the interrogation chair backrest. "Where are you from?"

"North Avedida."

"And your vocation?"

"I sell vegetables."

"And your relation to Gavriilan Spark?"

"I don't know what you are talking about." She averted her gaze, sobbing. She peered around Avyer to the reflective glass behind him. "You have to believe me!"

"That's what they all say," Avyer muttered. She blubbered and blathered until Kuzmin returned with the stun cuffs.

Avyer took the cuff controller while Kuzmin clapped cuffs on her wrists and ankles. *Primitive, yet effective.*

"Sir?" Kuzmin stood at attention.

"You will try again," Avyer replied.

The door opened with a metallic click behind Officer Kuzmin.

Half of Officer Petrov's head and cap peeked from behind the door.

"Sir?" Petrov sounded hesitant.

"Now what?" Avyer's brow furrowed. He relinquished the controller to Kuzmin.

"There's been a call about a possible curfew violation."

"Where?"

"The Vadim Stables. Unconfirmed, but there was a rider out and they supposedly haven't returned to the city limits."

"Is there a reason *I* should be bothered with this? You could have sent out two officers." Avyer frowned.

Petrov's jaw clenched. "General Stepanov just arrived. He's in your office right now, and sir, the Vadim Stable master mentioned very specifically that he is a friend of General Stepanov."

Of course he is. Connections. So, if he happens to be right and this is a Spark rebel, it would be in my best interest to be the one heading this up because if I don't, Stepanov will fry me in our monthly meeting. Or worse.

"He was trying to be helpful, I believe." Petrov cleared his throat. He did not miss the irritation in Avyer's eyes.

Avyer sighed. "Send two men in a car to pick me up."

"Yes, sir." Relief washed over Petrov's face before he disappeared behind the door.

Avyer turned to the prisoner.

"I don't get any enjoyment out of this. The sooner you talk, the sooner we can get on with things."

"Sir?" Kuzmin was glued to where he stood.

"Carry on. Report to General Stepanov when you have concluded with the prisoner," Avyer said. "I'll look into the stable report. Convey my apologies to the General. Our meeting will be somewhat delayed."

CHAPTER 2
TWILIGHT

KARINA IVANOVNA WAS grateful that the moon's face had ducked behind the clouds, leaving the woods in semi-darkness. A full moon glaring down on them would have been as good as a streetlight.

She and her gray stallion, Gladrion, drifted like ghosts along the wood path. It was nearly curfew. If the local police spotted them she would be in trouble. *Thanks for nothing, Bentuari. And thanks for nothing, blasted Bentuarian Loyalists! If my generation weren't a bunch of cowards, I wouldn't be in this predicament.*

The end of the path could not come soon enough. *Hurry, hurry, hurry. I hope no one else is there now. If I'm reported, I'll be arrested. If I'm arrested, I'll end up in jail. I can't believe I lost track of time today.*

The moon reemerged from the clouds, bathing the stable in sharp white light. Gladrion clopped into the dark stable yard, passing many closed wooden stalls. Karina's eyes darted all around them. *Good, no one is here now.*

She dismounted and draped the reins over a hitching post. She replaced the bridle with a halter and lead, tying him to a post. As she removed the saddle the horse stood still, occasionally twitching his silky tail.

Karina turned on the barn lights. *No one can say I missed curfew.*

She removed dirty straw from his stall, replacing it with fresh straw. She hefted a fresh bucket of food onto the hook and lugged in a sloshing bucket of water.

She pulled her hair tie from her ponytail, freeing a cascade of golden-brown hair. She smoothed a few rogue hairs on the top of her head before taming the long locks back into a ponytail.

The next step was to groom him. She popped plastic boots off his hooves and set them aside to clean them later. She pulled a low block beside her horse. She stepped up on it to work with the dandy brush. That finished, she returned the block outside, pulling her horse out of his stall into brighter light to survey her work.

"You look good, handsome."

She rubbed his nose and rested her forehead on his.

Footsteps thumped behind her, then a rough hand gripped her shoulder. "A bit late, aren't we?"

"I made curfew," Karina spat and shrugged away from the hand. Gladrion snorted nervously.

"Who's to say ya did? All I'd have to say is I saw ya outside city limits at twenty oh one. Yur word against mine. I can find someone to agree with me."

The hand wrenched her around. Her eyes landed on an emaciated, unshaven man. Probably ten years older than Karina's twenty-four. "That leaves ya in my debt, unless ya wanna be turned in."

"I'm not rich." Karina shrank back. Her face twisted in disgust as waves of unwashed body odor wafted from him.

"Oh, it's not money I want."

Karina swallowed. *What Uncle Misha taught me. Move!*

She twisted out of his grip, wrenching his arm the wrong way. Her knee found his groin, and as he doubled over in pain, she grabbed his hair to smash his head against the mounting block. Gladrion pranced and whinnied. He added a couple of kicks for good measure.

Yes! Exercise and drills doing their work. Karina's heart thundered in her chest. *Breathe.* Her head was spinning but she broke into a proud grin. It was the first in a long time she had to put her mixed Systema training into practice.

As she calmed Gladrion and hurried him into his stall, voices of more men echoed throughout the stable. Footsteps pounded. The voices yelled one word, but her panicking brain did not associate meaning with the syllables. She closed the stall.

Run! If I can get out of here and into a store, I'll be fine.

She had reached the dim, square courtyard before a man came out of nowhere to tackle her to the ground. He groped for her hands to restrain them behind her back.

Karina nearly fell flat on her face, but Uncle Misha's voice rang in her head. *Up!* She shoved herself back up with her hands. The man had a loose hold on her leg. Karina kicked him in the ear with her free leg. *Free! Twist his arm. Knee to the groin. Head against pavement. Free!*

Not so free.

Karina took stock of her situation. She identified two open doorways covered by two men—no, three. The third was a tall figure in the doorway that would have been her exit. He stood in the shadows behind the second man.

"I haven't done anything wrong!" Karina glared at each man in turn.

"You don't call assaulting police officers wrong?" The tall one's deep voice scoffed. She imagined him peering down a long, aristocratic nose.

Karina's eyes widened. "I didn't know."

"Doesn't matter. You started the show. You can finish it," he replied, his speech in deliberate cadence. He then ordered the two: "Make it interesting. I'd like to at least be entertained by this waste of time."

The shorter man attacked first. Karina fended off both men, never letting them get too close.

Neither of them understood her hybrid fighting style, but both were larger than she was, so she could not simply twist them around like the first two.

Her breath began to come in short gasps. *One down.* Her right leg threatened to cramp. *Relax.* She winced at a particularly painful blow she caught with her elbow. *Two.* As she backed away from the men groaning on the pavement, she considered running again.

The tall one stepped forward.

Of course. He was counting on them to wear me down.

"I enjoyed watching, but I'll take a turn."

As he stepped forward Karina took up a defensive stance. She blocked his first blow. *A basic punch.* Feeling bolder, Karina attacked. He casually deflected her first blow and his knuckle grazed her cheek.

He knows Systema. Karina's jaw dropped as she drew a sharp breath. *I'm dead.*

He matched Karina's every move and wore her down, slowly but surely. It ended when their shins met. He did not flinch at the painful blow while Karina gasped in pain and fell against the stable wall. He clutched her wrists in a vise-like grip, spread-eagling her against the wall.

Karina strained against him. She threw her body weight down. She jerked to the side. She scraped her wrists raw against the bricks. He towered over her and leaned in. At this distance Karina saw that he did indeed have a long, aristocratic nose. A police badge glinted on his shoulder.

"Didn't . . . do . . . anything . . . wrong . . ." Her eyes widened with fear as they met a pair of angry, deep-set eyes. *Can't he see that?*

"You have an unusual definition of wrong. It's a crime to attack police officers." He raised an eyebrow. "We shouted out 'Police!' at least five times. Are you deaf or just stupid?"

"Didn't—" Karina didn't have enough breath to finish the thought.

"Give me one very good reason to believe you." He took a step closer.

One of his hands released her left arm and grasped her throat. Karina choked in terror. He had swept one of her feet to the side, leaving her unbalanced and vulnerable.

"I was defending myself!" She coughed and gestured wildly with her left hand. "Check the cameras!"

An officer ran up to Chief Avyer Nikolai.

"We have another man in custody," the officer huffed.

"Hm. Interesting. We'll check the security footage."

Avyer released her throat and wrist, letting his hand drop to his stun gun. Karina weakly leaned against the wall, massaging her throat.

"Meanwhile . . ." he said casually as he shot her with the gun.

Karina slumped to the ground.

"I really must see what they're teaching the men these days." He looked in disdain at the two men who had fought Karina. One cowered on the ground and the other painfully stood up. He took out a radio. "Base, this is Nikolai. Bring a wagon around. Several men down and two prisoners to investigate."

He eyed Karina curiously before returning to his own cruiser.

ПОЛИЦИЯ

CHAPTER 3
AVEDIDA JAIL

EVERYTHING BLURRED white as Karina's eyes fluttered open. *Everything is bright. Hard. Uncomfortable.* Every bone in her body had been chilled by a freezing slab of metal serving as a bed. She sat up stiffly. She ran a dry tongue over equally dry lips. She jammed her frozen fingers into her pockets seeking warmth. As her fingers met with cloth, she sat up straighter. *No ID. No phone.* Nothing was left to her.

She blinked as she gazed around the bare white cell: barely three paces wide, no windows, and a metal mesh door. No way to escape. She leaned against the wall and shivered.

A guard came in nearly as soon as she had awakened. He clapped stun cuffs on her wrists and escorted her to an interrogation room, leaving her to stand in the center. Karina stood stock-still under a blinding white light.

"All yours, Kuzmin." The guard nodded before leaving Karina alone in the room.

"What were you doing out past curfew?" A male voice rang from a speaker, echoing in the cell.

Karina started and turned to look around her. The only gaze that met hers was her own, in a reflective glass wall. She stared at herself boldly. *Show no fear.*

"I made curfew. I was out on a ride."

Electricity surged through the cuffs. She felt all the muscles in her back, arms, and legs contract painfully, paralyzing her. Karina screamed as she fell to the floor.

"Answer the question honestly." There was a flicker of annoyance in the voice.

Karina's weak arms pushed her shaking body to stand again. She glared at herself in the mirror.

"I did answer you honestly—"

Round after round of electroshocks wracked every fiber of her body until she could barely stand.

"Well?" The voice paused, as did the electroshocks. "What do you know about the Gavriilan Spark Revolution?"

Her ears rang and her head was spinning as she swayed to her feet.

"I'm telling the truth," she said weakly. "I was out on a ride. That's all."

"Wrong answer."

More electricity coursed through the cuffs. Karina was too exhausted to scream. When her muscles tightened, she collapsed to the floor. She raised her head and stretched out an arm, but she had no strength left. She fell back down, smacking her cheek on the icy concrete floor.

The door swung open. Karina's eyelids were closing of their own volition and everything began to blur. When she squinted she barely made out a pair of black boots belonging to the person who had walked in.

"That's enough, Kuzmin," Avyer snapped. "Just because I authorized stun cuffs earlier does not mean you should use them in every interrogation."

He crouched beside Karina. Karina's unfocused eyes melded Avyer and the metallic walls into a mass of black and gray.

"Karina Ivanovna." Avyer cocked his head as he looked at her. "They say it's the quiet ones who are the most dangerous. Would you consider that an accurate statement?"

Silence.

"What? Afraid of me?"

"Kuzmin almost killed her," said a voice behind Avyer. A man in a doctor's coat came in and bent over Karina.

"Remedy that, then." Avyer stood up.

An officer brought in a chair. The doctor sat her up to check her pulse and heart rate. "I think she'll be fine," he pronounced, "but that was too much. Let her drink something, then sleep it off."

The two men, the cold metal walls and the cold concrete floor swam in Karina's head and turned into a huge black blur. Something hard met her parched lips. Hands tilted her head back, forcing a gulp of water down her throat.

So tired . . .

Everything went dark.

CHAPTER 4
INNOCENT

AS AVYER NIKOLAI observed the doctor tending Karina, his imperious gaze faltered for a fraction of a second. A security guard entered and broke his musing.

"We finished going through all security recordings," he stated. "She didn't arrive late. She just made curfew, and it would appear that the other man in custody did attempt to assault her."

"Who was he?" asked Avyer sharply.

"Just another citizen."

"You heard that, Kuzmin?" Avyer raised his voice.

"Yes, sir." Kuzmin's voice sounded meek over the speaker.

"Deal with the assailant. Harshly," Avyer told the security guard. "Thank the Vadim Stable master for me."

"And the girl?" The doctor pointed at Karina slumped over in the chair.

"Take her to the infirmary and release her when she wakes up," said Avyer, turning to leave.

The doctor cleared his throat. "Sir, there's a . . . em . . . a slight problem."

"Which is?" Avyer did not turn around.

"The infirmary is full. There's a virus going around a couple of cell blocks and we're trying to contain the spread. The last bed was just taken."

Avyer clenched his fists, closing his eyes. *Yet another irritation to deal with . . . or an opportunity for answers to a few questions?*

He opened his eyes before he turned to address the doctor. "Very well, then. I will take her to my quarters until she wakes up."

"As you wish."

Avyer signaled for a smirking guard to pick up Karina and follow Avyer.

Police chiefs were required to live on the base, as were all unmarried officers. Avyer was no exception. The interrogation room as well as the jail proper were a few hallways and an elevator away from Avyer's personal quarters.

The guard gawked at sumptuous oil paintings of horses and wolfhounds in gilded frames. They were spread out every few meters or so on the brown walls of Avyer's quarters. In his distraction he stubbed his toe on an armchair leg and nearly tripped on a rug. He reached a gigantic four-poster bed against the center wall, leaving Karina on the bed.

CHAPTER 5
AWAKE

KARINA'S EYELIDS FLUTTERED OPEN. *The light is softer here . . .*

A book snapped shut loudly.

"How are you feeling?" Avyer's voice was calm, controlled.

Karina's head jerked to the left, and her wide gray eyes met his. *Dark brown eyes. At least he doesn't look angry now . . .*

He sat back casually in a red armchair as though he were in the habit of entertaining prisoners in a soft bed every day. He slid the book onto the table beside him.

Her lips parted slightly. "Does it matter?"

"If I say it does." He stood and stretched. "It's been a long night. You look unwell."

"I feel the same as before."

"Before what?"

"Before I passed out."

He put his hands behind his back as he walked to the bed. "You're talented. I'm surprised you never joined the police. With a little training, you could rival even me. It's rare to find a plebeian so gifted, yet unheard of."

"You must not know many plebeians, then." The words came out before Karina could think them over.

Avyer laughed. "Why do you say that?" His eyes crinkled in amusement.

"There are many talented but ordinary people on this world," she said, choosing her words more carefully.

"Perhaps." He sounded unconvinced. "Sit up. What's the story?"

"There's no story," Karina said through her teeth as she sat. "Many years of mixed martial arts and minding my own business."

"Healthy. And what do you do other than mind your own business?"

"Karina Ivanovna. School teacher." She craned her neck to look at him. "And you?"

"Avyer Nikolai. Avedida Police Chief." Karina paled. "Surprise."

She lay back down. Black ringed the edges of her vision, threatening to overwhelm her again.

"Can I ring for anything?" he asked.

"Something to drink."

"Shot of something? Vodka?"

"Coffee."

"Very well." He pushed a button on a table. "Bring up a coffee."

When the coffee arrived, Karina sat up and swung her legs over the side of the bed. Avyer stepped in front of her.

"Stay there. I trust you won't spill a drop on my bed."

His bed? She grasped the mug with white knuckles as she sipped the coffee. A little color returned to her face. Between sips she glanced at Avyer but averted her eyes to the coffee cup when their eyes met.

"What do you want?" she finally asked.

"Pretty much everything."

"And do you get pretty much everything?" *Did I just ask that?*

"Pretty much." He smirked as her cheeks flushed. "What do you think of that?"

"That sounds like a pretty boring way to spend your life."

"Where did you learn Systema?" Avyer returned to his chair and sat. He toyed with a ring on his left hand. "No one uses that fighting style these days."

"You do."

"I was fortunate: my instructor was a professional. You?"

"My uncle was a professional."

"Was?"

"He's been gone a long time now." Karina gulped down the rest of the coffee.

"Interesting," said Avyer. "I have more questions, but I don't think you are ready for them, and I need sleep. Finish the coffee and go."

"I can go?" Karina echoed.

"Don't sound so disappointed. The security cameras cleared you."

Karina slid from the bed to the floor. Her wobbly legs supported her weight. She left the coffee cup on the nightstand. "Good night."

Avyer silently watched her leave.

———

Karina found her parents and her sister Sofia awake and waiting for her at home. The three were huddled on the couch when she opened the front door.

Her father, Ivan, leapt to his feet and spluttered in fury. "Where the blazes have you been? We've been worried sick." If he had been any angrier his thick gray eyebrows and mustache would have burst into flame.

"I was out riding and lost track of time."

"It's after midnight, young lady! Have you been riding all this time?"

"No."

"Then what?" Her mother, Viktoriya, stood. "*What* were you doing?" She chewed her lower lip.

"Do we have to do this now?" Karina rubbed her forehead. "I had a terrible night. Can't we talk about this tomorrow?"

"Not while you're still living in my house!" Ivan thundered. "What happened?"

Karina scrubbed her face in frustration. "I barely made curfew. I was putting Gladrion away and a guy came up and threatened me. Said he was going to turn me in for breaking curfew, which I hadn't. Then, he made it clear that he was going to rape me, so I did what Uncle Misha always said I should do. All good there. Then I heard a ton of people running into the stable and I thought it would be a good time to run. But it wasn't. Because it was the police. They knocked me out and jailed me until they saw I hadn't broken curfew."

"You *what*?" Her mother's voice reverberated off the walls despite the fact that the house was small, and the thin walls were lined with rugs.

"I was attacked at the stable, then the police attacked me. I was in jail," Karina repeated. "That's why I'm late."

"Was that *all* that happened?" Her mother's voice rose several pitches.

"All that's worth mentioning."

"Really?" Viktoriya shook Karina's shoulder. "*What* were you thinking?"

"Yes, that's all." Karina frowned and shrugged off her mother's hand.

"They could have killed you!" Ivan said. "What were you thinking?"

"I'm sorry, *ok*! I lost track of time. It's not like I did it on purpose. A lot of things could have happened, but they didn't. I'm ok." Karina looked her mother in the eye. "I'm tired and wanna sleep. I didn't do anything wrong, and if that guy hadn't attacked me none of this would have happened."

"None of this would have happened if you'd been more careful," Viktoriya snapped.

"Do you think I'm happy about this? They were treating me like I was with those Spark people, not like a victim," Karina snarled back.

Karina pushed past Sofia and bounded up the stairs two at a time. She locked her bedroom door behind her. Not that the locked door made her feel much better. *If anyone came after me, they'd snap it in half like a matchstick.*

CHAPTER 6
THE INTERVIEW

"GOOD MORNING." Sofia leapt from the sofa with teenage exuberance when Karina came down the stairs. "Or afternoon or whatever," she added.

"Yeah," said Karina.

"Let's go out and have some fun," said Sofia.

"I don't know . . ."

"C'mon, it's Saturday! I'm bored. Get looking nice, and let's go!"

"Fine." Karina conceded.

Avedida had little to offer in the way of entertainment. There was a mall, and when people went there, they went out as stylishly as they could.

Within thirty minutes Karina was dressed and made up. Sofia came in as she was pulling black boots over her pants.

"Hey, gorgeous!" she teased. "Looking nice! That purple tunic shirt thingy looks amazing. Ready to go?"

"Just about," said Karina as she pulled back her hair with a clip. She rummaged through her dresser. "Oh, shoot." Her face fell.

Sofia's smile faded. "What?"

"My ID." She clasped a necklace.

"What about it?" asked Sofia.

"I left it at the police station," she groaned. "Knowing my luck, today will be the day they ask for ID somewhere. I've got to go get it. I don't want to end up in jail again. And I'm all fixed up, too." She let her head fall with a bang on the dresser top and groaned again.

"So?"

"Kark! Do you know how the guards were looking at me? And that was when I had been beaten up and tortured. Don't tell mom that," she said. "I'm in for an earful later."

"Oooh. Not a word." Sofia put a finger to her lips. "Soooo now what?"

Karina massaged her forehead as she sat on her bed. "Let's get it over with and get my ID."

Sofia nodded. "I'll get the clunker warmed up." She referred to their mini cruiser.

It was a silent drive to the police station. *I really hope the chief is not in today. I don't want to see him.* Karina shivered as she stared out the window, listening to the cruiser creak and squeak as Sofia maneuvered it along the pothole-filled roads to the station. *How can you torture someone one minute, then have them in your bed sipping coffee the next?*

The trip felt shorter than the fifteen minutes it took to get from their house on the outskirts of town to the police station.

"Do you want to go in alone?" Sofia asked as she pulled into a parking space.

"Um, yeah." Karina pushed the button to open the cruiser door.

"Are you sure? I don't mind," said Sofia.

"No. I'm good."

"I'm coming in. Moral support." Sofia squeezed her older sister's hand, turning off her own gravity buckle.

The transition from a sunny day to the gray wall of the boxy building was a stark contrast. The walls closed in around them as they approached the desk sergeant.

"Excuse me." Karina used a polite but strong tone.

"Yes?" A gray-haired officer pushed his spectacles up his nose. "What's your business?" He looked down at them from the elevated desk.

"I left my ID here last night," said Karina.

"Wouldn't know a thing about it." The desk sergeant leaned back. "You'd have to talk to one of them officers that was on duty last night. Not me."

Karina swallowed nervously. "I don't know any names." The next words stuck in her throat. She gave Sofia a side glance. "The police chief was involved in my case."

"You're in luck then: he's in."

No! Karina bit the tip of her tongue but kept a pleasant look on her face. "Could you please ask him? I need it."

"Yes. Wait here." He stood and disappeared behind a door behind his desk. They heard another door open and close.

Karina tried to not fidget and sat down. Sofia gawked at the reception area, standing beside her. Karina critically eyed the yellow paint peeling from the wall.

"So weird," Sofia said. "It smells clean and the desk looks new."

Karina shrugged. "Priorities."

"So, what do you think they'll do?" asked Sofia.

"I don't know." Karina grimaced.

A door slid open and the desk sergeant reappeared. "He'll be down directly. Wait."

A lump grew in Karina's throat. She fingered her necklace and looked through the entrance doors to their cruiser.

Avyer Nikolai strode through a door to their right. Sofia ogled him in admiration. Karina's eyes roved his immaculate black and blue uniform. *Looks like the same one he wore last night.*

"You look smaller in daylight." He looked hard at Karina.

"You look the same," she replied, meeting his gaze. Her face flushed with heat but Karina refused to look away first. *Is that a flicker of amusement in his eyes?*

"You brought reinforcements." He averted his gaze to glance at Sofia. "Not that you need them. You did pretty well last night. Left me a bright purple souvenir." He rubbed his left arm.

"I need my ID," Karina told him. "Could you please return it to me?"

"It would be much more fun to fight for it." A ghost of a smile flitted across his face.

"I've got plans for today," said Karina.

"Very well," said Avyer, "but I still think it would be more fun my way. Follow me."

Sofia mouthed to Karina. *What should I do now?*

Stay there, Karina mouthed back.

Karina vaguely remembered the layout of the building. She followed him to a small brown lift that took them to the second floor. They passed his bedroom door on the left. Avyer led her to a long brown hall to the right, punching in a code to open the door. It slid aside.

"Have a seat." He gestured to the chair in front of his desk. He eased into a padded leather chair behind the desk.

Karina accepted, sitting up straight in the chair. She crossed her legs and kept her head up, trying to look relaxed as Avyer stared at her. His eyes flickered down from her eyes and lingered on her face before he sat back, lacing his fingers. He glanced at a data sheet on the desk, then back at her.

"Have you considered working for the police?" he asked.

Karina shook her head.

"You should. Consider this an interview," he said. "Tell me about yourself."

"I already have a good job." A pit formed in her stomach.

"That doesn't matter to the government. Tell me about yourself."

"My name is Karina Annushka Ivanovna. I'm twenty-four years old." She pressed her tongue against the inside of her top teeth.

"You look eighteen."

Karina trudged on. "I studied modern and ancient art at the academy. That isn't very lucrative these days, so I teach high school art during the school year, and manage HR for the school and a restaurant."

"Where does Systema fit in there?"

Karina's smile tightened. "What can I say? It's a dangerous world we're living in."

Avyer contemplated her incredulously. "You're too good." He shook his head. "You've never competed and no one knows about you. There's a story behind that."

"I told you last night: there's no story there. I just want to live in peace. I don't want a job like yours." She mirrored Avyer's posture and laced her fingers. "My uncle taught me to fight to take care of myself like I did last night."

Avyer flipped a data sheet over. "Family?"

Waves of nausea washed over Karina. *He's likely reading that right now.* "Father. Mother. My sister's in the lobby."

"Very little resemblance. Tall and blond. Who's older?"

"I am."

"Oldest and smallest. Does she know Systema, too?"

"No. She's useless in a fight."

"What's so special about you that your uncle taught you?"

"She wasn't interested, and my uncle knew that size doesn't matter in a fight. It's what you do with what you have that matters." She met his dark eyes when he looked up from the data sheets. *I should not have said that. Why do I keep saying these things?*

"Hmm." Avyer crossed his arms and sat back. "You hire and fire people as HR. What happens next in this interview?"

"This is your interview," she answered slowly. "If you like what you see, I'll hear back from you. If you don't, then we're done here today."

Once the interview was over, Avyer escorted her back to the lobby.

"Here." He fished her wallet and phone from his pocket and placed them in Karina's hands.

"Thank you." Karina swallowed.

As soon as they had walked outside, Sofia asked worriedly, "Is everything ok?"

"No, it's not," said Karina. "I have testing tomorrow afternoon."

"What? What in the world for?"

"Get in the cruiser first."

When the cruiser doors closed Karina answered her sister's question. "Police training. Chief Nikolai thinks I have great promise as a Bentuarian Loyalist."

"But," Sofia sputtered, searching for the right words as she turned on the gravity buckles. "You've got three jobs. How are you supposed to take on a police job and do what you're doing now? They can't do this to you."

"Yes, they can," Karina said. "And I'll do what they want, unless I want trouble for the family. Remember what happened to Caesar when he didn't cooperate?"

"Caesar? Caesar who?" Sofia frowned.

"Exactly. Come on! You know that chef with an amazing restaurant?"

"I'm drawing a blank."

"We went there once. His cooking was so popular that the governor sent for him to work as his personal chef. When Caesar politely declined, the governor executed him and his family."

"Oh." Sofia gaped in horror. "Do you really think the Chief would do that to us? He looks so nice."

"Seriously? If he's going to threaten me for defending myself, I'd hate to think what he'd do if I misbehaved."

Sofia's gaze was pensive. "Do you think it's always going to be like this?" she asked.

"What do you mean?"

"You know. Us. Bentuari."

Karina sighed as she leaned against her headrest. "I don't know. Why?"

"There are rumors, you know."

"We shouldn't talk about that." Karina's lips pressed in a thin line. "Not here."

"Some people are saying that he's dead, you know."

"Dead or not, here we are. Let's get out of here. I'm feeling creeped out in this parking lot."

CHAPTER 7

SUNDAY

SUNDAY WAS JUST another day for most people on Gavriila, but Karina's family carefully, quietly attended a small church in Avedida. Karina's heart and soul were zealous in prayer, but she heard next to nothing of the message. This morning's services ran late, cutting into what little time Karina had before the testing.

Karina bought a sandwich and water at a corner store to eat and drink as she followed the cracked paved road to the high school where she worked. *Had been working.*

Memories flooded her mind as she approached the brown-stained block walls. She had spent many hours here encouraging kids to be creative in a world that did not appreciate creativity.

She pulled a key card out of her dress pocket, inserting it into the huge lock of the art department door. The lock groaned and beeped. The creak of the heavy metal door sliding open reverberated off the walls of the room. There was not much inside to dampen the noise: the arts were a useless skill set, so an art department was one large open room with easels in rows. Karina left the door open.

She walked to her desk in the corner of the room to place a handwritten letter for the school director between two small paint bottles. She left the jumble of paint supplies littering her desk. She only wanted her paintings.

Karina carried the first and largest painting to the door, propping it against the doorframe. When she returned to her desk she did not hear anything, but she felt someone there. Her hands balled into fists low at her side. As she turned, she mentally prepared for a fight.

A tall figure was framed by the doorway.

"I'll be over later," she said icily. "I have things to take care of." *Has he been following me all day? I hope not. I was a sight during church.*

"I see." Avyer walked over to her. "Are these yours?" He admired the paintings, pausing to look at a bay horse head on Karina's desk. His eyes shifted to a wolfhound next to it, then the massive full-body painting of Gladrion still leaning in the corner.

"Yes." Karina bit her lip.

"Not bad. Raw realism here: your work is accurate but I enjoy the obvious traces of brushstrokes. Acrylic." He noted the supplies on her desk.

"Yes. It's more forgiving than oil."

"If you ever need money, I could take some of these off your hands."

"I'll keep it in mind. Did you need something?"

"It's standard procedure to check in on candidates." He eyed her.

Karina crossed her arms.

"I'm not going to run away if that's what you're worried about. You said to come in at four, right?"

"Yes."

"You're not in uniform," she said. "Can this wait until four? I have a lot of things to leave in order."

Now that she mentioned his clothing, she dared to take a better, longer look at him. He was less imposing in normal clothing. It suited his straight, solid figure. Her artist's eye lingered on his face. His facial features were distinct: long nose, well-defined cheekbones and a strong jaw with just enough curve that it wasn't harsh. That would have been tricky for her to capture with paint. The face was completed with imperious eyebrows and dark brown eyes. In daylight they were not quite as dark. All that was framed with short, thick black hair. Hair was always easy to paint. She loved a good head of hair. The facial hair, not so much. That would have been more difficult to paint.

He was aware that he now had her undivided attention. "Does my being here bother you that much?"

"Off the books?"

"Yes."

"I'd rather keep to the schedule and see you at four."

His eyes narrowed. "See you at four."

"Ok." Karina nodded and resumed stacking up paintings. Avyer made a show of exiting the building but stepped to the side of the door. He could hear her muttering to herself.

"Arrogant idiot! I bet he doesn't know the difference between acrylic and . . ."

Smart girl. She knows she's not coming back from this. If she behaves herself, she'll be an excellent addition. If not . . . well, that will be one less threat. Avyer left.

Karina had barely enough time to taxi the paintings home, change, and drive to the police headquarters.

She arrived in time for the testing, smartly dressed and ready. She looked herself over in the glass door. She straightened the dark tunic shirt over her fitted pants, dusted her boots, and straightened her already slick and perfectly set ponytail several times.

When they called her back she sped through the written, oral, and psychological tests. The last part was uncomfortable.

"Wide hips." One doctor had the habit of reading as he made notes in his datapad. "Better suited for babies than fighting."

Karina glared at him.

Combat testing was last. A guard led her to an immense training room. A large white circle painted in the center of the room took up more than half the area. Karina noted huge, closed cabinets lining the walls. *Likely for weapons.*

The guard pointed to the inside of the circle. Karina stepped into it. *I hope today's fight is fair.*

Karina jumped and drew a sharp breath when a voice boomed through loudspeakers: "Hands only, no weapons! Stay in the ring. Do not step outside of the circle."

A slight, masked figure stepped into the ring. The mask obscured all their facial feature except for the eyes. *Judging from their build, it's girl.*

"Don't hold back," the voice instructed, "and begin!"

Karina sent her opponent flying out of the circle within a minute.

"Sorry." Karina winced as they tumbled into a cabinet. Her opponent hobbled away.

"Next!" the voice rang out. *Are we reenacting the other night?*

She faced masked opponent after masked opponent. By the fifth one, she was winded, sweaty, and bruised. *How long have I been fighting? I'm going to be sore in the morning.*

The fifth opponent was lean and tall. *I know those eyes. Avyer—Chief Nikolai—again. This time I'll leave him hurting.* Karina's eyes narrowed as he stepped into the ring.

They circled each other to analyze the other's movements. When Karina hesitated for a split second he attacked swiftly, viciously. Karina barely blocked his kick with her elbow and he took advantage of her arm and threw her to the floor on her back. She gasped for breath. *That was very Systema of him. Why won't he leave me alone?*

She would not leave him an opening, even if she could not breathe. As he leaned down for a finishing blow, her foot connected with his nose. CRACK! His eyes watered. She whirled around out of his reach and leapt to her feet. She dodged his attempts to grab her arms and legs. What she could not dodge, she blocked.

If he grabs me, it's over. He's too strong. Her throat felt tight as she imagined his hand on her neck again. *No. I'm not letting that happen.* Sweat dripped in her eyes. Her lungs were running out of air. Her muscles burned and her hands hurt, but she kept going.

Her limbs shook and her sweaty palms slipped when she tried to grab him. He had shown no moment of weakness despite her strategic attacks. *I can't beat him. He's too good, and they wore me down again.* No one on the outside would have blamed her for losing.

He herded her toward the edge of the circle, covering all sides at once. Karina cast about for a non-existent opening. *There's no way out . . . but I owe it to myself to beat him. There's always a way, high or low.* That was it.

She let him goad her toward the outer white line. When they were close, she dropped to her hands, swinging her body around to bear her full weight against the inside of his knee. His leg gave way. Karina leapt to her feet and swept a leg behind his other leg to topple him completely. *Finally! Got him.* As she relished a second of triumph he caught her arm. She fell with him, her legs flung across his body. *No!*

"Done!" boomed the voice.

Karina slid her legs to the floor as she peered at the white line. His larger body was out of bounds more than hers.

"We. Are. Finished." She looked him squarely in the eye.

His brown eyes softened and crinkled slightly around the edges. He released her arm.

"Not too shabby." Avyer removed the mask and stood up. The smile in his eyes did not reach his mouth. Blood dripped from his nose down to his upper lip, which he carelessly wiped away with the mask. He offered her a hand. "Get a grip on your emotions and you'll be good."

Karina bit back a retort as he pulled her to her feet. *What do you mean by not too shabby? It was excellent.*

"Now what?"

"See you bright and early tomorrow. Have a good afternoon." He left as though a little girl hadn't just broken his nose.

"Of all the nerve," Karina muttered as she left the police head-quarters. She drove to the Vadim Stable, to Gladrion. She did not want to face her family, not yet. She had done too well in the testing.

Horses were a luxury few commoners could afford. Karina was one of those few.

A few years ago, her family had given her an emaciated foal as a present. The previous owners thought that the foal was dying but Karina nursed him back to health. Now she loaned the robust stallion to sire foals with richer folks' mares. That was a major source of income, and the only reason she could afford him.

Gladrion nickered as she approached. She brushed him until he shone, grooming his mane and tail to a flat, glossy sheet.

"I don't like how he looked at me." Gladrion was a good listener, nodding or snorting in all the right places. "He makes me feel . . . weird. I just . . ." She twisted a strand of mane around her finger. "I have a bad feeling about this."

CHAPTER 8
INTEGRATION

BAM! BAM! BAM! Karina sat bolt upright in her bed. The pounding of her heart echoed the pounding on the front door. Her father's voice resonated up to her bedroom. She dressed quickly. The soft glow of the wall clock said it was just past five a.m.

She cracked the door open and cocked her head to listen.

"We're here to pick up Cadet Karina Ivanovna." A calm, deep voice stood out in contrast to Ivan's agitated voice. *Avyer.*

Karina ducked back inside to stash clothing and personal items in a backpack. She slung it over her shoulder. *He wasn't joking when he said he'd see me early. Why did he come personally?*

"She's not here," Ivan repeated as Karina bounded down the stairs.

The sun barely raised its sleepy head to light up their side of the planet at this hour. The house lights dimly illuminated the scene: Ivan blocked two police officers and Chief Avyer Nikolai from the staircase. Ivan looked guilty and Viktoriya looked frightened. Sofia huddled in her pajamas on the couch, frozen in fear.

Karina pushed past her parents. Karina seemed to shrink as she stood in the middle of the five people. Her eyes searched for Avyer's. "I'm ready."

"You see." Avyer ignored her and gestured grandly toward Ivan. "There's no reason to get worked up over things."

"Sir?" One of the guards tensed up.

Avyer's eyes raked over Karina before meeting her gaze. She maintained eye contact.

"We got what we came for. No need to disturb these good people."

Uncharacteristically generous for a Loyalist. That is, unless he is going to send back an execution squad later. Stop thinking about that. She followed Avyer and the two guards.

Karina did not turn around to look at her family. They had shown enough weakness by showing how much they cared for her. *What was Papa doing? Does he want to die? Mama would be useless without him. Think!*

Pale light caressed everything outside, including a police cruiser waiting outside their house. Cool morning air blasted Karina as they walked. She shivered despite wearing a jacket.

A guard opened the cruiser's back door and motioned for her to climb in. Avyer took up a seat across from her. He asked no questions and offered no explanation as to his presence.

They drove to the police station, to the back where no civilians ever visited. They passed many gray one-story buildings until they reached two blocky u-shaped barracks wings forming a square. A half-dead garden filled the open square in the middle of the barracks.

"Home," Avyer announced when the cruiser stopped. "Gregor will show you where to go." He pointed at the guard exiting the front passenger seat. The cruiser left Karina and Gregor.

Karina followed Gregor inside the barracks. "Barracks are segregated. Women in the back. Men in the front. Don't even think about breaking the rule." He led her inside her wing, apparently allowed to break that rule.

Karina blinked in the blinding bright light. The floral scent of disinfectant mingled with fresh paint burned her nostrils.

"Hi." A pale young girl sitting at the reception desk greeted them.

Karina double took when their eyes met. She was as pale as Karina, with the exact same shade of brown hair and same round face. When the girl looked up from her desk, Karina's gray eyes met striking amber eyes. The golden hue framed with honey brown would have been incredible to paint.

"Karina, Sasha," said Gregor. "Sasha, Karina. Get her a room and get her some clothes."

Sasha heaved an exaggerated sigh. "Don't bother me. You know I'm on duty." Her intonation was odd, lilted. "What I'd like to know is how am I supposed to be on duty and help her at the same moment."

"Not my problem." Gregor turned his back on her, leaving.

Sasha stood up, nearly reaching Karina's height. "I don't have time for this. You can live with me. Just be quiet and respectful." She led Karina down the hall. "As you can see, there's many rooms on either side. This is ours."

Fourth door on the left. Karina felt slightly claustrophobic as they stepped into a white, windowless room with bare walls.

Sasha languidly motioned to one of six metal bunk beds in the room lined up against the three walls, two to a wall. "You're on top." She pointed at the bunk. "Don't move around too much. It bothers me. Leave your stuff on your bed. No one will bother it. Or chuck it in a trunk." She pointed at a chest of drawers at the end of their bed. "Follow me." Karina tossed her backpack up on the bunk before hustling behind Sasha.

"While on duty, you'll be wearing a uniform," Sasha explained. "So. We are going for you to get yours. Each of us gets three pair. Try them on and be sure about if it fits. What you get is what you have."

They walked outside through the dead garden. The rising sun cast deep shadows on the ground. The crusty stalks and stems were in sharp relieve.

Sasha led her around the men's barracks, to the back of the station. *Dining hall, another door leading to the gym, and a small store.*

"Hi, Artyom." Sasha sighed as a tall blond man came over and towered over the two girls. "Your problem. I've got work to do." She deserted Karina and left Artyom to fit Karina with a uniform.

"Where do I go now?" Karina asked once she had changed.

"Leave your clothes in your room. If no one's come for you, check with the desk sergeant."

"Thanks."

When Karina returned to the women's barracks Sasha had resumed her post at the front desk, staring into space. She ignored Karina until she stopped in front of the desk.

"What do you want?" Karina heard an eye roll in Sasha's voice.

"I just want to make certain I'm doing the right thing," said Karina. "Artyom said to check in with the desk sergeant."

Awkward silence.

"And?"

"Is that right?" asked Karina.

"Probably."

"Thanks!"

What have I gotten myself into? Karina groaned inwardly. *I hoped to find at least one friendly face in this herd of brain washed people. Do they all support Bentuari or do they just not care?*

The desk sergeant did not keep her waiting long and sent her to Avyer's office.

"Sit." Avyer did not look up from his datapad. He leaned back in the padded leather chair, reading.

Karina sat patiently. *He'll speak to me when he wants. This could be a test.*

She took a better look at the office. It was as customized as Avyer's bedroom, only more rustic and more comfortable than the bedroom. Her eyes roamed from modestly framed wild animal paintings to a mounted deer head centered on the wall behind him. She tried to not toe the huge rug spread out on the floor. Judging from the colors, it was cowhide.

Avyer shammed interest in his reading for a few minutes.

"You should be flattered." He broke the silence without lifting his eyes from the datapad. "I don't know where to place you. You'd do nicely in what serves as the HR department, given your track record."

"It's not a job for just anyone."

"Agreed. The position is currently filled, but she isn't half as pretty as you." He tilted his head to meet her eyes before returning to the document he did not need to reread. "Your combat skills are impressive for someone your size. Quite impressive." He placed the datapad on the desk and traced his finger down the bridge of his recently healed nose. "You still have much to learn," he reflected as he sat back. "So, you see my dilemma."

Karina ran along with everything Avyer said, nodding her head.

"So, you'll do a bit of everything. We shall see where your deficiencies lie and how to improve you. I'll decide where to place you later."

He tapped the datapad, selecting options.

"You'll be in the gym at nine with the other trainees. Enjoy the beating." He dismissed her with a wave of his hand.

Karina's face flushed. *I should break his nose again. I can't, though. Not if I want to stay alive. And keep my family alive.*

CHAPTER 9
BLACK AND BLUE

KARINA WAS NOT ABOUT to disappoint Avyer. *I'll let them rough me up a bit, at least for now. I don't know what they'll do if they see how well I can fight.* Two hours were practice and general instruction, while two more hours were a free-for-all. She hobbled out with the rest of the trainees for lunch.

They were twenty in total: fifteen men and five women. Only a few of them had an idea of what they were doing.

Karina caught a few names. The ones she remembered were either good in a fight or handsome. Tai was a young woman about Karina's age. She was responsible for most of the bruises on Karina's body. Victor was small but good in a fight. He had a scared but wholesome farm boy look to him. Handsome Jerod Ternovvy was useless in a fight. Illya was not as handsome, but he was a good fighter.

Karina kept her head down as she entered the sterile dining hall. She felt . . . exposed. All the walls facing the outside were black glass panes, allowing the diners to see outside.

She murmured her order to the servers then scoped out the tables and benches for the most isolated one. The corner.

Karina slid her tray on the dark metallic table. She glanced around her before clambering over the metal bench and sitting down. She bowed her head and closed her eyes to give silent thanks for the food. When she opened her eyes Illya and Tai were coming to flank her. Jerod had installed himself across from them with Victor.

"Well, guess this is life now." Tai spoke cheerfully.

I guess not everyone who came here was under duress, thought Karina.

"You mean all black and blue?" joked Illya.

"Technically, it's blue and brown," said Karina.

Illya rolled his eyes. "I'm talking police colors, not bruises."

"Oh." Karina reddened and crammed food in her mouth.

Illya laughed and elbowed her. "I'm kidding! Of course I'm referring to bruises!"

Karina tried to laugh it off with the two. "What comes next?" she asked.

Tai and Illya exchanged glances. "You really don't know?" asked Tai.

"No, I came in this morning," said Karina. *Don't mention being handpicked by Avyer. Nikolai. Chief Nikolai.*

"Not a volunteer, then?" asked Tai.

Karina shook her head.

"Doesn't matter," Jerod said cheerfully. "You'll get used to it. It's not that bad. Breakfast at six, walk at six thirty, gym at seven. There's a break until nine, when we train until noon. Lunch is an hour, then weapons training. That's Monday through Friday. Saturday is strategy and simulations for five hours, eight to one. Sundays are free until you've graduated and have been assigned a post."

Tai regarded Karina dubiously, but Jerod still seemed friendly.

Lunch ended quickly.

All trainees filed out to a field behind the barracks. All police funding must have gone to Avyer's office and bedroom, and the women's barracks. Shocks of grass surrounded the legs of a hodgepodge of circular and human-shaped targets placed at intervals in the poorly mowed, wide-open field. One long rickety table separated them from the targets.

Karina fell into the line leading to the table. Untidy lines of weapons were strewn on the table. The table creaked and swayed as trainees pushed to select or return a gun.

I don't know if I'll be able to hit the side of a barn door. Her father liked guns so she knew how to handle one. What she lacked was practical experience.

Empty plasma magazine out, loaded one in. Safety on until it was time to shoot. I wished I had a holster. Her gun hand rested at her side.

"Line up!" A voice boomed over the commotion of the trainees. *It's the voice from testing day.*

A middle-aged man with pale skin and sunken eyes stepped up. His voice belied his exhausted appearance. "Form a line behind the targets. Try to not shoot your fellow cadets in the foot. Seriously?" He slapped a slouching young man's backside. "Get your butt situated! You call that a straight line?"

Karina stood straighter between Illya and another young man. *I hope that's straight enough.* Her back hurt at this angle.

"Like that!" The trainer pointed at Karina's line. "Almost perfect! The centerpiece just needs a step stool."

Karina's cheeks turned crimson. She stuck out like a sore thumb. The only person close to her height was Sasha. *Hopefully we aren't the only two short people on the base . . .*

"Ok. My name is Oleg. I'll be your weapons instructor for two months. If you do an atrocious job with weapons, it's not my fault. Show me what you've got."

One by one the trainees stepped up, aimed, and fired. Oleg critiqued five rounds, yelling their individual strengths and weaknesses to each cadet. He was everywhere all at once.

Karina barely managed to hit the target.

———

The next morning Karina awakened with a pit of dread in her stomach. *I don't want to work for the Gavriilan police.*

She stumbled out of bed. Every muscle she had used yesterday was burning, bruised, or in pain. *And that's despite the fact that I'm used to training every day.* She gingerly showered and dressed, braiding back her wet hair.

Sasha did not converse. Even though Karina had fallen asleep and not moved around, Sasha looked angry from the moment she awakened until she was ready for the day. *I'll wait until later to know her better.*

Things were as Jerod had predicted yesterday: breakfast, walk, gym, break, train, lunch, train, supper and free time.

———

A week had passed before Karina visited her family.

"Are you all right?" Sofia observed bags under Karina's eyes.

"I'm fine." Karina forced a smile.

"You don't look well." Her mother's face twisted into a sad frown. She had not missed the bruise on Karina's cheek. "You could have at least called."

"Training has been intense." Karina brushed it off. "I'm fine. It'll be done before I know it. I'll call and come home more often."

"You can do it," said Ivan. He hugged Karina hard and whispered in her ear. "I know you. You're independent and think on your own. Make a difference, wherever you are." He kissed her forehead.

"Thanks. Try to not worry about me," Karina murmured. They both stood there with serious eyes.

Karina bit her lip and left her family to return to her barracks. *I can't see my family for a long time after this.*

She took her time walking back. "I don't know what to do," she said to herself. She kicked a stray rock and watched it bounce from the pavement to a patch of weeds. "Well, I do," she confessed, "but I don't want to admit it."

"Why does Mama have to look at me like that? I hate that sad frown. I know she means well, but I don't need a pity face! I need her to be strong!" She raised her voice higher than she had meant, so she lowered it. She did not want to share her monologue with the world. "I don't want to be here, but maybe I can make a difference."

Let everyone think I'm a simpleton or an idiot.

Ivan left her with food for thought. She needed to make a difference. Preferably without killing herself or her family.

CHAPTER 10
AVYER NIKOLAI

AVYER'S strong hands deftly dismantled and reassembled his gun, polishing the pieces as quickly as he took them apart and put them back together.

If only the world were as organized as his gun. It would make life less complicated. His good life was complicated on a daily basis: problems to solve, prisoners to torture, and prisoners to transfer. It was not difficult, just time consuming.

Had the guards gone alone to pick up Karina, they would have executed Karina's family. It would not have been the first time for an entire family to die for not cooperating. Avyer had lost distant family members when they expressed dissension with the government.

The time was not right for executing her family. Loose ends could be useful and keep people in line.

Once his gun was ready, he dressed in his black uniform. He stood straight as he regarded himself in the mirror. His shoulders stretched out the tight black undershirt that accentuated his lean but muscular frame. He buttoned on a dress shirt, slipped one gun into a shoulder holster over the shirt, shrugged into his coat, and tucked his pants in his boots. Avyer belted yet another holster and gun over the coat. *Time to look over the jail.*

Routine, routine, routine. That was how a police state was run and how life must be, whether Bentuari were dead or alive. This had been his life for thirteen years.

Without Bentuarian discipline, he never would have made police chief. Bentuari's regime had taken a raw eighteen-year-old, turning him into the perfect cog in their wheel, a model chief by the age of twenty-one. He had held that position for ten years, first in Desmarin and now in Avedida. In addition to the police chief position, he was Avedida's Police Major General, in charge of all police stations in the province. Both roles kept him busy all day every day.

Clang. Clang. Clang. The jail cells were in stark contrast to his luxurious quarters. Layers of putrid green paint peeled from black paint that had separated and flaked from yellow walls. Body odor and fluids combined to form one stench. A line of barred ventilators on the opposite wall mitigated the pungency, but the trade-off was no temperature control. On warm days the ventilators struggled to keep the inferno at bay. In the winter prisoners had to hope that their relations or friends loved them enough to give them a blanket.

For Avyer, the malodor was a part of life. *Life has ugly parts just as it has beautiful ones. It's a matter of learning how to tolerate the ugly ones.*

In Avyer's case, it was as simple as holding his breath to not smell the reeking prisoners. Avyer had developed that particular ability to an extreme. His current record was two minutes, if he did not talk to anyone while inspecting the cells.

After inspecting five floors of cells—prisoners, guards, and all as thoroughly as possible—he ate a private breakfast as he watched recordings of the trainees. It was amusing to watch the stragglers and satisfying to identify those with promise. He watched Karina with a mixture of curiosity and amusement.

Her gray eyes were serious while she stood to the side of the arena. Once she looked directly at the camera. She pinned up her golden-brown braid before fighting. She took up a typical fighting stance in the ring: her left foot rested ahead, the right foot slid to the back, she tilted her chin down and kept her right fist close to her face.

A broad-shouldered woman who waddled into the ring mirrored Karina's defensive stance. Avyer cocked his head as he observed the other woman's poor form. Her feet were weak. Karina should easily take her on with Systema. He took a sip of orange juice.

Karina shuffled to the side. Her strong stance inexplicably weakened. Avyer's orange juice glass froze in the air. *What is she doing?*

Karina *let* the woman punch her in the arm. Then box her in the ear. She barely deflected a punch aimed to her face, falling over from the force of the blow.

Avyer's eyes narrowed. *I'll have to address this.*

He moved on to recordings of target practice. Karina's movements told him that while she was not completely unfamiliar with a gun, she was not adept. She never gave up despite barely hitting the target. *Not her forte.*

He eyed the other trainees. Many were better than Karina on the shooting range, but none were as good the last one. *Sasha Bondaruk.* Another little girl worth watching. She was useless in hand-to-hand combat, but good with a gun.

Avyer chewed a spoonful of eggs. He would keep an eye on the two. Sasha had nearly finished the police law training and had shown no signs of insubordination.

Karina was an open book. He had seen how she had looked at her family the day he came for her. *She's terrified, and terrified people are much more manageable.*

Sasha was brutal, made for this kind of life. Her strength was guns and she was feral on the range. She annihilated whatever she aimed at. She would be useful.

The two golden girls. He scooped up the last bite of egg. Their careers would be well worth following.

CHAPTER 11
LAW

"YOU WILL BE ATTENDING a fast-paced law course." The Monday class instructor eyed Karina as she sat. "Passing grade is ninety-five. Failing isn't optional, so catch up."

Karina did not ask what would happen if she failed.

"I thought schedules were fixed," said Karina.

"They are," the instructor replied, "and they are flexible when Chief Nikolai requires an adjustment."

"Oh." *Just when I thought the hard part was over.*

Karina's schedule was turned upside down. She was in Sasha's group. Sasha fired off correct answers as well as she shot a gun. Karina limped along, barely keeping up with every day's new information.

Evening trainings left her with more bruises than ever. She called her family and spoke with them at least once a week on the phone to let them know she was fine. Had she visited home her family would have been in hysterics at the sight of her purple and brown blotched body. Bruises extended from her toes to a bright purple eye she recently sustained.

Sasha was the only trainee who could not beat Karina, despite Karina's poor form.

"So," Karina said to Sasha one day they were practicing in the training room. She panted and wiped sweat from her forehead before it could drip into her eyes. She dabbed around her tender eye. "I have an idea."

"Yeah?" Sasha sat cross-legged near the circle.

"Why don't I help you with combat and you help me with law?"

Sasha's forehead knitted as she considered the idea. "Ok." She shrugged. "Sounds like a fair trade. When do you want that we start?"

"Now."

"Yeah, ok. Sure."

From that day on they got up together, ate together, trained together, studied together, and talked together. Neither of them had anything in common with the others.

"So," Karina ventured to ask Sasha weeks later, "how did you end up here?"

"I was caught hunting for food. It was either work in the jail or go to jail."

"Oh." Karina had recently learned in law class that hunting was illegal in Avedida.

"You?"

"It's a long story."

"It's not like I got anything better to do." Sasha gave a snort-laugh.

Karina told Sasha everything starting with her late night ride on Gladrion to her appointment with Avyer in his office.

Sasha's eyes were wide as saucers by the end of the tale. "WOW. I think I like you. That is absolutely insane! How could you beat up the Chief and they not kill you?" She shook her head. "That's not normal."

"No, it's not," agreed Karina.

"So?"

"So what?"

"So why do you think he did that?" Sasha looked at her slyly.

"Oh, no!" Karina laughed nervously. "I know where you're

going! We're not going there. No!" She shook her head adamantly. "He was impressed with my fighting skills. He specifically said that."

"Uh huh," Sasha said in a singsongy way. "Well, if that's what you prefer to think, but I disagree." She winked. "You know what all guys want." She made an hourglass figure in the air with her hands.

Karina blushed. "He's demented if that's the case. Torture's hardly the way to a girl's heart."

Sasha shrugged. "Well, I don't know. Guys are stupid and girls are mean."

"That's harsh."

"You can't tell me you can't think it's true. You know it is."

Karina didn't argue the point.

"Ready for the next questions?" asked Sasha.

Law was not complicated in and of itself: the devil was in the details. There were many details, ranging from a series of prohibitions resulting in jail or torture or death when broken, to statutes governing degrees of robbery, to rape and murder. They also had to memorize officer ranks, jurisdictions and boundaries.

"What is law 2271?" Karina read from the textbook.

"2271 covers general theft and burglary," Sasha responded immediately.

"How many types of general theft and burglary?"

"Seven." Sasha named each and every one perfectly. "Your turn." She took the book. "Name the law concerning assault and battery."

Karina frowned and looked up at the bedroom ceiling for inspiration. "2272?"

"Come on, it's not that easy!"

"2273? 2274?"

Sasha rolled her eyes.

"I don't remember!" Karina huffed and lay down on her bunk.

"6081. If you don't know just stop guessing already." Sasha

continued with the next question. "What classes of treason are covered by law 8290?"

Karina pounded the bed with her fists. "Give me a hint: how many classes?"

"Five."

She squeezed her eyes shut. "Treason against the Bentuarian government includes insubordination, deception, selling or sharing of government private affairs, conspiracy with the enemy, and abandonment of the planet."

"Punishable by?"

"Death, death, death, death, and more death. Easy," said Karina.

Sasha glared. "Not that easy. General insubordination results in immediate execution of you and your entire immediate family. Deception results in imprisonment. Length of time depends. Selling or sharing of government private affairs results in capital punishment. Abandonment of the planet results in capital punishment."

"I was close."

"Close won't pass an exam," said Sasha. "You've got to remember everything. If you can't differentiate between what happens to Spark sympathizers versus Spark rebels, you'll get in trouble."

Karina made a face.

"My turn! What is the chain of command?"

"General of the Police of the Bentuarian Federation of Gavriila is General Stepanov, followed by various Police Colonel Generals, followed by three Police Lieutenant Generals over the Police Major Generals—one per province, Chief Avyer Nikolai being Avedida's Police Major General—then Police Captains and then the Police Officials, and the last being the lowly Police Officers that we will become." The words flowed glibly from Sasha's tongue.

CHAPTER 12
THREAT

TIME FLEW BY. Karina had been in training for two months. They had one month left before testing day. Everyone felt the pressure because performance determined ranking and job placement. Everyone was quiet, on edge.

Sasha and Karina used evenings to train and study. Night after night they sparred an hour, showered and studied. There was an optional mounted police test, so Sasha was panicking at the idea of riding a horse. Karina was far from a bull's eye, but at least she hit more targets than not these days.

"One, two, three, four," Sasha muttered as she practiced the moves Karina had taught her. She stepped forward, grasped Karina's arm, twisted it behind Karina's back, and swept her foot behind Karina's leg to throw her off her feet.

"Much better." Karina nodded as she leapt from the mat. "Now a little faster. If I had really been trying, you wouldn't have had a chance."

Sasha put the pieces together again.

"Hey!" Illya called out from across the room. "Trade partners?" he asked.

Sasha and Karina exchanged glances. "Sure." Sasha trained

with Illya, while Karina worked with the young woman Illya had been sparring with.

"Maria, right?" asked Karina.

Maria nodded, her tight bun of black hair bobbing. "Let's get to it."

I'm tired of being beaten up. Tonight she's going down, but I can't make it look too easy.

Karina did a terrible job of not making it look too easy: within a minute Karina had grappled Maria down to the floor. She gave Maria a hand up.

"Wow!" Maria gasped. Her eyes were wide. "Very nice. You'll get better at this soon!"

"Good show!" Illya clapped from his and Sasha's corner.

Maria left, so Karina sat in the corner opposite Illya and Sasha. They were the only ones in the training center.

Karina wiped her face with the inside of her training shirt. She closed her eyes and leaned into the corner of the wall, releasing the tension from her muscles. *It feels good to win. And it also feels good to sit and not think about things.*

As she lowered her head and opened her eyes an unwelcome shadow loomed over her. She did not have to look up to know who it was. No one had the same towering profile.

Avyer looked down at her as she stood straight at attention. She shuffled out of the corner into the open.

"You've underperformed up 'til now." He walked around her. "At ease."

"Underperformed?" She clasped her hands behind her back. She tried to swallow but there was no saliva in her mouth.

"Come now. After beating up two of my men months ago and taking me on, you should win every time you spar. You've been losing on purpose." Every word was with the same deliberate cadence he had used the night they met. His eyes narrowed as he circled her. Karina remained motionless. "I hope to see considerable improvements soon. When I say soon, I mean immediately, unless you want problems."

Their eyes locked. Avyer opened his mouth as though he were about to say something, but he closed it and his jaw tightened. He turned his back on her and left as abruptly as he had appeared.

So much for peace and quiet. Blasted Loyalist!

Karina's fingers trembled as she unclenched her hands from behind her back. Her unsteady legs took her to the showers.

She took refuge behind her shower's frosted glass door. Given that there were individual stalls, the showers were one of the few places that were safe to be vulnerable. She slumped against the wall, basking in the steaming hot water. Karina made all the faces she could not make at Avyer at the tiled walls.

She had fallen asleep in her bunk by the time Sasha returned. She awakened to the sound of Sasha sighing deeply as she dressed for bed and pulled the blanket over her head.

"Y'ok?" Karina asked groggily. She did not dare crane her neck over the side of the bed. Not that she would have been able to see her friend in the dark.

"Are you?" Sasha asked in an odd tone.

"I'm cold."

"Use your blanket."

"I am."

"Come on down, then." Sasha groaned. "For warmth."

Karina snatched her blanket from her bunk and climbed down, blinking sleepily. Sasha patted the scant space beside her. They hugged, chilled to the bone. Karina's hand brushed against Sasha's face as she pulled up her blanket. Sasha's cheek was damp. With tears.

CHAPTER 13
TESTING DAY

SASHA AND KARINA said nothing as they prepared for testing day. Anxious glances and helping each other tuck in a stray hair or adjust a belt sufficed. They slipped into long black tunics, belting them. The belts accentuated curves or showed a lack thereof. They nodded to each other, smartly turned out with their pants tucked into black boots.

Karina had been assigned to the first testing group. She glanced furtively around the testing room. *Whew.* Avyer was nowhere in sight.

She breezed through the law testing, both written and oral. Oleg presided over the afternoon physical tests with several other judges.

Karina defeated all three of her opponents in record time. *Avyer will be elated if he bothers to watch the cameras.*

Sasha's tips raced through her mind while on the firing range, but she barely met the mark for firearms testing.

"There is optional testing." Oleg looked up from his datapad after weapons testing. Nearly all the trainees exchanged nervous glances. Karina kept her eyes on Oleg. "The test for the mounted police. Follow me if you're up to the challenge." An officer led a bay gelding to Oleg. Oleg mounted it.

Silence. Karina stepped forward to follow Oleg. She bit back a smile.

"Just the little one?" Oleg raised an eyebrow. The remaining nine stepped forward. "That's more like it!"

He led them to the modest barn behind the station. Several saddled horses were swishing their tails, waiting for them.

"First part of this test." He rode to the line of horses and wheeled his mount around to face the cadets. "Mount up."

Karina did not step forward first. *Let the others make complete fools of themselves first.*

Three were unable to mount the animals. One swung too far and flung himself against the brick barn wall. He hobbled away in embarrassment. One was bucked off when she jabbed the horse's belly hard as she swung into the saddle. The third put one foot in the stirrup and twisted around too far. He wrenched his ankle and fell on his backside on the concrete.

That left seven.

Four including Karina put the horses through their paces. Three ambled around aimlessly and let their horses go where they pleased. Karina chocked back a laugh as one panicked and threw herself onto a hay bale.

"Very well." Oleg walked his horse in front of the remaining four. "Last part of the test. Follow me."

Karina moved her mare behind Oleg. He led them through several pastures to a large, open area set up as an obstacle course: mud, fences, inclines, and more. He pulled up in front of the course.

"It's simple. Do as I do."

He urged his horse to the starting point then took off at a steady clip. He ran quickly but efficiently through the obstacle course. When he returned to the small group his horse was blowing, and both horse and rider were coated in mud.

"Easy peasy." He laughed. The gelding shook his head and snorted. "Go for it, short stuff." Oleg nodded at Karina.

She walked her mare to the starting line. The mare was no

Gladrion, nor was she the worst animal Karina had ever mounted. From the feel of her mouth and movements, Karina knew she would give a good show.

They started off at a moderate pace, slogging through mud to a low jump. They progressed around barrels on dry ground at a faster pace before tackling graduated jumps. She slowed to go over the rocks and a bridge and carefully traversed more mud.

"Excellent time," was Oleg's only comment as he noted something on his datapad. "Next: Ives Sanderal."

None of the other riders matched Karina's time but held their own.

"That's all for today," Oleg announced after watching the last rider. "Scores up late tonight or early tomorrow morning in the dining hall. Dismount and leave your horse with the stable hands."

Karina's gut twisted as she rode the mare to the stable. With nothing better to do, she returned to the barracks to change her clothes and nap. She was brusquely awakened by Sasha shaking her shoulder.

"Scores are up!" Sasha was sweaty but not muddy. "Let's go check them!" She pulled a blinking Karina out of the bunk to the dining hall. Karina smoothed her mussed hair.

Two data screens glowed on the glass walls. Names flashed across them in alphabetical order, so Karina and Sasha parted ways.

Karina held her breath as she searched for her name. There it was. She exhaled when she found it. *Two hundred and forty-one. Must have been from horsemanship, because there's no way I passed weapons.* The minimum to pass was two hundred and forty.

Sasha danced her way to Karina with an odd smile on her face.

"Made it!" she shrieked as she drew closer to Karina.

"What'd you get?"

"Two eighty-four." Sasha jumped up and down in exuberance. "You?"

"Two forty-one."

"That's great! We're going to be ok!" Sasha threw her arms around Karina and hugged her.

"Oof! Yes," Karina said slowly. *At least, I hope so.*

Jerod and Illya ran over and threw their arms around Sasha and Karina. "We made it! We passed!"

"So did we." Sasha grimaced as she squirmed out of the hug.

"Fantastic." Jerod grinned at Karina as he released her and Ilya, mock-saluting. "So, Officer Karina, would you like to go out with me tonight?"

Karina's jaw dropped. "Um . . ." She looked at Sasha, who only rolled her eyes at Karina. "Yes?"

CHAPTER 14
OFFICER KARINA

"ONE, TWO, THREE, FOUR: MOVE OUT!" bellowed Sergeant Sergei as they ran around the track.

Sasha gasped for breath as she ran beside Karina. Her gun slung over her shoulder and the backpack straps dug into her shoulders. Being officers did not preclude exercise and drills.

"Breathe more quietly!" Karina hissed. "Unless you want to get in trouble."

"I know," huffed Sasha. "I can't."

"You should work out more."

"And stop!" A commanding voice rang out.

Whether they were familiar with the voice or not, all the new officers flinched before they froze to attention.

"Sir." Sergei saluted Chief Nikolai as he materialized from near a shed beside the track. "Form up!" Sergei ordered the officers.

Sasha panted as she took a place beside Karina.

"Quiet," Karina warned Sasha.

"I can't help it," Sasha hissed. "I've got asthma."

"Less chatter, more line." Sergei glared at Karina and Sasha.

Sasha elbowed Karina.

Chief Nikolai's eyes raked the group of twenty officers up and down, from the tip of their boots to the top of their heads. Sasha had barely caught her breath before he reached her.

"Tired, Officer Bondaruk?" he asked Sasha.

"No, sir!"

"Then you can run another ten laps with your gear," said Avyer.

"Yes, sir!"

"That won't be necessary," Avyer responded drily. "Thank you for your enthusiasm." He scrutinized a tall, thin man next to Sasha. "Officer Secily." He offered a hand to the officer.

Mistake, Karina's brain screamed.

Chief Nikolai twisted him hard and sharply. Secily folded like a human pretzel and sprawled on the track.

"Always be aware," Avyer told Secily sternly. "The Gavriila Police Force is all that stands between our citizens and the Inter-Planetary Government. I could have killed you twice. Step aside, officer."

"Yes, sir!"

Secily scrambled to his feet and staggered to the side with what little dignity he had left. Avyer continued down the line until he reached a blonde, heavy-set girl.

She's in trouble. Karina recognized the look in Avyer's eye.

"Ivanna Glorienka," he read her name badge. "You are quite a disgrace. Straighten up that jacket. Brush the lint off your pants. And don't eat so much. Join Secily."

Ivanna turned beet red. She shuffled over to Secily. Avyer concluded reviewing the row and turned to have a second pass at the remaining eighteen. Karina swallowed nervously and pressed the tip of her tongue against the inside of her upper teeth.

"Karina Ivanovna."

"Sir!" She nearly jumped out of her skin.

"You look upset."

"Sir?" *Now I'm in trouble.*

A gloved hand connected with her left cheek with a resounding slap that jerked her head to the right. She stumbled against Jerod. Jerod's hand caught her waist and his other hand rested against the small of her back. He was the only thing between her and the track pavement.

"Don't wear your feelings on your face."

"Yes, sir!" Karina straightened her back like a rod.

"Ten laps." Avyer lazily waved a hand at Ivanna and Secily. "And the rest of you: watch and learn."

When Avyer's back was turned to them Sasha poked Karina in the rib. "I don't think *I* need to worry about getting into trouble," she growled through her teeth.

"Tell me about it," Karina muttered, and she gave Sasha a side eye.

At the end of their final lap Ivanna and Secily were more winded than Sasha had been. Avyer signaled for them to rejoin their fellow officers.

"The IPG* and Gavriilan delinquents will not go easy on you. It is not enough to be good. You must be the *best*." Avyer regarded each officer. "Become the best."

---

* InterPlanetary Government, considered the Bentuarians' greatest enemy

CHAPTER 15
YOUNG REBELS

AS HE RETIRED from the running track, Avyer frowned. *How am I supposed to work with any of that? None of them are what I would have liked: too dumb, too fat, too weak—and in Karina's case, too emotional.*

He made his way to the jail proper. "Does Kuzmin have everything ready?" he asked a guard outside.

"I believe so, sir."

"That's something," Avyer muttered.

He made his way up to a special cell on the third floor. There were no screams or cries today, which was promising.

"Sir." Kuzmin saluted as Avyer entered the windowless white cell.

Kuzmin looked put out as he stood in front of three shirtless prisoners. Their hands were shackled over their heads and their feet chained to a peg on the floor. Blood oozed or dripped from their backs and chests, all in differing stages of coagulation. Kuzmin dropped a wet whip in a puddle of blood on the concrete floor before washing his hands in a sink.

"All yours, sir. After fifty lashes, they admitted to knowing things about Spark."

"Good work, Kuzmin." Avyer Nikolai sized up each of the glassy-eyed men. "You may leave."

Kuzmin dried his hands in a hand dryer then left.

"Now." Avyer turned to the prisoners. "To business."

All young, judging from the very sparse or complete lack of hair on their faces. An emaciated blond one with a swollen half-closed eye began sobbing. *The weakest link.*

"We'll start with you." He singled out the blond. "We know that you three belong to the Gavriilan Spark Revolution. What's their plan and what is your part in it?"

"We-we already told the-the other man everything." Spittle and blood dripped from the boy's mouth.

Avyer grabbed the boy's chin, jutting it up to look him in the eye. "Humor me. I won't ask again."

"We w-w-want the InterPlanetary Government's support. In a few weeks we will make contact." The boy slobbered and bled on Avyer's glove.

The cell door slid open behind Avyer. In stepped General Pavel Stepanov, Bentuari's regent for the planet.

"Chief Nikolai, I see you are busy."

"Somewhat." Avyer dropped the boy's chin.

Stepanov pressed a button to turn on an additional light. The three prisoners blinked and cowered as the imperious older man stepped forward.

"Would you like some assistance?" Stepanov stroked his graying mustache.

"As you please." Avyer deferred.

Stepanov took Avyer's place, yanking the blond boy by the hair. "So. Where are the rebels?"

"Shut up!" A young man with light brown stubble squawked. "You'll kill them a—"

Stepanov shot the protestor in the head. "The things I have to endure for order on this planet." He shook his head, clucking his tongue before he addressed the blond again. "Continue."

"Y-y-y-y-y-yes," the blond boy stammered.

After enduring ten minutes of tears and stammering, Stepanov gathered that in a matter of weeks or months the IPG *might* send support. None of them knew where the Gavriilan Spark Revolution might meet with the IPG.

"Good boys," Stepanov said as he left. "Continue to cooperate and perhaps you'll live." He removed his gloves and tossed them to the blood-stained floor. He only paused to speak to a guard. "Dispose of the dead. Send the other two to General Raize. He'll be interested," said Stepanov.

"And send maintenance in to sanitize everything," added Avyer.

They ambled down the hall together.

"Fine work," said Stepanov. "That's what? The fifth one this month?"

"Fourth."

"At this rate, you'll not have a Spark sympathizer within a hundred kilometers of your province." Stepanov clapped Avyer on the shoulder. "Keep up the good work, Nikolai. I'll see you next month."

"Very good, sir."

Avyer and Stepanov parted ways, Avyer returning to his office and Stepanov to catch a maglev.

Avyer discovered a figure as large as himself sprawled in one of the chairs in front of his desk. He recognized the mop of curly brown hair from behind. "Dima! What the kark brings you here?" Avyer's face lit up.

Dmitri leapt to his feet and wrapped Avyer in a bear hug. "Just thought I'd drop by." He gave Avyer a playful slap on the shoulder. "What have you been up to these days?"

"Sweating slobs and teaching revolutionist kids a lesson. Same old, same old. You?"

Dmitri ignored the question. "I think I know better than to ask if you're serious when you say both of those things."

"Be careful." Avyer's face fell. "That sounds unpatriotic."

"Not really." Dmitri gave him a quizzical look. "I am for

Gavriila, for its *people.*"

"As am I," concurred Avyer.

"Beating up citizens sounds a bit unpatriotic."

"Be careful," Avyer repeated, frowning. "Lesser comments have led men to the execution stand."

"Come, come." Dmitri tried to lighten the mood, "We're just having polite conversation."

"Be that as it may," said Avyer, "as your friend *I* suggest being more careful with what you say."

"So I shall." Dmitri gave him a mock-salute. "However, have you thought about how you might *convince* the people that the police are for Gavriila? The 'revolutionist kids' probably believe just as strongly as you that they're right."

Avyer hesitated. "I'll think about it."

"Good." Dmitri smiled as he looped his arm through Avyer's. "Lunch? I have had some issues in the mayor's office and thought you might have some suggestions."

CHAPTER 16
MOUNTED OFFICER KARINA

KARINA SAT bolt upright in bed when the bell rang. *It's today!* Despite being half-asleep she dressed quickly and practically bounced out the door to the dining hall. She ate breakfast before anyone else—well, almost anyone else. A husky blond officer sat finishing his eggs.

Karina finished after him, nearly inhaling eggs, oatmeal, and milk. She found herself following him to the stable. As she closed the distance between them she saw the insignia on his sleeve. *A higher-ranking officer.*

"I'm the mounted police commander." He was inspecting the stalls. "You must be Officer Karina Ivanovna." He stroked the nose of a brown horse. "You're early. Arya is in stall nine, and her gear is outside her stall. I trust you know what to do."

"Sir! Commander . . . ?"

"Mounted Police Force Commander Pyotr Kartrovich. You may call me Commander Kartrovich."

"Commander Kartrovich."

Karina slowed as she searched for stall nine, bouncing a little less. There it was: to the right, nearly in the center of the dim but airy stable.

Arya was a fairy-like name but the mare Arya was hardly a

dainty fairy creature. A bay, no-nonsense mare with a sturdy, well-built body awaited Karina in stall nine.

"Be careful," advised Kartrovich as Karina led the mare out. "She has a sensitive mouth. Her last officer forgot that."

"What happened to him?" Karina set Arya up at the crossties.

"He's in the hospital with a broken collarbone."

"Ouch." Karina winced.

"Exactly."

Karina brushed Arya and had her tacked up by the time her fellow officers arrived. Kartrovich inspected the mare from hoof to tail. Karina held her breath as he tested the cinch and straps.

"Excellent. You do know what you're doing." He nodded in appreciation. "Wait in the corral. I'll assign your partner shortly."

The remaining mounted officers filed out at the same time, lining up beside Karina. Kartrovich inspected all the horses as he had inspected Karina's.

"Good morning." Kartrovich strode along the row of thirty horses and riders. "The person to your left is your partner for the year."

Karina looked askance at a tall man with a salt and pepper beard. He was rail thin, hardly an intimidating figure. *If we get in a fight, I'm not counting on him to help.*

"Very well," Kartrovich said. "Mount up." Thirty pairs of legs swung into thirty saddles. "Officer Ivanovna and Officer Calandre will go to the north quadrant of Avedida . . ."

Karina's mind wandered after hearing her assignment. Preoccupied with her seat, her heels, and how she held herself and the reins, she stole glances at Officer Calandre.

She followed Calandre to the extensive north quadrant of Avedida, which covered part of town as well as a smaller rural area. Avedida City was divided into four large quadrants, which were divided into four smaller quadrants. Every day mounted police rode all over one or two quadrants, never going over the same one two days in a row. They worked evenings as well as day shifts. Every two weeks a pair of riders were assigned only evenings.

——

Weeks later Karina and Calandre were working an evening beat on the lower eastern quadrant. Not much usually happened there since it was a commercial area. All the small, barred shops had closed long ago.

"Go over there," Calandre told her with a bored wave of his hand. "Nothing's happening over there. I'll take this side." He turned his horse to clop in the opposite direction.

"Ok," Karina replied. *Calandre probably hates every minute with me, because I always find work to do.* Her mind drifted to a recent incident between homeless people.

A scruffy homeless man had grabbed an equally scruffy woman by the hair. The fragrance of sweaty bodies mixed with human excrement assaulted Karina's nose. Undeterred, Karina drove her horse between them.

"Leave her alone! You heard her!"

The man grabbed Arya's bridle. Karina kicked him in the chest. He sprawled to the ground. When he tried to sit up he gasped so badly for breath that he had to lie back down.

"Do I need to repeat myself?" Karina dismounted and stood over him, glaring.

"N-o-o-o," he gulped.

"Good." Karina signaled to the woman and mounted Arya. "Come with me. I know a place where you'll be taken care of and left in peace." She led her to the church.

Karina shook herself out of her reverie. A cool, light breeze caressed her face and sent strands of Arya's mane tickling her hands. The streetlights were softer since their only purpose was to illuminate shop signs. Everything here was calm, quiet.

Is it too quiet?

Karina turned up her coat collar. A stronger breeze began to whistle in her ears. That and Arya's hooves clopping on the pavement were the only sounds breaking the silence. No cruisers crossed their path.

Tomorrow will be nice, Karina mused. *I can't wait for the date with Jerod.*

The wind blew stronger, pelting Karina with rain. She donned a slicker and pulled the hood over her head. The glossy wet pavement reflected the glow of streetlights and business sign lights. Arya's hooves splashed through quickly forming puddles.

By midnight Karina had nearly finished her assigned part of the east quadrant. The rain turned into light sprinkles. She was passing a poorly lit side street when she heard scuffling. PLOP! Something heavy thudded to the ground.

She wheeled Arya around to face the street, gun in hand.

"Halt! Avedida Police! Hands in the air!" It was not the first time she had said that, but it was her first time alone. *If they get frisky, I'll shoot first and ask questions later.*

Karina squinted at three shadowy figures leaning over something—or someone—on the ground. What she did *not* see were any hands in the air. She fired a warning shot in the air.

"Police!" Karina called out louder.

The three figures froze then scattered.

Karina spurred Arya after them. She ran down one with Arya. He fell to the ground, motionless. He did not move, not even when Arya nearly kicked him.

"I'm on the west side of Fourth Street," Karina radioed Calandre. "Three suspects and a victim. One is down."

"I'm on my way," said Calandre. "I'll request back-up. Where are they headed?"

"One in the middle of Fourth Street," said Karina, "and the other two are running to Red Plaza."

"Take care of the first one. We should have at least one in custody," said Calandre. "I'll take care of the others."

"Understood," Karina responded. She scowled as she wheeled

Arya around. *I wanted to get the other two.* But Calandre was right: they could not afford to lose a culprit.

The man she had run down sat up in a daze. Karina clapped handcuffs on him, dragging him to a light post to cuff him to it and search him. *No weapons. He can wait here.*

She walked Arya back to what the three had left on the ground. The prone figure of a man lay face down on the pavement. Droplets of water rained from his glistening black hair as Karina strained to roll him over. His soaking wet overcoat added to the weight.

"Oh, God," Karina uttered in prayer as she covered her mouth. "Help me." She stared in horror at Avyer's face. His uniform was under the overcoat. "In Jesus' name amen," she muttered.

She reached to check for a pulse when Avyer groaned. Karina froze. *What's he doing here? What do I do?*

Karina heaved him to a sitting position.

"Ok, got an idea." Karina fought to pull off the overcoat. She draped it over Arya's neck. She shook Avyer gently. "Chief Nikolai, please wake up." She shook him harder. "I need you to work with me on this. What do you want me to do?"

"Hm-huh," he murmured.

What should I do? She analyzed the situation, trying to decide how to move him out of the middle of Fourth Street.

She squatted and draped his arms around her shoulders, halfway pulling him to his feet. His weight shifted to the side and he dragged her with him.

"Agh!" Karina groaned.

She counterbalanced in time and centered him over her back. She pulled Avyer to a light post. His eyelids fluttered and he was noticeably less limp. She helped him stand, propping him up against the post.

"Whew!" Karina sighed in relief.

Now that they were in better lighting, a gash oozing blood on his forehead was visible. "That doesn't look good," she said. "You're going to need a doctor."

Avyer grabbed Karina by her coat collar. "Call the desk sergeant and tell him to have the doctor waiting for us. Don't tell them anything else."

"Whoa!" Karina was prepared to catch him, but he remained leaning against the post.

"Get me on your horse." His eyes half opened as he rubbed his forehead and smeared blood across his face.

"Can you ride?"

"Obviously." His voice held a hint of annoyance.

"Ok."

Karina brought Arya closer to Avyer. He weakly grasped a handful of mane and raised his left foot to shove it in the stirrup.

"Give me push." He hung his head.

Karina bit her upper lip. *Awkward.*

"On three," she said. "One, two, three!"

She shoved his right leg up with all her might to give him a boost and he slowly mounted Arya. His face twisted in pain.

"Get on." He slouched over the mare's neck.

"I don't think she can carry both of us."

"And I don't fancy falling off a karking horse. Get. On."

Karina hopped up behind Avyer, reaching around him for the reins. Without warning he slumped lower on Arya's neck. "No, no, no!" She tightened her arms around him, grabbing two handfuls of mane. The horse nickered nervously. "Don't fall! Don't fall!"

Her arms and hands ached from the effort of keeping him on the horse. *God, please help me get him back to base without him falling off Arya or he'll kill me when he wakes up.*

She jammed her chin against her radio button as she rode. "Officer Ivanovna to base. Please put me in to the desk sergeant. Yes? I have an injured person. Chief Nikolai says to have a doctor ready where you are. Also, send a wagon to Fourth Street. There's a perp handcuffed to a light post. They need picked up."

"Got that. Sending a wagon," responded the dispatcher.

Karina took the shortest route to the station. She dismounted, leaving Avyer outside. He was conscious enough to not fall off. She ran to the desk sergeant.

"It's Chief Nikolai." She pointed outside. "Help me."

"What the kark—?" The desk sergeant peered through the entrance doors.

"Help me get him down. And where's the doctor?" She looked around. No doctor was in sight. Her eyebrows furrowed.

"He's on his way." The sergeant groaned as he helped Avyer out of the saddle. As the sergeant helped Avyer dismount, the doctor appeared.

"What happened?" The doctor took the sergeant's place once Avyer had his feet on the ground.

"I don't know," said Karina, "but I have a night watch to finish."

"Go," said the sergeant. "Report to Chief Nikolai first thing in the morning."

Karina resumed what little was left of her night watch. That meant she did not go to bed until three in the morning, which gave her three hours before she had to report to Avyer. If it had not been for the incident she would have slept in this Saturday.

"Officer Karina Ivanovna." She presented herself to today's desk sergeant. "Here to report to Chief Nikolai."

"Go on back. He is in his quarters."

"Not in his office?" Karina's chest tightened.

"No, in his *bed*room. I'll ring you in." The desk sergeant pressed a button on the desk.

She hesitated a few seconds before she forced herself to take the elevator and walk up to Avyer's bedroom door. She screwed up her courage and knocked.

"Come in!" Avyer sounded more like himself.

The door slid open. Avyer lay in bed, looking as sleepy as Karina felt. *It must be nice, being the boss and doing whatever the blazes you want, like sending people to your room so they have to get up early and you don't.*

"Come closer," he ordered her.

And he's shirtless. Great. She glued her eyes on his face and eyes.

"I apologize if I'm too early. The desk sergeant said to—"

"He was perfectly right," Avyer cut her off. "You look uncomfortable. Turn around while I dress." He paused. "If you wish."

Karina did an about-face, studying the bedroom door. *At least he hasn't slapped me this time. Or put me in stun cuffs. Or wanted to spar.* He rustled through clothing. She cleared her throat. "How are you?"

"I'll live."

A hand settled her left shoulder, and Karina flinched. Avyer walked to stand in front of her, now dressed. She lifted her gaze from his chest to his eyes.

"Why did you help me? You could have done any number of things. You could have shot me."

"That goes against my religion." *Oops.* Karina tilted her head and tried to decipher the expression on his face. Avyer's eyes shuttered.

"That must be quite the religion," he said as he opened his eyes.

"Even if it didn't, I'm not so stup—, um, foolish enough as to shoot the Chief of Police. The shot would be traced."

Avyer looked amused. "I have questions. Have you eaten?"

Karina shook her head, dazed.

"Very well. We'll discuss this over breakfast."

Avyer opened the door and motioned for her to follow him. They walked down the hall to a closed door to the right. The door slid open to reveal a modest dining room with no decor on the brown walls. He installed himself at the head of a dark wooden table in the middle of the room. Karina sat directly across from him. She rested her arms on the chair armrests. She clenched and unclenched her fists while Avyer rang for food.

"So, I want to hear your side of things." He dug into the food as soon as he had been served. "What happened last night?"

Karina gave him all the details he required. She ate just

enough to look as though she were not rejecting breakfast. When he was satisfied, he dismissed her. Karina strode through the lobby. She forced her weak legs to walk at a normal pace to the dining hall.

Jerod was there, finishing breakfast. "Good morning!" His face lit up with a good-natured smile. "Everything ok?"

"Yes," Karina said. "Just had to give a report on an incident last night."

"So I heard." Jerod tousled his brown hair. "Last night's desk sergeant has rumors swirling like crazy. Do you know what happened?"

Karina shrugged. "I don't think I should say anything. Let's just say that it was very weird, but everything seems to be ok."

"Silence is wisdom." He wiped his mouth with a napkin. "You ready?"

"Yeah, just let me eat a bit before we go." Karina was relieved that he didn't ask more questions. "Where do you want to go first?"

"I was thinking we could walk around Avedida Park for a bit. I can tell you all about my promotion."

"Oh?" Karina smiled as her heart fell. "Congratulations. What promotion?"

"To Captain."

"Wow. That's amazing. What does that mean for you now?"

"I'll tell you about it on our walk," said Jerod. He put his hand on Karina's.

Karina smiled. "Sure. Sounds good. That means you'll be transferred soon. That's great news. Nothing big ever happens in Avedida City." *And there goes my potential boyfriend.*

CHAPTER 17
DIMA

"OVER HERE." Avyer leaned back in his chair, waving his friend over as soon as he had entered the small cafe. He shoved the chair opposite his with his foot and pocketed his phone.

Dmitri took the chair and sat, noting they were surrounded by empty tables and chairs.

"Coffee," he said to a wizened woman who appeared to take his order. As soon as she was out of earshot, he turned to Avyer. "Quaint place." He eyed the rugs lining the walls before returning his gaze to Avyer. "Old world Gavriila feel. How was the weekend?"

"It's still the weekend, you know." Avyer took a swig of his drink.

"Rumor has it some idiot went out last night undercover, chasing after Gavriilan Spark people." Dmitri leaned toward Avyer, lacing his fingers. "Do you know who the poor devil is? They say he took a beating."

Avyer gave him an undisguised look of annoyance. "You can just ask, Dima. It was me. You know it was me."

"Uh-huh." Dmitri sat up straight and crossed his arms. "What were you thinking?"

"I suppose I wasn't thinking," Avyer said. "Happy?"

"Not really," said Dmitri. "Who or what saved your skin this time? The details were a bit fuzzy."

"There shouldn't have been any details. Last night's desk sergeant will be getting an earful," Avyer said. "In my defense, I was surrounded by three men and shot with a stun gun. Officer Karina Ivanovna saved me. She was on night patrol."

"What?" Dmitri's eyes widened in disbelief at first. He burst into laughter. "You can't be serious? That little girl you roughed up months ago?" He shook his head.

Avyer did not laugh. "The very one." As he eyed his glass, he remembered the panic in Karina's serious gray eyes when she had entered his bedroom this morning.

"You *are* serious, then. But how?"

"That's exactly what I asked her this morning," said Avyer.

"And?"

Dmitri's coffee arrived.

"Anything else?" wheezed the waitress.

"That will be all, thank you." Dmitri sipped his coffee. When she had left he repeated the question. "And?"

"She said it wasn't easy. I'm heavy in a soaking wet overcoat."

"I should think so." Dmitri laughed. "But hadn't you suspected her of working with the Gavriilan Spark people?"

"I had." Avyer nursed his drink. "But I looked into her. She's so clean that I would have to fabricate something to implicate her with them. Church-going good girl. All she's ever done is work hard. And believe me, I did some digging. There is *nothing* interesting about her other than the fact that she knows Systema. And I still don't know where in the world she learned that. Well, she said it was her uncle. Who knows?"

"I'm not going to lie," said Dmitri. "Little bugger has me impressed. You have to be double her size."

"About," Avyer confirmed, downing the last drop of from his cup. "What do you make of it?"

"She's clever. Be careful, or you'll lose her."

"Why?"

"She's good. The higher-ups will have her in their sights."

"In what sense?" Avyer sat up straight. This conversation could go in only one of two ways—either keeping a sharp eye on Karina or . . . "Is there a problem?"

"Not for you."

Avyer shifted, clearing his throat. "Someone like her . . . do you think they'd put her through the Saratov Trials?"

"If she's as good as you're saying, I don't doubt it," Dmitri said. "Does that matter?"

"Perhaps." Avyer crossed his arms.

"Well, you must do as your conscience dictates," said Dmitri, "for the good of Gavriila." He mirrored Avyer's crossed arms.

"You mock me," said Avyer, frowning. "I would just like to know what she's thinking. She could have left me there. Or kicked me. Or shot me."

"You sound disappointed." Dmitri rolled his eyes. "Just ask her."

"I did."

"What did she say?"

"First she said it went against her religion, then she said she's not stupid."

"There you go." Dmitri shrugged. "Does that not satisfy you?"

"Not particularly," said Avyer.

"In all my years of knowing you, you have never let anyone bother you as much as this girl. How old is she? Is she pretty?" Dmitri goaded.

Avyer hesitated. His mind strayed to Karina's eyes, her hair, and her dangerous habit of immediately responding with what came to her mind when he asked her a question.

"She *is*, isn't she?" A grin spread across Dmitri's face. "If I didn't know you better, I would say you liked her."

CHAPTER 18
STEPANOV

"SIR." Chief Avyer Nikolai stood at attention in front of General Pavel Stepanov's desk. "I repeat, respectfully, that Avedida is under control."

Stepanov had been listening to Avyer's monthly jurisdiction report.

"I'm not so sure of that," Stepanov responded in a deliberating tone. "Of all the provinces, yours is one of the few in which some liberties are still taken. You have a good track record squelching the Spark people, yet some areas seem to be lacking." He swiveled in his chair and turned over a data sheet.

"I follow the law to the letter. If you consult with General Raize he will confirm my total cooperation and contributions to track down Gavriilan Spark Revolutionists. There have been no uprisings the entire time I have been in charge."

General Stepanov had been studying Avyer carefully. Aside from a flicker of annoyance in his eyes Avyer was unwavering, but one could never tell exactly how far a subordinate's loyalties would lie until put they were put under pressure.

"A show of power is in order," Stepanov continued. He rose from his desk. "It's good to have that sort of thing every once in a while to keep the rabble in check, so that they see they need us.

We will launch a chemical attack on one of your smaller towns. Desmarin will do nicely."

Avyer did not react.

Stepanov walked around the desk until he was face to face with Avyer. "You will do nothing and say nothing. If the weapon is found you may dispatch a team, but they'll be sacrificed. I will leave that to your discretion, who to keep and who to sacrifice." Still no reaction from Avyer. "Any questions?"

When Avyer did not answer, he returned to his desk chair. Avyer swallowed hard when the General turned his back on him.

"When will this take place?" Avyer asked.

"Within the week."

"Very well. Should I be concerned about contamination to outlying areas?"

"Negative. We'll be using a non-persistent Genya chemical weapon. Purely cutaneous absorption."

"Any other instructions?"

General Stepanov shook his head. "You gave me a thorough enough report. I'm looking forward to hearing about the progress of the new upstarts. Sound promising."

"Yes, sir. Thank you, sir." Avyer curtly nodded.

"Very well. Dismissed."

Avyer's stoic face belied the immense lump in his throat. He took his phone out of his pocket and called Dmitri once he had left the Avedida Capitol Building.

"Dima, I need a favor."

CHAPTER 19
DESMARIN

KARINA WHEELED ARYA AROUND. The outer neighborhood of Desmarin center was a cacophony of voices and cruisers.

"Please evacuate to the designated meeting site," Karina yelled through the megaphone. "All citizens must arrive at the evacuation site within ten minutes." *I doubt they'll resist.*

When an anonymous call had come in two hours ago warning that the Spark people had planted a bomb in Desmarin, most of the townspeople began to scurry out like a swarm of ants fleeing a flooded mound. Unfortunately, Desmarin was such a dense city that the ants jammed the streets, causing further mayhem.

Avyer had ordered his upper officers to send special teams to assist the Desmarin local police with the evacuation. They had mobilized within the hour. A maglev sped them the twenty kilometers within five minutes, leaving the mounted police to direct crowds out of the city and round up stragglers.

"Captain Tolstoy?" Karina phoned her commander. "How are we on time? This sector is almost empty."

The phone crackled loudly in her ear and she winced. "Calandre is working out sector six. There is a huge traffic jam there. Ivanovna, proceed to sector five and extract several upper-class families. They seem to think they're safe. Get in and get out."

"Understood, sir. On my way." Karina sighed after she turned the phone off. "Why do people have to be so stupid?"

She rubbed Arya's neck soothingly as they walked through swarms of people. They trotted through a nearly empty side street to sector five, where four obstinate families had formed a group in the front yard of a tall, elegant house.

Of course the stragglers are rich. Rich people always think they know better.

She rode up to a tall mustached man who looked like he might be the leader.

"I must ask you to vacate the premises immediately."

"No." He crossed his arms.

She took out her stun gun. "I was being polite. What I really meant was this: there is a mandatory evacuation going on so you must leave. Once we receive the all-clear signal you may return to your homes."

The man stepped closer, grabbing Arya's bridle. The mare pinned her ears back. "Not happening." He jerked the bridle to point the horse in another direction. Arya whinnied in pain.

Karina stunned him. He slumped to the ground. "Pick him up and get in your cruisers." She waved the stun gun at the remaining stragglers. "Now!"

Now the families were anxious to leave. *They're more afraid of getting arrested than a bomb.* They were soon speeding down the road in their cruisers.

"Captain, I'm done here," she called Tolstoy again.

"Get out of here and go to the evacuation site immediately."

"What?" Karina's mouth went dry. "What is it?"

"Chemical weapon." Tolstoy sounded grim. "The team found it. Get to the site now."

"Understood. Moving out." She spurred Arya to canter down the emptiest streets, following her AutoMap's shortest route.

Arya sensed Karina's urgency and flew through the streets. A few minutes later they had reached the outskirts of Desmarin. An explosion rocked the ground as a rocket shot into the air and exploded. Karina felt as though her heart exploded with the rocket.

No ordinary bomb does that. She spurred Arya on to a gallop. *We're still too close to ground zero. If that touches me . . .*

She covered her head and face with a hooded jacket and pulled on gloves. She rummaged through her emergency kit and pulled out a gas mask. She jammed it over her face.

Probably too late . . . Karina's lips pressed into a thin line. They were three kilometers from the explosion's origin point according to the AutoMap, but given that a rocket had exploded in the air, Karina was not far enough.

Arya's skin was lathered in sweat. Karina did not dare push the mare anymore. She slowed to a canter then a trot. Arya's breath came in heaving gasps.

One kilometer from the evacuation meeting site Arya collapsed. Karina was thrown onto soft grass. Arya trembled and twitched as her breathing became more labored. The mare attempted to roll over and scrambled to get her feet on the ground. Karina jumped to her feet and pulled on the reins.

"Roll over! Roll over!" Karina begged.

The mare showed the whites of her eyes and whinnied weakly as Karina pulled. Karina looked into Arya's eyes. *Her pupils are pinpointing.* Karina let Arya rest her head on the grass. A tear ran down Karina's cheek.

"I'm so sorry." She stroked Arya's velvety nose. "I'm so sorry!"

Karina shot her in the head. Arya's head thumped to the ground in a rapidly growing pool of blood.

No time to cry. Run. Run. Run. Please, God, help me get to the site!

She ran. Karina's eyes began to blur. Her lungs burned.

Keep going. You can't die now.

Her legs grew heavy. More than once she felt as though she could not take another step.

Her legs crumpled under her weight, mere meters from the

rendezvous point. Soft green grass came up to meet her face. Karina gulped for air. Medics in blinding white contamination suits ran out with a stretcher, unceremoniously heaving her on it. They removed her gas mask and deposited her in a decontamination wagon. Everything blurred and everything around her moved in slow motion.

She heard a radio. It sounded far away. "Yes, sir. This is the chief medical officer. Yes. As far as I know. The last one made it in but doesn't look good." He paused a moment. "Ivanovna. On foot. She's gone through decontamination. Yes? Very good. Yes, sir. I will do that." The radio beeped off. "Take this and jab that girl who just arrived."

Karina barely felt a long thick needle pierce her arm. A rough plastic circle smashed against her face. Icy oxygen blew through the circle and forced its way into her lungs. That was the last thing Karina felt before losing consciousness.

CHAPTER 20
HOSPITAL

KARINA DID NOT HEAR Sasha make a fuss over her once she had arrived at the hospital. She was unaware of her family coming in and out to check on her. She had even less idea that Avyer himself had entered her private hospital room.

Sasha stood up from sitting on Karina's metal bed when Avyer entered the tiny room.

"At ease." He nodded to Sasha.

Sasha sat back down.

"How is she?"

"Better. The doctor said she should wake up soon. What happened?" Sasha asked.

"I'm not at liberty to discuss all the details," he said. "What I can tell you is that she saved many lives. She saved several families at the last minute, right before the bomb went off."

"Of course she did," Sasha muttered more to herself than to Avyer.

"I came to leave this for her." Avyer Nikolai retrieved a small box out of his deep coat pocket. "Hardly a consolation prize for nearly dying, but it's standard issue. Hero of the Gavriilan Federation." He hesitated a moment before handing the box to Sasha. "Would you give this to her when she wakes up?"

"Certainly." Sasha took the box, looking at him curiously. "Who were the families she saved?"

"Upper class nobodies."

Sasha squinted in suspicion as she watched him leave. A nurse entered to administer Karina's daily injection and IV, so she turned her attention to the nurse's work with needles.

A syringe fell with a clatter on the nurse's metal tray. Karina's head tilted to the right.

"Karina?" Sasha's eyes lit up.

"Mmm?"

"Karina!"

"Yeah?" Karina turned her head to the left to look at Sasha.

"Karina!"

"Yes. Sasha." Her eyes half opened.

"I thought you were going to die on me already." Sasha smiled. "Welcome back. What happened?"

Karina blinked. "Everything feels fuzzy. I was riding Arya and I . . ."

"Yes?"

"I . . . I had to shoot her." Tears filled her eyes as she remembered. Sobs racked her body as tears streamed down her cheeks. "She was poisoned."

"Are you seriously bawling your eyes out over a horse?" Sasha smacked Karina's bed. "That should be one of the last things on your mind."

Karina sobbed the entire time the nurse was medicating her. Sasha rolled her eyes. "Love your priorities. You almost died!"

When Karina managed to contain the tears, questions flooded her mind. "What's happened? How long have I been here? Does my family know I'm ok?"

"Your mom, dad, and sister have visited. They're distraught. Chief Nikolai visited. I've been here since forever. Several families came to pay their respects. And you've been in this particular hospital five days now."

"What? Five days? And Avyer? What? Why? And what families?"

"Calm down or I'll ask a doctor to sedate you," Sasha said drily. "You're recovering from chemical poisoning. You're the *only* one who was poisoned and survived. The only one. Nearly half of Desmarin died. And as far as the visitors, it's the families that you saved that came to see you. One of them," she said, savoring the drama, "looked very familiar."

"What?"

"Do you remember the guy you stunned?"

"Yeah. Man with a mustache?"

"The Nikolai family." Sasha raised an eyebrow.

"It's a common enough name." Karina sat up.

"It's no coincidence." Sasha grinned. "I took it upon myself to research them. You shot Chief Nikolai's father."

CHAPTER 21
RETURN TO DUTY

KARINA ENDURED three more days in the hospital before being cleared for duty. She reluctantly attached the medal to her dress coat. The Hero of the Gavriilan Federation medal was a simple purple bar overlaid with an ornate silver star. Sasha said it was awarded to police officers that nearly died in the line of duty.

Karina eyed her uniform nervously, wriggling as Sasha wound her long hair into triple buns. Karina looked at Sasha in the mirror as she stood behind her.

"You'll be fine." Sasha patted Karina's shoulder with tranquility.

"I know," said Karina. "I would just feel better if I knew how this were going to go."

"Come on." Sasha grinned mischievously. "We both know he's either going to kiss you or kill you."

"Shut up."

"You saved his family."

"So what? He probably hates them," said Karina. "I don't think he likes anyone. If he cared about them, he would've gotten them out personally."

"I doubt that," Sasha said. "He would've looked angry when

he came to the hospital. I don't know how to describe his face, but angry it was not."

Karina rolled her shoulders.

"Relax. If nothing else, you'll get through this with your natural charm."

"I'm not charming."

"Don't be silly," chided Sasha. "Go." She gave Karina a gentle shove. "Don't want to be late!"

"Yeah." Karina let Sasha's push impulse her out the door.

The spring breeze pushed dark clouds across the sky. All around everything was green as though in preparation for the next season. Buds had sprouted in the once-dead garden in the middle of the grounds, the crackly brown stems replaced by fresh green stalks. A damp, earthy aroma hung in the air.

Rain. Karina inhaled deeply. *This is getting to be a bad habit, constantly reporting to Avyer.*

She reported to the desk sergeant. "Officer Ivanovna to see Chief Nikolai."

The same grizzled man who attended the desk every other day barely looked at her. "Go on to his office. Knock on the door. He's expecting you."

"Ok."

Her heart began to pound in time with a downpour outside. When she reached his office she rapped on the door smartly. He might not hear her over the rain. Karina leaned forward, straining to listen over the torrential rain.

"Come in." Avyer's strong voice rang out, slightly muffled.

The door slid open. As soon as she had entered it closed behind her.

"Sit, Ivanovna. This is an official conversation and will be recorded." He pressed the record button on his datapad. "Officer Karina Annushka Ivanovna, report on the events of March twentieth."

"Yes, sir." She recounted the fateful day, careful to include every detail. "I was riding police mare 212." A lump grew in her throat toward the end. "She was poisoned but she had galloped through Desmarin. She collapsed approximately two kilometers from the rendezvous point and couldn't get up." *Don't cry. Don't cry.*

"You're certain it wasn't fatigue?"

"Very. Her pupils were tiny, and signs of poisoning presented themselves before she collapsed. She was a good animal, sir. The run we made was not enough to kill her."

"I see. Continue." His gaze was fixed on Karina, as he weighed her every word.

"I shot her and ran to the rendezvous point. I'd tried to cover myself with a coat and other equipment, but some of the poison made contact with my skin. I passed out on site. I don't know what happened between then and when I woke up in the hospital."

"Very well. Thank you for your report." He stopped the recorder. "I have a few questions for you, not on the record. You wasted a bullet on the mare, did you not?"

Karina stiffened. "She was suffering."

Avyer sat back. "I see." He laced his fingers. "Minus the wasted bullet, you are to be commended. Stand."

Karina stood.

"Turn around slowly. Keep turning." He waved at her until she had revolved in a complete circle and faced him again. "Good. I require an escort for the annual gala at the Gavriila Royal Palace. You'll do. Better a hero from my own ranks than a paid escort."

"Permission to say something, sir?" Karina's voice cracked at the end of the question. She nearly sat, but jerked back to attention when she remembered that he had told her to stand.

"What?"

"I don't dance."

"All the better. Neither do I."

"You're taller than I am."

"You're the one who has emphasized that size doesn't matter."

A pinkish tinge spread across Karina's cheeks. "What do I need to wear? Dress uniform?"

"No." Avyer rolled his eyes. "Gala means dresses for women. I'll see that you're provided for. Can't have you waltzing in looking like a country bumpkin."

Karina stood there for a few seconds with her mouth slightly open, no argument willing itself to her lips. *What is worse? Being insulted or being forced to go with him?*

"That's all," Avyer said. "I will send for you." He waved her away.

Karina left in a daze and feeling like a dog dismissed by its master. *I'd like to find Sasha and tell her everything, but I have a patrol to cover.* She returned to her room for her raincoat before going to the stable.

Since losing Arya, she sent for Gladrion to be brought to the police stable. He had been wasting away in the Vadim Stables. A few weeks ago she had found a reputable breeder to breed him with several mares. This time the only charge was the foal of her choice. *Just in case.*

She strapped on a blast proof and bulletproof vest before she saddled up to make her rounds. Calandre had died in the Desmarin attack, so now Illya was her partner.

"Good morning, Karina!" He greeted her with a smile when she found him in their quadrant. "Everything ok?'

Karina nodded. "Yeah, just . . . can we talk about things not related to work?"

"Of course."

Illya was a more pleasant partner than Calandre. He understood what she meant by her request and talked all kinds of pleasant nonsense while they rode.

The beat was calm despite the rain. The deluge drenched anything not covered by their heavy raincoats. Feeling cold and being preoccupied with dreams of a steaming hot shower helped Karina forget all about Avyer.

The miserably wet day concluded with a wonderfully dull

evening. After taking care of Gladrion, Karina basked in a hot shower and a change of clothing. She ate alone because Sasha had already eaten and was out on a date.

Karina peered out the dining windows as she finished eating. She made out part of the well-lit exercise track peeking between two buildings. It appeared to be empty. Since the rain had stopped the air was probably cool and refreshing. She wiped her mouth and left the dining hall for a solitary walk.

As she approached the track, her heart fell. It was not empty. One other person was walking around. Avyer.

What in the world is he doing here? He's never in common areas.

She could not turn around. That would be too obvious, especially since he strode straight toward her.

"Don't let me stop you," he said as he drew closer.

"I won't." She walked at a brisk pace, but Avyer easily took her two strides with one.

"You're not on duty. Is there a problem?"

Karina clenched her sweaty palms. "The last time I showed how I felt you slapped me. I'd rather not spend a night in stun cuffs or in trouble."

"Ah. I shall leave you in peace, then." He left the track abruptly, leaving a bewildered but relieved Karina looking after him.

CHAPTER 22

BREAK

SOMETHING HAD TWISTED in his gut when his eyes met Karina's. Avyer maintained his facade as he returned to his room. It broke only after the door slid shut behind him.

"Why does she keep getting in my way? No matter what I do, I end up using her for something. And she's too good to get rid of." He ground his teeth as he recalled his conversation with Dima at the cafe.

CHAPTER 23
THE PROJECT

KARINA WAS AWAKENED by someone shaking her shoulder. Her bleary eyes struggled to focus on the night receptionist standing over at her. "Yeah?"

"Dress. You're wanted at the front desk." The receptionist left.

"Great," groaned Karina. She blinked as she struggled to read the clock. It was an hour before they normally got up.

"Whaizit?" Sasha mumbled as Karina slid to the floor.

"Dunno," said Karina. "Can't be good, not at this time."

Her unsteady hands fumbled to dress quickly. She stumbled to the bathroom to splash cold water on her face. She slicked her hair back into a ponytail and smoothed her eyebrows with the water dripping from her fingers. She traded her hairbrush for a cap and belted her gun over her tunic. *Hopefully whoever it is won't be about to shoot me.*

Or perhaps they would. Avyer stood in the lobby with his hands behind his back.

"Sir?" She stiffened to attention.

"We are going for a walk." He pointed at the misty track they had walked on hours before.

Karina cleared her throat when they reached the track. "This seems highly irregular."

"It is." His normally deep voice went a pitch higher than normal. Karina looked at him sharply. "What would you say if I told you that the Desmarin attack wasn't all that it was cracked up to be?"

Karina's gut churned. *This is a dangerous conversation. If he's trying to trick me, I'm dead.* "I wouldn't be surprised. I'd be angry. We lost good men, not to mention all the civilians that didn't make it." *That's a safe answer.*

"Be angry then. And what would you say if I told you that all the . . ." His voice trailed off and Avyer swallowed hard. "What if," he continued, mastering himself, "survivors from the city were shot down like dogs, on the pretense that they had collaborated with the bombing?"

"All of them?" Karina breathed.

"Every. Single. One."

"Why are you telling me this?" Karina stood still. "Are we not, as Bentuarian Loyalists, to turn a blind eye to this sort of thing?" She sized him up, more afraid of his answer than the consequences of a borderline rebellious question.

"And are we to not waste munitions, even on a measly, dying animal?" Avyer retorted.

Karina's legs shuddered under her weight. Her palms sweated, and everything else quivered in fear. *What did I just say? He could kill me. My family. Just for that question.*

"What?" he asked after several seconds of silence.

"Nothing. Sir."

Breathe. Just keep breathing. Don't hyperventilate, not now. Breathe, not too loudly.

"Then keep walking," he said.

Karina forced her rubbery legs to move. "With all respect, sir, you haven't really explained anything. Why tell me this?"

"I needed to see your reaction."

"Oh."

"I need a lower officer to move to the HR department. You will be that officer."

"Will there be an interview?"

"No."

"Oh. Does this require . . . personal favors?"

"Hardly." Avyer's face twisted in disgust.

"What do you want from me?" Karina pried. Anything would be better than an awkward silence.

"Total commitment to the project."

"That's what all of us are expected to give."

"I don't know who I can trust right now," said Avyer. He stopped walking and grabbed her by the arms. "Can I trust you?" He drew back. "You're shaking like a leaf."

"I'm fine," she replied coldly. She pulled away from him. "And yes, you can trust me."

Neither dared look at the other as they silently paced halfway around the track. Karina's body trembled uncontrollably, while Avyer scrubbed his hand down his face in bewilderment.

When he peeked at her first, he shoved down strange feelings demanding to settle in his chest. No one would suspect her: everything about her was innocent, from her wiry build to her soft gray eyes and small face. He looked at his watch.

"We'll continue this conversation later."

"Very well, sir."

When Karina returned to the barracks, the glowing clock marked the hour as ten to six. Still shivering, she took off her boots and coat to climb into Sasha's bunk. Sasha awakened with a squeal when Karina's cold fingers brushed her arm.

"What the kark? I just fell asleep."

"Avyer," said Karina quietly.

"Wha—? What happened? You ok?"

"I don't know . . . Yes, I guess I'm ok."

"Well?" Sasha gave Karina a sleepy grin. "You'd better tell me all the details. And don't leave out any of the juicy stuff."

РАСПРОДАЖА
МАНГО
РАСПРОД

CHAPTER 24
GALA

KARINA'S FACE was plastered everywhere: signs, newspapers, and news. Karina hated being the talk of Avedida but she could not very well run away from citizens coming up to praise or thank her for her bravery in Desmarin.

The dawn of the morning of the gala, Sasha awakened to keep Karina company while she dressed.

"Do you think he's crazy?" Karina whispered as she dressed in the bathroom.

"No," Sasha reassured her. "His family must be dead now. You know." She lowered her voice. "What if he may not be all that bad?"

"Not all that bad?" Karina echoed. She popped her head out of her stall to give Sasha an incredulous look. "Hello! Are you ok? He still talks in threatening undertones. One day he slaps me, and then he takes me to a political party!" She disappeared behind the door to finish dressing. "Why should I trust him?"

"It wouldn't be a bad thing," Sasha reflected. Karina could hear the eye roll in Sasha's tone of voice. "The Chief's good-looking."

"So what? Torture and cruelty are just minor details?" Karina came out to do her makeup while Sasha did her hair. They traded places when they finished.

"You are beautiful. He's brain dead if he doesn't see that. As soon as you hit the red carpet, all the guys will drop dead."

"I don't think they have red carpets at these things." Karina laughed nervously. "But I'll try to remember that. It makes me feel better." She hugged Sasha. "Don't get into trouble while I'm gone."

"I won't. You, too." Sasha hugged her back harder.

"I'll be careful." Karina balled her fingers into fists, breathing deeply as she left the women's barracks. *There's nothing to be afraid of. Avyer's had plenty of opportunities to hurt me again. He hasn't yet.*

She kept telling herself that as she entered the main office and was directed to Avyer's office. She was about to knock on his office door when Avyer barreled around the corner at a brisk pace, in full dress uniform.

"Let's go," he said. "Cruiser's waiting."

She trotted to keep up as they went out to the cruiser. She climbed in one side and he on the other.

"Enjoy the view. It's a five-hour ride." He reclined his seat and fell asleep.

Karina did just that. There was nothing of interest in the sumptuous cruiser so she watched the scenery slip by—town, countryside, city, countryside and more countryside. Between the window and stolen glances at sleeping Avyer, time flew by and they were in Chita before she knew it.

Normal Gavriilans were not allowed free passage from province to province, so Karina was unsure what to expect. The capital city of Chita was not as horrible as she had anticipated.

A cacophony of cruisers, wagons, and freight vehicles traversed the streets, winding around multi-storied structures built in a colorful, ancient onion dome style. More sleek and modern buildings curved up to the sky like giant white teeth.

Karina eagerly glanced at everything all at once. She was

unaware that Avyer had awakened and was observing her child-like enthrallment of the metropolis.

The cruiser drove through a nice side of Chita. They passed at least fifty boxy and domed condo buildings in a row before turning off the main street into a commercial area.

"You will wear what I choose." Avyer's voice broke her reverie as the cruiser parked in front of a purple boxy building. There was no sign out front.

He stepped out of the cruiser to the sidewalk. He held a hand out for her as she followed him. It was the same one that had been on her throat months ago. She could feel it on her throat again as she eyed it.

"Come on." He beckoned impatiently with his hand. "We don't have much time."

Karina accepted the hand. It closed around her hand, strong yet gently pulling her out of the cruiser.

"Welcome, welcome." A clothier smiled and bobbed up and down as they entered the automatic doors. "It's been a while."

Karina gawked at the shades of purple drowning the interior. An indigo carpet squished under her boots with each step she took, strings of lavender wrapped around the walls, and the chandelier lights glared off a vaulted amethyst tiled ceiling.

"Since the last gala," Avyer said curtly. "She needs clothes." He tilted his head at Karina.

"Do you have a theme in mind?"

"Mature innocence."

The clothier stroked her chin, looking Karina up and down.

"Well." She walked all around Karina. "I think I would go more for the mature part. Forget the innocence. She's got too much of that."

"She's in your hands. I will wait here to see the results." Avyer nodded and installed himself in a chair outside the dressing room.

Avyer insisted on seeing everything she tried on. Karina had no say in the matter, with Avyer or the dresser.

"Pink chiffon," announced the dresser as Karina entered with an overly fluffed dress.

"She's not twelve."

"Red nights." The dresser flaunted a dress wrapped tightly around Karina like bandages.

"It's a gala, not a mummy festival."

"Airy heights." The dresser presented a simpler, white gown.

"Gala. Not a country wedding." Avyer glared at the dresser. "Dark and striking colors. Mature."

The clothier returned. "How are things going?"

"Terrible. Find something better or I'll take my business elsewhere."

The clothier and the dresser exchanged glances.

"I'll take care of this," the clothier said confidently. "We'll bring out the gold. Yes, that one! Look for *Golden Age*." She sent the dresser to find it while Karina waited in the changing room.

"I hope this works." Karina sighed as they bustled her into the dress. Avyer's foot tapped impatiently outside the changing room.

When Karina saw herself in the wall-to-wall mirror, her stomach dropped several floors at the thought of Avyer seeing her in this one.

It would have been difficult and a delight to paint: the velvety forest green bodice was overlaid with delicate golden lace flowers. A silky golden sash at the waist divided the bodice from the long shimmering green skirt. The only color breaking up the swath of silky green cloth was golden paisley teardrops creeping from the hem of the skirt, their points trailing upwards.

When she came out, Avyer's eyes lit up in approval.

"That's it," Avyer said. "Let's go." He paid and they returned to the cruiser.

Daylight waned as the cruiser navigated more congested streets. They wound around to stop at a professional stylist.

Avyer gave her a warning before opening the cruiser door. "From here on out, only speak when spoken to. Smile and look pleasant. You're not allowed to have an opinion even if asked for it. Understood?"

"Yes, sir." Karina's palms began to sweat.

The stylist had Karina complete within an hour. *I wish I felt as confident as I look.* She ran a finger along the vine-like outlines of the golden choker around her neck. It matched a long bracelet encasing her left arm.

"You'll pass." Avyer's eyes lingered on hers as he considered the eyeshadow and mascara the stylist had used. "Let's go."

The cruiser dropped them off at a long, white staircase leading to an elegant archway beckoning a multitude inside an immense blue and white vestibule. Before Avyer weaved his way through the crowds his hand found Karina's, lacing his fingers through hers. He guided her behind him as he pushed his way inside.

Karina felt as though the crowd had disappeared when they stepped into a ballroom. She found herself gawking at the ornate blue, white, and gold decorated ceiling vaulted at least three stories above them. She was captivated by intricate cut-glass chandeliers hanging from the ceiling, modern imitations of light fixtures from hundreds of years ago. Avyer's hand tugged her back down to reality, to the ground floor, to him and the less than desirable company they were keeping tonight.

He limited himself to commands and brief comments, such as "Take my arm," or "Don't slouch," or "Keep your eyes up."

What a charmer.

Avyer mingled with the dry, military types. Most of them greeted her upon introduction before pretending that she no longer existed. Karina amused herself by soaking in her surroundings, appreciating the paintings hanging on the walls or admiring the intricacies of the walls themselves.

"Hello, Avyer!" A man with a curly mop of brown hair called behind them.

"Dima." Avyer nodded stiffly, but his eyes flickered with amusement. He released Karina's hand.

"And who might this be?" Dmitri asked as he bowed his head at Karina. A few curls strayed into his eyes.

"Dmitri Janiv, this is Karina Ivanovna."

"A pleasure." Dmitri took her hand. "Might I have a dance?"

Worry lines creased Karina's forehead as she glanced between Avyer and Dmitri.

"You might not." Avyer pried Dmitri's fingers from Karina's hand. "Mine." He laced his fingers through Karina's. "We'll talk later."

Dmitri shrugged but gave a good-natured laugh. "Sure."

"Mine?" Karina muttered to herself with an unladylike snort as Avyer led her to another group of people.

"Yes." His arm tightened around her.

"As always, you have taste." A greying, stiff man greeted Avyer. He took Karina's chin with his hand to force her to look him in the eyes.

"General Pavel Stepanov," Avyer acknowledged him.

"You're not a typical escort," noted Stepanov. Karina lifted her chin out of his hand.

"She's one of my officers," explained Avyer.

Stepanov let his hand fall to his side.

"I see," he said without any emotion.

A chill ran down Karina's spine. *It's as though his eyes were dead.* Avyer Nikolai was a hard man, but she knew what to expect from him. General Stepanov . . . there was something frightening about him . . .

"Blind obedience. Unswerving loyalty. We need more of that these days. What's your name, my dear?"

Out of the corner of her eye Karina saw Avyer nod. "Karina Ivanovna."

"That sounds familiar."

"It would," said Avyer. "She barely escaped the Desmarin attack."

"Ah, that would be it." The General nodded. The pleasant smile on his lips did not reach his eyes. "Brave and beautiful.

Good choice." The conversation turned to mundane, work-related topics. He looked at her sharply when there was a lull in conversation.

Karina zoned out of the conversation. *The General's comment about blind obedience was pointed.* She considered things in Avedida. *Our people aren't all blindly obedient. Some are. Not all of them.*

"Wine?" General Stepanov accepted a goblet and offered her one when a server came around.

"No, thank you."

The server turned toward Karina and tripped. The contents of a full goblet splashed in her face. Tears streamed down her face as Karina blinked her burning eyes.

"You should be grateful and accept what is offered," General Stepanov said. He took a sip of wine as though nothing had happened.

"The restrooms are in the corner," said Avyer.

He spun her around in the general direction of the restrooms. Karina walked blindly and blinking furiously. She had not taken five steps when a hand wrapped around her waist. Karina stiffened.

"That's got to hurt," Avyer said. He guided her but she pulled away from him "Don't do that. You're going to run into someone or fall and hurt yourself." He drew her closer and released her at the restroom door.

She rinsed her eyes for several minutes. She patted her face dry, careful to avoid smearing the makeup. *Where would we be without waterproof mascara?* She dried her damp dress under a hand dryer before returning to the gala.

Avyer leaned against the wall next to the restroom door. He uncrossed his arms. "Better?"

"What do you care?" She looked at him, red-eyed and now every inch as imperious as Avyer.

He peered at her eyes, first one then the other. "I don't want them to . . . nothing."

Avyer took her by the arm. As he made his rounds, his hand

fell back down to her waist again. Karina squirmed and wriggled out of his grasp, but his hand always returned to her side.

"Behave," Avyer said sharply, in such a tone that Karina did not dare resist him again.

Avyer spent the entire evening swirling an untouched glass of wine with his right hand. His left hand did not leave her unless he were shaking hands. Otherwise, it lingered behind the small of her back or was wrapped around her side. He ate nothing, nor did he encourage her to eat, so Karina did not accept food from the servers. By the time people started leaving her stomach was audibly protesting.

Just when she feared they would spend the entire night in the palace, Avyer began giving his farewells. Twenty-four handshakes, a few embraces, and more than one witty remark later found them outside the Gavriila Royal Palace to their awaiting cruiser.

Avyer opened the door for Karina to climb in. When he entered he leaned back in the seat and stretched his legs.

"Ugh." He unbuttoned his dress coat and pulled out his shirt. Karina stared at him, waiting for him to say something. "What?"

"I had a question," she said.

"What?"

"Are we going to eat?"

Avyer chuckled. "Noticed that, huh? I don't trust anyone."

"Nor do I."

He pressed the cruiser comm. "Take us to eat. The usual place."

"Yes, sir," the comm echoed slightly.

Avyer sprawled out in the back seat and fell asleep again. Karina eyed him uncertainly. She could not get comfortable. She could not, would not change clothes, not here. She sat back and stared at Avyer. Questions with no answers ran through her mind.

Avyer slept until the cruiser stopped at a restaurant. He groggily lifted his head. "We're here. I'll go in and order. You can change in the cruiser if you want." He ran a hand through his hair and yawned.

After he left, Karina changed faster than she had thought possible. "I just don't know," she contemplated the restaurant. "I just . . ."

Avyer emerged from the restaurant entrance. Karina opened the cruiser door and stepped out.

"I was beginning to think you'd gotten lost in there," Avyer said as they walked inside.

"It was a lot of fabric to wade through," said Karina.

"I've already ordered. Food will be ready soon."

Karina had no idea what they were eating, but she was too hungry to ask questions. She tried everything they served her.

"So." Avyer watched her eat. "You're not worried that I might poison you?"

Karina stopped mid-bite. "No."

"Why not?"

"If you wanted to kill me you would have done that a long time ago."

"True." Avyer downed a shot before pouring another from the tall bottle the server had left them. "You don't drink."

"No. And you do," Karina noted as he drank the second shot.

"One of my few vices."

Karina snorted.

"You disagree?" asked Avyer.

"I don't think you want to know what I think."

"You'd be surprised. Why don't you drink?"

"It goes against my religion."

"What is with you and your religion?" Avyer scowled as he poured another shot.

"Even if it weren't my religion, I'd rather be in complete control of my faculties." Karina took another bite to avoid conversation.

"Huh." Avyer did not pursue further conversation.

They finished eating quickly. As they left, Avyer grabbed another bottle to take with him. Karina looked askance at him.

"One for the road."

He drank. And drank. And drank.

Karina was no expert, but whatever he had been drinking had him wasted an hour into the drive home. That or he was so tired that exhaustion combined with alcohol knocked him out.

He began mumbling incoherently. "Yes . . . sleep . . . no . . . yes, I want to . . ." After mumbling a few minutes he raised his head and blinked at Karina. "Y'know why I don't care if I fall asleep around you?" he slurred.

"I don't."

"You're the only good person working . . . I *know* you're not going to kill me in my sleep. Y'know what we should do?"

"No."

Avyer's eyes shut and his head fell to the side. Karina tentatively leaned over him. *Still breathing.* She sighed with relief.

"And I probably don't want to know," she said aloud.

CHAPTER 25
ROUTINE

"COME ON!" Karina awakened Sasha. "Today's the day."

Sasha made a low growling sound.

"You asked me to teach you how to ride," Karina reminded her.

"Yeah, but not this early on our day off."

"What time do you think it is?" asked Karina.

"Eight." Sasha refused to open her eyes.

"Nope."

"Nine?"

"It's noon."

"Wha—" Sasha's golden eyes fluttered open. "It's lunch time!"

"Yes! Get dressed and let's go!"

Karina was bouncing with energy. She had gotten up early to check on Gladrion, find a horse for Sasha, go for a run and take a shower.

"Tone it down a bit, would you?" Sasha said crossly as she stumbled behind Karina to the dining hall.

After a quiet lunch, they walked to let their food settle.

"I don't want to get sick on a horse," Sasha had said. It was a valid point.

Karina was too pleased that her friend was willing to learn, to push Sasha much more. After the long walk they went to the stables.

"This is Ron." Karina introduced Sasha to a plain brown animal. "He's a gelding, so he should be easier to manage than Gladrion."

"What's a gelding?"

"He can't mate," said Karina. "Compare him and Gladrion. You'll see a difference." She pulled Gladrion closer to Sasha. Sasha eyed Ron warily. "Put a hand out. He's gentle. He won't bite." Karina gave Ron an affectionate pat on the neck. "Don't be shy."

Sasha stretched out her trembling fingers for Ron to sniff. When he showed no inclination to bite, she delicately patted his velvety nose.

They took everything in baby steps. Meet Ron. Pet Ron. Brush Ron. Put the tack on Ron. Mount Ron.

Sasha did not feel confident enough to tell Ron what to do, so Karina mounted Gladrion and led Ron while she corrected Sasha's riding posture.

"Relax and let yourself move with the horse."

At the end of the session Sasha felt confident enough to give Gladrion a pat without shaking.

"Same time next week?" asked Karina, grinning.

"I guess so," said Sasha. "That wasn't too bad."

"It can only get better."

———

Life had settled back into a routine. Karina rode on rounds with Illya nearly every day. She got to intimately know the streets of Avedida, because Illya pointed out many places and areas she had not even known existed.

Illya was the opposite of Calandre, and he never asked Karina to split up.

"So, you and Sasha," he said one day. "You're close, aren't you?"

"Yeah, pretty close."

"Can I ask you something and you keep it a secret?"

"Maybe. Is it good or bad?"

"All good." Illya laughed. "Don't look so alarmed."

"Go for it."

"Does Sasha have a boyfriend?"

Now Karina laughed. "Nope, she's free."

"Do you think I'd have a chance?"

"I'd think so. Just give it a try. Wouldn't you prefer a regular person, though? I think it'd be more stressful, both of you being police and all."

"You really don't know much about police culture, do you?" asked Illya.

Karina shook her head.

"It's normal to go out with fellow officers. I'd go so far as to say it's encouraged. There are generations of families in the force," he explained. "Take my family, for example. My parents both work in Lonok. They met in the force like their parents did before them."

"Odd."

"Not really. Think about it. It makes sense, even for the government."

"Give it a shot with Sasha, if you think you're up to the task," she said. "And good luck!" Karina's mind wandered. *What would happen if I dated someone here?*

"What about yourself?" Illya interrupted her thoughts.

"What about me?"

"Anyone special?"

"Maybe. I don't know. I had a boyfriend a couple of years ago but it didn't take. Like he was a taker and didn't give anything back. I'm a bit busy these days. No one has their eyes on me, anyway."

Illya rolled his eyes. "You're oblivious. There's Jerod, for one. Well, he's not around anymore. Quite a few of the guys have their eyes on you, especially since Chief Nikolai hand-picked you."

"Who told you that?" Karina pulled the reins a little harder than she meant to.

"Must be true, judging from your reaction." He grinned.

"Who?"

"It came down the grapevine. Maybe Kuzmin, who shocked you silly." Karina drew a sharp breath and her cheeks felt hot. "Maybe the doc. Maybe the desk sergeant on duty the night you rescued the chief," Illya said. "Certainly not Chief Nikolai and definitely not Sasha. She's silenter than a grave."

Karina smirked. *That's true. Sasha wouldn't tell anyone anything.*

"So it's all true," Illya mused as Karina did nothing to deny the claims. "Then there's the fact that he took you to the gala the other week."

"So?" Karina's face was flaming red.

"So normally ranking officers either have a paid companion or they bring a girl they fancy. Didn't know that either, did you?"

"Nope." She leaned back over her saddle to grab her water bottle. She gulped water, hoping to cool her face.

"You look shocked," Illya said. "What are you going to do?"

Karina rolled her eyes. "Finish our shift. We've one more round to make." She hurried Gladrion into a trot.

"That's not what I meant!" Illya called after her. Sighing, he spurred his horse after her. "C'mon, it wouldn't hurt to share a bit with everyone. A little gossip livens up life."

CHAPTER 26
MOVEMENTS

"GOOD AFTERNOON, GENERAL RAIZE." Avyer Nikolai extended his hand.

General Raize accepted his hand and gave it limp shake before Avyer sat in a posh red chair. Avyer eyed the many empty chairs. No one was in the bar, the library, or this tea room. *Must have bought out the place for his meetings today.*

"Afternoon," grunted the white-stubbled man. "Let's sit and get down to business." He heaved his hulking frame into a leather easy chair. "How are things in Avedida?"

"Good." Avyer did not hesitate as he sat back in his chair. "We've had no problems, especially after the Desmarin maneuver."

A server offered both men a drink. General Raize accepted a glass of whisky, as did Avyer.

General Raize grunted. "That's relative. We have serious trouble stirring in the south."

"How far south?"

"In Oryol province."

"That's quite far," said Avyer smoothly. "I doubt that dissent there will affect my jurisdiction."

"Have you heard of the Lomans?" Raize leaned toward Avyer.

Avyer let out a hiss of disgust. "Who hasn't? There's only one or two of them left. What could they possibly do to shake the Bentuarian Empire?"

"You'd be surprised. General Joseph Loman is a formidable general in the IPG Special Air Forces. His sister joined the ranks, and it's been coming down the grapevine that they are moving closer to Bentuari. There was an altercation in Yashu last year. We've covered it up well, but Bentuari is shaking in his boots, and people are beginning to feel it."

"What could an upstart general and a little girl possibly do to change things?" A lump came out of nowhere to settle in Avyer's throat.

"It may sound like absolute nonsense, but a lot. And Karura Solari has joined them."

"Is there any good news?" Avyer's throat tightened.

Raize paused. "You have been an outstanding officer. This is not to go beyond this room."

"Understood, sir."

Raize cleared his throat. "What I just said . . . all that happened around five years ago."

"What?" Avyer sat up straighter and set his glass on a side table. "Why were we not informed?"

"The Bentuarian Empire exists, even if Bentuari himself does not. Do you understand?"

Avyer sat back and his hand returned to his glass. "Yes, sir. It's just . . . a lot to take in. What do we do?"

"There will be arrests and executions. If they're directly from General Stepanov or myself, you'll do nothing. Empty your jail cells now. They're about to fill up."

"As my senior officer, how would you suggest I empty them?"

Raize gave a careless wave. "Your problem. I'd suggest killing them. It saves time in the long run."

"Understood, sir."

"How much?"

"All of it," said Avyer.

"Repeat it back to me."

"We'll make an example of people. I'm to not get in the way or intervene in any form or fashion, and I am to follow direct orders from you or General Stepanov."

"Beautiful." Raize clapped. "Stepanov chose wisely. Keep this up my boy. It'll take you far."

"Thank you, sir. Will there be anything else?"

"No, that's all. Send a waiter here on your way out."

Avyer left the club looking thoughtful. *That hardly went the way I would've liked. There is much to decide now.* He returned to the Avedida police station.

The first step was to clear out the jail cells. Avyer shipped prisoners out in truckloads. The trucks went far, only to come back empty. Daily executions began, with murderers and rapists sentenced to the firing squad.

That was just the beginning.

General Stepanov made arrests in Avedida province's major cities. The detained were filtered to the Avedida jail, which filled to bursting. Tension ran higher.

Arrests were based on severity of the crime. Who had flagrantly broken the law? Who had spoken out against the government? Who was suspected of anti-government sentiment? Neighbors reported on neighbors, engendering a sense that you could trust no one.

Neither Stepanov nor Raize set foot in Avedida to oversee the arrests, so Avyer was out front and center. He spent hours poring over the lists of people to be arrested the following day. He needed to see his men and their reactions so in addition to selecting the day's executioners, he observed the executions.

Strategically, none of the officer's families were arrested. The Bentuarian regime was at least aware that would have been a morale killer. The day would come soon enough when they would thin their own ranks.

Avyer removed all women from mounted patrol, assigning that task to men. The women were allowed to ride shotgun in patrol cruisers or perform other menial tasks. Sasha was reassigned reception duty more often than not, and occasional sniper duty for raids.

Karina was reassigned guard duty, which was the best and the worst. It was quiet work, but prisoners grabbed at her or threw things at her.

She was cleverer than the older, larger male guards. They would get lazy or cocky because they were larger. Karina took nothing for granted. That was what got you in trouble . . . or killed. More than one guard had been strangled to death or tricked because they had underestimated the prisoners.

Avyer did not fail to notice her dedication, which resulted in his posting her on guard duty more frequently. Given that the jail was full, Avyer took it upon himself to make more daily rounds to inspect the cells. He inevitably passed Karina at her post.

Karina always stood at attention when Avyer passed without a word. She remained at attention even when he was far from her, because he occasionally glanced back at her.

Despite her reassignment, weeks had passed without him uttering a word to her. Her eyes widened with surprise the day that he did speak to her while she was on guard duty.

"Come with me," he told her. He motioned for an officer outside to take Karina's place. Once they had strolled out of earshot of the guard the conversation began. "At ease. What do you see here?" he asked.

Karina clasped her hands behind her back. "A lot of trouble waiting to happen."

"Explain." Avyer crossed his arms as they ambled down the hall.

"I'm not so certain it's a good idea to explain in here," she said nervously. She took a faltering step.

"Say it," Avyer commanded.

"If the idea is to have a tighter grip on people, it's a bad one, at least for Avedida. We've always been compliant and I don't think people will put up with this for much longer."

"How do you know this?"

"Look around you." She gestured at the full cells. "I see and hear things in here, all day."

"Uh huh."

They continued their walk down the hall.

"Just ask any of the other guards," Karina broke the silence.

"Don't think that I haven't asked them," Avyer retorted. "You're the last one. They're concerned with logistics. You *see* the people. I have a proposition to make. Could we meet in Liski Park on Saturday? We can finish this conversation there."

"What kind of proposition?" Karina asked slowly. Liski Park was a huge public forest, not a typical meeting place for work.

"We can discuss that there," he replied. "I won't ask again. Take it or leave it."

"Yes. When and where?"

"Ten a.m. on the Southern Ridge." One of the less-used hiking trails.

"I'll be there."

"Here." Avyer held out a slip of paper. "Call me when you arrive."

Karina grabbed at the paper and pulled it, but Avyer did not release it immediately. Karina stood in resignation waiting for him to let go.

"There is no going back from this," Avyer warned her. Only then did he let go of the paper.

Karina's brow furrowed as she tried to read his expression. His face betrayed no emotion. She shuddered as though someone had stepped on her grave. "Ok."

CHAPTER 27
LISKI PARK

KARINA PULLED the cinch tight on Gladrion. She tied her bag of breakfast to the tie strap holder so she could eat on the go. Liski Park was an hour away by horse, and Gladrion needed exercise.

"Well, here goes nothing." She swung into the saddle.

She munched on crackers and sipped coffee as she rode. The summer morning air was warm, but not so warm that hot coffee was stifling. When she had finished eating and drinking they went at a faster pace.

Gladrion trotted along the treelined road leading to Liski Park. Karina basked in the glimmers of early sunshine that peeked through the tree leaves, even when a particularly bright ray nearly blinded her.

She tugged her long, loose shirt over her gun. The knife in her right boot pressured her calf as Gladrion trotted. *If Avyer gets any ideas, I'm ready. I could take him on, given a fair chance.*

She called him on her phone as she neared the park. "I'm riding in on my horse," she said.

"I'm over by Big Head Rock," Avyer replied. That was a major landmark anyone would know.

Karina walked Gladrion into the park. He champed at the bit, wanting to trot again. Karina rubbed his neck. "Calm down. We're on time."

They clopped down a treeless side trail close to the park entrance. This particular dirt trail led to an enormous lookout over a valley of trees, and a huge rock that looked as though the rain had carved a face into it.

Avyer could not have chosen a more scenic area to meet. Wind blew through the trees in the valley below, rustling the leaves in a natural symphony.

Avyer sat on a small boulder leaning against the rock. He stared into space with the air of a person who had been waiting a long time. He looked like a civilian, except for the gun he openly wore on his hip.

Karina reined in her horse next to him, not dismounting. She felt less vulnerable looking down at him.

"Timeliness is the courtesy of kings," said Avyer.

"I know," said Karina as she flashed her watch at him. It read ten a.m.

"Let's walk."

Karina reluctantly dismounted. Avyer scanned her and Gladrion with a hand scanner.

"No bugs. Scan me."

Karina gave him a sideways glance but did so. "Clean." She returned the scanner, which he pocketed.

"You know," Avyer said, "I can usually peg people right away. But you, you're something else."

Karina waited for him to continue, uncertain whether his tone was one of annoyance or confusion.

"Everyone loves their family. Well, almost everyone. That's predictable. The day we came for you, no fuss on your part. Nice and quiet. You knew what you were doing.

"In training you kept a low profile, which was easy for you. Everyone underestimates smaller, quieter people. What they don't know is that you use your brain. You could beat anyone to a pulp if you put your mind to it. Except me," he amended.

"What don't you understand, then?"

"You. Getting up despite multiple rounds of shocks. Sasha. The wasted bullet. Helping me again and again, no questions asked."

"What can I say? I'm a sucker for lost causes."

"That's not incredible, given your track record, but humor me and explain."

"Is that an official order?" asked Karina. Gladrion jerked his head up and snorted, sensing her unease.

"No."

Karina chose her next words carefully. As they trod the dirt path, she kicked the rocks at their feet. *He seems sincere.*

"It's friendship, compassion, and godliness," she said. "And if you really don't understand those things, that's pretty pitiable." Her mouth was set in a thin, tight line.

"What?"

Karina cleared her throat nervously. "It is incredibly hard to find a good friend. When I find one, I'm not about to let it go. And as far as the other two . . . if you know someone or something is suffering, you should do something about it if you can. And I wasn't kidding the times I talked about my religion."

"I see." They hiked farther before he spoke again. "This isn't easy for me." Avyer's voice fluctuated. Karina could not pinpoint what she heard in his voice, but it was not his usual confident tone. "I need your help."

For someone that treats everyone like dirt, of course it would be difficult to ask for help. Certainly not what Karina expected to hear. *But then again, I wasn't sure what to expect.*

"If you're in, I have to know that you're in all the way. Can I rely on you?"

"You know that you can," said Karina.

"How far can I?" Their eyes locked.

"You know what I've done since you recruited me," said Karina. "If that's not enough, I don't know what is. What do you want me to do?"

"It's simple. You're promoted to official and will work in the human resources offices. Your first task is to interview candidates that I send you. They must fit this profile." He retrieved a chip from of his pocket and placed it in her hand. "Ask no questions and answer none."

"Is this on the level?" Karina eyed the chip.

"I promise to keep your family safe."

Karina bit her lip.

"You've put on an incredible act, but you and I know all too well the Bentuarians will find you and your family out. If I let them."

"Why would we be in trouble? We haven't done anything wrong." Karina's voice went a pitch higher.

Avyer laughed and pressed his tongue against his cheek. "Oh, let me count the ways. You're anticipating trouble. There's a bulge on your right hip." Avyer had seen the gun. "Your reactions. Not to mention how your family reacted when I came for you. I've seen the same thing happen so many times it bores me. You are in silent, complete disagreement with the Bentuarians. If you're found out, it's over for you and everyone you love or care about. I'm the only thing that could stand between you and death."

Silence.

"We're on the same side," said Avyer.

"Are we?" Karina cocked her head and squinted at Avyer. "Everything you just said sounds threatening. How am I supposed to know you're not going to turn around and shoot me when you're done with me?"

"Don't be ridiculous," said Avyer. "As you yourself pointed out, I've had too many opportunities to either take advantage of you or kill you. Why would I start now?"

They followed the trail along the ridge until they had looped back to the main road. They stole glances at each other in turn when they thought the other was not looking.

"It's a deal," Karina said as they reached the end of the trail.

"But include Sasha. Like I said, good friends are hard to come by. Anything else?" She rubbed her forehead.

"No. It's a deal. One wrong move, though," he warned as she mounted, "and the deal is off. Tell no one."

"Got it." Karina kicked up Gladrion.

CHAPTER 28
THE INTERVIEWS

KARINA TRAVELED all over Gavriila with the special pass that Avyer had given her. One day she was in Avedida, and the next she was in a random house in Barnaul, hundreds of kilometers north of Avedida.

Her task was easy enough: she interviewed hundreds of people—officers and civilians alike—to fit a specific profile. After years of HR work for the high school and restaurant, she was exceptional at filtering profiles. She soon connected the dots to pinpoint who Avyer was searching for.

Avyer wanted anyone who was able-bodied, between eighteen and forty years of age, in good physical condition, with analytical skills or working knowledge of military or police operations. They needed to be able to use a weapon or willing to learn. Most were lower-income and very opinionated. The latter was the most subjective demographic and Karina concluded that Avyer referred to dissension.

Karina selected one out of every ten people interviewed and sent their data directly to Avyer. She never saw them again personally.

She kept her word and told no one, not even Sasha. Sasha knew better than to ask what was going on.

"I'm safe," Karina had reassured her. "I just can't talk about it."

Sasha was distracted these days. After a few months of intense dating, Sasha was engaged to Illya. Illya kept her busy.

Avyer began to involve himself personally with Karina's work. At first he had been content with her reports, but when he was able to spare the time he traveled to observe the interviews. He waited for her to finish, which took hours because he never scheduled fewer than ten a day, often up to twenty. At the end of the day he gave her more criteria and they discussed the interviews.

"What do you think of them?" he asked after a grueling ten hours in Barnaul.

"Waste of time I'll never get back." Karina stretched in her leather chair. "Only three of them match."

"I agree. How do you feel about this?"

Karina sighed. "What does that have to do with anything?"

"Everything," said Avyer. "Tell me. That's a request, not a command."

"I hope I'm not sending them to a slaughterhouse, that's what I think."

Avyer laughed grimly. "Would it comfort you to know they're not?"

"Only if you were being honest with me."

"I am," he said.

Is that his way of answering the question? Karina's eyes locked with his, searching for his soul. *If he has one.* They stared at each other in silence.

"What?" Karina broke the silence with a nervous laugh.

"You hate me," said Avyer. He snatched the data sheets from her hand and thumbed through them.

"I don't hate anyone." Karina's face darkened.

"You hate me," said Avyer quietly. "Not that I blame you. I'd hate me, too, in your position."

Karina waited for him to thumb through the sheets and her notes. He frowned at the pages.

"These two." He handed her two sheets. "Trash the rest." He sat back and crossed his arms.

Karina stood to retrieve a folio on a small desk. She put the sheets in the folio. Avyer showed no inclination to get up, so she sat across from him.

"Let's stretch. We have a long ride home as it is." He stood up and stripped his jacket. He draped it on the back of his chair.

Karina's heart began to pound. He shoved all objects on the floor and furniture against the walls. Her pounding heart slowed. *Was he . . . ?* He was.

"Show me what you can do with Systema. I've wondered how good you really are. You think you're up to fighting me. Get comfortable." He pointed at her jacket.

Karina slipped out of her jacket, leaving it on her chair under her gun belt. She pulled her hair back in a bun and rolled up her sleeves. Avyer watched with a bemused smile.

Karina turned her back to Avyer a moment, rolling her shoulders and closing her eyes. *Breathe.* She took in a deep breath. *Relax. Just like Uncle Misha taught me.*

She opened her eyes and turned to Avyer. *What's the point in this? He never does anything without reason, but this makes no sense.*

Karina scanned the room searching for anything useful in a fight. Little in this stuffy government office could serve as a weapon. A pen. *No, I don't dare do that.* A chair. *Too heavy.* A clock. *That would hurt if I threw it hard enough.* She nearly smiled at the ludicrous thought. *Nothing useful.* She did not dare maim Avyer.

No echoing voice moderated the fight, nor was there any signal or bell to start them off. She let Avyer lead. It was his game, after all.

As long as he doesn't grab me by the throat . . .

His first move was to strike out with his foot. A bold move, and a bad one. Karina ducked back and blocked what was left of the blow with her elbow. She grabbed his foot to twist his leg and send him sprawling, but he twisted out of her grasp before she completed the move. As she stood up his knuckles grazed her face. She grasped his fist and twisted it behind his back. She swung around behind him to straddle his back and put her arms in a chokehold around his throat.

Her bracers protected her arms from punches, but she strained to keep him from prying her arms from around his neck. *Bad idea.* She was so focused on her stranglehold that she was taken off guard by a punch to the ribs. She gasped for breath and loosened her grip with her arms and legs. She swung around under him and found herself hanging in his face.

Flashbacks from the Vadim Stable raced through her mind. She dropped to the floor, scrambled to her feet, and backpedaled to the desk. She groped behind her for something to work with.

Desk. Book. She snatched a book from the desk. She barely dodged Avyer's hand as it shot out for her arm, and she smashed the book against his forehead. He took a step back, stunned.

"You're still holding back, aren't you?" He shook his head and rubbed where the book struck him. "How many times do I have to tell you to give it everything?"

"I'm not the only one holding back," Karina spat. *You could have hurt me badly several times, but you chose to bruise me. So that's the point: that you're better than me.*

They both took a step back to size each other up before exchanging kicks and blows again. The cycle lasted several minutes. Everything seemed to move in slow motion. Hands punched, feet stepped back, blows slashed through the air, furniture crashed to the floor, more than one item broke, they jumped back, someone swung in for another punch, a hit landed on its mark—they repeated the process over and over again.

"Tired yet?" he asked with a glint in his eye.

"You?"

"You'll tire long before I will," said Avyer.

"Don't tell me that." Karina panted and glared at him.

They edged closer to the chair where Karina had left her jacket. *Don't grab the gun. Don't grab the gun.*

Avyer slammed Karina against the wall next to the chair. *No.*

He did not have her by the throat, but he did pin her left hand to the wall. Avyer caught a glimpse of her right hand. The barrel of her gun pointed directly at his head.

Avyer smiled grimly. "I told you."

"What did you tell me?" Karina froze.

"Just one pull of the trigger . . ." He dropped her hand and backed away.

"Would bring me problems," Karina finished tersely.

She lowered her gun and turned her back on him to slip into her jacket and belt the gun back on. When her eyes met his she felt an overwhelming urge to slap the supercilious look off his face.

"It's all in here, so use it." He tapped his finger on her forehead. Karina flinched at his touch. Fear and doubt reflected in her eyes. Avyer did not miss it. "I am not going to hurt you." His eyes softened.

"Oh, no!" The words escaped her mouth before she could stop them. Karina was more alarmed by his sudden gentleness than anything else he had said or done before.

"*Oh, no*, what?"

"Nothing," Karina said quickly. *Sasha was right. Illya was right. Everyone was right. Is right. I wanted them to be right, but I don't want them to be right, not right now.* She picked up her bag.

"Can we go now?" she asked. "It's late, and I've a lot to do tomorrow."

"Certainly."

The cruiser brought them back to the station later in the evening. Karina was prepared to flee to her barracks, but Avyer's hand fell on her shoulder before she took a step out of the cruiser.

"Follow me." They returned to his quarters. "Wait here," he instructed her before leaving her alone in the vast bedroom.

She stood where he left her, looking around. It was the same as always.

A few minutes later the door slid open to reveal the doctor. "Sit." He tended to her cuts and bruises until there was not a mark on her body. It was as though nothing had ever happened.

"Chief Nikolai says you are free to go," said the doctor at the end.

"Thank you," said Karina.

She strode out of the building quickly and quietly, her eyes and ears on the lookout for Avyer.

Her tired mind clung to one thought: *He could have hurt me, more than once. But he didn't.*

Now she had something else to fear. The way he had looked at her terrified her and left her feeling . . . something else.

CHAPTER 29
BUST

KARINA AWAKENED WITH A START. She was relieved to find Sasha warmly snuggling her. She hugged Sasha so hard that Sasha awoke with a grunt.

"Now wha—?"

"Sorry, bad dream."

"Think of something happy and let me sleep," growled Sasha, rolling over and jerking more of the blanket toward herself.

It was still dark outside when the alarm clock went off. Karina and Sasha sat up blinking the sleep from their eyes.

Karina stumbled out of bed with glazed and unfocused eyes. She dressed slower than usual.

"Hey." Sasha slapped Karina's backside when she saw how distracted she was. "Wake up! We have to get to the cars in five minutes."

"Yeah." Karina yawned. "Sorry. Dream's still on my mind."

"Tell me about it later. We have work to do."

Had it not been so dark, a group of twenty officers would have been seen crossing the commons to waiting vehicles. Exhaust fumes cut through the cool morning air.

Black trucks and wagons were manned by their respective drivers. Including the drivers, there were four officers to a vehicle, all armed to the teeth. Each officer had their own specialty: driver, weapons, guns, and hand-to-hand combat.

Avyer stood beside a truck. He said nothing as Karina and Sasha were sorted into his truck. Waves of last night's emotions came crashing over Karina when Avyer signaled for her to climb in the back with him. Karina eyed Avyer as she sat but he said nothing. Sasha rode shotgun with Illya.

Their destination was the Avedida slums. The caravan of police vehicles silently drove down a fairly smooth road, passing burned out buildings and jagged chain fences. As they approached their destination, everyone donned their helmets and checked their weapons. They pulled up to a dimly lit parking lot that was more pitted and cracked than any parking lot had a right to be.

Avyer left the truck first to move all teams into position. Drivers followed up in the rear while hand-to-hand combat experts and weapons experts were in front. Karina took a place beside Sasha. They exchanged solemn glances.

We'll be fine, Sasha mouthed.

Karina nodded. They would take care of each other.

Four men marched with a reinforced battering rod. They charged it before bringing it to bear down on a hefty bar door. The door exploded inward, and light streaming out of the building pierced the darkness. All teams plunged forward.

"Everyone, freeze! Avedida Police!" Avyer's voice rang throughout the bar.

The majority of partygoers did not freeze. Several screamed. Most ran. A few took up fighting stances when they realized it was a bust.

Karina took up a defensive position as people fled. Her gun was at the ready but she physically took on anyone who came too close to Sasha. One prisoner. Two. Three. Four.

Karina cuffed and herded them in a corner against the wall. Sasha guarded them but was distracted looking between the prisoners and Karina.

"Don't worry about me," Karina barked at Sasha. "Just do your job."

Karina spotted a small group running past the bar. No one was stopping them. "Halt!" she called out.

Karina's feet crunched glass littering the floor as she pursued them. She was so focused on the group that she was oblivious to a kid standing across the room. He glared at Karina as he tossed his long hair over his shoulder.

Sasha turned her back to Karina. "Be still!" She scolded one of the prisoners.

The kid drew a gun. He aimed it at Karina.

Avyer's arm shot out of nowhere and shoved Karina behind him. A blast blew through where Karina's head had been a second before, sending shards of shot glasses and bottles in every direction.

Karina gasped and ducked. She squeezed her eyes tightly shut as glass rained around her. When she opened her eyes the first thing she saw was the kid slumped to the ground, stunned unconscious.

"You are a mediocre shot on a good day," Avyer snapped at Karina. His eyes burned with fury. "Stay behind me unless you want to be used for target practice."

"Yes, sir."

Avyer glanced back at her, as though expecting her to disobey. When she made no move to go anywhere he ran after the three people trying to escape.

It was over in a matter of minutes. Survivors were cuffed and escorted to the prisoner wagon. After the prisoners were secured, Sasha and the other officers returned to their vehicles.

Karina was about to follow Sasha when a private cruiser pulled up. Avyer stepped over to the vehicle, opening the rear door. He paused to look around for something . . . or someone. When Karina's eyes met his he waved at her.

Surely, he doesn't mean me . . .

Karina stole a glance at Sasha's truck. Avyer waved more insistently. *Yes, me.* She marched to his cruiser.

"Sir?"

"Get in." He tilted his head from her to the cruiser interior.

After Karina sat in the back seat Avyer took a seat opposite her. He glared at her intensely before loosening his left combat glove strap with his teeth. He pulled off the glove with his teeth and winced slightly as he removed the other glove with his bare left hand. When he winced Karina noticed blood soaking his right arm. It oozed from a circular hole in his forearm.

"Are you ok?" she gasped. Horror settled in her chest.

"Yes."

"Is that because you pushed me?" Karina's eyes widened. Horror was replaced by guilt.

"Yes." His eyes shuttered. "Did you do as I told you?" he asked as he opened his eyes.

"Yes. I always do exactly as you tell me," Karina said with calmness belying her pounding heart. "Is there a problem?"

Avyer frowned. "I don't know."

Karina toyed with the hem of her coat. *He looks more intimidating like that.* "Is there something I should know or you need me to do?"

"Possibly. I'll let you know later. No matter how ludicrous it sounds . . . just go with it. Here." He pulled several data sheets out of a pocket and handed them to Karina. "We've ten cities to go this month. You have ten days."

Karina's mouth dropped open when she saw the list. These were some of the biggest cities: Urlyu, Agar, Pravda, Jennifer, Ulitsa, Virlam, Myrna, Visitre, Argye and Lovna. These were nothing like the slums she and Avyer had been frequenting in Avedida, or even the modest locations in Barnaul.

Then she saw the names on the lists under each city. The symbols beside the names indicated they were middle-class or upper-class citizens. Karina's eyes darted from the list to Avyer. "Permission to ask a question, sir?"

Avyer stifled a laugh. The laugh turned to a grunt as the movement jostled his arm. "Unless I've told you to shut up, there's no need to ask permission. I think we've moved well beyond that point."

"We have?" Karina bit her lip. "At some point, am I going to know what's going on?"

"Yes."

"When?"

"When it's time."

Karina's mind raced. *Ten cities in ten days? Some of these places are halfway across the planet.* Panic rose in her chest and threatened to strangle her.

"That's a lot to cover in ten days."

"You can do it. You've always exceeded expectations, even mine."

"I'm flattered."

Avyer yawned. "I'm sending you via maglev." As though to tell her to not be an idiot fretting over minor details. "Grab what you need when we get back. Ivan will drive you to the station. Tell the contact in each city who you choose, and write the names on a data sheet for me. And do your best to act like someone. You will be soon."

ПОЛИЦИЯ

CHAPTER 30
FOREST OF HUMANS

THE MAGLEV CLIPPED along at a dizzying pace. Tall firs close to the maglev melded into a green and brown blur as they sped down the track. Had she opened the windows, she would have been able to nearly touch them. An occasional rush of orange, red, or yellow fall foliage broke the green blur.

Karina settled back into the gray cushioned seat as she watched the blurring colors. *I bet it smells good outside.* The train was cool and clean but cramped. *We can't arrive quickly enough to Pravda.*

A total of twenty provinces covered their modest-sized planet: Avedida, Inna, Jerson, Zarvii, Ternopil, Oryol, Poltava, Gavriila, Azya, Kadix, Volga, Iszmail, Don, Nizhni, Samara, Barnaul, Irkutsk, Ulan, Kursk, and Dnipro. Each province had its own capital. Pravda, her first stop, was the capital of the farming Inna province.

Karina had not bother to change out of the morning's combat gear. *It won't hurt to look intimidating, since I'm alone in a big city.*

As she stepped off the maglev she was awestruck by towering skyscrapers surrounding her. An official received her and glanced at her permit. "State your business."

"Official Ivanovna. Her for interviews for the Avedida Police Chief." She came out of her daze.

The official scanned her document. "Approved. Go this way." He pointed to an adjacent parking lot in the distance.

"Thank you." Karina nodded.

She soaked in the bustling environment as she slowly stepped off the boarding platform. All below was steeped chaos: loads of wheat being shipped, boxes being unloaded, and a myriad of Bentuarian officials in their khaki and black uniforms going about their business. *What's Avyer doing sending me here alone? Am I in over my head?*

A familiar face bobbed through the crowd: Captain Jerod Ternovvy. At first Karina exhaled in relief at the sight of a familiar face. *Blast it! If he gets nosy, I'll have to feed him Avyer's story about searching for new talent . . .* Which actually was an ingenious one, given that it was not uncommon for the police to want outsiders to work in their cities.

"Karina!" He waved, hurrying over to her. "How good to see you!" He wrapped her in a warm hug. "What brings you out here?"

"Official business." She stood at attention.

"Aren't we all? At ease." He broke into a grin. "I may have been promoted but I'm not your boss. Have you eaten yet?"

"Yes, thanks. On the maglev."

"I was on that one, too!" He thumbed the maglev Karina had left. "How did I not see you?" He raised his cap to scratch his head.

"I was in the back," Karina said lamely. The back car was normally for cadets and private officers.

"Chief Nikolai knows no shame." Jerod shook his head.

Yeah, I'm not telling you I chose the back to be alone. "Is it wise to speak that way about a Police Chief?"

Jerod shook his head. "Forgive me. I forget that Avedida is so concerned about rules and regulations."

"Very much so." Karina pretended to look over her shoulder at something so he did not see her clench her teeth.

"We should meet for dinner." Jerod put a hand on her shoulder. "I know I haven't called or anything. It's not that I didn't want to. I've just been swamped with work." He fished out a piece of data sheet from his pocket to scrawl his number on it, folding it neatly and placing it in her hand.

"Thank you," Karina interrupted him, "but I'm afraid I really can't. I'm in and out today. It's a short trip."

"Shame," Jerod said, sounding disappointed. "Maybe when I'm back in Avedida? I miss you."

"Perhaps." Karina pasted on a pleasant smile.

"If you need anything." He pointed at the scrap in her hand. "Don't hesitate to call. Until then." Jerod gave her another enthusiastic hug, before he left her alone.

"Whew." Karina felt a twinge of longing and guilt as she looked after Jerod. *If he had just bothered to call me, just once . . . Avyer.*

She remembered the leather dispatch folder tucked in her jacket. She slid out the folded data sheets, straightening the precise crease Avyer had made down the middle. She read the first few lines.

Her contact, Sergeant Victor Ivanovich, appeared nearly as soon as Jerod had disappeared. He whisked Karina away in a cruiser to a mansion in the heart of the thriving metropolis.

Three floors rose above her as she exited the cruiser. Karina gawked at a columned porch lining the entirety of the mansion, stretching out a massive five hundred meters to the right and left.

"Whoops!" Ivanovich caught her by the arm when she stumbled over a step.

"Sorry."

Karina's eyes were fixed on the atrium ahead. The mansion's gaping maw swallowed them to even greater heights of decadence: long hallways lined either side with many open doorways and a red carpeted grand staircase spiraled upward with wide golden rails stretching right and left.

Karina followed Victor to the right, down a long hallway pitted with doorways. He led her to a ballroom. Filled to the brim with traditional decor and rug-covered walls, it was the epitome of gaudiness. *And I thought Avyer was flashy.* His quarters were nothing in comparison to this place.

A lonely desk and two chairs waited in the middle of the room. Karina deposited herself in the chair, waiting for interviewees to be ushered in. *What am I doing here? I have fifty people to interview, and this has to end by midnight.* She sat up straighter.

A round-faced young man with black hair padded into the ballroom.

"Anton Timurovich?" Karina looked up from her data sheet.

"Yes." As he sat down he pinned a pleasant expression on his face.

"Age?"

"Thirty."

"Occupation?"

"Doctor. Um, surgeon." His soft eyes wavered.

"Studies?"

"Medical degree completed."

"Physical capabilities?" Karina doubted he had anything of merit as she watched him twiddle his slender fingers on his paunchy stomach. "Why should we choose you? Include your political stances."

After ten minutes she dismissed him. If she were to finish by midnight, she had to finish each interview quickly. As she interviewed she drank and ate. *Is this why Avyer acts the way he does? Because he has so little time in the day?*

Avyer was rigid to the point of discrimination: anyone over the age of fifty, ill or obese was automatically dismissed. Slightly round candidates such as Timurovich were acceptable.

She finished just after midnight, at which point Victor came to put her on the maglev to set off for Ulitsa.

Ten days rushed by in an exhausting blur. Karina slept on the train between towns. She exercised and drilled whenever she wasn't completely exhausted, her only reprieve from the forest of humanity surrounding her.

Five hundred people in ten days. She selected ten or twelve out of every one hundred, writing their names on data sheets to give them directly to Avyer.

Fifteen of the interviewees boarded her maglev as it retraced its route back to Avedida. *Anton, Stepan, Yury, Yakov, Maria, Mikhail, Pável, Jaír, Faddei, Alexei, Oleksaandra, Zaria, Albert, Geordi, and Vyacheslav.* Despite her exhaustion, the names were fresh in her mind. *The best and the brightest.* Karina frowned as they filed into her car. They were not cuffed but had been escorted on board and were never allowed to leave the car.

"Don't look so serious," Anton said when he saw Karina's concerned look. Karina glowered at him as she removed herself from the new passengers. She sat in a corner next to the restroom.

As the maglev set off she ducked into the restroom, securing the door behind her. She dug into her coat and pulled out the ten data sheets with the chosen candidates' names. She folded the sheets in half several times. She removed her gun from its holster. There was space between the leather and the holster's lining. No one would look there.

She jammed the data sheets in until they were so far down in the holster that the bump was not visible. The gun slid back into the holster easily.

Karina fought sleep for twenty-four hours. She paced from her car to a second empty car. She splashed water on her face and drew on a few spare data sheets.

Karina stretched in relief as the maglev pulled up to the Avedida City platform. She sat back and watched a group of officers escort the fifteen in police wagons. Her heart sank as the wagons disappeared down the road.

She stumbled off the maglev to the platform. She rubbed her blurring eyes as she searched for a cruiser. *Who's picking me up?*

She touched her shoulder to hitch her bag up higher. *And where's my bag?* She shook her head and returned to her seat on the maglev to retrieve the bag.

As she reached under her seat, strong hands grabbed her from behind and pinned her arms behind her back. Karina twisted around but a second pair of hands restrained her head and blindfolded her. A needle pierced her arm.

Karina had a hazy sensation of drifting in and out of consciousness. Reality and a citrus mist meshed together. As she inhaled, an odd, tropical odor filled her lungs. She had the strangest sensation that she was inside an orange.

"So, dear." Jerod Ternovvy's face blurred into view as she forced her heavy eyelids open. His tone was anything but endearing "Why did Chief Nikolai send you outside of his jurisdiction?"

"Dea—" Karina's jaw fell limply open.

"Speak up!" A hand yanked her chin up at an uncomfortable angle.

"Gave her . . . too much . . ." A second voice echoed in the distance. ". . . your girlfriend."

"No matter." A new face came into view. Karina had never seen this one before. "Please tell us. We just want to help."

"Kill . . ." Karina managed to pronounce. It was easier to enunciate than 'death.'

"Why did Chief Nikolai send you outside of Avedida for interviews?"

"Kill'em," Karina mumbled. "All . . ."

Everything faded to black and she was in a hospital bed. Again. Sasha sat beside her, rubbing Karina's hand briskly. Illya was beside Sasha.

"Karina!" More color leapt into Sasha's face. "You're awake!"

"What happened?" Karina asked weakly.

Illya and Sasha exchanged glances.

"We were hoping you could tell us that," said Sasha. "I don't know. Chief Nikolai said he'd sent you on a mission. I didn't know anything else until he told me that you were mugged getting off the maglev."

Karina frowned. That didn't sound right, not at all. "I wasn't on a . . ."

Sasha shook her head and interrupted. "The doctor says you're out of danger. You were drugged with some crazy kind of cocktail. You'll be released tomorrow if you're fine." Sasha gave her a hug.

"I'm hungry."

"You should be. You've been here a day," said Illya.

They brought her food.

"Where was I?" Karina chewed slowly.

Sasha hesitated. "Officially, they found you on the floor of a back room in the maglev depot."

"Unofficially?"

There it was again, Sasha and Illya exchanging glances.

"You know I don't want to hide anything from you, right?"

Karina nodded. Relief washed over Sasha's face.

"The Chief wants to talk with you personally. Ask him."

CHAPTER 31
RECONCILIATION

"YOU HAVE A MESSAGE." The attending nurse poked her head in the room.

"From whom?" Karina's fingers trembled and fumbled as they buttoned her jacket.

"No idea. It's from police headquarters." The nurse shrugged as she handed Karina a folded data sheet:

Meeting today at 10 a.m.—Chief Nikolai

Karina bit down hard on inside of her lip. *Of course. I'm just being released and I've got to go see him.*

"Thank you."

She tried to not look at herself too much in the mirror as she freshened up. Ten days of poor sleep and irregular meals had left her face gaunt, with bags under her eyes.

She basked in the morning sunlight as she plodded to the office. She dragged out the walk to arrive on the hour. The desk sergeant directed her to Avyer's office.

Avyer looked serious when she entered. "Sit." She sat. He

laced his fingers and leaned forward across his desk. "What did you tell them?"

Nice to see you, too.

"It's hazy," said Karina slowly. "I'm not sure what was real and what wasn't."

"Tell me what you remember and what you think was real." He leaned on one elbow, propping his head up with a hand.

"It might sound . . . ridiculous," Karina hesitated, remembering the orange and citrus sensations.

"Doesn't matter." Avyer tilted his head, frowning. "Did they do more than drug you?" His frown deepened and his fingers ran up and down his scruffy goatee.

"No." There was a slight slump in his posture after she enunciated the word. "It's just weird." She recounted what had happened at the station, the blindfold, the needle, the strange citrus sensation, Jerod and the questions.

"And what did you say?" asked Avyer when she mentioned the questions.

Karina's mouth went dry. "It was hard to talk. I tried to say, 'Kill them all.' I don't remember saying anything else." She bit her lower lip.

Avyer sat back, sighing deeply. He tapped a button on his desk. "Send for Doctor Gorbachov." He eyed Karina stonily.

"Did I do something wrong?"

"No. My doctor did some blood work while you were in the hospital. He's going to do a quick scan."

The same doctor she had seen before reappeared: he had treated her when she had been shocked senseless, he had treated Avyer that one night he was mugged, and he had treated her bruises after she had sparred with Avyer.

"I'm not in the mood for more poking and prodding," Karina said crossly.

"No poking or prodding involved." The doctor pulled up a file on his datapad, showing it to her. "Take a look." Karina accepted the datapad. He pointed at a list of drugs. "First, they gave you a sedative. Next, they pumped you full of these." He pointed out several long, unpronounceable words. "These are normally used to get information out of people. A truth serum of sorts. It was a cocktail, and a risky one at that. You should be fine, though."

"Encouraging," Karina mumbled and returned the datapad.

"Stay positive." The doctor scanned her. Elevated heart rate and trembling hands. "Try to relax. You're not in danger. Have you eaten?"

"I'm fine," Karina growled.

"Ring for some food," the doctor told Avyer before he turned back to Karina, "Unless you do prefer to die, you need to eat and get your strength back."

He showed Avyer the scan results. Avyer's eyes flickered between the datapad screen to Karina.

"All normal," the doctor pronounced. "Give her some time to rest. She shouldn't overexert herself," he told Avyer. "And eat." He pointed at Karina as he walked out the door.

Avyer raised an index finger. A heavy silence filled the air between them, which Karina did not dare break.

"Do you have the data sheets?" Avyer asked after a minute.

"Yes." Karina stood up, sliding her gun out of the holster. "I hid them in my holster lining." She pulled them out, crisply folded but intact.

"Do you think Ternovvy found them?"

"No. I folded them exactly like this," she said.

The papers wavered in the air as Avyer accepted them from her unsteady hand. He scanned them with a small device, then pulled a lighter from his desk drawer and set them on fire. Small flames devoured the sheets as he deposited them on a plate on his desk. Karina's eyes widened.

"That never happened."

"Yes, sir," she said.

"Your hand is shaking."

"I still feel shaken up." *Why did I admit that?*

"You're safe. You've been cleared and they won't bother you

again. Let's not talk about that. Let's eat." Avyer led her to his private dining room.

He took his place at the head of the table. When Karina sat directly across from him waves of deja vu threatened to drown her. Her head was spinning. *What does he mean I've been cleared?* She clutched the round claws at the end of her armrests to ground herself. *Why did Ternovvy attack me?*

There was only one place set, but soon a servant came in to set another one. They ate breakfast despite the fact that it was nearly lunchtime. Avyer finished first, then silently watched her eat.

Karina was famished and kept her eyes glued to the plate of bacon, eggs, and toast. She only looked up at Avyer between sips of coffee.

"I don't need you passing out on me," Avyer said as she had drained her coffee cup.

"Why?" She averted her eyes and stared at the coffee grounds in the bottom of her cup.

"We've a lot to do. Would you like to walk with me?" he asked.

"Why not?"

"I asked if you would *like* to walk with me."

Not particularly, but . . . "I don't know."

"Then do as you will. You have three days off. Rest, eat, ride your horse, see your family." A ghost of a smile crossed his face when she looked up at him with visible surprise.

"Thank you. Am I dismissed?"

"Yes. Go." He nodded at the door.

Karina paused at the door when the same thought returned to her mind.

"What is it?" Avyer stood.

Karina turned around. "Should I be worried about Ternovvy?"

"I submitted a report to Ternovvy and his boss." Avyer thrust his hands into his pockets, balling them into fists. "The fact that you're alive says no, you should not be worried. You passed whatever test they had in mind. I doubt he'll bother you again. If he does, let me know. I'll take care of it." He said it as casually as though he were offering to take out the trash.

"Thank you, sir." As soon as the door slid closed behind her, Karina's eyebrows shot up. *What was that about?* She mouthed to herself.

She returned to the barracks to sleep the day away. Hunger pangs awakened her the next morning. She broke her fast with Sasha and Illya.

As they ate, a guard came and handed her a data sheet. He waited for Karina to open and read it.

"What is it?" asked Sasha.

Karina showed her the message:

Would you like to walk with me?—A.N.

"Wow." Sasha's eyes were wide as saucers. "What are you going to say?"

"Is there a reason you're still here?" Karina asked the guard.

"I'm waiting for your reply."

"What is it?" Illya elbowed Sasha.

"He's serious." Sasha grinned and elbowed Karina.

"Seriously nuts," mumbled Karina.

"Who's seriously nuts?" Illya raised his voice.

Sasha glared at Illya. "Stop asking questions," she hissed. "How many years of your life do you want to continue to enjoy?"

"All of them. What's going on?"

"It's better to not know," Karina said to Illya before she turned to the guard. "Am I supposed to write on this or are you just going to tell him?"

The guard shrugged. "I'll tell him whatever he wants to know, but I think he expects a written answer."

I'm eating.—K.I.

"Shouldn't you go see what is it that he wants?" asked Sasha.

"He'll ask again," Karina said with conviction.

After eating she retired to the barracks to sleep all day, only coming out to check on Gladrion and join Sasha for supper.

"How you feeling?" Sasha looked up from her plate at Karina.

"Better." Karina bit a piece of bread. "I think the doctor was right. Whatever they did to me, plus a rough ten days did a number on me."

"Yeah. Sure." Sasha nodded as she chewed.

"You up for sparring?" asked Karina.

"Sure."

The gym was busy by the time they arrived, but they found a free corner. Karina went as hard as she could but had to stop when Sasha landed a blow that left her ear ringing.

"You're ok, no?" Sasha looked at Karina worriedly.

"Yeah. I just need to get my strength back."

"I'm sure sleep helps, but you should train more maybe."

"I know."

They were about to continue sparring when another guard came up to her with a message. The girls exchanged glances.

"I told you." Karina grinned.

"You did," conceded Sasha.

Karina unfolded the message:

Come out to the track.—A.N.

"Tell him to give me five minutes," she told the guard. After he left Karina wiped a bead of sweat from her forehead. "I look awful."

"He's seen you worse," Sasha said drily. "Weren't you worried about stun cuffs and death and stuff?"

Karina glared at her. "I'm going to get this over with."

"Sure. Good luck. Have fun. Or whatever." Sasha waved goodbye.

Karina found Avyer in front of the track. His hands dug deep in his pockets.

"Good evening," said Karina. "I was sparring."

"I didn't ask what you were doing."

"I know."

"Would you like to walk with me?" Avyer asked.

Karina pondered the question. *Would I?* "Not today." *I should have said yes.*

"Why not?"

"I'm tired."

"Take another couple of days off," said Avyer. His lips pressed together tightly as his eyes raked over Karina. "Good night." He spun on his heel, leaving a bewildered Karina looking after him.

She gratefully accepted the time off and continued the cycle of oversleeping. *I should probably do something more productive,* Karina thought guiltily the next day. She crunched on an apple and pocketed another as she headed to the stable.

Gladrion whinnied and poked his head out of his stall as she came in. She struggled to keep him at a trot as she rode out to Liski Park, to the ridge trail where she had met up with Avyer weeks ago.

Despite the fact that leaves were falling from the trees en masse, humidity clung to her skin and beads of sweat began to roll down her neck and back. The lack of a breeze was stifling, but Karina did not care. *It feels good. I feel alive.* Insects chirped as they only did in early fall, and the sickly-sweet smell of wild flowering vines and decaying leaves crunched under her horse's hooves.

She dismounted at Big Head Rock, where she had found Avyer sitting that day. She leaned against the rock, watching the yellow and orange leaves in the valley flutter weakly in a light breeze. The leaves whispered dryly as they rubbed against each other.

"So beautiful," Karina murmured as she tied her hair back in a loose ponytail. Gladrion nudged her shoulder. She dug the second apple out of her pocket and offered it to him. Gladrion happily crunched away at the apple while Karina observed the leaves.

What would happen if I walked with him?

When her horse had finished the apple, she slapped one of her loose reins in a rhythm against her palm. She found herself toying with the idea of accepting his offer. By the time she finished riding around Liski Park, she had decided. She returned to the police station. She took care of Gladrion before eating a late lunch in the dining hall.

Her head swiveled right, left, ahead and behind her. No messenger. No Avyer. Karina took a deep breath. *Guess now is a good time to train.*

It was early, but there were people in the training room. She did not hold back today. Each opponent left her sweatier, battered and bruised. Karina kept getting back up. She needed to regain her strength. That meant no holding back.

Night fell before she knew it. A hot shower and change of clothes later, she went to the dining hall to meet with Sasha.

"You look good." Sasha sniffed Karina's freshly washed hair. "Smell good, too. How's vacation treating you?"

"I feel better," said Karina as she slid her food tray on the table.

"Lucky dog." Sasha sat down beside Karina.

"Why don't you ride with me Saturday?" asked Karina.

"I have plans with Illya," said Sasha. "Sunday morning?" She stuffed her mouth with an enormous spoonful of purée.

"Later in the day. Church in the morning, remember?" said Karina.

Karina jumped when a shadow behind her towered over her and her food tray. Karina covered her mouth with her hand, massaging her jaw.

"Whadizit?" Sasha mumbled through the mouthful of potatoes when she saw her friend stiffen, then she saw Avyer out of the corner of her eye. She nearly choked as she swallowed quickly. Karina patted Sasha on the back and handed her a cup of water.

"Could you give me a minute?" Avyer's tone was icy.

Sasha took a gulp of water and waved Karina away. "I'm fine," Sasha croaked.

"Sure." Karina followed Avyer outside. When she looked back at Sasha, her friend was forming heart shapes in the air with her hands. Karina glared at her. *Please don't look back, Avyer.*

"I trust you're feeling better," Avyer said as they walked through the automatic door.

"Yes. Thank you, sir."

"I'm not going to ask you to walk with me, if that's what you're worried about."

Karina bit her lip. Her heart sank. "What is it, then?"

Avyer looked straight ahead at a fountain in front of them. His jaw twitched slightly as they stopped in front of it. Water splashed loudly from ring nozzles set into the sides. They were alone, and if anyone came here, it would be difficult to hear their conversation over the water.

He sat on the fountain edge, beckoning for Karina to sit as well. She hesitated for a fraction of a second, but sat, leaving a healthy distance between them. Avyer's eyes locked with Karina's, his jaw clenched. Aside from the tension, his eyes were soft. *Warm even.* These were not the same eyes that had threatened Karina months ago.

"I just wanted to apologize for hurting you when we met." The words sounded unnatural coming from his lips.

Karina's jaw dropped. She recovered enough to say, "Ok."

"Was that 'Ok' as in it's all right or as in you heard me?"

"Um . . . " *What if saying the words changed things?* The next words tumbled out of her mouth. "Well, it was not ok, but I forgive you."

All the tension seemed to drain out of him. His jaw unclenched and his posture shifted to what likely was relaxed for him.

"Thank you." He stood. "Enjoy the rest of your evening."

For the second time in twenty four hours he left Karina alone

and perplexed. She was perplexed by his sudden change of atti-
tude, to say nothing of her own confused feelings.

CHAPTER 32
RAIN

A HINT of rain permeated the air on her final official day off. Karina packed a raincoat in Gladrion's saddlebag. All smells were more potent in the encroaching rain: the well-used leather saddle, the fresh straw in the stable and manure. Over all those scents was the odor of rain and decaying leaves.

Today they traversed the police horse training grounds behind the stable, twenty acres of varying terrain. As they picked their way along a grooved dirt path all was quiet.

Karina stopped at a fork in the trail. A masked rider in police gear approached from the opposite direction. Karina squinted. *Is it a man or woman?* The rider pulled up, waiting for Karina.

"Race horses?" A muffled, feminine voice came from behind the mask.

Karina wracked her brain for the name of a female rider, but none came to mind.

"Why not?" Karina shrugged. Her opponent's horse was nowhere nearly as good as Gladrion. "Where?"

"The back loop," said the rider.

"Signal when to start," said Karina. She wheeled Gladrion around. Gladrion twitched his ears nervously, sensing Karina's eagerness.

"Go!" signaled the rider. She shot forward on her horse.

Karina gave the unknown rider a head start.

"Let's go!" she told Gladrion. He charged forward.

It was all too easy: they went fast on the straight track, lined up for the jumps, eased around curves, plunged up then down a steep hillside and around to the finish. The other horse slipped more than once, clearly unaccustomed to going over such a track. At the end Karina was several lengths ahead.

Gladrion blew hard but nickered with his head held high. The other horse was exhausted and walked to the finish. Both riders dismounted.

"You have excellent form," said Karina. "You just need a better horse."

"Thank you."

"I'm sorry, but I don't remember your name," Karina said.

The other laughed. Karina thought she could hear a smile in the reply. "How could you forget?" The other rider lifted half of the face mask. It was Oleksaandra, one of the fifteen people who had traveled on the maglev with Karina.

"Great interview, by the way." Oleksaandra laughed at the shock on Karina's face. "Have a little more faith in Avedida's Police Major General." She winked before replacing the face mask and riding away.

Karina walked Gladrion down another side trail. *What was that about? Did Avyer not execute everyone?*

CHAPTER 33
EXECUTION

KARINA WAS ONLY a few bites into her solitary dinner when a messenger arrived with a crisply folded data sheet.

Come to my office at 18:00. Full dress uniform.
—A.N.

Karina looked at the dining hall clock in alarm. *Half an hour.*

"I'll be there," she told the messenger.

"Very well."

Her stomach churned with unease, but she shoveled food into her mouth as quickly as possible and ran to the barracks to change. A few drops of rain pattered on the roof as she changed clothes. She snatched her raincoat before she ran back out. She dashed past Sasha on the way out of the lobby.

"What's going on?" Sasha's eyes widened when she saw Karina's formal uniform.

"Don't know!" Karina pulled the raincoat over her uniform as she sprinted out the door. Drizzling rain soon left the raincoat slick.

"To see Chief Nikolai." She panted as she spoke to the desk sergeant.

"Go on back," he grumbled. "As much as you come here, I wonder you even bother to ask."

Karina gave him a withering look. *Let him think what he wants.* She strode to Avyer's office and rapped on the door. She straightened her uniform and tried not to pant.

"Come in." The door slid open.

A smartly dressed high-ranking official sat in the seat in front of Avyer's desk. Karina automatically stood at attention.

Is this a Special Agent? A knot of fear formed in Karina's throat as thoughts of Ternovvy came to her mind. *What's his insignia?* All ranks and insignia meanings had left her brain.

"You're joking, right?" The official raised an eyebrow at Avyer as he pointed at Karina.

"Don't let her looks fool you." Avyer's icy tone left no room for argument. "You requested the best official on this base. Here she is." They stood up. "Let's go. Come." He motioned to Karina without sparing her a glance.

Avyer's cold eyes sent a chill down Karina's spine. She trailed behind them as they walked down the hall to the jail cells. Seemingly at random, the official pointed out prisoners. "One, two, three, four." He paused before motioning to the last one. "Five. Get what you need." He nodded to Avyer.

Avyer assented with a barely perceptible nod. "Ivanovna, with me." He nodded in turn to Karina.

"Sir."

Avyer studiously ignored her. He led her to the weapons room, which was maintained far from the prisoners. Karina peered at an enormous black door with a complicated locking mechanism. *It looks like a giant safe.* Avyer placed his right hand on a bio scanner beside the weapons room door. A blinding white light scanned his palm. A robotic voice chirped. "Avyer Nikolai. Accepted."

The door slid open, but he did not enter.

"Avyer Nikolai, add left hand," said Avyer.

He seized Karina's left hand and flattened it against the scanner. The scanner flashed up, down, left, and right. "Avyer Nikolai. Bioscan saved," the machine announced.

"Grab a rifle," Avyer told her. Karina paused as she contemplated the weapons before her. "Now!"

She turned her back on him. As she selected a rifle from the rack his hand gripped her shoulder. She drew a sharp breath.

"You will do exactly as I tell you, no matter what," Avyer said. "Understood?"

The lump in her throat grew tighter and bigger. Karina forced herself to turn around to face Avyer. He had positioned himself between her and the weapons room security camera. His hand loosened its grip, gently brushing her cheek as she turned around. His hand was warm to the touch.

"You've made yourself *quite* clear." She met his dark eyes without blinking. He holstered a gun as she inspected the rifle. "It's good." *Clean and loaded.*

After closing the weapons room, Avyer led her to the execution grounds.

No. I don't want to . . . Karina had done this before, just not at night, and certainly not with Avyer to scrutinize her marksmanship.

The official had lined up the five prisoners against the wet concrete wall. Karina dragged her unwilling eyes to look at them.

An older man with a mop of white hair and a tired, lined face. A kid who couldn't have been more than eighteen, at most. A middle-aged woman with high, sharp cheekbones and eyes that pierced through Karina. Two young men with sullen expressions and angry eyes. They stood with their backs to the wall, feet shackled, and hands restrained behind their backs.

"Are we ready?" asked the official.

Avyer and Karina nodded in unison.

The official strutted in front of the five prisoners. "You know why you are here," he said in a tired voice.

"You," he signaled the older man and middle-aged woman. They nervously exchanged glances. "Have committed treason against the government, colluding with Gavriilan Spark rebels. And, you refuse to divulge their current location."

"And you two." He shook a finger at the young men. "Have been given many chances to reform. Perhaps too many." His eyes lit on Avyer briefly. "In any case, it will be good for Gavriila to be rid of you."

He came to the kid. "And you." He shook his head and clucked his tongue. "Killed your parents. You are a shame to society. Any last words?" He directed the question to all five.

Silence reigned. The scene was indelibly inked onto Karina's brain. She eyed the five condemned prisoners blinking under the glaring white floodlights trained on them, shivering in the drizzling rain.

"Fire when ready," the official told Karina. He stepped back.

She advanced and shouldered the rifle. She took aim.

"Please!" the kid cried out in agony.

She set her sights on the kid first. *Don't think about it. Don't miss. Don't make them suffer. Aim slowly. Squeeze the trigger.* She shot the kid first, then the old man, then the other three. Clean headshots.

Guards dragged the bodies to a wagon parked beside a private cruiser. Karina stood at attention, waiting for Avyer. Her mouth filled with excessive saliva. *Don't puke.* She swallowed hard.

"That concludes my business here," said the official. "Until you find more rebels, that is."

"The sooner we rid Gavriila of this scum, the better." Avyer sounded pleased.

The sound of his voice grounded Karina, but she shivered when she looked into Avyer's emotionless eyes.

"My thoughts exactly." The official smiled. "Generals Stepanov and Raize will be most pleased when I turn in my progress report." The official boarded the cruiser, leaving Avyer and Karina alone in the rain. The rain was cold. The light was cold. Karina shivered despite her raincoat and dress coat.

I don't understand anything . . . Avyer saved the people I interviewed, but he is killing Gavriilan Spark Revolutionists? Did he call me just to add my hand to the weapons room scanner?

"Dismissed." Avyer loftily waved her away. "Return the rifle."

"Yes, sir."

She returned the rifle to the weapons room before she walked to the barracks. Sasha was cross-legged on her bunk, mending a shirt. Her face lit up when Karina appeared in the doorway.

"You're back! Are you ok? You look pale as death."

"Poor choice of words," Karina said thickly. She hung her dripping raincoat on a wall peg. Their room was empty, so she spoke her mind. "I shot five prisoners."

"Oh." Sasha's golden eyes were full of pity. "I'm sorry." Her mending lay forgotten on her lap.

"I've done it before. Once."

"I know."

"They had it coming but I don't feel any better about it."

"I know," Sasha echoed.

"I think that's why . . ." Karina's voice trailed off as she thought aloud, "that's why he was like that."

"What? Who? What did I miss?" Sasha's brow furrowed.

"Avyer took me to get a rifle. He added my hand to the weapons room scanner."

"That's weird." Sasha raised an eyebrow.

"What do you think?" asked Karina.

"Either he was protecting himself or you."

"Or both," Karina mused as she sat beside her friend. "Yeah. I'd thought as much."

"Did he say anything?" asked Sasha.

"Don't get comfortable." A voice came from the doorway. It was Maria, this evening's receptionist. "Message." She handed Karina a folded data sheet with her name scrawled on it.

Karina groaned once Maria had left. She threaded her fingers through her hair. "No!" She recognized the handwriting on the outside. "Again? I don't feel like doing this right now."

"What does he want this time?" asked Sasha.

Karina unfolded the sheet. "For me to change into something comfortable and meet him at the barn."

"That sounds promising," Sasha sang. She waggled her eyebrows at Karina.

"I don't think that he meant *that*." Karina shrugged out of her dress coat and hung it over the edge of her bunk. She fished through her trunk for dark-colored civilian clothing.

"Take your gun." Sasha watched Karina finish changing.

"I planned to," said Karina, "even though I'm a lousy shot." Karina tucked her pants into her boots.

"Still. Good idea. You do good at close range. Stay safe."

CHAPTER 34
NOCTURNAL EXCURSION

AS SHE APPROACHED THE BARN, she noticed all lights were off. Her breath caught in her throat until she saw Avyer in front, also dressed in civilian clothes. He had two horses ready. He scanned her to check for bugs. After the scan he motioned for her to mount a brown horse.

Karina followed Avyer behind the barracks, to the land beyond it. The dark trail led through dense woods. Raindrops dripping from overhanging branches fell at regular intervals, threatening to soak them. Karina slipped on her raincoat and pulled her hood over her head.

Branches scritch-scratched as they scraped the horses and riders alike. The horses' hooves clopped dully on the pine needle and leaf-covered ground, occasionally snapping a tree branch or striking a stray tree root. The scent of rain and crushed pine needles permeated the air.

"What time is it?" Karina asked quietly. *It feels like we've been out here forever.*

Avyer pulled up his horse. Caught off guard, Karina's horse was next to him before she reigned it in. He pushed up his jacket sleeve.

"It's 22:11." Avyer glanced at his watch. "We've a ways to go."

"We'll be out all night?"

Karina could not make out the expression on his face but thought she heard a smirk in his voice. "What? You have somewhere else to be? A hot date, maybe?" When he received no reply, he added, "You'll have all of Saturday and Sunday to get over an all-nighter."

Unable to think of a safe reply, she changed subjects. "I'm sorry about your family." *Oops. That was not the best conversation starter.*

"Causalities of war."

"What war?" *Why did I ask that?*

"Don't play dumb with me. You know the answer. Let's discuss something else." His deep voice held little enthusiasm. "How old are you?"

Karina rolled her eyes. "That's in my file."

"Humor me. A police chief has better things to do than to memorize all their personnel files. There are hundreds of them."

"I'm twenty-five. Just turned twenty-five the other day."

"Congratulations. You don't look it."

"And you?"

"I'm thirty-three."

"I thought we were going to be honest with each other," said Karina.

"I am being honest. You can see my ID in the light once we arrive."

"I thought you were older."

"Experience ages."

"I didn't mean you look bad, just older," Karina amended.

"Do you have a boyfriend?" he asked.

"That's a pretty serious question." Karina frowned to herself.

"Not half as serious as what we're doing tonight," Avyer said.

"No. Do you have a girlfriend?" Karina clapped a hand over her mouth, berating herself for prolonging the small talk.

"No. No family, either. All of them lived in Desmarin. One friend in the force. A police major general can't be fraternizing with employees, even though they are the only people I see every day."

And what am I?

Around midnight a light glimmered in the distance, breaking through the darkness. As they came closer Karina saw light bleeding through cracks between boarded up windows of what had likely been a politician's old summer house.

Guards in nondescript clothing stood watch around the house. *Not Gavriilan. Not Bentuarian.* They had a different air about them . . . the air of people who, unlike the Gavriilans, had not lived trodden underfoot for several decades.

Avyer strode to the front door and flashed a small metallic disk. Karina's brows knit together as she watched the exchange. The front door guard shone a light on the disk. She squinted but could not make out what he was looking for. The guard opened the door for Avyer and Karina.

A musty, stale smell assaulted their noses. The spacious summer house had once been very homey, but dust coated the elegant wood-patterned floor, interrupted only by booted footprints. The footprints led down a dark hallway directly in front of them as well as to a living room to their left.

Avyer stepped to the left through the living room doors. He approached a table set up with a few chairs and military equipment. Karina's eyes darted behind them as the front door closed. She took a step closer to Avyer and nearly walked into him. She jerked back away from him just in time.

A lone man sat at the table. His bronze skin, thick black hair and nearly black eyes confirmed that these people were not Gavriilan. He spread his legs out as he leaned back in the wooden chair. One hand rested on his knee near his gun and the other rested on the table. If his chiseled features and brawny hands were any indication, he had a good body under the light armor encasing him.

"Karura Solari," said a soldier in the living room doorway. "Chief Nikolai and um, accompaniment."

The soldier in the doorway interpreted for Avyer and Karina.

Karina had to work hard to understand the conversation because her English was not the best.

"This is the closest thing I have to a right hand at this moment," Avyer explained to Solari in perfect English. He sat down without an invitation. "Official Karina Ivanovna."

Karura Solari's black eyes bored into her. Karina averted her eyes and studied the dusty floor.

"Have a seat," Karura told her then turned his gaze to Avyer. "She's safe?"

"She wouldn't be here if she weren't."

"How do you know?"

Avyer did not look at Karina. "She loves her family and best friend too much."

"Hm." Solari took stock of Karina. "Official Ivanovna, please share your *true* feelings and opinions about the current Gavriilan government."

As the translator confirmed Solari's message, all the blood drained from her face. She gripped her chair with white knuckles. *Breathe.* Her right ear rang. She winced from the sound.

"Jay"—Solari signaled one of the men—"bring us some coffee."

An officer in the corner of the room nodded and hurried away.

"Relax, kid," Solari said. "I'm not threatening to go kill all your loved ones." He glared at Avyer. "With friends like you, no one needs enemies."

"I'll take a walk," Avyer said.

"Please do." Solari's eyes were fixed on Karina.

Jay returned with a steaming mug for Karina.

"Jay will go with you," Solari told Avyer.

"Yessir." Jay saluted before escorting Avyer outside.

Karina hid her face behind the mug as she sipped scalding coffee. She took deep, slow breaths. *What's worse? Being left alone with Solari or being left alone with Avyer?*

The interpreter stood beside Karina.

"Breathe, kid." The interpreter said as Solari's hard eyes bored into hers. "I don't know Chief Nikolai personally, but if my intel is correct, he's not as bad as you think. Have you heard of me?"

Karina shook her head and sipped more coffee.

"Not surprising," Solari grunted. "The Loyalists have done a good job keeping me and the Lomans hush-hush. You do know about the IPG, right? The InterPlanetary Government?" Karina nodded. "Great. We'll start there. I work with the IPG. We've been chipping away at Bentuari's hold on a number of planets."

That sounded good.

"We're interested in helping yours. As I understand, rumors have been flying for a while. The rumors are true. Bentuari's dead so there's no reason for Gavriila to be under the heels of his generals and wannabe dictators."

That was even better.

"We need to know where you stand before we can consider letting you or Nikolai in."

Is he telling the truth? Karina considered the implications of her answer. "Is my side that important?"

"Yes."

Once she began talking, words gushed out all at once: meeting Avyer, Desmarin, her family, dissenting families, weird interviews, Sasha, the unrest and the execution she had carried out tonight.

Solari considered her story. "Interesting. Call him back in," he told the guard.

When Avyer returned to the living room, Jay reappeared with more coffee. Karina sat back in her chair sipping a second cup of coffee while they talked about "redistributing" people. She struggled to keep up with the conversation and listened to the interpreter. Avyer's command of English was well beyond her own. Karina found out that some of the people in question were ones she had interviewed.

"They know who will join and who won't," Avyer explained to Solari.

"It's a calculated risk."

"All of this is, but it's worth it," Avyer insisted.

Should I be listening to all of this? Karina was rooted to her seat, too terrified to leave the room.

Avyer finally stood up, looking at his watch. "It's two in the morning." He turned to Karina for the first in a long time. "We need to get back."

Solari shook hands with both of them. "I'll arrange to pick up the redistribution. You send them to me and the IPG will pick up where they leave off. And you," he addressed Karina. "This conversation never took place."

Karina nodded, stumbling after Avyer as they left Solari. Jay showed them out to their horses and they mounted up to return to the station.

Karina quietly asked Avyer questions the entire ride back, to help her stay awake as much as out of curiosity. "Who is Karura Solari?"

"He's a very famous, ruthless mercenary working for the IPG."

"Why does the IPG want to help us?"

"It's good for them and us. Gavriila has many resources."

When they arrived at the station, weak rays of sunlight were blushing over the stable. They left the horses with a stable hand.

"Good night." Karina turned to return to her barracks.

Avyer's hand wrapped around her wrist. "No, you need to come with me." He pulled her after him.

"Where?"

"My place."

Karina no longer felt sleepy and her mouth went dry. No words willed themselves to her mouth, at the moment they would have been most useful. Avyer tugged her behind him. As she dug her heels into the ground he wrapped an arm around her shoulders and stopped pulling.

Avyer sighed. "For appearance's sake, please don't make me carry you." When he looked down at her he perceived terror in her eyes. "I'm not going to do anything to you."

She gave him a side eye but stopped straining against him. He gently escorted her to his quarters. She wavered as he opened the door for her, but he took her by the wrist to reel her in after him, pushing the button to close the door behind them.

"Make yourself comfortable. Take the bed."

He removed his boots before opening his closet to rummage for something. He dug out a thick bedcover and unceremoniously rolled up in it on the floor, clothing and all.

Karina gaped at him. *What in the world?* After staring at the bedcover on the floor for a few minutes, exhaustion overcame her suspicious mind. She slipped out of her shoes and coat before burying her head under the velvety blanket in his bed.

CHAPTER 35

DANGEROUS THINGS

KARINA GROANED SLEEPILY. She rolled onto her side when a strong hand moved from her shoulder to her arm. Another hand sank into the blanket next to her waist. The hands were cautious but insistently pulled at her. When she refused to open her eyes the hands gently shook her.

"Let's eat, and then if you want you can go to your room and sleep." A deep voice resonated close to her face.

Her eyelids flew open. She inhaled sharply when she saw Avyer leaning over her.

"I've sent for lunch."

Karina sat up, trying to look calm and natural. "Thank you." She readjusted her ponytail, smoothing out hairs that were sticking out at odd angles. "What was the point of this?"

"Of what?"

"Sleeping in here."

"We were out late last night. I'd rather the world think inappropriate things than dangerous things. Wouldn't you?"

Karina nodded. She swung her legs over the side of the bed, pulling her boots on before following him to eat.

They stole glances at each other as they ate. More questions flooded Karina's mind, none of which were safe to ask, not here and not now.

"I'm not going to hurt you again." Avyer wiped his mouth as he finished eating and leaned back in his chair. "Nor do I have the slightest intention of harming Sasha or your family."

"I thought I knew that, but you sounded threatening last night in the weapons room," Karina said coldly.

"You know why I did that." Avyer crossed his arms.

"Tell me. I need to hear the words," said Karina.

Avyer loosened his arms and shrugged. "First of all, the special official specifically requested my most trustworthy officer for the execution. Second, we are all on the edge of a knife. If there had been even a moment of hesitation on your part, it would have been fatal to you and who knows what to myself. I don't want that to happen." There was a flicker of emotion in his eyes.

Karina shifted uncomfortably. "What are we going to do?"

A tight smile crossed Avyer's face. "We are going to continue what we started. You'll interview people and I'll have them redistributed."

"And the rest of the population?"

His smile disappeared. "We can't save everyone."

"Can we include Sasha's family?"

"Consider it done. I will assign her to travel with you. I don't want you alone, not after Ternovvy attacked you."

"Why?" Karina froze. "Do you think they'll come after me again?"

"No, but I would feel better knowing you weren't alone. I can't go right now, and Sasha is the most logical choice."

CHAPTER 36
WEEKEND

AVYER NIKOLAI RETURNED to his room to sleep in his own bed after Karina left. While Karina was blissfully asleep, he had lain on the floor considering his next steps. As he pulled the sheets over his head, a fresh, sweet fragrance wafted in his face. His bed smelled like Karina.

He awakened hours later to darkness. He stretched the stiffness out of his joints before he went to a small desk to write a brief note. He rang for a guard.

"Call Sasha Bondaruk," he said.

"Yes, sir."

Fifteen minutes later the guard returned with Sasha. When the guard left Avyer spoke.

"Deliver this for me." He handed her the note. "Do so at first light tomorrow to the address indicated. Read it yourself before you deliver it. Don't tell anyone. That includes Karina."

Sasha blanched as she read the note. She nodded before placing it in an envelope he handed to her. "Are you sure about this?"

"Yes." Avyer regarded her. "Just do it and be there for Karina when it's time. And take this." He handed her a small device.

"A phone?" Sasha's forehead wrinkled in confusion.

"I know you don't have one. Keep it on you at all times. If there's an emergency, call me. There's only one number in there and it's mine."

CHAPTER 37
FRIENDS ON THE ROAD

SASHA WAS NOT GIVEN to pacing back and forth, but as the train sped toward Sarchi, pace she did.

"You've hardly said anything to me this weekend," Karina said.

"Lots on my mind."

Karina shrugged and reviewed the extensive lists Avyer had given her. This route had Sarchi in Azya province as the first stop, followed by time in Oryol and Barnaul, mostly concentrated in middle-sized cities in the two provinces. There were over fifty people at each location, but this time Avyer gave her two days per town.

Soon they pulled into Sarchi. The only thing Karina knew was that at every stop a man named Taras would meet them. He would flash a small flat disc like Avyer had shown the guard at the summer house. She was to tap a button on her uniform first, then he'd tap his. A little over the top, but that was the plan.

Taras was a blond, gangly young man with blue doe eyes.

"Official Ivanovna." He nodded briskly. "Taras, at your service."

He took off his cap. She tapped a button on the cuff of her jacket and he tapped his in turn, in the inside of his cap.

"We have a cruiser for you," he said.

Karina and Sasha hefted their backpacks into the back of the cruiser. They sped through a medium-sized town with a medium hustle and bustle to it, not unlike Avedida. Sasha sat back gazing in fascination at the gray, dingy skyscrapers built in old-style architecture. After so much traveling, Karina no longer craned her neck to see everything at once. She memorized the route in case they had to return to the maglev alone.

Taras was disinclined to converse and Karina made no attempt at conversation. Eventually they reached a large apartment building on the outskirts of town. It was an unimpressive cold gray slab with a square courtyard in the center open to the sky.

Taras led them to a lift and guided them to a room on the fourth floor. As Sasha sidled through what served as a kitchen, she nearly knocked over a coffee maker and toaster. She held her backpack over her head to squeeze past a narrow table filled with paraphernalia and finally reached the bedroom at the back of the apartment. She dropped the backpack on a bed under a fogged-up window. She kneeled on the bed and wiped the window with one sleeve, peering through the grimy pane to look out over the courtyard.

Karina noted a bathroom to her right as she followed Sasha. She wrinkled her nose at a grimy toilet jammed between a low sink and a standing-room only shower. A tiny glass partition hanging from the wall by two screws was the only thing keeping the toilet bowl dry.

Sasha eyed the bedroom curiously as Karina left her backpack next to Sasha's. Everything was stored on shelves or on the floor in plastic boxes: clothing, toiletries and all. Sasha turned her nose up at a bag of rusty razors resting on canned food.

"It's not pretty, but I call it home." Taras confirmed the girls' suspicion.

"We just need a place to sleep," Karina said. "It's not a problem."

Sasha glared at her to let Karina know it *was* a problem for her. She pasted on a fake grin before turning around to face Taras.

"Where will the interviews be held?" asked Karina.

"In the kitchen," said Taras.

"What? Here?" asked Sasha. She wrinkled her nose.

"Uh, sorry. No! There's a communal kitchen downstairs that was turned into a conference room."

"Let's get started, then," Karina said.

Sasha nodded at Karina and patted the gun on her hip. Taras guided them back down to the ground floor, to the repurposed kitchen.

Karina did fewer than half of the fifty interviews slated for Sarchi, despite interviewing for twelve hours straight. Sasha's jitteriness did nothing for Karina's concentration. Her friend alternated between pacing around the room and sitting to read a small book. The book did not alleviate Sasha's boredom or anxiety. She did not get past five pages. She began to read, was distracted, and had to re-read the page to remember what she had just read.

Both girls were relieved to go to bed. Taras slept on an old, patched blanket in front of the bolted door. Karina and Sasha cuddled on the twin bed and fell asleep almost as soon as their heads rested on the pillow.

Karina awakened to the aroma of coffee and Sasha's arm hugging her tightly. Karina grimaced as she squirmed out of Sasha's grasp without awakening her. As soon as Karina stood up the front door slammed open. Sasha jerked awake.

"Well, that was a waste of effort," Karina growled to herself before snapping at Taras. "Sasha *was* asleep. *Was* being the key word."

"Sorry." He turned beet red. "But it's already six."

Karina served herself and Sasha a coffee. "First interview is at seven." Karina handed Sasha a mug. "I'm going to shower and stretch."

"M'kay."

Karina showered then took a walk around the building. She

had fifteen minutes before the first round of interviews for the day. Karina had barely warmed up when her watch told her to return to the apartment.

Taras was nursing another steaming cup of coffee. Sasha broodingly stared out the window, champing the lip of her coffee mug with her teeth.

"It's time?" Sasha turned to face Karina.

"Yes," said Karina. "But is there anything we need to talk about?"

Sasha shrugged. "Like what?" The pitch of her voice was a little too high.

"Come on, I know you. Something's wrong," Karina said.

"Yes," Sasha drew out the single syllable. "But I can't talk about it anymore than you can talk about what you're doing for Chief Nikolai."

The words were like a punch in the gut. "So that's how it is?"

Sasha nodded.

"But we're ok, right?"

"Of course we are."

CHAPTER 38
SARATOV TRIALS

AVYER HAD HIS OWN PROBLEMS. He had a splitting headache, which had not yet been eased by the medication he had taken minutes ago. His second problem sat in his office: visiting Police Colonel Vernal Allen Mognari.

"I've been reviewing the new recruits from this year. There are several promising names." Mognari huffed through his drooping gray mustache. "I would like to see them put through the Saratov Trials. No point in their wasting away here where nothing ever happens."

"I see, sir." Avyer swallowed. "Which ones did you have in mind?"

Mognari handed him a data sheet with a list of names, six circled in red. Avyer drew a sharp breath as he read:

Gregor Ivanovich

Arya Leonari

Victor Chekov

Ivan Gregorovich

Karina Ivanovna

Sasha Bondaruk

"Sasha is out of the question. Her weapon skills are

formidable, but she is not physically capable of going through the Trials." He drummed his fingers on the desk as they continued the discussion.

"Is there a problem, Chief?" Mognari asked after enduring several minutes of Avyer's finger drumming.

"There is an . . . issue with Officer Ivanovna."

"I'd think you'd be glad to send her. She's exceptional. General Stepanov himself made this recommendation. She's wasting away out here in this outpost of a town. What possible objection could you have for NOT putting her through the Trials? She'd be top of the class."

"I'm aware of her capabilities, sir," said Avyer, swallowing hard again. "She is indeed exceptional."

"Then?" demanded Mognari as he lifted his cup of wine to his lips.

"She's with child."

Mognari sputtered over the wine. "But how is this possible?"

"How is it ever possible?" Avyer's tone resumed its normal deliberating cadence even as he tapped his desk nervously.

"Do you know whose child it is?"

"Yes, sir."

"Whose? We'll make an example of the—"

"Mine."

The single word cut Mognari short, and his facial expression changed completely. He roared with laughter. He was forced to abandon the wine glass on Avyer's desk as the liquid precariously sloshed about. He laughed until tears filled his eyes. Wiping away the tears and still wheezing, he walked behind Avyer's desk to give him a hearty slap on the back.

"Ah, well, a Chief has his right to a little fun every once in a while. You'll have to tie the knot, you know?"

Avyer nodded.

"Young scamp, it was about time anyway. You're what? In your thirties?"

"Thirty-three," Avyer confirmed.

"Thirty-three?" Mognari echoed. "It's good to start early. No sense in wasting your youth while you've got it." He returned to his armchair with a thump, shaking his head. "You're a sly rascal, you are. Didn't know you had it in you!"

CHAPTER 39
THE SPECIAL AGENT

MOGNARI WAS NOT KNOWN for his discretion. The news spread like wildfire, from the Avedida Headquarters all the way to General Raize and his right-hand Jerod Ternovvy in the Gavriila Palace.

"Special Agent." General Raize sauntered into the Opal Room. "You hardly seem surprised by the news."

"What news?"

Jerod lay on the couch studying the intricacies of the iridescent opal-like patterns swirling on the ornate ceiling. He ignored Raize as he limped to a gaudy white desk and settled into an embellished wooden chair.

General Raize snorted. "What else? The big news about Official Ivanovna and Chief Nikolai."

"It was a long time coming," Jerod remarked. "I wonder it didn't happen sooner."

"So, you really do believe they're together?" Raize's chair moaned in protest as he shifted his weight.

"Of course." Jerod sat up and turned to look at Raize. "Never a doubt in my mind. Should there be? I lost track of how many times she ended up in his office or in his bedroom."

Raize wove his fingers together and settled them on his desk.

"Sir? Do you have a doubt?"

"I guess not," Raize said, "but it's odd that such a talented girl was hidden for so long. Are you certain that she is a Loyalist?"

"Quite. She is too ingenuous to be otherwise." Jerod shrugged it off.

"What about Nikolai?"

"Rigid as a board. Aimless young man who found his place in the Bentuarian Loyalist ranks fifteen years ago. He has a track record that probably made his mother blush when she was alive. He's never hesitated to kill or enforce a law. He executed his uncle on his mother's side, some cousins on both sides, and other relatives during his police training. But you know all that."

General Raize grunted noncommittally.

"What?" Jerod yawned and stood. "Do you *want* to get rid of them?"

"No, not me," Raize huffed. "Something's bothering Stepanov. Every time I ask him about it he always says the same thing. Something's bothering him, but he can't put a finger on it."

"So what? An officer got his subordinate knocked up. What else is new?" Jerod paced around the couch.

"Nothing, I guess."

"If it's bothering him so much, he can send out an execution squad to get rid of them." Jerod said. "What's my next assignment?" He leaned on the back of the couch, toward the general. "So little time, so many headquarters to infiltrate."

CHAPTER 40
INDISCRETION

KARINA AND SASHA stumbled off the maglev after a ten-hour journey, both of them bleary-eyed from lack of sleep. It had been an ordeal completing the interviews on time and vetting the interviewees well enough to avoid spies in the ranks.

Avyer had sent his driver to pick them up at the train station. The driver handed Karina a data sheet as she and Sasha climbed in the cruiser.

We need to talk.—Chief Nikolai

"I do *not* like the sound of that." Karina blinked her burning eyes furiously. "I just wanted to get some sleep."

"Yeah," yawned Sasha. "You have fun. I'm gonna go sleep while you . . . whatever."

The driver dropped Sasha off at the barracks before he left Karina at the office. Something felt odd when she stepped out of the cruiser. *Is it me or is everyone looking at me strangely?* She walked straight to the desk. The desk sergeant did a double take when she came in. *Ok. So it's not just me . . .*

"Go on back to the office." The sergeant chewed thoughtfully on a pen. "He's waiting for you." Karina felt his stare on her back as she went to the lift.

A pit of dread grew in Karina's stomach as the lift took her up. It had made itself at home by the time she was in front of Avyer's office door. Karina steeled herself as she rapped on the door.

"Come in."

The door slid open.

"Have a seat." Avyer's jaw tensed as the door shut behind her.

Karina's eyes were glued on Avyer as she sat.

"We have a bit of a . . . situation."

"Which is?"

"There's bad news, then good news, and more bad news."

"What's the bad news?" Karina leaned toward Avyer, clenching the arms of her chair. The pit of dread must have shot up from her stomach to her throat, because now she felt as though she were choking.

"You were put up as a candidate for the Saratov Trials."

Karina's mouth dropped open. "They are REAL?"

"Very much so. The good news is that you've been removed from consideration."

She released the armrests and her shoulders sank with relief. The pit of dread moved out. She had nearly relaxed against the chair back, then she remembered. "What was the other bad news?" She pronounced each word slowly. The pit of dread in her stomach returned in full force.

"Getting you out of the Trials came at a cost." Avyer swallowed and shifted his weight in his chair. "I told the commander in charge of candidates that you are pregnant. With my child."

"You told him *what*?" Karina leapt to her feet. The room began to sway around her. "You've got to be kidding me."

"I was going to let you rest a day or so before telling you," said Avyer. His lips were in a thin line. "But rumors are flying."

"Of course they are!" Karina threw her hands in the air as she sputtered. "That's what people do when they hear their chief slept with a subordinate and got her pregnant!"

Avyer stood up. "Would you rather have faced the Saratov Trials?"

"Yes!" Karina glared daggers at him and took two steps toward his desk. She leaned on the desk for support.

"Do you know what they involve?" His tone was maddeningly calm.

"No. Just that they're dangerous and . . ."

"One moment." Avyer raised a finger to silence her. "I'll indulge you," he said. His eyes narrowed in annoyance.

Avyer unbuckled his gun belt, dropping it on his desk. He unbuttoned his jacket and hung it carefully on the back of his chair. As he loosened the tie Karina's initial shock was replaced with horror. She averted her gaze to look at his desk.

"Don't look away," he ordered as he unbuttoned his shirt.

By the time he reached the black undershirt, Karina was holding her breath. It was impossible not to stare once the undershirt was peeled off. Irregular, zig-zagging scars marred his lean, well-toned body. Shorter, parallel lines wrapped around his chest and jagged along his side. When he pivoted to show off the rest of his torso Karina noted more uneven gashes on his left arm as well as odd marks on his back. *What in the world would make those scars?*

"Saratov Trials aren't anything you're going to experience. Seen enough?"

"Who are you to make this decision?" Karina snapped.

"I need you *alive*." Avyer leaned toward Karina with an alarming intensity in his dark brown eyes.

She took a step back but refused to be cowed. "What happened to you?"

"That's not up for discussion. Not yet." He slid the undershirt back over his head. "This does mean that we'll have to marry. It's one thing if a ranking officer is messing around. It's a completely different matter if he's gotten an officer pregnant."

Karina's empty stomach churned. "I need to sit." The room was spinning around her faster than before.

"Please do."

Avyer put his shirt back on and buttoned the cuffs. Karina sat, bowing her head between her legs. Both her ears rang. *This is a nightmare.*

"I . . . don't know how to feel about this," she said thickly.

"Well." Avyer paused as he tucked his shirt back into his pants. "You're either stuck with me or you're going to die. Even if I let you go into the Trials, if you pass you would be forced to join the Red Guard. I assure you they do not share your ideals."

"Were you with the Red Guard?" Karina looked up sharply at Avyer. She winced as the movement made her ears ring more loudly.

"Yes." Avyer crossed his arms and looked at the floor.

"How would this work?" asked Karina.

"As in?" Avyer's eyes did not meet Karina's.

She took a deep breath. "Am I supposed to marry you and get pregnant?"

"No."

"Then what do you have in mind?"

"We'll marry and a month or so later I'll sadly report that you suffered a miscarriage."

Karina raised an eyebrow. "Why don't you do that now and tell them that happened? That would be easier."

"Two excellent reasons." He raised his head and met Karina's gaze. "One." He raised a finger. "Police Colonel General Mognari told me we must marry immediately. Two." He raised a second finger. "If we did as you suggested, that would make the lie obvious, and they would send you to Saratov on the next maglev."

"Mmm," Karina responded. Her shoulders sank.

"I'm sorry," said Avyer.

"Not half as sorry as me," Karina snapped as she pinched the bridge of her nose.

"Are you in love with someone else?" asked Avyer.

"No, but that's beside the point. Was there no other way?"

"Aside from maiming or crippling you, no."

"Did you know this was going to happen?" Karina's eyes narrowed in suspicion.

"Your candidacy for the Saratov Trials? I had little doubt that the day would come."

"Come on." Karina stood on rubbery legs. At least the room had nearly stopped rotating. "Why bother with me? No one here is irreplaceable. You could easily find someone to replace me."

Avyer's jaw tightened. "*You* are irreplaceable. I need you. I'm not sending you to certain death."

"I'm offended you think I'd die, given that I'm a fair combatant for you."

"Because?"

"I'm strong and I don't need your help."

"That's what you think."

"And what little reputation I have has been completely shattered," Karina sputtered.

"To blazes with your reputation," scoffed Avyer as he adjusted his tie. "If you were so worried about your reputation, you shouldn't have had anything to do with me in the first place. You're going to need the reputation I've given you."

CHAPTER 41
PREPARATIONS

AT SUPPERTIME SASHA found Karina in bed with her head buried under a pillow. She shook Karina's elbow.

"Hey," she said tentatively. "I don't know if you're asleep or not for real, but we need to talk."

A tear rolled down Karina's damp cheek as she turned to face Sasha.

"Yeah, I heard," Sasha said. "You want to clean up your face then get out of here?"

Karina sniffled and nodded.

"Stay here. I'll bring you something." Sasha dashed out of the room to return with a cold damp washcloth. "Wipe your face and press that against your eyes, nose, and mouth. Won't get rid of all of it but will help."

"They're saying awful things." Karina sobbed as she dabbed at her face. "I heard them when they thought I was asleep."

"Don't talk right now." Sasha shushed her. "Not until we're out of sight and sound."

Sasha searched through Karina's clothing until she found a hooded jacket. Once Karina had calmed down Sasha coaxed her out of the bunk, helped her into the jacket and covered her face with the hood. They slipped outside.

"Where do you want to go?" asked Sasha.

"The barn." Karina sniffed.

Sasha rolled her eyes. "Of course."

"The day watch has already left. No one will bother us for a while," said Karina.

When they reached the barn Karina turned on a light and hefted a rectangular hay bale into Gladrion's stall.

"Come in." She tilted her head at the stall.

Sasha cast a sideways glance at Gladrion but followed Karina inside. Gladrion nibbled at Karina's hood as she sat on the bale.

"So," Sasha said simply as she sat beside Karina.

"I don't know where to start."

"The beginning will do because I'm your best friend and have no idea what in the world I should think." Sasha frowned.

"I didn't know about any of this until I spoke to Avyer."

"And?"

"I was put up as a Saratov candidate."

Sasha's jaw dropped in horror.

"And this is Avyer's way of saving me from it."

Sasha clapped a hand over her mouth. "I can't believe it. I mean, I can. You're strong and really good at stuff. But . . . what ever are you going to do?"

Karina held her head in her hands. "I don't know. I mean, get married. I guess."

Karina leaned on Sasha's shoulder, sobbing. Sasha awkwardly patted Karina on the back, unsure what to say. Karina continued sobbing for several minutes but her head shot up. She wiped her very wet nose on her sleeve. Her eyes were wide.

"My family," she whispered. "They are going to kill me."

"Really? Why?"

"I'm supposed to be a virgin."

"And you are?"

"Yes."

"Shoot." Sasha grimaced. "Good luck with that one. Why don't you just . . . tell them the truth?"

Karina stared at nothing until Gladrion nuzzled her hand. She rubbed his velvety nose absently.

"I don't think I can," she mumbled. "Because of . . . you know, we're not supposed to . . ."

"Oh, yeah. I forgot you can't really talk about what you're doing. Shoot. Eek!" Sasha squawked when Gladrion snuffled her hair.

Sasha backed away so quickly that she tumbled onto the hard floor. Karina muffled a laugh under her hood.

"I know you love your horses." Sasha leapt to her feet. "But could we continue this somewhere else?"

CHAPTER 42
FAMILY

KARINA WAS ENJOYING a dreamless slumber when a hand shook her shoulder. Karina groaned and turned her back to the waker.

"He's outside and wants to talk to you," Sasha's voice whispered in her ear.

"Wut?" Karina rolled and yawned. "What is it?"

"Chief Nikolai is outside the barracks waiting for you," Sasha said.

Karina's eyes snapped open, and she kicked off the blanket. "Did he say what he wanted?"

"No. He did say to ask you nicely to get dressed to go out with him."

Karina rubbed her swollen eyes. The damp washcloth last night had not alleviated all the puffiness.

She stumbled off her bunk and rifled through her clothes to find something nicer than her everyday civilian clothes. She held up a red dress and shoes she normally wore on Sundays.

"What do you think?"

"Probably."

"Help me out here! What's he wearing?" Karina frowned.

"Regular stuffs. He looks nice. You probably should wear that," said Sasha.

Karina slipped into the dress and pulled her hair back with a clip. She looked at herself in the mirror. She sighed as she dabbed extra makeup under her baggy eyes.

"What do you think?" She turned in a circle.

Sasha gave her two thumbs up and gave a fake, toothy grin that looked more like a grimace. "Great. Good luck."

Sasha walked Karina outside, leaving her with Avyer. She gave Karina an encouraging glance behind Avyer's back. Karina bit her lower lip.

"Good morning," said Avyer.

"Good morning." Karina looked at him for a moment, then lowered her eyes, studying his clothing. *Mostly blacks and browns. He was smart, wearing a jacket. I should have worn one.* A stiff breeze already nipped at her exposed arms.

"You look beautiful. How are you?"

Avyer's hand tilted her chin to force her eyes to meet his. Karina's breath caught in her throat and her stomach dropped. His eyes were concerned. *Did he see the bags under my eyes?*

"Very not ok." She tried to modulate her voice.

He let her chin drop. "I'm sorry."

"What do you want?"

"We need to finalize wedding plans." Avyer offered her his arm.

"Now?" Karina weakly accepted his arm.

"We're running on borrowed time," said Avyer. "The sooner we're married, the sooner we can fake a miscarriage. If we wait too long people will wonder why you aren't showing."

Karina shivered as the wind whipped at her cheek. *If I stay to the side maybe he'll block the wind.* As they walked through the center garden she pretended to be fascinated by the withered plants that had drooped their crispy brown heads.

"What's the plan?"

"Before we do anything else, we'll meet with your family."

Karina balked and her arm pulled Avyer to a halt. She leaned on him more heavily than she meant to.

"What is it?" He gave her a quizzical look.

"I just thought that . . . I'd have time to tell them. Is it really . . . necessary for you to talk to them?"

"Yes. Family is important. Is there a problem?"

Would he even understand if I explain they'll disown me over this? She looked up at him with pained and conflicted eyes. She opened her mouth once but closed it. *I don't even know where to begin.*

When Karina did not answer he gently pulled her arm to continue walking. He led her to an awaiting cruiser and opened the door for her. She sat facing the driver's seat, relishing the cruiser's warmth. Avyer sat across from her. He closed the window between them and the driver.

"I don't know what you're thinking or what's between you and your family. I can imagine quite a few things," he said. "You can't tell them the truth right now. You know that, right?"

Karina nodded.

"Would it be better for me do the talking?"

Karina nodded again.

"Ok. Give me your phone."

Karina's eyebrows knit together but she dug her hand deep in her dress pocket and retrieved her phone. She unlocked the screen and handed it to him. Avyer's fingers flew across the screen.

"There. You have my office number. Call there if I don't answer the other one." He returned her phone.

The cruiser stopped in front of her house sooner than she would have liked. Karina drew a deep breath as she looked out the window. No one appeared in the grimy living room window, but the family cruiser rested under the rickety metal slats that served as a garage. The cruiser being there was a fairly accurate indicator they were home.

"You're not alone." Avyer leaned forward to take her hand in his. "I'm here."

Karina looked at him uncertainly.

"Take my arm." He directed. "And don't let go."

Avyer stepped out as though he had visited her house many times before, approaching the worn metal front door with familiarity. He rapped on it smartly. He did not give the lower-class wooden house a once-over. Then again, it was not his first visit.

Sofia opened the door. "Karina!" She stopped mid-squeal at the sight of Avyer and backed away in alarm as she opened the door wider.

"Are Papa and Mama home?" asked Karina.

A wide-eyed Sofia nodded. Her eyes fluttered between Karina and Avyer.

"Would you mind getting them?" Avyer asked as they stepped inside.

Sofia tripped over her own feet as she did an about-face. She continued nodding as she picked herself up. She bounded up the stairs to the second floor, taking them two at a time.

Avyer glanced at Karina, who stood frozen as though she were a statue. She looked after Sofia and clung desperately to his arm.

Hushed whispers drifted down the stairs, but no audible words. After a few minutes of murmuring, Ivan and Viktoriya descended the staircase with Sofia.

"Good afternoon." Avyer shook hands with Ivan and Viktoriya.

"Good afternoon," Ivan echoed. His eyebrows furrowed with worry.

"Noon," mumbled Viktoriya. She gave Avyer a once-over then glued her eyes on her hands clasped in front of her.

"I'm probably the last person you would like to see right now. I'll go straight to the point." Avyer cleared his throat.

"I'm in love with your daughter." Sofia audibly gasped behind her parents, but Avyer ignored her reaction. "She has changed me and my life for the better. I am not whole without her. I can't imagine what I would do or where I would be without her. Whenever she's not around, I think about her every waking moment. There is no one, nothing on all of Gavriila as perfect and beautiful as Karina is. I will do my best to give her everything she needs and deserves. She has and will always have my undying devotion."

Karina felt her cheeks warm as she studied the living room rug. She toed the tattered brown fringe. Her fingers had a life of their own and had Avyer's arm in a death grip. He covered her white-knuckled hand with his own, caressing it. If Karina did not know better, she would have been convinced of his affection herself. *Where in the world did this smoothness come from?*

"I love Karina too much," he said. "I *have* loved her a bit too much," he amended.

Ivan and Viktoriya exchanged alarmed glances. Karina eyed the rug one last time before forcing herself to face her parents.

"Police protocol dictates that we marry as soon as possible. We will be marrying next week."

And there went all the subtly and smoothness. Karina met her parents' gaze with distraught eyes.

"What?" Viktoriya's eyes bulged as she glared at Karina. Her lips visibly tightened downward.

Avyer ignored Viktoriya's question. Karina heard his words droning on, but her brain tuned them out. Sofia peeked from behind their parents and mouthed *Really?* to Karina. Karina set her lips in a thin line and shook her head nearly imperceptibly. Ivan's eyes flitted between Avyer and Karina. He had noticed Karina's subtle gesture.

Viktoriya's eyes were fixed on Avyer. Her mouth was paralyzed into a scowl. She listened to Avyer's discourse, but refused to look at Karina until he had concluded. When she did make eye contact with Karina, her eyes narrowed until they were thin slits.

"Very well," Ivan picked up the conversation. "Thank you for letting us know. I'm sure you will take good care of her."

Karina saw a glimmer doubt in her father's eyes but did not dare to make any more signs. Ivan wrapped her in a warm embrace. Karina hugged him back, clinging to him a few seconds longer than she normally did.

"I love you," was all Ivan said when he let go. Tears welled up in his gray eyes.

"We'll be in touch," Avyer said. "We need to run errands to prepare for the wedding, so we will take our leave."

He steered Karina back to the front door, which Sofia had left ajar. As he opened the door a chill breeze whipped Karina's skirt around her legs. Ivan and Sofia followed outside. They echoed perfunctory goodbyes as Avyer opened the cruiser door for Karina. She reclaimed her previous seat. This time Avyer slid beside her. He touched her arm.

"You're cold."

Karina shivered involuntarily. Avyer turned up the cruiser heat before rapping the back window to signal the driver to go.

"How are you feeling?" Avyer rested his left arm behind Karina's head.

"Awful. You?"

Avyer half-shrugged. "I would say that went well under the circumstances."

He took her left hand in his much larger palm. Karina drew back as he traced the outline of her ring finger.

"I want to make this clear, once and for all." Avyer stared at her finger. "As my wife, I will take care of you and do my best to keep you safe as long as I'm alive. I'm never going to hurt you again, nor is anyone else allowed to hurt you."

Karina's stomach churned between a lack of breakfast and the sea of emotions she had been fighting since last night.

"Will we stay married?" she asked.

"If that is what you wish."

"Marriage is a serious thing," said Karina. "It's supposed to be for life."

"You're very traditional," Avyer said drily, yet with a pleased air. "Is that your religion talking again?"

"Yes."

"Then yes," said Avyer. "We will remain married."

Karina's stomach groaned for her, more loudly than she would have liked.

"When's the last time you ate?" Avyer's eyes narrowed.

"Yesterday."

"Yesterday, when?"

"Yesterday afternoon."

Avyer leaned forward to open the window between them and the driver. "Change of plans. Take us to eat first." As he slid the window closed he gave Karina a stern look. "Don't even think about trying to lose weight for the wedding. You're already ridiculously tiny." He crossed his arms.

"I-I . . . That wasn't . . . I just didn't have an appetite after everything yesterday."

Avyer grunted and cast a skeptical eye at her. Karina leaned back and closed her eyes. As the cruiser moved along she tried to not let her head graze Avyer's arm.

He's still looking at me. I can feel it. The warm car feels so good. It would be perfect if I weren't so hungry.

Her mind drifted and Karina nearly nodded off. The top of her head brushed against Avyer's arm when the cruiser made a sharper turn or sudden movement.

When the cruiser stopped and the engine turned off, she opened her eyes. Avyer offered Karina a hand out of the cruiser. When she hesitated, he took it upon himself to take her hand.

"Need to work on appearances." He leaned over her and mumbled in her ear. "We're supposed to be madly in love."

He gently led her into the restaurant. Karina glanced at a dark sign above the entrance. A brown bear head graced the left of the restaurant name, but the only word she read before she was whisked inside was "Probka."

Karina stared at the old paintings and antiques covering the gray walls as a waiter led them to a round table in a darker corner. She had never been in such a place before. Avyer pulled out her chair and helped her sit at the table.

"Waiter." Avyer seated himself and thumbed one of the menu options. "This tea for her. Black coffee for me."

They silently waited for the beverages. Karina was entranced by the restaurant and peered at the oddities on the walls. Avyer leaned back in his chair contemplating her. When Karina realized he was staring at her, she became even more interested in an oil painting on the wall next to her.

As soon as the drinks arrived Karina took a deep sip of the herbal tea. Its warmth traveled down her throat, warming her belly, infusing her with warmth. *He chose well. So good.*

"I take it you like it." Avyer broke the silence.

"Yes. Thank you."

"Before we eat and before we go out, I need to tell you a few things."

Karina gazed into her cup as she sipped her tea. She nodded at him.

"First of all, get your act up. People will see through this fast if you don't change how you behave around me. Look at me," Avyer said.

Karina's head jerked up.

Avyer shook his head. "That's got to stop. Relax. Take a few more liberties. Be daring. If I were someone you *really* liked, you wouldn't have raised your head so abruptly. You would have lifted your head with a more relaxed, more tender gesture."

"I'll work on it," said Karina.

"We can work on it now." Avyer moved his chair to face Karina. He pulled Karina, chair and all, to face him.

"What are you doing?" Karina gripped her seat nervously.

"Practicing."

"What?"

Avyer leaned into her face. *He smells like . . . fresh soap.* His right hand traveled the back of her neck to cradle her head while his left hand caressed her cheek. Adrenaline surged through her body, but Karina willed herself to remain in her chair.

"You don't have to like me. You don't have to love me or sleep with me. I'll sleep on the floor. You take the bed. Just focus on staying alive. I'll make it easy for you: I don't like you."

With that last word, he closed the gap between their faces. Karina's hands flew up from the sides of her chair and landed on his chest. As soon as she felt his heartbeat and his chest expanding as he took a breath, she clasped her hands and threw them back in her lap. *Do I want to feel . . .* His nose brushed hers as their lips met. *No, I do not want to feel this.* She squeezed her eyes shut, terrified of what she might see in Avyer's eyes.

But she did feel everything that she did not want to feel. His lips were warm and strong, and as they pressed into hers it was as though everything around them had disappeared—the table, the waiter, and even the restaurant itself.

She tentatively opened her eyes after his lips released hers. He tilted his head as he sat back in his chair, as though waiting for her reaction.

"Was it that bad?" he asked after a few seconds of silence.

"No." She blinked. "I just . . . was not expecting that."

"Might as well get used to it now, because we'll have to do a lot more of that."

CHAPTER 43
I DO

AVYER ACCEPTED her outstretched palms in his own with reverence. Karina gazed at her long lace sleeves as she listened to the minister drone on about vows. Sasha was visible out of the corner of her eye when she pulled Karina's long, white dress train straight. The silky cloth shimmered perfectly behind her.

Karina dragged her unwilling eyes from Avyer's black dress uniform, past his white starchy shirt with a stiff collar. She studied his neatly groomed facial hair. Her eyes lingered a moment on his lips before rising to meet Avyer's eyes. It was impossible to not feel anything.

She felt as though she could get lost in his dark brown eyes, but even as the thought teased her, Avyer's words echoed in her mind. *You don't have to like me. You don't have to love me. You don't have to sleep with me. I'll sleep on the floor. Just focus on staying alive.* Karina's throat tightened. *I'll even make it easier for you: I don't like you.*

The minister was finishing his discourse. ". . . as long as you both shall live?" He looked expectantly at Karina. *How fortunate that we don't have to vow to like each other.*

She turned to the minister with a vacant stare. "I do."

Sasha handed her a dull silver band. Karina held her breath as she slid the ring on Avyer's ring finger. His hands were warm and strong.

Very different from mine, Karina thought as his large hands delicately placed her ring on her ring finger. *And to think . . .* Her thoughts faltered as her eyes locked with Avyer's eyes again. She was in danger of getting lost again.

"... kiss the bride."

I hope this looks natural. As his face came closer, she felt an odd flutter in her stomach. His lips met hers, warm and gentle. They clung to hers longer than they had been practicing the past week. *I suppose he's trying to be more convincing.* She closed her eyes and leaned into it. He threaded his fingers into her hair as his hand supported her head and he leaned more passionately into the kiss. Karina closed her eyes. She did not dare open them. Her stomach dropped as though she had been shoved off a high cliff. His lips began to pull away from hers. *Open your eyes carefully. Can't let anyone see I'm panicking.* Her eyes shuttered before she broke into her practiced smile.

Kiss done. Big smiles, applause from the audience.

Sasha remained by her side the entire time. When no one important was in earshot, she gave Karina a devilish look. "Are you going to sleep with him?"

"No. I'm not that far gone."

"Yet," Sasha snickered. "You got a prime specimen: tall, dark and manly."

"Yeah, I know. Shame to waste it," said Karina.

"You're not dead, right?" Sasha elbowed her.

"You're not making me feel better," said Karina.

"So?"

"I don't know how to feel."

"Get over it." Sasha stopped speaking as high-ranking officials approached Avyer to congratulate him and greet his bride.

"Love isn't just an emotion," Sasha hissed between handshakes.

Karina had no time to answer.

"I would like to present my wife, Karina Annushka Ivanovna," said Avyer. "Karina, this is General Raize, General Mognari, Lieutenant Glav, Lieutenant Chekov, and Doctor Tolstoy."

Karina greeted each in turn, but was surprised when she saw the doctor. She knew him.

"A pleasure," said the round-faced man. "I've heard so much about you."

"The pleasure is mine." Karina studied his face. Where had they met? *The interviews?*

"I do hope things won't slow here," said Lieutenant Chekov. "I heard that you're due double congratulations. Boy or girl?"

"Girl," said Avyer just as Karina said, "We don't know."

He laughed and put an arm around her. "It's a bet," he explained. "I'm betting on a girl." He gave Karina another long kiss. She smiled and ran her hand along his jawline.

"Whatever it is, may it be a good strong Gavriilan child just like its parents," concluded Raize.

"I'll drink to that." Mognari toasted.

As they toasted Karina desperately searched for Sasha. Sasha was several meters away. When Karina caught her eye, Sasha shook her head.

Even General Stepanov made an appearance. His cold hand grasped Karina's tightly, his dead eyes staring into hers.

"Best wishes for you and the baby." He icily congratulated them with a tone more menacing than congratulatory.

When Karina's parents and sister came over to the couple, Viktoriya refused to speak and looked as though she were about to burst into tears. Ivan and Sofia offered typical pleasantries. Karina sighed with relief when they left to eat cake.

When there were fewer officials, Sasha reappeared. "Just think about it," she whispered not very quietly. "You and that hunk."

"I can hear you, you know." Avyer glared at Sasha. "If you weren't her best friend . . ." He let the threat hang in the air.

Hours later Karina sat at a newly installed dresser in Avyer's room, staring at herself in the mirror. Everything was so surreal: the veil, the unrevealing but fitted white silk dress, and two silver rings gracing her left ring finger.

Avyer's voice broke her reverie. "You did a good job today." He gave her shoulder a reassuring squeeze.

CHAPTER 44

HONEYMOON

AVYER HAD BEEN GRANTED a week off, so they set off on a brief honeymoon excursion. Both had pre-packed their bags, so it was a matter of eating breakfast and boarding a train.

"Where are we going?" asked Karina once they boarded the maglev.

"You'll see," said Avyer.

Karina resigned herself to staring out the window. They were passing the Avedida flatlands, toward the Don hills. Avyer busied himself with his datapad. When she grew bored of the scenery, Karina drew horses and trees on a sketchpad.

So passed the hours. The maglev sped past the Don hills and on toward the Ulan Woods. Their destination was a small station in a clearing in the woods.

It was early evening when they arrived. The sky was turning a dusky orange and blue color. A cool breeze wafted the fresh scent of leaves and pine needles in their faces.

Avyer sent the luggage ahead of them, and they walked along a dirt trail that eventually led to a cabin.

"We can talk, you know," said Avyer.

"I don't know what to talk about."

"The usual," said Avyer. "Family, friends, and favorites would be a good start. If we want to pull this off *successfully* we need to know everything about each other."

"Probably." Karina soaked in the forest around them. The idea of sharing her entire life with him right now was overwhelming. It was easier to focus on one thing at a time, starting with the trees, the dirt road, the fresh breeze, the smell of pine needles crushed underfoot, and finally Avyer's deep voice.

"Why not now?" asked Avyer. "Start here." He put his hands on her shoulders and positioned her squarely in front of him. He took her chin and slowly tilted it up at him. "Like that. Relax your face. You look like you're about to be executed."

Karina pulled away in annoyance.

"What is it?" Avyer's face fell.

"I don't know," said Karina. *Too many emotions.*

"Ok." He hesitated as though he were considering what to tell her. "Think about how you would treat a husband, one you loved. I can give you tips and hints all day, but that'll only get us so far. Do your part."

"Ok." Karina stared at nothing in particular on the ground. She gave a half-hearted tug on his arm. "Let's keep walking."

"That's it. Just give it a little more enthusiasm." Karina shrank back when Avyer put an arm around her. "It'll get easier with practice." His hand found her waist and pulled her closer to him.

"I'm sure you've had plenty of practice," said Karina.

Avyer laughed. "You flatter me, but not as much as you think. You?"

"Not that much."

"Tell me about your family."

Karina stiffened. "What do you want to know?"

"Well, their less-than-friendly behavior would be a good place to start. Do they hate Loyalists that much, or is there more to it than that? Your mother did not even want to look at you, which seems extreme even to me."

"Um." Karina tried to swallow but all the saliva had left her mouth. "They're mad because they think we slept together before we married."

"Oh." Avyer raised an eyebrow. "That makes a lot more sense. Why didn't you tell me that sooner?"

"There's nothing you could have done about it. You said I couldn't tell anyone the truth."

The comfortably furnished cabin in the woods was a good place to rehearse. Avyer took her by the hand until it became second nature for her to reach for him. He opened doors and helped her with everything.

"I can do it," Karina often said in annoyance.

"My helping you has absolutely to do with your capability or lack thereof. It's how I would like to show respect to my wife."

CHAPTER 45
MARRIAGE ROUTINE

WHEN THEY RETURNED TO AVEDIDA, they fell into a routine. Karina remained close by his side while he spoke with someone. She wrapped an arm tightly around him. She gave him attention non-stop. She brushed his shoulder, ran a hand down his arm, or rubbed his back.

Avyer was just as convincing. He pulled loose strands of hair from her face or gently caressed her cheek.

When Sasha saw them kissing off-duty, she blushed. "Just watching that made me feel dirty," she told Karina one evening they met at a cafe to chat and watch the news.

"Get some practice with Illya," advised Karina.

Sasha made a face.

"He's a sweet guy," said Karina. "Are you not feeling it?"

"I'm really feeling it." Sasha hesitated. "Maybe a little too much. I don't think right now is a good time to get married." She eyed the news broadcast showing another execution. "You still feel the same way about Avyer?" She lowered her voice.

"I don't know," said Karina. "I'm trying to not die right now and keep everyone I love safe."

"Yeah," Sasha mused. "Now is not the season of love." Her eyes roved back to the TV.

Bentuari was locking down on things. Ulan had been razed two days ago and a week ago in Jerson several hundred Bentuarians arrived and mass executions began. The streets were filled with black and khaki uniforms. It was a matter of time before that came to Avedida.

Dissenters were dragged out of their houses and shot in the streets. The TV broadcasts were all of the blazing houses of the dissenters and their dead bodies splayed out in front of them.

"It's weird." Sasha lowered her voice. "I really don't like watching this but I need to know."

Karina reached out to give Sasha's hand a squeeze. "He said he would keep your family safe, too," she said.

"It's just my dad, mama, and me. They don't care about me."

"But it matters," said Karina.

"I doubt it. This world is falling apart. And isn't your marriage something platonic?" Sasha asked slyly. "Since when did you start asking him for favors?"

"I ought to get something out of it."

Karina returned to the base with Sasha. She found Avyer waiting up for her in the bedroom. He sat in the chair he always seemed to sit in, his long legs crossed in front of him. "Have fun?"

"Not particularly." Karina removed her jacket and gun. "I don't go out for fun."

"What's the point, then?"

"Distraction." She slipped out of her boots.

"Just because you're my wife doesn't mean you can do as you wish without consequences. It's late," he said.

"I didn't do it on purpose."

"You never do." He uncrossed his legs. "Be careful."

Karina's jaw tightened. "Same old Avyer." She crossed her arms and stood beside him.

"What is that supposed to mean?" He stood up.

"Just what I said." Karina met his gaze without blinking.

Avyer glowered a moment, but his expression softened. He shook his head and laughed.

"What?" demanded Karina.

"Unless things change, none of your business," he said. "Are you going to bed?"

"If you let me."

"Seriously?" Avyer retired to his rolled-up blanket on the floor.

Karina showered before she beat a hasty retreat to the bed. She settled on her right side. First she had to change sides. Then she was hot. Then she was cold. Then she needed a drink of water.

After she moved around for the umpteenth time Avyer broke the silence. "Are you ok?"

"Yeah."

"You don't sound ok."

"I'll try to keep the rustling down to a minimum," Karina replied.

There were several minutes of silence. Karina tried to shift again, very quietly.

"Is there anything I could do?"

Karina sighed. "For example?"

"I don't know. You tell me."

Karina didn't really have to think it over. The big question was whether or not to ask him.

"Are you sure you can keep my and Sasha's families safe?"

"Yes." He answered without hesitation. "I told you I could."

Pause.

"Just like that?"

"Yes."

Silence. Karina was uncertain what to say next. "Thank you," was what eventually came out.

"Think you can sleep now?"

"Yes."

"Good."

Karina fell into an uneasy sleep. Avyer was keenly aware of Karina's every move. He got up several times to cover her up when she kicked off the blanket in her sleep. Nights were getting chillier and chillier.

Avyer was always up and ready before Karina. He never explained what he was doing. He would come and go at times. Occasionally she awakened to him sitting in the room watching her. He always left without a word.

It came as no surprise to Karina the next day to see he had already left the next morning. What was a surprise was finding Captain Ternovvy in her office when she arrived for work. Had he not seen her walk in, she would have turned around and fled. Unfortunately, they made eye contact.

"Wonderful to see you!" He extended a hand and gave that disarming smile of his. "I understand that congratulations are in order. We're peers now."

"Thank you," said Karina as she unenthusiastically accepted his handshake.

"And congratulations again." He put a hand to his belly and pointed at hers. "How's that going for you? You look a little peaked."

"Ah, normal." She mirrored his gesture.

"That's good."

"Yes." Karina's face warmed.

"Don't overdo it," said Ternovvy, "It'd be a shame to overexert yourself and lose the baby."

Karina's emotions finally made their way to her face. *How dare he come here, invading my space?* It would be so easy to beat him up. *I could close the door. No one would know.*

Something in her eyes made Jerod take a step back. "Don't take it the wrong way. You know what I meant."

"Of course." Karina smiled icily. "What brings you here again?"

"I'm on tour."

"What does that involve?"

"A little bit of everything. Please excuse me." He gave her a superficial pat on the shoulder and practically ran out the door.

Tai laughed from the desk next to Karina's. "His loss. I would've made a comment about him picking on someone his own size, but we all know you. No one wants to take you on, pregnant or not."

"Thanks." Karina laughed with her. She vaguely wondered when they would end the pregnancy story.

Karina finished her checklist for the day, so she made a new list for the following day. She reviewed several anomalies picked up by security, double checked the assigned posts, and arranged prisoner transport details. By then the morning had flown by.

Next came lunch, then finalizing tomorrow's schedules. That gave her time in the afternoon for training. Sometimes Avyer joined her.

Today he did. Karina smiled as soon as she spotted him. He did not smile with his mouth, but there was a smile in his eyes.

Anyone in the room dropped everything when Avyer and Karina stepped into the ring. Everyone knew that this couple was the fiercest pair of fighters on the base.

Bets were always made on who would win, even though Avyer always made sure that no one actually won.

It was not for a lack of trying on Karina's part. She tried to beat Avyer but he always was several steps ahead of her.

She had been working out more and harder but she would not challenge him today. They would keep things even. It was boring, but she was not about to start something she could not finish. At the end both of them were sweaty and panting. They retired to the room to shower, one at a time.

Karina dressed and waited for Avyer as he showered. Every other evening that she wasn't with Sasha they ate together. She sat on the bed, tracing the outline of her right hand with her left index finger. Outline completed, she toyed with the wedding band on her left ring finger.

Avyer came out half-dressed, toweling his hair. "What is it?"

She jumped guiltily. "Nothing. You'll catch a cold with no shirt on."

He finished toweling his hair and slipped into a shirt. "Unhappy to not beat me?"

"I could if I wanted to."

Avyer laughed. "We both know you've tried. You got lucky the first time you knocked me down."

Karina stiffened and glared at him. "If you're better than me, teach me what I don't know."

"Perhaps I will." Avyer arranged his hair. "Meanwhile, good luck."

"It's what you do with what you've got," Karina continued stubbornly.

Avyer shrugged it off. "Let's eat." He offered her a hand, which Karina took. "Just one more thing."

"What?"

"Be careful with what you say in the dining hall," said Avyer. "The officers have been a little rough with people lately. Just following orders, a situation which I believe you are quite aware of."

They sat in the ranking officers´ dining hall. Tonight it was nearly empty, so they sat alone. Avyer threaded his fingers through her slender left hand. Karina had been looking down at her plate until his hand touched hers. The instant they locked eyes it was impossible to feel annoyed with him. His gaze was . . . longing.

He lowered his voice. "Try to look less angry. People are watching us."

Happy thoughts. Sasha. Her new foal, Kyra. Karina smiled broadly and laughed. "Better?"

"Much," he smiled back. "I understand you saw Ternovvy today."

"Yes."

"What did he say?"

"Congratulations and he advised me to take it easy so I don't lose the baby."

"Hm." Avyer frowned.

"It wasn't even a halfway decent attempt at a veiled threat," said Karina.

"What happened after that?"

"The secretary said I gave him a scary look and he left."

"Do you really think you could take on Ternovvy?"

"Yes."

"Why?"

"I've taken on you. Has he gone through the Saratov Trials?"

"Curiously enough, no."

"I'd be fine, then."

"You really don't know your size, do you?" Avyer shook his head.

Karina rolled her eyes. "Please. I've met many huge cowards." She changed the subject. "Something's off," she told Avyer. "I can feel it. The prisoners have been restless lately."

"And the men?"

"Normal. I think they're just grateful that things are quiet. They're just glad that there hasn't been an uprising here like in Jerson and Ulan."

"Possibly."

"What really bothers me is that Ternovvy is here."

"Let me know if he bothers you again . . . I'll take care of it," said Avyer.

"Why?"

Avyer's eyes hardened. "No one bothers my wife."

CHAPTER 46
SASHA AND AVYER

PALE SUNLIGHT PEEKED through Avyer's office window. Sasha squinted at him through the darkness. *Is he too stingy to turn on the lights?*

"No need to sit." Avyer stood as she sat. "We need to go out and talk."

"Ok." She raised her right eyebrow.

He led her out to the better lit exercise track. A chill breeze nipped at their faces as they walked around alone.

"I need your help," said Avyer.

"With?"

"Don't interrupt and I'll tell you." Sasha did not squint at him again but imagined the miffed expression on his face. "It's done. You and Illya will be in contact with Timurovich. He'll give you details."

"Ok, but what is it that you need help with?"

"I will be in a meeting when all this goes down. Make certain Karina goes with you. Knock her out, if necessary."

"Are you being serious?" Sasha's eyebrows raised and her body stiffened. "Firstly, there is no way I could beat her in a fight. Secondly, Illya can't either. Thirdly, I doubt she'll be a problem."

"And I don't doubt she will be, when she finds out the truth. Do you need anything?"

"I don't think so." Sasha tilted her head. "When will that thing you mentioned happen? *That* would be more the time to knock her out."

"This morning. I'll be going right after we're done with this little chat," said Avyer. "Everything's been arranged."

"Kark," muttered Sasha as they rounded a bend in the track.

"What?"

"I hope everything goes to your plan," Sasha replied. "If not, we're going to be in big trouble."

"We won't," Avyer said grimly. "I've timed it down to the wire. There was no margin for error or Ternovvy and his special agents would have beat me to them. It won't be pretty. Just . . . be there for her."

"You don't have to tell me *that*," said Sasha, "but the question is: when will you be there for her? I really think you should tell her."

"We also need to end the baby act. I'll tell her. Soon." He looked at his watch. "Go before anyone important sees us."

Sasha nodded silently. Avyer watched her trot back to the women's barracks.

It was a mundane day for Sasha: desk duties in the main office, a little paperwork, and a short report to turn in. She sighed through all of her tasks. The minutes on the clock passed too quickly. As she typed up the last report, the clock showed one minute left before lunch break. Sasha sighed again, stretching in her desk chair. "I don't want to . . ." she groaned. She clicked to send the report.

CHAPTER 47

DEATH

"HOW'S IT GOING?" Karina slid along the food line with Sasha. She pushed her metal tray to the next part of the buffet. When she looked at her friend, she realized that all the blood had drained from Sasha's face. "What's wrong?" Karina pressed.

Sasha said nothing. Her eyes were frozen on the dining hall TV screen.

Karina gripped the buffet bar tightly and dragged her unwilling eyes to the screen. They were witnessing the televised executions and burning down of houses. *What's happening? Is Sasha's family in trouble?*

A familiar wooden blue house appeared on screen. It was surrounded by a complete Avedida police unit. Three cruisers and a wagon waited off to the side. All means of escape were cut off. *No, no, no!*

"This morning there were raids on houses suspected of collaborating with the Gavriilan Spark Revolution group," the newscaster commentated. "What you are watching right now was . . ."

Two officers kicked the door in. *I always knew that door was bad.* Three officers plunged inside, guns up and ready. Karina held her breath. Five seconds passed. *What were they doing?* There were no gunshots. Ten seconds, fifteen seconds. She was forced to exhale.

"While there was circumstantial evidence for colluding with this criminal activity, the denounced families were immediately scheduled for execution."

Avyer promised me . . . Karina had not blinked for a while now. Her burning eyes were glued to the screen. *How could he?* Tears began to fill her eyes and forcefully lubricated them.

Through the stream of tears, she saw three people were pulled out of the house They offered little resistance. They were hand-cuffed and wore brown sacks over their heads. The officers forced them to their knees. Karina knew their clothing all too well. *Papa. Mama. Sofia.*

"This morning the family of Ivan Petrov, Viktoriya Trotsky, and Sofia Ivanovna . . ." *Blast it! Why does the private dining hall always have the TV volume up so loud?*

Karina watched in horror as the officers put their guns to the prisoners' heads.

Bang. Bang. Bang. Karina jumped at each headshot and leaned against the buffet bar for support. The cameras panned over to Avyer. *Cool, calm, and collected.* Karina's ears rang so loudly that they threatened to deafen her. The dining hall spun around her. She gripped the metal bar tighter.

"He is going to die," Karina's voice rasped. She ignored the ringing in her ears and the floor swaying under her feet. Sasha's voice echoed, muffled and far away. Karina strode off.

"What is it that you're going to do?" Sasha jogged to Karina's side. She looked around the dining hall. The few people there were staring at them. So much for subtlety. Avyer had said to stop her.

"I told you."

"But he's your husband."

"And?" Stall. Stall. Stall.

"This is suicide."

"And?"

Sasha bit her lip as she stepped in front of Karina to block her way.

"And now you defend him?" Karina spat. "You're the last person who should. He and I had an agreement. He promised to keep them safe!"

"Stop and think, Karina," Sasha said coldly. "This is wrong. I know you're upset but this isn't the time or place . . ."

Karina shoved Sasha. Sasha sighed, jogging to keep pace with Karina. She pulled on her arm and pled with Karina through the garden in the center of the barracks, all the way to the training room. Karina marched into the gym where Avyer was observing new recruits.

Avyer stood off to the side. When he saw her walk through the door his face fell. The fury and grief in Karina's eyes told him everything he needed to know.

As soon as she was within range, she launched herself at Avyer. Avyer easily deflected and redirected her blows. Both of them gravitated to the center of the training area, Avyer on the defense and Karina on the offense.

"Yeeeeeah!" Several recruits applauded in excitement, supposing this was part of the program.

"Stop making a scene. I don't want to do this." Avyer lowered his voice. "We can talk later."

Karina punched him in the face. "So you know why I'm angry."

"We need to talk later." Avyer frowned as he took up a defensive stance.

Karina lashed out with another fist. A fraction of a second too slow. Avyer moved to the outside of her arm and twisted it behind her back. "You're making things worse, Karina. I don't want to hurt you," he growled.

"Then don't." Karina grimaced but dropped to her knees using her full weight to tug on Avyer. He loosened his grip enough that Karina had time to rotate her leg and strike behind his knee. He lost balance. She wrenched her arm away.

Karina continued attacking. Avyer maintained a defensive

stance, which frustrated her more. She glared, daring him to attack her with the same fury she directed at him.

Calm down. If she spent herself, he would eventually come on the offense and take her out easily. *As he always does.* The realization set in too late. As if cued, he attacked.

Karina heard a collective muttering in the training room. Some were criticizing, others were analyzing. When Karina did a drop-roll somersault to avoid a punch she glimpsed Sasha's worried face in the crowd.

Should I have listened to her?

Avyer turned away most of her punches toward his face and midsection. She twisted and dodged his punches and kicks. She was running out of energy. A strong kick cracked her left shoulder so hard that her eyes watered. *Is it broken?* A warm sensation radiated from her shoulder, down her arm and into her chest.

Don't stop.

Gritting her teeth, she landed an equally painful kick to Avyer's lower back. He doubled over.

I can't keep this up. He looks done. Karina stepped forward. *I'm going to end this.*

She landed with a crack on the training mat, the breath smacked out of her. Tears streamed from the corners of her eyes. She blinked and gasped for breath.

Avyer stood up straight. "I think that's enough for today." He addressed the audience. He smoothed back his hair and pulled his uniform straight. "Take note. Keep a cool head. Be calculating."

Sasha helped Karina sit up. Karina's breath came in heaving gasps. Now that her fury and adrenaline were subsiding, her shoulder screamed with overwhelming pain.

"Carry on." Avyer dismissed the crowd and pulled Karina to her feet.

Karina tried to speak, but only hoarse gasps shuddered from her chest. The pain in her shoulder mounted to excruciating as Avyer half-carried her to their bedroom.

"Leave us," Avyer told a wide-eyed Sasha once Karina had been deposited on the bed.

"No!" protested Karina.

"Yes, sir." Sasha shook her head sadly at Karina.

Avyer paced the room as Sasha left. Karina gingerly sat up. The movement made her aware of more aches and pains from the fight that she had not felt before.

"You're a smart girl." Avyer scowled. "How could you possibly do something so idiotic? Really? I really, truly thought you'd use your brain for this one." His eyebrows knit together as he winced in pain. Karina must have hit him harder in the back than she had realized. "You're making everything so difficult! I told you I wasn't going to hurt you and what do you do? You decide to try to take me out in front of everyone!"

"You're one to talk about promises," Karina gasped. "You *promised* me that nothing would happen to my family!" She doubled over as pain stabbed her shoulder. "But what do you do? You televise a public execution of my family and burn down my house for all of Gavriila to see."

"You're overreacting. If you would just let me explain—" Avyer began.

"I'm *not* overreacting," snapped Karina. The pain was nearly unbearable. "We had a deal. Not everyone is going to be as cold-hearted as you when they lose their family." She lay back down with a groan.

"That was . . ." Avyer stopped pacing and raised a finger. "Fine. Think what you will. I *was* going to explain but I'll leave you with your murderous thoughts. I'll also send the doctor to look in on you. Don't go out or so help me I'll . . . I'll . . ." He raked his hand through his mussed hair, thought better of what he was about to say, and left Karina alone in the room.

By the time the doctor arrived, Karina's shoulder had turned into one giant bruise. The doctor healed all her injuries, with exception of her shoulder.

"It's fractured. Don't lie down completely. Keep something

cold on it and try to not move it," he instructed her before leaving. "I'll return tomorrow and take a look at it. That will heal slowly." Meanwhile, he injected her with strong painkillers.

Karina spent the rest of the day in the bedroom. When she was not dozing off in bed, she stiffly paced around the room.

My parents are dead. My sister is dead. Dead. How could Avyer say everything's ok? The three hooded figures were them. I recognized their clothing . . . they are dead. All I have left now is Sasha.

Karina had dressed to sleep and hid under the bed covers when Avyer returned. She kept her back to him. She heard rustling as he changed out of his uniform to sleeping shorts.

She felt the bed shift as Avyer sat down on the other side of the bed. "Not a word: my bed is huge and I'm sleeping in it. My back is killing me. You have your side and I have mine."

Karina stiffened. The covers and the bed moved as he settled himself on the right side, close to the door. He did not attempt to move closer to her, so she fell asleep.

The next morning when Avyer's alarm went off she tried to sit up. She moaned when she twisted her shoulder. Avyer's hand settled on her chest and pushed her to lie back down. Karina sputtered. Despite the fact that he had condemned her family, her heart rebelled against her, hammering wildly under his gentle touch.

"Sleep in," he mumbled. "You're staying in this room for a few days." His hand left her chest and rubbed her good arm.

"Why?" Karina pulled away, ready for another argument.

"We're pretending you had a miscarriage. I sent a mass memo to the higher-ups and your coworkers informing them of your current condition and telling them that you're indisposed."

"Oh." *Good point.* Karina lay back down. "Great. How did they take it?"

"Well, you know higher-ups. They could care less, but they were polite. Tai started bawling her eyes out. Are you ready to hear what I had to say yesterday?" Avyer yawned.

"No." Karina's shoulder ached too much to turn away from him.

"Ok. Your loss. When you're ready let me know."

Karina scowled, biting back a retort.

"Ok?" he pressured.

"Ok."

CHAPTER 48

BASE ONE

KARINA KEPT up the good wife act despite her stiff shoulder. Beyond their public facade she had avoided speaking with Avyer the past two weeks. When she emerged from the bedroom with her arm in a sling she was met with a deluge of condolences.

"I'm so sorry, Karina." Tai gave her a gentle hug when Karina returned to the office. "Are you feeling ok?"

"Mostly," said Karina as she gingerly sat at her desk.

"Let me know if you need anything. Take it easy! We're all here for you," Tai said.

"Thank you." It was not necessary to conjure fake tears. Her eyes began waterworks of their own volition. "It's been a lesson hard learned: don't spar hard while pregnant."

This Friday Karina would have eaten alone, but Sasha and Illya insisted upon accompanying her, so she ate in the general dining hall. Avyer was in a meeting with several generals and had said he would be a while.

Halfway through the meal gunshots rang out. Sasha and Illya exchanged glances. Karina froze. As soon as she stood to run out the door, they dragged her out a side door.

Karina winced in pain as they pulled her stiff shoulder. "What are y—?" began Karina.

Sasha clapped a hand over her mouth. "Shut up and come with us." They had an iron grip on her arms as they hauled her to the stable. The only thing that kept Karina from fighting them was her throbbing shoulder.

They released her when they arrived at the dark stable. Karina made out several horses saddled, waiting in the darkness. Gladrion was in the crossties, his saddle to the side.

"Get him saddled. We're leaving," Illya ordered as he loosened his grip on Karina.

"*What* is going on?" Karina turned to Sasha.

"We're rebelling. The revolution begins now, courtesy of you and Avyer and the people you interviewed," said Sasha.

"What?" Karina staggered back a step.

"You may not have seen this coming, but you have to have suspected," said Sasha. "We're pulling out, with you."

"But why? Why?"

"Saddle up this thing," Illya insisted. "He won't let us touch him. Saddle first, questions later."

"But he killed my family."

Karina eased the blanket and saddle on Gladrion's back. She winced as she pulled the cinch tight, and checked the straps. She and Illya exchanged their police uniform jackets for plain brown ones. They gave one to Karina.

Sasha snorted. "You think? They're alive and waiting for us. He tried to tell you."

"Is that true?"

Karina's breath caught in her throat as she put a foot in the stirrup. Gladrion snorted and champed at the bit as she pulled his rein to the side.

"It's true, and we need to go," Sasha huffed. "This is not the time to think about your family."

"I told you we shouldn't tell her yet," Illya said.

"And Avyer?"

"He's a big boy," said Illya, "He can take care of himself. Get up and we're going."

Karina sized up Illya and Sasha. Both were tense, alert and ready to pounce on her.

"Ok." She ungracefully swung onto Gladrion, trying to avoid jostling her sore shoulder. As Sasha and Illya mounted, Karina spurred Gladrion in the direction of Avyer's office.

"Karina!" Sasha shrieked behind her. Hoof beats pounded behind Karina, but she had a head start.

Gunshots coming from the jail cells were making their way to the main office. Karina rode to the weapons room without hesitation. She put a hand on the control panel to open it up and fill a saddle bag with plasma magazines. She grabbed several guns and left the door open behind her.

Sasha and Illya caught up to her. "What are you doing?"

"And Avyer?" Karina thrust a gun in Sasha's hands then Illya's.

Sasha and Illya exchanged glances. "We don't know."

"Exactly."

"This is not the time to get sweet on him," said Illya.

"I'm not leaving him," said Karina. "Grab what you need and follow me."

"He's in a meeting, and said to not interrupt," said Sasha. "Stop her!" Sasha turned to Illya.

"Yeah, right," Illya grumbled. "*I'm* not getting my butt kicked, not right now."

They rode to the offices. Karina dismounted and pulled Gladrion into the building.

"You can't take a horse in the building," Sasha protested.

"We can't get out of here if our transport is dead."

They left their mounts in the empty reception. *Where is the desk sergeant?* Karina pointed out the security cameras and Sasha shot them as they made their way down the halls.

"How many people are in the meeting?" asked Karina.

"Don't know," hissed Sasha.

"Three or four, I think," said Illya.

"How do you know that?" Sasha looked sharply at Illya.

"Saw them come in this afternoon."

"Oh."

As they rounded the corner, Karina realized what a half-cocked idea it was. Two guards in the hall and two more flanking Avyer's conference room spotted them before they ducked back around a corner.

"What are you doing here? Stop!"

"Stay and shoot them!"

Karina ran back to the lobby desk, launched herself over the desk and went through the door behind it. *I knew it.* A short hallway led her to the other side of the guards. They would be pinned between Karina and Illya and Sasha. As she peered around the corner of the hallway she saw two guards dead on the ground. The other two were distracted by Illya and Sasha. It was an easy kill, even for Karina.

She ran to the conference door as soon as the two guards hit the floor.

"Wait!" Illya warned. He had a hand to his shoulder. Blood streamed between his fingers.

Karina pressed the door panel open and ran to Avyer. "Are you all right?" She flung her arms around him. Her back was to the four men in conference with him. "There were shots!"

Sasha and Illya were hot on her heels and closed the door behind them.

"What the—" began a general.

"Choose your next words very wisely." Another general scowled at the trio. His bushy eyebrows glowered over his eyes.

"What are you talking about?" One of Sasha's braids fell to one side as she cocked her head. "We're here to help."

Karina shot the general next to Avyer. Before the others could react, Sasha's gun was out and the other generals were on the floor with the first one.

Avyer shot out the cameras. "Did you get the cameras in the halls?"

"Done." Sasha scanned the office.

"I'll destroy the security room." Avyer's neutral expression changed to pure rage. "What the kark are you doing here?" He eyed Karina before glaring at Sasha and Illya. "I gave you direct orders."

"I directly disobeyed them." Karina pulled on his arm.

"*You* are never in charge again." Avyer pointed at Sasha.

"We need to get out of here," said Karina.

"There is no *we*." He removed her hand from his arm. "You need to leave."

"It would be easier," she began, then corrected herself. "It *would have* been easier if you'd told me your plans."

"I tried to and you would not listen. You decided I was a homicidal fiend."

"This is *my life* you're playing with." Karina's face reddened. "Do you want me to play with yours?"

"I am playing with *our* lives." Avyer corrected her. "We'll talk later. You have five minutes before this place is in lockdown. I'll finish things here. Go!" He turned his back on her to gather a binder of data sheets and a datapad before walking out the door.

"Don't you make me . . ." Karina called after him.

"What?" Avyer stopped, but did not turn around. When Karina did not respond he kept walking. "That's what I thought."

Shots rang out from his general direction after he had disappeared.

"We're losing time," Illya said. "Your family is waiting for you. Let's go."

Karina reluctantly followed him to reception, mounted Gladrion and rode out. They dodged shots and explosions on the way back to the stable. Illya led them back to the trail Karina and Avyer had taken the night they met up with Solari.

All horses and riders were flecked with sweat and small cuts by the time they arrived at the summer house where she and Avyer had met up with the IPG weeks ago. A bulky cruiser with a horse wagon awaited, ready to drive them all to a place that Sasha referred to as Base One.

For five hours the cruiser rolled over unpaved country roads until it reached a large field. The weak rays of dawn were blocked by a small mountain looming over the field, but slowly lit up carefully organized chaos. As they drove across the field Karina was struck by the size of things. They plowed past swarms of busy people. The leaders wore brown jackets and directed everyone.

"Camps to the left," called out a woman. She sent refugees to a hodgepodge of tents and tarps stretched out over sturdy tree branches.

"Food to the left." A man next to her signaled a ramshackle structure composed of thin metal slats that would have been a welder's nightmare. Even Karina could see that an inexpert hand had put together the building labeled as a kitchen. "You have three hours to get rations."

"Medical services! Keep the way clear," ordered a man in scrubs a little further to the right.

Their vehicle did not turn right or left. They went straight ahead. It was slow going but they eventually reached a rickety building complex at the end of the road. Several people appeared to unload the horses.

"Put hers next to the little filly," Illya told the handlers. "They're both hers."

"She's here?" Karina's eyes lit up.

"We thought of everything." Sasha grinned.

Karina hugged her and Illya.

"Let's meet some people," said Illya.

Karina and Sasha followed him into the makeshift buildings. Every board groaned as though theirs was the last weight it would bear, but they did not crash through the floor.

"Your family isn't here," Sasha said as they reached the back of the building.

"Then why did you say they were waiting for me?"

"They are," Illya reassured her. "But they were taken farther out, for their safety. We had to say something to get you out of Avedida."

Karina recognized many people she had interviewed or rescued. She also spotted a few IPG people in the mix. She was glad Karura Solari was not here this time. She felt uneasy around him.

A group of ten people sat or stood around a small wooden table, examining a map and various documents. Each greeted Karina in turn.

"Would someone please explain what's going on?" Karina asked weakly.

Stepan spoke first. "A revolution. The IPG and the Lomans are well on their way to defeating Bentuari. It's a very long story, but the short of it is that Bentuari himself is dead. He's been dead a while. We're dealing with the leftovers of his regime. Some of his heads wish to maintain the empire. While they're distracted with maintaining other planets, we'll strike here. All of us in this room are leaders. You will be at the forefront with us."

"Why me?" Karina's eyes widened and glanced around the room at everyone. "I'm no one special."

Oleksaandra laughed and shook her head.

"It's not funny." Karina's forehead knit in annoyance.

"Sorry," Oleksaandra said. "I know you're not in on everything yet. No offense. It's just that if you had not come along, Nikolai would never have joined Gavriilan Spark and organized things better. We wouldn't be here if it weren't for you."

"Let me explain," Stepan said. "All of us were selected according to Nikolai's parameters. The people you interviewed all had one thing in common: they have weight in their sectors. People look up to them. Perhaps none of us are special at the end of the day. I don't feel special. However, all of us are recognizable figures in our communities.

"You're Avyer Nikolai's wife. You're also an excellent fighter. Above all that, you serve only the people. Do you really think that your kindness and mercy have gone unnoticed?"

Several people smiled.

"But what am I doing here? I've no experience in war."

"You'll train people to fight."

"And Avyer?"

"He's the engineer of all that you see," said Stepan. He gestured at all the leaders and the equipment in the room. "He's established quite a few cells like this one. He will join us in his own good time."

Karina bit back many questions. She would wait to talk with Avyer. *And apologize.*

"The time for you to dodge bullets may well come," Stepan seemed to read her mind. "But right now we need you here."

CHAPTER 49
IN CHARGE

AVYER EYED the four dead bodies in the conference room before turning his back on Karina. *This had not been a part of the plan. Illya and Sasha had only one job. I have my own job to do.*

Avyer strode down death row. Some of the prisoners deserved death, while others did not. Avyer shot the murderers and left the innocent alive. Soon Special Agent Ternovvy's team would reach this area.

Avyer ducked out a side door in search of the IPG operatives. Their five minutes were almost up. A swarm of Loyalists shoved past him to enter the jail as he left.

"Search the premises," he called out sternly. "They've assassinated the generals!"

As soon as the door slid closed behind the Loyalists, Avyer reached into his pocket for a small device with a button. He pressed it.

An explosion rocked part of the complex close to his office as the security room was torn apart by explosives he had planted there earlier in the day. That should buy him a few more minutes.

Avyer broke into a run. It would not take long for even the densest of Loyalists to question why Avyer was alive while the four generals had met an untimely demise.

Karura Solari and Spark leader Danylo Ponomarenko were in a cruiser waiting for him a few blocks away. Avyer took off his police jacket and took the black one Danylo proffered him.

"How are we on time?" asked Avyer.

"Tight. What happened?" asked Solari.

"My wife," said Avyer. "Let's go."

He sat in the back with Solari while Danylo drove.

"First of all," Karura said as he showed Avyer his AutoMap, "we have cells going off all over the place. Here." He tapped on Avedida. "And here." Now Barnaul. "And here." Ending at Oryol. "These sectors are rebelling. The IPG is prepared to aid you, but you must do the heavy lifting. This is *your* planet, after all."

"You're no negotiator," said Avyer.

"No, I'm not." Solari pocketed the AutoMap. "The IPG cannot be everywhere all at once. We're here because you expressed interest in signing an alliance with us once you have taken back your planet."

"Look, those sectors are strong. We have some of the strongest patriots in our ranks. We're doing what we can."

"The IPG needs more than assurances," Karura replied. "If we're about to stick our neck out for you, you need to do more than that."

"What do you propose?"

Karura Solari shrugged.

"If you're going to mention more problems, the least you could do is offer a few solutions," said Avyer.

"If I saw a solution I would offer it," Solari said. "At this point, speed is key. Move fast, before the Loyalists have time to react."

Avyer shook his head.

"You're the one who started all this," said Karura.

"I'll finish it," Avyer snapped. "Don't worry about that. Let's get to where we're going." *There are no fast or easy solutions to the lack of manpower.* He took out his phone to text his second in command. *Dima, make sure the Sparks have Karina and Sasha training people ASAP. Solari needs to see that we have the manpower necessary to win this war. We don't have much time. Stepanov, Raize, Mognari and Ternovvy will be looking for us.*

Several hours on the road did not bring him new ideas. They abandoned the cruiser at a farm and took a ship to a remote base in the Barnaul Mountains on the edge of Barnaul Province.

Avyer shivered as he disembarked on the mountaintop. Someone handed Avyer a warmer coat. Danylo led them into a warehouse dug out of the side of the mountain. It was an ideal location, hidden from prying eyes. As they entered a stark concrete room serving as their main operations room, Avyer realized that the sun glimmered over the pale snow. *How is it morning already?*

Someone else handed him a hot coffee. He was soon standing in a crooked circle of twenty people. He looked around at the somber faces. He took a gulp of coffee and nodded at Solari.

"I started all this, so I guess I'll open the meeting officially. We're off to a good start. Solari here." He pointed at the IPG representative. "He says the IPG is willing to support us, but that we must put in a little more effort."

"We don't have any more people at this moment," a man spat at Karura Solari.

"Do you want allies?" Solari wiped the spittle off his armor with a gloved hand and flung it at the man. "Or would you rather be dead?"

"Allies," croaked the Gavriilan.

"Excellent. Now, are you going to figure things out or should I leave?" Solari eyed Avyer.

"We'll figure things out," said Avyer. "Kuryagin is just tired. Aren't you, Kuryagin?"

"Yessir," Kuryagin mumbled sullenly.

"Very well. Let's have a summary, shall we?" Avyer turned to Oleksaandra.

"Karina, Sasha and Illya are at Base One. They're receiving instructions right now if they haven't already. They're fine, but there have been many civilian casualties. Anton is on it." Now she nodded to Anton.

"Yes." Anton rubbed his stiff hands. "I have connections in every base, and they're doing everything they can to milk their connections. There will be no lack of medical support."

"And medical supplies?" asked Solari.

"We're still determining that."

"I need a full report on medical supplies as well as weapons supplies," said Solari, crossing his arms. "To get a better picture of where things stand."

"Understood," said Anton.

Avyer motioned for the doors and windows to be closed. He set a small device down in the circle of people, turning on a 3D map. "Gavriilan Spark Revolutionists have been hard at work and highly instrumental in locating safe areas for bases. This information must not go outside of this room. If you breathe so much as a word to your friends or family, I'll shoot you myself. Not even my wife knows about this."

CHAPTER 50
THE LOYALIST'S FURY

"BLAST IT!" General Stepanov's fist slammed his desk. Data sheets flew into the air and the few medals he displayed on the desk rattled. "I told you Nikolai was up to no good! But no, everyone insisted that he was the model civil servant."

He turned to the man in an armchair to the left.

"And you, Special Agent Ternovvy," he growled at Jerod. "You said the girl was innocent."

"Sir." Jerod swallowed and considered his answer as he responded. "I doubt she knew what Chief Nikolai was having her do. She always did as she was told. I spent hours with her. Even if she were, or is, part of the revolutionists, I have a hard time believing that she is the mastermind."

"Raize." Stepanov's eyebrows knit together until they formed a unibrow. He pointed at Raize. "You said Nikolai was the best of the best."

Raize's face was serene. He crossed his arms as he rocked in his seat. "Yes, he was. Until he wasn't. These things happen. You yourself witnessed how he pursued and jailed Gavriilan Spark people. He was dedicated. Then he fell in love. Just goes to show, you never know. Why do you think I proposed sending special agents to inspect different jails, prisons, and government buildings? I foresaw this type of thing happening."

"I want both of them *dead,*" Stepanov hissed the last word with venom. "I don't care what it takes and I don't care how you kill them. I want their carcasses on my desk as soon as possible."

"All right, then." Ternovvy swaggered to the desk. "I'll have my people track Nikolai's and Ivanovna's whereabouts. If they're smart, they will have split up."

"And." Stepanov thrust his index finger in Ternovvy's face as Ternovvy leaned toward him "If you do not get the job done, next time it will be *your* head"—he jabbed the desk with his finger—"on my desk. So stop strutting and get something done. Special Agent, you are dismissed. General Raize, you are not."

CHAPTER 51
TRAINER KARINA

EVERYONE and their assistants showed up at the checkpoint meeting bleary-eyed and swaying. Karina's body ached with exhaustion. She took the closest available chair and sat. Someone wisely began passing around coffee.

Anton was there, as was Oleksaandra. Karina had not seen either of them in a while. The usuals—Yakov, Stepan, Zaira, Andrei, Illya and Sasha—were present. After a few minutes of small talk and a second cup of coffee Karina was more awake.

"Who's going to get this started?" Yakov voiced the question in Karina's mind.

"I will." Oleksaandra did not hesitate. "It won't take too long, so don't get comfy." Everyone took a chair despite her warning.

"As I'm sure you all know," Oleksaandra said, "Avyer Nikolai is heading this up with the support of the IPG, all at great personal risk."

Karina zoned out when she heard that. *He's . . . in charge of everything? It all feels so . . . big.* She returned to reality in time to hear, ". . . and we'll be moving Sasha, Illya and Karina from base to base to do the same."

"Sorry," Karina interrupted, and her face turned beet red. "Why are we being moved again?"

Sasha glared at her.

Oleksaandra repeated herself. "Nikolai sent a covert assessor last week. The troops are in decent enough condition. You'll go from base to base, identify the best fighters, train them on how to fight, and get things in halfway decent shape. You've done an excellent job here. No reason to waste that talent."

Sasha sighed loudly.

"Very well." Karina glared across the room at Sasha.

"We'll talk privately later," Oleksaandra said to Karina before continuing with other points of interest.

By the time the meeting concluded, it was past breakfast time. Food was brought in and they ate a silent breakfast.

"You ok?" Oleksaandra put a hand on Karina's shoulder. "You look unwell."

"I'm exhausted," said Karina. "Everyone here is."

Oleksaandra gestured with a thumb to the door. "Let's go for a ride."

Karina nodded. "I'll get a couple of horses ready." She went to the lean-to serving as a stable. Sasha was busy flirting with Illya, so she went alone.

"Morning, Borys," she greeted the animal keeper.

"Good morning, Karina. Gladrion is in the corner."

"Thanks."

Karina saddled Gladrion and a gelding, then rode over to the shack to hand the gelding over to Oleksaandra.

"Let's go a little further into the woods," said Oleksaandra. "I imagine you have a few questions."

"Just a few," Karina said dryly.

They followed a narrow, unkempt path overgrown with dry dying weeds. Evergreens pressed around them. They rode five minutes out from the base to a more open area of the forest. Oleksaandra dismounted and Karina followed suit.

"Your husband has been very busy," said Oleksaandra. "He's doing an excellent job. We couldn't have asked for a better leader. You should be proud of him."

"I am."

"But you can tell him that yourself." Oleksaandra smiled as they rounded a corner and came to a larger clearing.

Karina's heart skipped a beat. Avyer was leaning against a tree waiting, his arms crossed. He had traded police attire for the brown leather jacket and dark clothing that set leaders apart from the followers. As soon as he saw them he straightened.

Karina's eyes lit up. "You could have just told me that Avyer was here."

"Sure," Oleksaandra said. "I'll leave you to it." She mounted up and left the couple.

Avyer uncrossed his arms as he walked toward Karina. He eyed her. "Are you still mad at me? You look like you're either going to kiss me or kill me."

Karina's heart fluttered in her chest. "I . . ." her voice trailed off.

Silence.

"You look well. I'm glad," he said. "Do you want a divorce?"

"No! Do you want one?"

"Not unless you've been sleeping around."

"I haven't. Have you?" Karina toyed with her jacket cuffs.

"No."

"So?"

"Then I don't want one. Do you?"

"No."

Avyer rubbed his chin. "What do you want?"

"The truth," said Karina. "All of it, starting from the beginning. Were you always with Gavriilan Spark? If not, what happened? Was it a coincidence that I survived the Desmarin attack?"

"That's a lot of questions." Avyer raised an eyebrow and leaned toward her.

"Just start from the top."

"Ok." Avyer took a deep breath. "When you met me, I was with the Bentuari Loyalists . . ."

"What changed that?"

"You did."

Karina swallowed a lump in her throat. "I didn't do anything."

Avyer laughed and shook his head. "What did you not do? You're beautiful. You're determined. You're fair and kind to everyone whether they deserve it or not. Do you think I forced you to join the police to make you marry me? I had no intention of falling in love with you. I was perfectly happy torturing kids and cracking down on locals." His eyes sobered.

"Dima tried many times to get me to question my loyalties. Nothing doing. Then I met you, and I started having doubts. The Loyalists slaughtered what was left of my family, with all of Desmarin, and that removed any last doubt I'd been entertaining.

"No, it's no coincidence you survived Desmarin. I had an idea when the attack would be and sent my doctor with vials of antidote for you and my family. There was a vial of antidote for everyone. It was a good thing, too, because they had to give you three of those."

"Really?" *So he did love his family.* Karina's throat tightened.

"You would've died if they hadn't dosed you. Anyway, after all that I started thinking—a lot—about what I might possibly do, and you came to mind."

"Me? Why?"

"You're a good person, and you're good with people. Have you seen how they look at you? Do you know how hard it is to inspire Avedidans to look up to the police? I never knew any Avedida police officer who received the admiration you did while you were roaming the streets. Everyone talked about you. Then came Desmarin. You did not hesitate to help people, even if it cost your life. You're the reason the Gavriilan Spark Revolution has its leaders now."

"And you're on top?"

"Unfortunately, almost."

"And the IPG?" Karina took a step toward him.

"Luck. One of the people you interviewed had connections with connections."

"And now?" Karina took another step.

"I'm overseeing everything." Now Avyer came closer. There was barely a meter between them.

"Like a president?"

"I just want Gavriila to be free." He laughed. "What? Do you want to be married to the president?"

"No. I'd rather be living in the obscurity of a cave."

"I'll keep that in mind and look for a nice cave for us when the time comes."

"You know what I mean." Karina pursed her lips.

"So, you want to stay married?" asked Avyer. "This is the last time I'm going to ask." He took another step. If he reached out he could touch her.

"Yes." Karina shuffled toward him.

"No second chances."

"I said *yes*."

Avyer closed the gap between them. "You have no idea how famous we are." His fingers brushed her cheek as he tucked a stray hair behind her ear. "I need to know that you are sure."

"I am." Karina wrapped her arms around him.

"What would you like now?"

"A kiss, for real." Karina's knees felt weak. She leaned against him for support. She felt as though she were resting against a strong tower. His arms enveloped her like impenetrable walls.

"All my kisses were real." Avyer touched his forehead to hers.

He leaned down to press his lips to hers. Karina closed her eyes and leaned into the kiss, savoring his warm lips locking with hers, his warm face next to hers, and the strong smell of woodsmoke that permeated his jacket and his hair. Her entire body trembled, but this time it was not out of fear.

"I thought you said you didn't like me." Karina gasped when the kiss ended.

"I don't like you. I love you."

Avyer kissed her again and this time Karina kept her eyes open. Somehow the forest, the chilly air, the war, and everything that happened up to this point no longer existed as she gazed into his dark brown eyes. It was as though she were looking at him for the first time.

"I need to say something." Karina swallowed when the kiss ended.

"What?" Avyer took her hand.

"I'm sorry."

Avyer's eyes widened. "Whatever for? I can't think of anything you've done to me that is worse than what I did to you."

"Well . . . I did throw out your back when I thought that you'd murdered my family."

"Oh. That. I'm fine now."

"And there's messing up your exit plans in Avedida."

A smile flitted across his face. "That *was* rather inconvenient, but I'm glad you did."

"What? Why?"

"You wouldn't have done that if you didn't have feelings for me. I knew then, that . . ."

"What?"

". . . that I had a chance with you," he said thickly.

Karina hopped up and flung her arms around his neck to pull him closer and kiss him. Avyer laughed as she awkwardly hung from his neck. Next thing she knew, Avyer swept her off her feet and planted another kiss on her lips. Karina's cheeks blushed furiously but she leaned into the kiss. He sighed as he put her back on the ground.

"What is it?" Karina gave him a timid look.

"I need to go. There's a lot going on."

"You just got here. I've not seen you for nearly a month. I don't want you to go," Karina's shoulders slumped.

Avyer's eyes crinkled around the edges. "I don't want to go," he said. "If I could, I'd tell you why, but I don't want to risk your safety. They'll move you regularly to keep you safe." He gave her a squeeze and turned to go but Karina clung to his hand tighter.

"What?"

"Please come back alive."

"You know I can't promise that," he said. "General Stepanov wants me dead."

"I'm not asking for a promise. Just take care of yourself."

"I will." He ran his hand through her hair, letting his fingers fall from her hair to run along her cheek. "I'll be back. You'd better get back to camp. Oleksaandra is going to move you, Sasha, and Illya to Ternopil. You should find a surprise waiting for you at camp." He left Karina alone in the clearing.

Karina watched him until he was out of sight. She mounted Gladrion and returned to the camp, where familiar faces were waiting there for her. For the second time today, Karina's heart skipped a beat as her family ran to her with open arms.

CHAPTER 52

CONFLICT

KARINA DREW a sharp breath as the wagon hit another pothole. Her stomach lurched up and down with the vehicle. She halfway expected each dip to be an explosion that would rock everyone inside.

She eyed her fellow occupants. Half of them were alert, while the other half slumped against the walls or leaned on one of their comrades. Occasionally an alarmed snort followed the jolts as a soldier was rudely awakened. Would they do as they had been trained?

Get a grip. That's what Sasha would say.

She peered out the wagon window, but her eyes met with black and gray shadows. Sasha was in a wagon behind her. Karina imagined her friend peering out through the darkness just as she was.

Everyone bounced upward as the vehicle discovered a crater in the road. CRACK! Several heads collectively smacked the roof. The battered soldiers groaned in pain.

There are advantages to being short, Karina mused.

After an eternity of jostling and banging in the wagon, it came to a halt. They had reached the edge of the small town where they were running this operation. Karina had already forgotten its name.

"All right." Her head did not graze the roof as she stood. "This may be practice for everyone here, but that doesn't mean it will be any less dangerous. There are quite a few Loyalists here. Find the weapons bunker, load up the wagons, and get out. Do not lose focus. If you see any soldiers, use the signals we practiced. If you get shot, get away and get out. Questions?"

Several soldiers exchanged glances. Two shook their heads.

"Let's do this, then."

Gravel crunched underfoot as Karina stepped out of the wagon. Lights from the town glowed on the thick fog rolling in behind them. She signaled for her group to follow her as she followed Stepan's squad. He was this excursion's leader. Karina was moral support and there to observe her trainees in action.

Karina had described the mission simply enough. However, her explanation was an oversimplification. *No sense in scaring the newbs.*

Karina glanced behind her. The other wagons had emptied. Sasha and her squad came up five hundred meters in the rear. Karina had to squint to see through the thickening tendrils of fog to make out the last wagon.

She shouldered her rifle and half-ran to catch up to Stepan and his team. By the time they reached a halfway paved street the fog had rolled into town with them. Stepan raised his hand palm outward at Karina's squad, then raised one finger. They stopped.

Karina looked left, right, and straight ahead. There was no one in sight. Two of her people began to mutter. She waved and glared at them, putting a finger to her lips. The muttering stopped and they nodded in understanding.

Sasha's squad reached them. Karina pointed at Stepan then held her palm outward at Sasha. Sasha's mouth formed an O as she nodded at Karina.

Stepan waved at Karina and Sasha. He signaled for them to

turn right. They tailed Stepan's men as they turned onto the side road.

Harsh streetlights pierced through the fog to the battered pavement. Everyone skirted puddles, ditches, and wide crevices breaking up what had been a nice road. Two high walls rose on either side of them, obscuring parking areas and small gardens belonging to twenty-story apartment buildings looming over the walls.

The lights came at more regular intervals and illuminated an approaching intersection with no traffic signal. Stepan signaled to turn left.

As Stepan set foot on the curb to the left, a motor roared to life and a blinding spotlight glared on Stepan and half of his squad. Stepan fell over himself as he backpedaled and signaled for his men to retreat.

It was not a cruiser or a wagon. It was an infantry fighting vehicle. *Loyalists have pulled out the big guns.*

"As practiced!" He mouthed and pointed to either side as they beat a hasty retreat.

Karina ran with her squad back the way they had come, to a side road on the left. They ducked down the side road, straining their ears for sounds of pursuit behind them.

"We're gonna die! We're gonna die! We're gonna die!" One of the younger trainees gasped as he slammed his back against the wall, clutching at his chest and gulping for air.

Karina scowled even as she fought the same panic rising within her. She signaled for the others to stop as she walked back to the man. She jammed a hand over his mouth to muffle his loud breathing.

"Only if you're not quiet," she whispered. "We are at war. You die here a hero, or you die later in peace. Try to not die a coward." She glared. "Ok?"

The wide-eyed young man nodded. Karina removed her hand from his mouth and wiped his spittle off on her pant leg. "Great."

Karina moved everyone down the road again. Chills ran up

and down her spine. *Is this how Avyer feels when he's rough with everyone?*

A roaring motor approached and the ground shook as treads rumbled over the pitted pavement. Karina urged her squad to move faster, signaling them to go left.

The spotlight illuminated where they had been running seconds before. Karina paused. The rumbling temporarily slowed, but it continued. The spotlight crawled up the road behind them. It would not take long for the vehicle to catch up, should the driver go faster.

Hurry! Karina pushed them faster and to the left again. They were back where they had started at the intersection, where they had first run into the vehicle. Karina cast about for a sign of other vehicles. She strained her eyes to look down the road. *Where's Stepan?*

"Ma'am." One of the men stepped forward.

"Yeah?" Karina looked at his nameplate. *Abramov.*

"What if we try attacking the vehicle?"

"How?" Karina crossed her arms.

"We've stayed ahead of it. Let's just run around the block and jump it," said Abramov.

Karina's mind raced. Infantry fighting vehicles were agile and heavily armed. *Under normal circumstances, it wouldn't be advisable to attack.*

"It doesn't seem to know what it's doing," he continued. "I think this is the perfect time to attack. Four of us can climb inside, and the rest can provide support."

"And avoid the cannon," Karina added wryly. "Fine. Abramov, you lead. Gorky, Makarov, and Zolotov will help."

They ran back around the block, slowing when they caught up to the vehicle. It crawled at the same pace, oblivious to Karina and her men. As she came closer she spotted a rectangular opening in the back. *A port.* A few men inside were chatting.

"Hey!" One of the Loyalists sounded the alarm when he caught a glimpse of Karina and her men emerging from the fog.

The vehicle screeched to a halt.

"Don't stop!" Karina yelled and charged forward. If they did not defeat this vehicle now, there was every possibility that they would be blown to smithereens.

Abramov dashed past her, jammed his gun in the port and fired off several rounds before clambering on top of the vehicle. Gorky and Makarov followed suit and dove inside. Zolotov kept pace with Karina. Karina tripped over a hole in the pavement but Zolotov grabbed her by the collar to steady her. They had nearly reached the back of the vehicle when a rifle muzzle stuck out the port.

Many things happened in a fraction of a second.

I'm sorry Avyer. Sasha. There's nowhere to go. Karina could not stop running. Should she duck to the side? Run faster and grab the rifle?

Inside, Makarov landed a solid uppercut on the Loyalist holding the rifle. The barrel dropped down sharply as the soldier squeezed the trigger.

Something exploded against Karina's Strev* vest and sent her flying backwards on the pavement. She struck the back of her head on the ground and lay in a stupor, trying to breath as the fog and slivers of night sky drifted into her field of vision.

"Are you ok?" Zolotov's face appeared above her. He sounded far away.

Karina could not respond.

"She's fine," Stepan's voice chimed in, muffled. "Look, the Strev vest took the brunt of the impact. She's just stunned. Carry her back to the wagons."

"No," Karina protested as Stepan's men flanked her and pulled her to her feet. She shook her head.

"I'm in charge here," Stepan reminded her. "And you need to get that head checked out. That's an order. Everyone did a great job. We can use this to get in." He pointed at the vehicle.

---

* Bulletproof and somewhat blast proof material

"Just . . . need . . . to catch my breath," Karina panted. "Let me sit in there." She nodded at the vehicle. She looked down at her Strev vest. The bullet had hit the lower torso of the vest. A twisted shred of metal poked out of it.

Stepan frowned. "Fine. But if you die, I'm telling Nikolai it was your decision." He nodded for his men to help Karina climb up the infantry fighting vehicle. "Sit still and tell medic Andrin if you need anything," he called after her.

"Will do." Karina climbed down the metallic green ladder after the medic.

"Watch your head," Andrin warned her.

Water-stained dingy green and khaki walls closed in around her as she made her way inside. She was able to sit without having to bend over. She leaned back against a metal opening behind the seat. It served as a shelf with metal instruments sticking out at weird angles. She pushed the instruments back so that they were not stabbing her in the back.

Andrin sat beside her. "Take off that Strev vest. You need a new one and I want to take a quick look at where you were hit."

Karina unstrapped the vest. Where the bullet had hit the vest began to sting. Andrin lifted up her shirt. There was an angry red welt surrounded by a purple bruise.

"Breathe deeply," he instructed her.

Karina breathed in and out as deeply as she could. She coughed. The stinging sensation was turning into pain.

Andrin pressed on her ribs above the bruise. "That hurt?"

"No." Karina shook her head. "It hurts down lower."

Andrin pulled a bioscanner from his belt and scanned the wound. "No internal bleeding," he announced. "It's just going to hurt like the blazes."

"I can tell." Karina tucked her shirt back in.

"Here." Andrin shrugged off his vest and gave it to her, donning hers on in its place. "Get this thing on before you really start hurting."

Karina strapped on Andrin's vest quickly. The slightest movement or jolt to the bruised area ached.

"Is it going to be a problem if I'm in physical combat?" Avyer's comment about her shooting skills echoed in her head.

"Other than being debilitated by pain, no. I wouldn't suggest it. Want something for the pain?"

"I don't but give me something just the same."

Andrin dug in his pouch and fished out a tiny packet of medicine. He ripped off the top. "Drink this shot. Should work pretty fast."

Karina put the open end of the pouch in her mouth, tilting her head back to drain it down to the last drop. She grimaced. *That tastes like someone boiled a cracker in sugar water and packaged it to go.*

"Great stuff, huh?" Andrin grinned at the look on her face. "It's the best we got."

"Thanks," said Karina.

"Close the ports and be quiet," the driver barked at them.

Andrin closed the open ports. Karina looked around the dim interior as the vehicle shook over the bumpy streets. There was not much to see. The turret and guns inside were ready for use and the radio had been turned off.

The shot of medicine was taking effect, but when Karina twisted to look around her side ached. She pressed her lips in a thin line. *Don't let them see I'm in pain. Don't wince. Don't blink.*

The vehicle ground to a halt, throwing Karina against Andrin. He was like a pillar that kept her from sliding off the tiny metal bench. She grunted from the impact.

"You ok?" he asked.

"Yeah." Karina nodded tensely. She strained her ears. Voices echoed around the vehicle.

"Whatever happens, stay in the rear, Ivanovna," one of the men said. "I don't care what the blazes Stepan says: if you die we will all face very unpleasant consequences."

Karina did not argue. After that last jolt it was all she could do to breathe without groaning in pain.

The voices were amplified, swelling in intensity. Shots began ringing out all around. Karina recoiled at the sound of projectiles striking the vehicle walls.

"Move out!" Stepan roared.

The vehicle shuddered to life. Someone clambered into the turret, and the entire vehicle vibrated as they fired the guns. Round after round pierced the foggy night.

"What's going on?" Karina shouted over the cacophony.

"Don't know. Stepan's moving us out," barked a man.

"I knew *that.*" Karina scowled to herself, then yelled back, "Shouldn't we get out?"

"Not until we're told."

They bumped and vibrated along the road, bullets thudding and explosives going off all around them. Karina's heart pounded wildly. She balled her hands into fists. *Anything would be better than being stuck in this tin can. I'm both helpless and useless here.*

"Get ready!" Someone near the front called out. "Stepan signaled."

Karina crowded behind Andrin as everyone filed to climb up the ladder.

Andrin yelled back at her. "If you start feeling bad, signal me!"

"Ok!"

Everyone shot up the rungs at top speed except for Karina. She grit her teeth as she emerged from the belly of the mechanical beast.

She was immediately blinded by glaring floodlights and bright streetlights all around. They had halted in the center of an open square. Barely twenty meters from the vehicle, Bentuarian Loyalists pressed around on all four sides, one for each Spark squad.

Karina looked left, right, behind, and before her. *Where's my squad?* There it was: Stepan had commandeered them. She climbed down the side of the vehicle, half-falling on the last step. She followed Andrin.

Can I do this? I have to. She glared at the Loyalists and joined the fray. Karina opted for a knife as she launched herself at the closest enemy. Most of them were wrestling with the Sparks.

Easy enough. The medicine numbed enough pain that she could whirl around the Loyalists, slash throats and avoid punches. What little pain remained was forgotten with the adrenaline surging through her veins.

She had no idea where she was going. She only knew that she needed to create a gap for the Sparks to move out.

Her fellow Sparks watched in astonishment, mouths agape for a millisecond as she carved a path through the Loyalists. When they had recovered from their shock, they rallied around her and the path became larger.

They made their way up low stone steps to a brick building emerging from the fog. Light from the windows pierced the fog and illuminated their path.

"This is it!" one of the men announced as he charged forward.

"It is?" Karina winced. The last Loyalist had smashed his rifle butt in her shoulder before she took him down.

"Stepan." The same man clicked on his radio. "It's over here. Boyko with Ivanovna."

Static crackled. "Got . . . we . . . be over," Stepan's voice sputtered.

"They're on to us," Boyko muttered. "Already trying to jam signals."

"Now what?" asked another man.

"We take the place before they can lock down." Stepan's voice came from behind them.

Karina clutched her shoulder. She followed up in the rear as Stepan made his way to a back door. Two of Stepan's squad rammed against the door and sent it careening wildly off its hinges. Sasha's squad filed past her and Andrin. In a matter of minutes the Sparks had stopped the transmission jamming and had captured or killed the Loyalists inside.

Stepan wiped a bead of sweat from his forehead. "Well," he

sighed as he leaned on the communications desk. "You did good," He eyed Karina appreciatively.

"I did not do anything," said Karina.

Stepan laughed. "I was referring to the men. I mean, you did fine out there, but I'm impressed with how . . ." He looked up at the ceiling. "How efficient they are, I guess, given that they've been training only a few weeks." He returned his gaze to Karina. "Keep up the good work, Ivanovna. You and Bondaruk are doing great. Might just win us the war. Let's go get us some guns."

CHAPTER 53

BASE TWO: TERNOPIL

THE OLD CRUISER banged and jolted its way down the road. Karina's teeth rattled uncomfortably. The bone-jarring bumps set Karina's nerves on edge, but it was yet another inconvenience they all had to deal with. They were close to the Ternopil base. Just a few more minutes.

Karina looked at Sasha beside her. Sasha's clenched teeth and eyebrow raise said it all. *Why are we on this road again?*

Illya was oblivious to the horrible conditions. He sat up front chatting with Oleksaandra and the driver.

"Probably a good thing we didn't eat breakfast." Karina's teeth gnashed when they hit another pothole. "Otherwise I'd be sick now."

"I *am* sick." Sasha pressed her lips together.

It was a relief to make the final jounce to the next base.

"Wow," said Karina when she saw Ternopil.

"Wow is right." Oleksaandra turned around in her seat to look at Karina. "It gets worse."

Sasha desperately poked her head out the window and vomited over the side of the cruiser. She choked when she saw the panorama before her.

Out Sasha's window a pile of cadavers was being hauled out

for burial. Mangled, burnt, and blasted uniforms as well as civilian clothes enveloping what was left of human beings formed tumultuous mountains of limp bodies with arms and legs at strange, uncomfortable angles. Those in charge of burial wore face masks as they jammed bodies into small wagons.

After passing the bodies they passed tents, tents, and more tents. Some were marked as medical, others as sleeping areas, and a select few as command centers. The two largest tents off to the side served as the hospital and the official center of operations. They parked at the latter.

Inside the tent, Karina took a deep breath and looked at Sasha.

"Yeah." Sasha drew a breath and tried to not gag.

"It's just for a bit," said Illya. "Not the end of the world."

"I think I'm going to be sick again." Sasha covered her mouth and ran outside the tent. Illya and Karina heard her retching.

They looked around the bare bones that was the command center tent. Karina played around with an old AutoMap jammed between a couple of old computers on a folding command table. She sat on a wooden crate, while Illya sat on a plastic one. Five higher-ups in brown jackets approached them.

Oleksaandra presented them to the leaders. Karina did not remember them from her interview days, but the names were familiar. *Alexei, Vladimir, Olaf, André and Merlé*—the latter two clearly brothers.

"I'm in charge." Olaf gave her a firm handshake. "Anything you need, let me know. We may not have much, but I assure you what we lack in current physical resources, we make up with resourcefulness."

Sasha returned, wiping her mouth on her sleeve. "Carry on," she croaked. No one gave her a second glance as she pulled up a plastic crate beside Illya.

"What's the plan?" asked Karina.

"Do like you did on Base One," said Olaf. "We've designated the back field as a training area. Half goes to Sasha and Illya for weapons training and the other half is for Karina's combat training. Here are the rosters." He handed data sheets to Karina. "Divide and conquer."

"How safe is this place, really?" asked Sasha. "It feels . . . exposed."

"Don't let the bodies fool you. We're far from the action."

Karina flipped through the sheets. *How long are we going to be stuck here?* "Do you actually have this quantity of people on-site?"

"Not at the moment. They'll be trickling in over the next few days."

"Oh."

Sasha sighed.

"Let's get started with what we have, then," said Karina. "There's no reason to wait until we're flooded with people to train."

They set off for the rocky field. Sasha's first step was in a hole. "Kark!" she spat as she twisted her ankle and her backside landed on the hard ground.

"Are you ok?" Illya gave her a hand up.

"Not really." She wobbled. "Good thing my thing is shooting." She limped the rest of the day.

They followed the same procedure they'd established at Base One: test known fighters and train new ones. They taught the excellent fighters how to train and assigned them to assist Karina.

While the names were in alphabetical order, it was impossible to group them perfectly because not everyone had arrived. That complicated things.

Trainees from this area thought they already knew how to fight. Several even wanted to challenge Karina. She said nothing. When the moment came, she left the trainee groaning in pain on the ground.

"There's a reason she's the boss, you idiot!" Sasha would yell from across the field.

Olaf dropped by to observe, but he never criticized their work. He left the three to their job. Training at Ternopil was painfully slow. Most of the people had no skill or knowledge of fighting or shooting. That plus those who thought they knew it all drastically slowed the process.

"We're never going to finish here," groaned Sasha every night they bedded down. "If I have one more nincompoop try to fire their gun with the safety on, it'll be too much. I swear I'll kill them." There was always someone who did that the following day. Sasha managed to survive, as did the trainee.

The lists narrowed down day by day. It took longer than at Base One to establish training leaders because there were no outstanding trainees.

"Everyone's at the same level," Sasha concluded.

"Bad." Illya didn't mince words.

"They're trying hard." Karina tried to be positive.

"Could've fooled me. They'd do better to recommend these people for manual labor," Illya said. "We're sending them to their deaths."

"I agree," said Sasha.

"We need to give them a chance," said Karina. "Not everyone is able to learn quickly." She did not add the *like us* on the tip of her tongue.

After several more weeks the trainees scraped by, barely. The next stop was Oryol, the home base in the Vladislav Forest.

"Just take the lead," Illya told Karina when they arrived. "You've always had a better idea as far as training. Might as well make it official."

"I don't really agr—" started Karina.

"Shut up!" Sasha snapped. "You're in charge of training. Period. You do all the talking from now on, and we'll just do our thing. You're Nikolai's wife anyway. People will listen to you, if for no other reason than that."

"Ok." Karina was too tired to argue. "Karina Ivanovna." She offered her hand to the Oryol base commander.

"Abram Victorovich," he said. "A pleasure."

"Sasha and Illya, my trainers," said Karina.

"Welcome." He shook their hands. "Let me show you around."

Oryol was little better than Ternopil. At least here Karina and Sasha slept in a shack next to the command area, which was half-cave and half-tent. The tent part was sheets crudely painted to camouflage the structure.

At night a chill wind blew through the cracks in the wooden walls and floor. Sasha and Karina huddled together, wrapped up in all the clothing and blankets they possessed. Illya sneaked them a candle to warm their hands.

Abram Victorovich awakened them early the first day. "This is what we have to work with." He led them out to the lines of volunteers. The ranks of men and women were broken up by the trees.

Karina and Sasha looked the people over: their tired faces, their hands, and their gaunt frames. Too-thin clothing provided little protection from the chilly fall that was the harbinger of the encroaching winter. Karina was shivering with her layers of tunics and thick wool coat. She shuddered to think how these people must feel.

"Do you think they'll survive?" Sasha whispered.

"I think the bigger picture is 'Will we survive?'," Karina hissed back in her ear.

Sasha snorted.

"I think we've seen enough," Karina pronounced at the end of one of the lines. "We have a few things to discuss."

Sasha nodded in agreement.

Abram regarded the two girls uncertainly, then Illya. "Are you sure? Many of them would like to see you first."

"See us?" asked Karina.

"See you. It's not every day that General Nikolai or Karina Ivanovna drop by a camp," said Abram.

"I understand," Karina replied evenly, "but they can see me on the training field. We need to plan to get ready."

"Very well," Abram motioned to a man who had been trailing behind him. "Please dismiss them." He and the three trainers went directly to command, leaving the subordinate to deal with the rows of shivering people.

"Ok," said Karina as they entered command and someone closed the sheets serving as doors behind them. "I'm concerned. I don't know where to begin. If these people don't die from starvation, the cold will kill them. I understand that my place is training, but are they going to have enough clothing or am I going to wake up one day to lines of corpses? And if there's not enough clothing, where and how could we get more?"

Abram sighed as he leaned on a crude desk formed by two barrels and a flat plank of metal. "We're working on it."

Sasha raised her eyebrows and jerked her head up at Karina. *Go on.*

"Listen," said Karina. "I respect your position, but I'm not about to train an army of pneumonic skeletons. What are we looking at?"

"Oryol is pretty tight." Abram crossed his arms. "You've been through some of the cities, right?"

"Yes."

"Saw the security?"

"Yes."

"Saw the poverty?"

"Not so much."

"Imagine poverty twice as bad as security is good."

"I have an idea," Illya piped up. "Remember the elite teams we've been working on? Form one first. Send them after supplies."

"That's not in your orders," Abram objected.

"Neither is freezing to death," said Sasha. "We're not as scrawny as your volunteers, but we'll get that way or worse very soon unless you fix the supply problems."

"Let me think about it."

Karina frowned. "Don't take too long. Do you have a list of recruit names?"

"Not yet. You'll have to make it."

Karina shook her head. "That will slow us down even more. We'll make up the initial list today," she said, "but after that someone else needs to do it."

"Anything else you'd like to know before you begin?" asked Abram.

"I think that's all for now," said Karina. "I'll let you know if I need anything."

Abram left the trio to get to work.

"We're doing this differently this time," she told Illya and Sasha once they had the names written out in alphabetical order. They split the letters up amongst the three of them. Karina took ten letters and gave Illya and Sasha each the rest.

The plan was simple: the weaker and thinner people would shoot or do menial tasks such as writing lists, while the healthier and more robust would train under Karina.

What she did not mention was that with or without permission she had every intention of forming elite groups of fighters to get food and supplies. *I doubt it will be difficult to persuade them to help me. They're starving, and who wouldn't want to help Karina Ivanovna form an elite group?*

CHAPTER 54
REBELS

"HELLO?" Avyer answered his phone. Dmitri stood to give Avyer space to speak privately. "Yes." He waved for Dmitri to sit. Dmitri lowered back down to his chair. "No, I don't think we have the resources for that." Pause. "Yes, I understand it would look good to do that, but it's not a priority right now." Pause. "Yes, I'll keep that in mind." He pursed his lips. "Ok. Love you. Stay safe and don't do anything without consulting me first." Pause. "NO! That doesn't—" He sighed and shook his head. Karina had cut the call off.

Dmitri regarded Avyer with worry. "What was that about?"

Avyer sighed. "She got wind of the situation in Kursk. She wants to send her special team to pull out some orphans before the strike takes place."

"In the interest of kissing babies that would probably be wise. I assume you have your reasons for not making that a priority, but do you have her under control?"

"She is my wife."

"Come on, I know you better than that. Her moral compass is stronger than you credit it."

"Oh, I credit it." Avyer collapsed in an old half-backed chair. He loosened his collar. "Karina is impetuous but she can take care of herself. If I didn't believe that I would have rushed her here by my side long ago. She's just as safe there as here."

"Very true. Bombs have an equal chance of falling there as much as here," agreed Dmitri. "What are you going to do, meanwhile?"

"What do you mean?"

"Aren't you going to stop her?"

"Why would I do that? She'll hold that against me if I do." Avyer looked at Dmitri. "I'll help her, then we'll secure Kursk."

CHAPTER 55
ORPHANS

CHRISTMAS EVE. Every breath produced a thick puff of fog. Stray snowflakes drifted down lazily, coming to rest on them and the Kursk orphanage. All was quiet and calm. The snow crunched dangerously loud as she shifted from her crouching position to stand.

Karina felt the biting air through several layers of clothing and gloves. She also felt a flicker of guilt as she contemplated the snowy scene before her.

Don't do anything stupid.—A.N.

was the one-liner Avyer had sent. He knew she was up to something.

"As planned," she spoke quietly into her radio.

She watched the elite team she had formed with Sasha and Illya. They crept up to the doors of the orphanage. She felt a sliver of pride as she observed them at work. They snapped the locks on the doors. After a moment, one of them flickered a light in a window three times. *They made contact with the caregivers.* Blackness, then two more flashes. That was her cue to meet up with the team through the side door.

Captain Trishandaw beckoned for Karina to enter the door. The team closed all the curtains and the door behind her. She blinked when they turned on a bright light. No one had been restrained or injured.

"Clear." Trishandaw nodded tersely. "Do your stuff."

"Who's in charge?" Karina scrutinized three homely adults before her.

"I am. I'm Rannia." An older woman tucking in wisps of gray hair flying out of her long black braid stepped forward.

"Cook." A younger woman.

"Schooling and the boys. I'm Parsha." The middle-aged man had likely been a real looker in his youth but had been worn down by life in Kursk.

"Parsha, wake the boys. Have the older ones pack what they *need* in a bag or sack. Clothing, food, a blanket. No dead weight. Rannia, same with the girls."

"Why should we?" Rannia looked suspicious.

"Rebel forces are about to attack the city. We were sent to evacuate." Karina's explanation satisfied Rannia. "Don't turn on any lights."

Trishandaw and Rodrick flanked the door. Illya escorted Parsha while Maria accompanied Rannia. They sent children out as soon as they were ready. Karina ticked off their names and sent them in single file to the seven awaiting buses.

Hurry up, hurry up! Every fiber of Karina's being screamed. *Any minute now . . .* They were spread thin: three of them to each bus, and over two hundred orphans to evacuate. Karina's heart pounded like a drum. *Come on!*

One-hundred thirty-five, she counted. *Hurry up! The last thing I want is to die here, doing something stupid Avyer told me not to . . .*

A resounding BOOM exploded somewhere in the city. The ground shook.

"It's started," Karina groaned. She moved the children faster.

"Don't cry, sweetheart," she told the younger children that were frightened and had begun to cry. "It's just like the sound of fireworks. Walk quickly in line!" She told the older ones, "Comfort the little ones. Keep them quiet."

Gunshots rang out in the night. More explosions came crashing closer and rocked the ground. Others sounded far off. *Move the kids. Move the kids. Smile. Don't let them see my legs are shaking with fear. One hundred . . .*

Something large and dark flashed in the yard, felling a swath of forest bordering one side of the orphanage. The children in the line screamed in unison, many of them thrown to the ground by the blast. Karina's ears rang as she poked her head out the door. The outline of a small flaming ship burst into brighter flames, illuminating the yard.

"It's all right!" Karina reassured the children then radioed, "Sasha and anyone on a free bus, get out and get these kids moving. No, better yet, Sasha, get on the bus roof and keep watch."

Two drivers ran pell-mell through the snow, following the special teams' tracks. A few guards trailed behind them. Everyone hoisted the youngest screamers to their shoulders and motioned for the older ones to do the same. They plowed a bigger path as they ran back to the buses.

Karina's heart was in her throat. Her hands shook so badly that she struggled to steady the list in her hands. She forced a smile as they moved the rest of the children out. It took time, but she was soon alone with Trishandaw and Rodrick. The caregivers, Illya, and Maria were out.

"Let's get out of here." Rodrick saluted her.

They ran to the buses. They scooped stragglers as they ran. Karina snatched up a little boy who was fighting to walk against the deep snowdrifts. She swung him around to her gunless hip and boarded a bus.

"Hit it," she told Illya as soon as Sasha had clambered down the roof and into the bus. "Everyone accounted for?" she radioed the other buses.

"Yes," the other buses confirmed. Illya closed the door and revved up the engine. He drove as quickly as he dared. Hitting a hole too hard could strand the bus.

Karina and Sasha stood next to Illya as he drove. Karina sent the little boy she had carried to a nearby lap. Karina and Sasha exchanged glances.

"Don't tell me it'll be ok," Karina said.

"I won't," Sasha said grimly.

"I won't either," Illya quipped, "just so you two don't feel lonely."

Sasha rolled her eyes.

As the buses rumbled over the ground, groups of hover bikes flanked them. A rider in the lead motioned to Illya.

"Who's that?" Karina gawked at their escort. There were in full military gear.

"Help," said Illya.

As he pronounced the word, the bus rocked violently. Sasha and Karina were thrown to the floor. Bombs and gunshots rang out as the road drew them closer to Kursk.

"Everyone down!" Karina screamed and she motioned for the children to duck.

"Stay sharp and don't let anyone shoot me," Illya said. "I don't doubt you'd be able to drive this trash can but would prefer to avoid that."

"Yeah," chorused Sasha and Karina. Karina positioned herself behind him and Sasha remained beside him, prepared to shoot at any enemy soldiers. Illya accelerated.

The bus rumbled through twisting, rambling, pothole-ridden side streets on the outskirts of Kursk, always avoiding areas of conflict. The hover bikes directed their path, and between the bikers and the shooters on the buses, they left the town behind them with few injuries.

"If we get out of this mess alive, what are you going to do?" Karina asked Sasha.

"Sleep."

"I don't mean getting to camp. I mean in general."

Sasha snorted. "Sleep even more."

"We have a surprise for you." Illya changed the subject.

"What do you mean?" asked Karina.

Illya grinned. "You'll love this!"

They drove out to a snow-covered field where three Z-130 cargo ships waited for them. They drove the seven buses straight into the ships.

Illya laughed at the look on Karina's face. "IPG isn't interested in helping fight, but apparently someone guilt-tripped them into taking in any and all Gavriilan orphans until the conflict is over and they can be relocated."

One of the bikers drove alongside their bus, cuing Illya to open the door.

"Can't imagine who must've done that." Illya parked in one of the last ships. He opened the door. "Can you?"

"Impressive," Karina said.

The biker pulled off his helmet.

Karina's cheeks flushed. *Avyer.* She stared at his mussed black hair. "What are you doing here?"

"Helping." Avyer stepped into the bus, planting a passionate kiss on her lips. "You're welcome. Stay safe. I'll see you later." He put his helmet back on. A speechless Karina smiled after him.

"So, we'll say you liked the surprise." Illya chuckled.

It took half an hour to load and secure the buses on the ships. The three-hour flight ended when they landed at an IPG organized refugee camp to the far south. It was a safe distance from the primary areas of conflict.

A gust of warm air flowed through the bus windows as they landed. Karina yawned. "What are we doing now?"

"Leaving the buses, then we'll be escorted to another ship that will take us back," Sasha said.

They abandoned the buses and left the orphans to the camp organizers. An IPG official beside the waiting ship motioned for them to remove their weapons. He said something in English. Karina needed no interpreter to explain.

"We just saved a lot of kids." Karina scowled. "We're not about to shoot up a refugee camp."

A voice inside the ship laughed and interpreted in English. A second voice made what sounded like an amused grunt.

"Good girl," the interpreter appearing in the ship doorway spoke Russian. "But that won't be necessary." It was a young woman. She brushed dust off her gray armor and flipped her gold non-IPG regulation braid behind her back. "Let's go."

The IPG official nodded. "Very well." He stood down for the trio to board.

"Hi, I'm Nicole. Let's get going. It's going to be a bit tight but we'll manage. Sit wherever you want. Just don't mess with the crates in the back. It's a mix of books and explosives."

"You're kidding, right?" Sasha gave her a side eye.

"Nope." With another flip of her braid she strode to the cockpit.

"Are we ready, Nicole?" Karura Solari whirled around to look at the young woman.

Nicole looked over the crowded back of the *Venge*. "Everyone good?" she called back in Russian. "Yeah?" She answered Solari in English: "Yeah."

"Great." Solari closed the ramp and took off.

CHAPTER 56
THE VOTE

AVYER SEATED himself at the long conference table in the capitol building. It had taken so much to get to the city of Kursk. They had lost quite a few men, to say nothing of the casualties. This would not become their permanent base of operation, but for today's purposes it was an important meeting place.

Avyer eyed each of the representatives in turn as they entered the repurposed ballroom. There were two for every province. He and Dmitri represented Avedida province.

Avyer knew all thirty-nine representatives by name, but only few personally. *Karina did a good job,* he mused as he looked around the table. *Her work was and continues to be important.*

He should probably tell her that one of these days, especially before she decided to tackle more crazy rescue missions. The IPG ate that up, but it was unnecessary and could be risky.

Sergei Bok stood to preside the meeting. "I require everyone's attention." Instant silence. "Thank you. I believe that at this point we are all in agreement that it's time to make leadership decisions. The InterPlanetary Government is pressuring us for an official list of leaders. If I'm not mistaken, Tatyana Yolkinka has details regarding the IPG demands." He cued an older woman at the far end of the table before he sat down.

As she stood and all eyes turned to her, she self-consciously smoothed back her auburn hair. "I would label them more as requirements than demands. The IPG is spread thin, especially with the assassination of Darrell Bentuari several years ago. They need to see that we're in earnest."

Several leaders muttered unintelligible remarks while others silently nodded their heads.

"They want to know what form of government we will choose. *Obviously*, it must be a free government of some sort, such as a democracy or a republic."

Obviously, thought Avyer, *or we will receive no support.*

"At this point," continued Tatyana, "we must elect an interim president and have an official counsel per our declared governmental system. Once we have publicized this decision the IPG will give us more aid."

"What kind of aid?" Gray-haired Larion Nemtsov huffed. "Just for the record."

"Of course," Tatyana replied. "Several IPG planets offer us much-needed resources. Batai is willing to provide food and some prestigious institutions wish to send interpreters and translators to help with communication. Other planets such as Qinir, Zephyr, Amuyakim, and Pentura are willing to send tech experts and possibly soldiers. In return, we will join the IPG's list of allies and agree to the IPG Humanitarian Standards. That is the current offer."

"Sounds reasonable," Dmitri muttered to himself.

"That's because it's more than reasonable," Oleksaandra piped up cheerfully. The staider Larion glared at her.

"That is all." Tatyana concluded and sat.

"Thank you." Sergei rose to his feet. "Are there any questions?" He was met with silence. "Or shall we begin?"

All heads nodded in unison and a few verbal affirmations echoed around the room.

"Very well. We will proceed to discuss and choose the best form of government. It must be the best possible *working* governmental structure for Gavriila given that our decision is irrevocable. We cannot make a decision today, only to make a new one tomorrow. We must show the IPG resolve and determination." He sat.

Fyodor presided over the ensuing discussion and debate. The sun had set by the time they chose their governmental structure.

"I motion we adjourn for thirty minutes." Avyer stretched after the vote. "Tired minds don't think well. We need to make the decisions today, but it would be wise to rest."

"Let us put the motion to a vote," Fyodor said.

The vote was unanimous. Everyone rushed outside for air or took a brief turn about the capitol halls. Dmitri lost sight of Avyer as the swarm of leaders cut him off from his friend.

He had to search the building for half the break time before he found Avyer outside at the back of the building facing a park. He was leaning against one of the bronze columns, looking up at the stars.

"Beautiful night," Avyer said appreciatively. "It would have been a good night to go out for a walk in Avedida. You can see for miles around, just with the moonlight and starlight."

"I guess," said Dmitri. "I'm fine here in the city."

"What do you want?"

"What do you mean?"

"I wished to be left alone. You *had* to have been looking for me."

"Come on." Dmitri slapped his arm. "Aren't you the least bit excited about the vote?"

"It was the right choice but I'm not about to celebrate until Gavriila is secure."

"I'm not talking about that." Dmitri scoffed. "The presidency."

"Not particularly. Either Leo or Sergei should lead. They have the experience and wisdom."

"What about *you*?"

"I'm not an appropriate choice." Avyer shifted his weight to one leg then another as he leaned against the column. "Historically speaking I'm too young. I'm not going against hundreds and hundreds of years of tradition."

"What about all your heroic deeds?" Dmitri shook Avyer's arm. "You've been saving orphans, evacuating cities before conflicts, and that's to say nothing of how you organized the Sparks."

Avyer pulled away from Dmitri. "I did not sign up for this to become president."

"You should have thought of that before sending Karina to do interviews," Dmitri reminded him. "But that's all the more reason that you're better suited to the position . . ."

Avyer cut him off. "Spare me any more motivational quotes. I know what I want, and it's not the presidency."

"What if they force you to?"

"They won't, not when everyone remembers what I did under the Bentuarians." Avyer walked in the direction of the meeting room.

Dmitri sighed and shook his head before he traipsed behind Avyer.

All the leaders returned punctually. A potpourri of coffee, food, and smoke permeated the air. Dmitri and Avyer took their former places.

Oleksaandra presided the next session. "Good evening and welcome back. I will make this as brief and to the point as possible. I realize this has been a long day and we all have many duties and preoccupations at hand. As mentioned, we will be voting for an interim president. Each of you may cast one vote. You must nominate one person per vote. We have sheets for everyone. Write your name at the top." She demonstrated with a sheet. "Then the candidate's name in the center. Fold the sheet and leave it in the center of the table. We will vote until only one candidate remains. The final candidate will be the interim president and will choose his or her vice president. Any questions?"

She was met with silence, so she distributed the sheets.

Avyer did not hesitate. He scrawled out:

Avyer Nikolai

Sergei Bok

Most of them knew who they would choose. Only a few glanced around the table, licked their lips, frowned, or did a combination of the three. Once the last vote had been cast in the center of the conference table, Oleksaandra took them up.

She read each sheet aloud as she unfolded them one by one while Boris noted the results.

"Please read the totals," Oleksaandra requested.

Boris went through the list. "Fyodor Lebedev from Inna, ten votes. Leo Vasiliev from Inna, two votes. Tatyana Yolkinka from Ternopil, ten votes. Avyer Nikolai from Avedida, ten votes. Sergei Bok from Zarvii, six votes. Andrei Yartsin from Oryol, two votes."

Andrei rose to his feet. "I motion to remove those of us with two votes from consideration."

No one voiced disagreement. Leo looked as relieved as Andrei. Sergei did not stand to remove himself.

Avyer nearly knocked his chair over as he rose to his feet. "While I appreciate the honor of being under consideration, I object my nomination."

"Here we go," Dmitri grumbled and glanced around the table as though searching for support.

"Dima, please." Avyer turned his weary gaze to his friend before giving his fellow representatives attention. "I am too young to be under consideration." He took his seat.

Oleksaandra stood. "If there is any objection to Avyer Nikolai's withdrawal, please make it known at this time . . ."

A steady muttering traveled around the table as the leaders spoke in hushed tones. Avyer gave his forehead a deep massage.

"Avyer Nikolai removed from consideration as Interim President. Let the next rounds begin."

The end of the second round: "Sergei Bok, twenty-one votes. Tatyana Yolkinka, ten votes. Fyodor Lebedev, nine votes."

Tatyana stood. "I request that I be removed from further consideration. My countrymen Sergei Bok and Fyodor Lebedev are better suited to the task than I am. Moreover, I have matters at home to attend when this war is over."

"Decision accepted," pronounced Oleksaandra when there were no objections.

Final round: "Sergei Bok, twenty-two votes. Fyodor Lebedev, eighteen votes." A round of applause broke out in the room.

Avyer closed his eyes with relief. *Sergei will do the job well.*

"Thank you." Sergei got to his feet with a tired but regal air. He raised his hands to signal for the clapping to cease. "That leaves one final decision this evening. That of my Vice President. I have spent quite some time pondering the question, and there is only one man up to the task. The one man who left everything he had built, to build us. Avyer Nikolai." He gestured grandly at Avyer.

Avyer's eyes snapped open. Hands clapped and leaders seated near him offered congratulations immediately. *I'm not . . .* He caught Sergei's eye and was about to refuse the position, but Sergei tilted his head and gave him a stern expression, barely shaking his head at Avyer. The message was clear. *Be silent and deal with it.*

Avyer Nikolai rode out the deluge of well-wishes.

CHAPTER 57
SECOND LADY

"THERE'S someone who wants to talk to you." Sasha shook Karina awake. "Now!"

Karina blinked sleepily, her heart in her throat. The door to their room was wide open and Illya stood outside the door. She rubbed the sleep out of her eyes, straightened her jacket and ran her fingers through her hair. *Who could it be? Did someone die?* Many thoughts raced through her mind, but she was too afraid and too sleepy to verbalize them.

Illya led her to the communications room. Avyer's serious face was on the video screen. Karina's body slumped in relief. When she sat, Illya left and closed the door behind him.

Avyer cleared his throat. "How are you?"

"The same as usual," she said.

"Do you need anything?" he asked.

"Only what everyone else needs: more food, more clothing, and no fighting."

"We're getting closer to that," said Avyer.

"Is everything ok? Sasha scared me half to death, waking me up like that."

"I know I could have just made a phone call, but I wanted to have this conversation face to face. I've been chosen as interim vice-president to the interim president."

"What?" Karina gave an incredulous laugh.

"What do you think of that?"

"It's amazing. Uh . . ."

"'Uh' what? Do you think it was the wrong decision?"

"No, no, no! They couldn't have chosen better. I just wasn't expecting to wake up and hear that my husband was the vice president."

"You don't have to do anything special right now, if you're worried about that."

"Ok." Karina took a deep breath.

"What you're doing right now is important. Illya told me that you don't feel particularly important."

Karina cocked her head as she looked at him. "I'm not. Anyone else could do what I'm doing."

"You're *the* reason we're taking Gavriila back." Avyer scowled. "Could just *anyone* have helped me interview hundreds of people within a few days? Could just anyone organize and train an insane amount of people with limited resources, little time, and practically no support?"

Karina shifted uncomfortably. *Probably not.*

"I want you with me now." Avyer came to his point. "As my wife you'll be in the spotlight more and more. I would feel better if I knew exactly where you were all day."

"Could I think it over?" asked Karina. "I have a lot in my head right now."

"Of course." Avyer nodded. "But be *careful*. No more orphan rescues or half-baked ideas."

"Ok," Karina promised. "Is there anything I can do for you?"

"Just one thing." Avyer eyed her. "Respect what I tell you to do. We're married, but that's all I ask of you. If you have a differing opinion, I will respect whatever you have to say. Perhaps not do everything you'd like, but I will respect *your* opinion within reason. Is that not reasonable?"

Karina swallowed. "It sounds reasonable."

"Do you agree?"

Karina bit her lip. "Yes."

"Ok," said Avyer. "I'll send you and Sasha warmer winter coats tomorrow. Good night."

"Good night." Karina sat and stared at her reflection on the screen after the video call ended.

After a few minutes of silence, Sasha opened the door, cautiously peeking into the room. She assessed her crestfallen friend. "You ok?" asked Sasha.

Karina nodded but a tear rolled down one cheek.

"What is it?" Sasha wrapped her arms around Karina.

"I don't know." Karina sniffed. "I just feel . . . overwhelmed."

"It'll be ok." Sasha gave her a squeeze. "It's a lot to take in." Her words confirmed that she had been eavesdropping.

Karina wiped her tears with a sleeve. "Avyer will be sending us better coats tomorrow."

"Yes!" Sasha punched the air with her fist. "I'm tired of my butt freezing off."

CHAPTER 58
VICE PRESIDENT

DMITRI FOUND Avyer pacing his new office. "Did you even sleep last night?" He peered at Avyer's red eyes.

"Enough," replied Avyer. "Have the coats been sent to Karina's current base camp?"

"Yes. It's done."

"You needn't fret any more about Karina doing anything foolish."

"Don't tell me you bargained with her with a couple of coats?"

Avyer snorted. "Hardly. We just had a talk. That's all."

"A talk," echoed Dmitri. "That's reassuring."

"There's nothing to talk about."

"Ok." Dmitri shrugged it off. "President Bok wishes to meet with you."

"Right now?" Avyer rubbed his forehead. He straightened his coat and collar. "Let's go."

"I don't know where the *let's* part should come in," muttered Dmitri as they left the office.

"I heard that," Avyer said coldly. "You know full well you're my right hand."

"I thought your wife had influenced you more than my warmongering monologues."

"Don't sell yourself short. You know what I mean."

Their footsteps echoed eerily on the marble floors as they marched down the long capitol halls to the Interim President's office. Sergei Bok awaited them, seated in the only chair in his office. The dark circles under his eyes rivaled Avyer's. Sergei yawned as they entered.

"If I had chairs, I would offer them," he said.

"Chairs aren't necessary," said Avyer. "Is it fine if Dmitri stays with me?"

"Perfectly. There's no reason to stand on formalities. My man Viktor accompanies me as well, unless we're discussing confidential items." He thumbed a servant standing in the corner.

Dmitri closed the door behind them.

"I don't intend to be here long. First of all, I'm old," Sergei said. "For all I know, I may die tomorrow. In my brief time here, I want to see Gavriila free from the Loyalists and for our planet to be what it used to be.

"The *council* has made a good decision as far as our government. I have a number of ideas and propositions that I'd like to discuss with you. If I do die unexpectedly, please keep them in mind . . ."

CHAPTER 59

BARNAUL BOUND

HOURS, days, weeks, and months melded together. Karina, Sasha, and Illya were constantly moved from one camp to another. Azya to Jerson to Kursk to Ulan to Inna to Zarvii . . . One week here, two weeks there and four weeks elsewhere.

Since Avyer had expressed he wanted her off the field, in her spare time Karina scrawled a rough training guide on scraps of data sheets. Illya and Sasha contributed their own points to the rough draft. Once the draft was done, she sent it to Avyer and the council.

Poltava will be our last training ground, then I'll go be with Avyer. Karina paced in the spartan Poltava main office and flipped through her datapad's calendar. *A year and a half. How am I still alive? The bombing in Samara, an ambush on the road to Volga, a night attack in Dnipro, several skirmishes in Gavriila itself, Jerson, and Kursk. I'm pretty sure I've forgotten something.* She closed the calendar and set the datapad down on a wooden desk.

Sasha sat behind the desk. She gazed at the ceiling, supporting her head with her hands.

"Don't get too comfortable," Karina joked.

Sasha rolled her eyes. "Please tell me how could I? Every time we start to relax something happens. It's like the *'relax'* word is unlucky."

"You probably shouldn't have said it, then." Karina sat on the desk.

Illya came in from his evening rounds.

"Anything I need to know about?" Karina asked.

"Nothing new," Illy said dully. "Just the usual. Trainees who think they know it all. Several that can't fight to save their life. Literally. I got one guy who couldn't hit the wide side of . . ."

BOOM! Karina watched Sasha and Illya soar as she herself flew across the room. Her head smashed the wall. Everything went dark.

Sasha flew backwards and landed on all fours like a cat behind the desk. Shrapnel and debris riddled the heavy wooden desk, which was the only thing protecting her.

"Karina!" she screamed over gunfire and yells following the huge explosion. She shielded her eyes with her arm as she scrabbled on all fours to Karina. Metal shards, pebbles, dust and dirt rained down.

Blood trickled from a cut on Karina's forehead. Sasha drew a sharp breath when she saw slivers of metal protruding from Karina's right leg and side. Blood soon soaked the right side of her body.

"Illya!" She shuddered. He was nowhere in sight. Sasha jammed her trembling hands in her pockets. Her fingers fumbled with her phone in her left pocket. There were too many explosions and screams to make a call. She sent a message to Avyer.

> Emergency. Under attack. Karina injured needs immediate medical attention. Possibly blood. Gunfire and explosion. Poltava. —Sasha
>
> P.S. Please respond as soon as possible.

CHAPTER 60
EMERGENCY

BEING MESSAGED after midnight was not a good sign.

"What?" Avyer exclaimed and nearly dropped his phone as he responded.

Sending help now.—IVP Nikolai

He ran out to Dmitri's tent with a lamp.

"Dima." He shook his friend awake. "Have someone on-site in Poltava get Karina to a secure location."

"What is it?" Dmitri blinked as Avyer blinded him with the lamp.

"Karina is injured and Sasha is alone. In Poltava. Send a team to extract them to the Barnaul site. Get a transport for me to go to wherever they are. I'm going now."

"Is this a good time for you to go?"

"*Do it.* I'm going to inform President Bok."

"Very well." Dmitri stumbled out of the tent in his underclothes. He shivered as he wrapped up in a blanket. "I'll call you as soon as I have info on the situation."

Avyer returned to his room for a bag. He checked his phone. Nothing from Dmitri or Sasha.

He half-ran to the Kursk governor's palace to the Interim President's door, rapping hard and insistently until a bleary-eyed Sergei opened the door. He was flanked by his bodyguards. "Yes?" Sergei stifled a yawn.

"Good evening, sir. Apologies, but I must leave. There was a sudden attack on Poltava and Karina has been badly hurt."

"I'm sorry to hear that." Sergei looked little more awake. "Keep in touch. Bring her back."

"That is my intention, sir."

"Very well." Sergei was unable to hold back another yawn. "I bid you a good night. My thoughts and heart go with you."

"Thank you, sir." Avyer gave him a cordial nod. "Good night."

A now dressed Dmitri rode up in a cruiser as Avyer left the palace. "It's not safe to fly between here and Poltava. Bentuarians have quite a few ships in the air, as do we."

"Ok." Avyer ran a hand through the stubble on his jawline. He climbed into the cruiser with Dmitri. "Push this thing as fast as possible," he told the driver.

"Yes, sir."

Avyer rested his head on the headrest. "How bad is it, Dima?"

"Medics have made contact with Sasha. They've moved her and Karina to a more secure location. The attack took them completely by surprise," said Dmitri. "Karina, Sasha, and Illya were in the main office, which was directly in the line of fire."

"How's Karina?"

"She's not ok, but she's stable. They're removing shrapnel. It could have been worse. Illya's dead." Dmitri scrutinized Avyer. "Are you ok?"

"No." Avyer scrubbed his hand down his face.

Hours dragged on as the cruiser barreled down the most intact highways leading from Kursk to Poltava. They jounced along pothole-filled side roads and raced along side streets until they reached a low, yellowed building that was twenty kilometers from the current skirmish. As soon as the cruiser had stopped, Avyer climbed out and ran through the automatic doors.

A group of officers off to the side spoke in hushed tones. When Avyer entered, the talking died down immediately.

"Vice President Nikolai." A woman with a green surgical mask hanging around her neck greeted him. "This way." She guided him through the strange square building.

Whatever it had been, it had been repurposed into an emergency hospital. They passed long open rooms with floors lined with patients. Half of them groaned or moaned and the other half suffered in silence. IVs and monitoring devices were jammed in the scant space between patients. More than once Avyer had to sidestep feet protruding from a doorway.

Avyer's eyebrows knit together and he turned up his nose at the sterile atmosphere. While the odors of blood, body fluids, and sweat hung in the air, an acrid smell akin to new plastic left a tangy sensation on his tongue. He clamped his mouth shut but the flavor had already corrupted his palate.

"Karina is out of surgery," said the woman.

"How is she?"

"She'll pull through. She had to have some transfusions during the procedure. We did several scans and have confirmed that no shrapnel or foreign objects remain."

"Can she be moved?"

The woman paused. "As in?"

"To a more secure location."

"You'll have to consult the surgeon in charge." She resumed their walk along another dingy yellow corridor.

She guided him past offices to the end of the hallway, until they had reached the last door on the left.

"Go on in," the woman said. "This was the best we could do under the circumstances. I'll let the surgeon know you're here."

"Thank you."

Avyer reached the bed with four strides.

Karina was unconscious. Her slow, steady breaths fogged the oxygen mask adjusted over her face. Other than an angry pink welt on her forehead where her skin had been fused together, she looked as though she were peacefully sleeping. A sheet had been draped over her body, so her injuries were not visible.

Avyer pulled up a thin metal chair beside the low hospital bed. He brushed his hand across her forehead through the top of her hair, avoiding the fused skin. He cleared his throat but whatever he was about to say was interrupted by the entrance of a frazzle-haired middle-aged man wearing a doctor's coat. An equally frazzled young officer trailed behind him.

"I know who you are, so let me introduce myself. Fedir Borysov, the attending surgeon." He stretched out a hand to Avyer.

"Thank you." Avyer shook his hand.

"Nurse Bohdana mentioned that you want to move her. Is that correct?"

"As soon as possible. This location may be safer than Poltava center, but it's not out of the line of fire."

"Very well then." Fedir's brow knit together. "Normally I would not advise moving someone in her condition but given that she's your wife I understand your concern. My professional suggestion is you take her out in a medical ship or wagon. The advantage of a ship is speed, but the wagon might be more inconspicuous. Either way, there should be at least three medical personnel on board in case she takes a turn for the worse."

"I understand. Which is available now?" asked Avyer.

"Most of the wagons are occupied in Poltava. If I call one, it could be here within an hour. There's a ship a few kilometers out."

"Get everything onto the ship. Report, officer." Avyer turned to the young man.

"Sir." The young man's hand snapped up to his mussed hair peeking out from a dirty cap. "It was Stepan and Ternovvy. Intel came through right before the attack. They are targeting your wife. And you."

CHAPTER 61
HEALING

KARINA FLOATED in thick black fog. *Or is it gray? Or white? White is a normal fog color.* Debilitating pain shot through her, as though a million splinters had impaled her entire body. *Is that Sasha crying?* As the fog evaporated, Karina landed in a mountain of soft, plush blankets.

As she wiggled her stiff fingers, she realized she was swaddled in many blankets. Her vision cleared to reveal that she was in a low bed in a small room. Everything was made of wood, from the bed, to the walls, to the floors, to the bookshelves lining one wall. Curtains filtered most of the light peeking from a window off to one side. Karina was so tightly wrapped she could not move.

"He-llo?" she called out. "Is anyone there?"

A door across the room cracked open. Light streamed in, blinding Karina. *Ouch.* She squinted, unable to make out the person's face.

"Karina Ivanovna." A dark figure surrounded by light bowed. "I'll let your family know you are awake. Is there anything you'd like or need?"

"Just Sasha," said Karina.

The figure nodded and closed the door. Darkness reigned once more. Karina strained her ears. *Where in the world am I?*

Save occasional footsteps outside, all was silent. When someone outside walked by, the footsteps echoed for some time as though they were following a long corridor or making their way around a large room outside her room.

When a new set of footsteps approached her heart jumped. *Who was it?* Each time the footsteps faded away Karina's heart sank in disappointment.

Karina was about to give up when her door opened and closed with a squeak. She squinted at her visitor. They were tall.

"Hi." Avyer's tense voice cut through the air. He pulled a chair next to her bed and sat. "How are you feeling?" He rested a hand on where her arm was hidden under the blankets.

"I don't know." Her throat tightened. "Do I look that bad?"

"No."

"Your face is scaring me."

Avyer cracked a smile. "My face?"

"You look like I'm dying or something."

"You've been unconscious for several days," said Avyer.

"What happened?"

"Stepanov and Ternovvy found you and blew up the office." Avyer's smile waned. "The doctors spent hours picking splinters and shrapnel out of your body."

Karina shivered. "Am I going to be ok?"

"They got everything out and have fused the skin together, but you're on bedrest for at least a week. There's only so much they can do, even for the Vice President's wife."

"And Sasha and Illya?"

Avyer's jaw twitched. "Sasha is very well. It was all I could do to pry her from your side when we got here. Illya's dead."

"What?" *Poor Sasha.* "Could you help me sit up?"

"I don't know." Avyer hesitated.

"Please. I feel like I'm suffocating." She swallowed down rising panic.

Avyer unwrapped the blankets and eased her up in a sitting

position against the wall. As he lifted her, heavy bandages scratched her left side and leg.

"Can I see it?" She brushed her fingers along her side. "I don't feel any pain."

"If you don't feel anything now, you won't feel anything for a while," said Avyer. "I had them shoot you up with the strongest pain meds they could find."

"You didn't really answer my question. Am I going to be ok or am I maimed or disabled?"

"No, thank *God*." Avyer's eyes shuttered.

"What is it?" Karina placed her hand on his, alarmed at his reaction.

"Nothing." He blinked. "I'll send Sasha, if you'd like." He met Karina's gaze. "You both have done enough. It's time for you to rest."

A lump formed in Karina's throat as she stared into his brown eyes. *So now this is where I don't do anything?* "So . . . after I'm better what will become of me?"

"You're going to stay where you belong." Avyer's jaw tightened. "With me." He stood. "I'll have Sasha come so you're not alone."

"Thanks." A million questions suddenly danced in Karina's brain, but she was unable to verbalize any of them before Avyer walked out the door.

Karina sighed. *Alone again. Didn't even get a kiss in that time.*

Sasha came in later than Karina would have liked. Then again, time dragged by interminably since she had no way to measure it.

"You look well." Karina surveyed Sasha's slight figure clad in a new uniform.

"You don't," Sasha replied. "I'd hug you, but you look delicate."

"Probably," Karina said. "Now catch me up on everything Avyer didn't tell me."

Sasha sat on the bed. Prominent bags sagged under Sasha's red-rimmed eyes.

"I-" Karina stammered. "If—if this isn't a good time, we can talk later."

Sasha sniffed, rubbing her nose.

"It will help me not think about things. What *did* he tell you?" asked Sasha. "I'm not exactly a high-class official here. We're on the outskirts of a small town in Barnaul. This is an old hunting cabin, and apparently your husband's personal hideout this past year or so."

"He told me about Illya." Karina squeezed Sasha's hand. "I'm so . . . so sorry." She choked on the words.

"Yeah, me too." Sasha stared at nothing in particular on the wall. "It's not ok."

They sat there holding hands. Sasha hunched over as she unsuccessfully blinked back tears. Karina held Sasha's hand when tears began to flow and Sasha sobbed, at times choking in her grief. She tried to stay awake, but Karina's head drifted down to her chest and she had nearly fallen asleep when Sasha mastered herself.

"Well, what would you like to know first?" Sasha dried the tears from her face and wiped her nose on her shoulder.

Karina jerked her head up sleepily and blinked like an owl suddenly awakened. "Everything." Karina shook her head, trying to wake up. "No particular order."

"Avyer came for you when you were hurt," said Sasha. "I didn't see him until later because they had me tied up with Illya's body and refused to let me be with you until he brought me here. He was pretty upset. He looked more dead than alive. I think he crawled out of bed and drove straight to the med facilities to bring you here." She blew her nose on her sleeve. "All base camps have been moved again, and the president and vice president are based here in this quaint little forest area for now. This past week all of Gavriila has been on a mad offense, attacking the Bentuarian Loyalists."

"Avyer shouldn't have dropped everything for me. He has too many important things to—"

"You *really* are pretty stupid," Sasha interrupted and glared at her. "He *adores* you. Yeah, ya stupid idiot, he's got karking tons of stuff to do but he dropped it all to make sure you didn't die."

"I just feel weird," Karina said haltingly.

Sasha snorted. "Stop being mopey and miserable while we're here and alive. Talk to your man. It'll make you feel better."

CHAPTER 62
SASHA'S GRIEF

ASIDE FROM HER daily check on Karina, Sasha went about her business, speaking to no one. She was a slight shadow flitting around the cabin most of the time, occasionally alighting in the nearby village. No one bothered her.

I don't want to be bothered.

Karina was fine and no one needed her, so Sasha trudged up a large hill behind the cabin. She brushed snow off a large rock next to one of the few trees on the crest and sat to contemplate the scenery.

Several trees that huddled over her provided a windbreak. A deafening wind sang through the ocean of fir trees surrounding the cabin behind her. Before her the wind lashed mercilessly at a few sparse pines on the plain.

The trees on the plain are Karina and me. How had they not snapped under the straining winds?

Sasha sat trying to think of nothing. *The trees bent and writhed under the wind. Will the wind stop soon? The trees are about to snap.*

She hoped so.

CHAPTER 63
LOVE

AVYER NIKOLAI SIGHED and ran a hand through his short but currently tousled hair. Piles of data sheets were lined up and awaiting him in neat stacks on his desk. Five, five, and four. That was average these days.

When Dmitri dropped in he found Avyer standing over the piles, rustling through the sheets more quickly than normal.

"If you're not going to sit, can I take that?" Dmitri pointed at the wooden chair behind the desk full of sheets.

"Yeah, here." Avyer passed Dmitri the chair.

"Aw." Dmitri sprawled back as he sat. "Feels so good to sit."

"Mhm."

"Would you like some help?"

"I'd be beyond relieved. Grab a stack," replied Avyer. "How are things out there?" He did not look up.

"You were right: spreading the news that Bentuari is dead shattered a lot of Loyalist confidence. The people are rallying to take back their communities, and the little fires of resistance are burning across the globe. As long as we can keep this up, the Loyalists will have little left to keep fighting. The IPG sent us some supplies yesterday. Oh, yeah . . . speak of the devil. Do you remember the IPG rep, that Karura Solari fellow?"

"Couldn't forget him even if I wanted to."

"His wife is an interpreter and the IPG would like to send them down as consultants."

"Yes, why the kark not? Let's get everyone and their wife involved." Avyer threw his stack down on the desk, which sent a flurry of sheets in the air to rain back down on them.

Dmitri picked up and sorted the sheets. "Let me take over for today. I've nothing better to do. Go take care of yourself—whatever that involves."

"I have a lot to do," snapped Avyer.

"We all do, but you won't be worth a kark in this state. If anyone asks, I'll say you're busy. Go eat or sleep or something."

"Fine, Dima. For the good of Gavriila, though," Avyer growled. He slipped on a brown coat and cap and left Dmitri sorting through the mess of data sheets.

Avyer strode halfway down the huge hall toward the front door but stopped in front of Karina's door. He did not knock. He entered and removed his cap. The pile of blankets in the bed stirred at the sound of the door opening and closing.

Karina blinked sleepily. "Yes?"

"I wanted to see you," he said. "If that's all right."

"Of course." Karina sat up on her own.

"How are you feeling?"

"Better, I think. I'm still tired but not like before."

"That's to be expected, given the extent of your injuries." He removed his coat and left it with his hat on the chair. "Do you mind if I sit?" He eyed the bed.

"Please do." Karina squirmed, trying to move to the side and make space for him.

"Allow me."

Karina drew a sharp breath as he gently lifted her and slid her to the side. The mattress sank as his tall frame descended beside her. Long, strong fingers enveloped her own smaller hand.

"How are things?" She could not stop looking into his eyes.

"Busy. Normal." Avyer's gaze remained as steady as hers.

"Is everything going well?" asked Karina.

"I would say yes."

"I'm glad." Karina pulled her hand out of the blankets and ran her fingers along several days´ worth of stubble on his cheeks. "If you don't sleep soon, you're going to look like a wild animal. You need to take care of yourself." She yawned. "I'd like to talk." She pulled Avyer's arm to draw him closer to her. "But I'm tired. You're tired. Let's sleep."

"What?" Avyer's eyes lit up. "You want me to sleep with you?"

"I know I look terrible, but I—"

"No, no, no," Avyer interrupted and bent over to slide off his boots. "You're beautiful. That's fine." Since she was no longer swaddled in blankets, it was a matter of pulling one of her blankets over him after lying beside her.

"Mm." Karina pulled his arms until they surrounded her. When she closed her eyes she fell asleep almost immediately, a soft smile on her face.

Avyer lay gazing at her in complete bewilderment. This had been the last thing he would have expected. He caressed her hair and face until he also fell asleep.

CHAPTER 64
DAWN

KARINA AWAKENED the next morning to a strong, warm arm wrapped around her—not too tightly—and the sun trying to peek through a crack in the curtains.

"Are you awake?" She tried to roll over to put an arm around Avyer but his hold on her was too strong for her to move.

"I am now," he muttered and lifted his arm so she could move freely.

His nose nearly touched hers. Karina drew back slightly. She smiled uncertainly. When he opened his eyes she was struck by the longing in them.

"Good morning," he said.

"Good morning."

"How are you feeling?"

Avyer cupped her face. Karina closed her eyes and savored the touch of his warm hand.

"I would like to go outside. I don't want to stay in bed all day."

"You did see what happened to your side, didn't you?"

"I did. It looks terrible but it's stuffy in here."

"All right." Avyer sat up. "I'll ask the doctor on duty what he thinks." He dug his phone out of his jacket and sent a brief message. He swung his legs to the floor.

Karina seized his hand. "Don't go."

"I'm not going anywhere." Not while he had her full attention. "Anything else you'd like, other than getting out of here?"

"Yes. What happens next?" she asked.

"What do you mean by 'What happens next'?"

"Well, Sasha told me that she heard your friend Dmitri talking with someone about our replacements—meaning Sasha, me and Illya."

"What?" Avyer asked. "Do you want to go back to training country bumpkins?"

"Be nice. It's just that . . . I don't want to be doing nothing."

"What would you *like* to do, then?" Avyer asked.

Karina considered her answer for a moment. "I've not had much choice about what I've wanted to do—"

"Really?" Avyer interrupted. "What about the men you beat up the night we met? And every single blessed time you've defied me to my face and behind my back?" He looked amused. "Do you seriously expect me to believe you've ever done less than what you wanted to?"

Karina glared at him. "Has the doctor answered yet?"

"Yes, change the subject." Avyer checked his phone. "He says to be careful but that it won't kill you to go out. There's a patio to the side. Shall we?"

"Is it private?" asked Karina.

"Relatively."

"Is there anywhere outside where no one will bother us?"

"Yes, but it's farther."

"I can handle it. Let's go." Karina spoke with more energy than her body had. "I can manage," she complained as Avyer helped swing her legs to the edge of the bed.

"I'm sure," he said. He took her arm and grabbed a blanket as they stepped out.

Karina leaned on Avyer as she shuffled to the door. He opened the door, careful to keep pace with her.

"Oh, no," Karina groaned after several people in the hall greeted them.

"What?" asked Avyer.

She smoothed her hair down. "I look terrible."

"Nonsense. You're beautiful, and no one is going to judge your looks. If they do . . ."

"You'll slap stun cuffs on them." Karina finished the sentence.

"I most certainly would not." Avyer flushed. "I would just have something to say to them." Avyer made a loud "Hmf" as he pushed the door open for Karina.

Karina's breath shot up in puffy clouds in front of her face. "Wow." She watched her breath hover in the air. "I had no idea it was this cold."

"We're in the Barnaul mountains," Avyer said. He wrapped the thick blanket around Karina. She bowed slightly under its weight. "Ok, we're not doing that." He scooped her up bridal style.

"Oh." A huge puff of breath flew from Karina's mouth. She looked into his eyes, now closer to her than they had been seconds before. They were warm and crinkled slightly around the edges as he met her gaze.

Avyer carried her several steps before settling her on a well-worn wooden bench. He tucked the blanket around her carefully so no cold air could seep in. Only when he was satisfied that she was completely bundled up did he sit next to her and put an arm around her.

"Fifteen minutes, max," he said. "I'm not letting you add illness to injury. Now: how do you really feel?"

"Like something ran over me," Karina admitted. "Everything is stiff."

"How's the pain?"

"It only hurts to move."

"Very funny."

"It wasn't meant to be."

"What hurts?"

"A better question is what doesn't hurt?" Karina amused herself watching clouds of breath rolling away from her as she spoke. "Right now, that is my head and stomach."

"I'm asking because you have a ridiculously high pain tolerance. If you feel bad let me know and I'll get something for you."

"I don't want to take pain meds all day every day. I'll be fine. How are you?" asked Karina.

"Fine."

"I don't mean that. I mean us. I think it's a good place to start, if we want things between us to work out." Karina did not give him time to shoot a cheap answer to put her off. "Just tell me how you feel. If I can handle nearly dying several times, I can handle knowing how you feel."

"I'm tired." Avyer looked deep into Karina's eyes. "And I adore you." He pulled Karina closer to him. "What do you want to do when this is all over?"

"What's my limit?" asked Karina.

"As long as I'm not tried for crimes against humanity, the sky's the limit."

"What?" Karina sat up straight. "They're not going to throw you in jail, are they?"

"So you *do* worry about me," Avyer teased.

"Yes, I do. Just answer the question."

"Sergei says it's possible but highly improbable, given my contribution to the Sparks. Now answer my question: what do you want?" He pulled her close enough that she felt his thigh touching hers through the blanket.

"I want a farm away from everyone and everything, and to breed horses."

"Kids?"

"I don't know. This isn't exactly time to be thinking about that."

"Well, that's not good," said Avyer.

"What? Why?"

"I was thinking about having four or five."

"*What?*"

"Oh, well." Avyer heaved a sigh. "Hopefully we'll have time for me to convince you of that. Or argue over it. Or whatever."

"W-w-why's that?"

"Because no one else will be having my babies," Avyer said. "If it's not you, no one."

He pulled her into his lap, tilting her back so her new view was his face and the icy blue sky. Her eyes widened at the new view but she did not resist as his lips met hers, a welcome warmth in the cold. She saw the smile in Avyer's eyes as she pressed her lips harder into his, licking his lower lip before they unlocked lips.

"Let's finish this war and not die first," Karina said breathlessly.

"Agreed." Avyer kissed her one last time before he stood up with her in his arms. "It's cold. I think it's best we go back inside."

They returned to the much warmer cabin, inside Karina's room. As he settled Karina back in bed Avyer was interrupted by a call. "Really?" He sighed when he ended the call. "They need me back at the new capitol."

"What about me?"

"You're coming with me," said Avyer. "I need to pack. I'll come back before we have to leave. I promise."

Karina's eyes swam with tears. She looked to the left and studied the blankets on the bed, trying to hid the fact that she was crying. She turned her head aside a second too late.

"Hey." He tilted her chin up until her teary gray eyes met his. "What is it?"

A tear overflowed and rolled down her cheek. "I don't want you to leave right now." Her voice was thick with emotion.

"I don't want to." Avyer desperately searched for something to say to stop the tears. "It's not worth crying over. I'll be back in a few hours. It's not like I'm going off on a long trip."

"How do you know that?" A stream of tears followed the first one. "Anything could happen. I almost died. You could be next."

"That's not going to happen again." Avyer traced the tear trail on her cheek with his thumb until he had dried her face up to her eye. "We're targets for Stepanov and Ternovvy now. If I have to die atoning for my sins I want you to be the last thing I see before I go."

CHAPTER 65
ZHOVKVA

THEY FLEW into Zhovkva early the next morning. Sasha had gone ahead of them. While Avyer conversed with Karura Solari in the cockpit, Karina fell asleep on a bunk in the back. She awakened to the engine whining off.

Avyer sat beside her bunk. At some point in the journey he had changed into a dress uniform. When she opened her eyes to find him there, Karina gawked at him, at how well the dark gray suit fit him. Yellow and silver bars and a pale silver star ornamented the left chest. As he leaned over to kiss her he removed the black visored military cap.

"Good morning." Avyer smiled.

"Good morning." Karina was entranced by his dark brown eyes. *I hope I don't have bed hair.* Her stomach twisted as though it were an acrobat about to fall off a high wire.

He cupped her face with one hand and leaned into the kiss. His hand caressed her face, traced her jawline, and smoothed back her mussed hair.

"Let's go." He offered her a hand. "You're getting cleaned up and going back to bed. I think you've been trying to do too much lately."

"I haven't been doing *anything* lately." Karina frowned. She pulled from his hand but he tightened his grip.

They stepped off the *Venge* in front of an extensive garden asleep under the snow.

"Appearances."

"I don't care," said Karina, "and I'm not a child to be put to bed."

"Is that what you think?" Avyer laughed. "Don't be ridiculous. You've barely gotten your strength back. Let me do something that makes *me* happy. Let me take care of you."

Karina's breath caught in her throat, from the sight of Zhovkva as much as from Avyer's words. She soaked in the sleeping garden and elegant buildings before them. "So Zhovkva is the new capital of Gavriila?"

"Yes," he said. "No one wants Chita to be the capitol anymore, not after the Loyalists used it. Zhovkva isn't too bad. It's large and the economy is good. Nothing fancy, but serviceable for what we need."

"I like it. It feels . . . right." Karina appreciated the skyline. There were a few onion dome buildings sprinkled on the horizon, some sort of palace, and an interesting mix of modern buildings that somehow harmonized with the palace and onion domes.

There were signs of people trying to improve the city. Impressive construction sites for military quarters and offices loomed on the horizon. Repair scaffoldings wrapped around pre-existing buildings, homes, and stores.

"There's a considerable military presence here," Avyer explained. "Here we're on alert 24/7. We'll know long in advance of any possible attacks. What just happened in Barnaul is not going to happen here. As far as cities go, this is the safest area by far."

"But isn't it also a target, since you and President Bok are here?"

"Yes and no," said Avyer. "I'm here and yes, I'm a target. Bok is moved once a week. We decided it would be safer. That way if one of us dies, the other has a fair chance of escape. Just this week we're making an exception. We have to make some government decisions together, so most days I'll be leaving you to confer with him."

They walked through the sprawling garden to an elaborate building capped with a singular blue helmet dome. A few dry brown stems or weeds lifted their heads out of the snow, beseeching the bright sun for more warmth.

"But you're a much bigger target just sitting here," Karina objected.

"Perhaps." Avyer laughed without a trace of humor in his eyes. "This is the governor's mansion. We'll be living here."

Karina faltered. "It's too big." She pointed at huge marble columns that towered over them to support an immense, vaulted roof. That was just the back entrance.

"Ah, yes. I forgot that you wanted a cave." Now the smile reached Avyer's eyes. "This modest area is part of the hallway."

They passed many open rooms. Karina spied a dining hall, a vast room that could be a ballroom, a library, a sitting room . . .

The hallway branched off left and right. "We are over here." Avyer steered her to the right. "There is a spare room upstairs. Sasha can stay there if you want her nearby." They wound around a curving staircase to the second floor.

"Are there many rooms?" asked Karina.

"Up here? No, just two: one spare room and the governor's living space. There's a nursery but it's full of storage items."

"Where are you sleeping?" asked Karina.

"That depends on you," said Avyer.

"Where are you sleeping now?"

"The governor's room," said Avyer.

"Then that's where I'll be," said Karina. Every fiber of her being trembled with joy when she imagined lying beside Avyer.

"Very well."

CHAPTER 66

WORK

AVYER NIKOLAI MARCHED down the street to his office in the Capitol Building. It was only a few minutes from the governor's mansion.

Dmitri reclined on his couch.

"When did you get here?" Avyer asked. "I thought you were going to stay behind with the troops in Barnaul."

"They're not *my* troops," said Dmitri.

"True," said Avyer. He sat at his desk. "Anything worth discussing?"

"I don't think there's anything to discuss." Dmitri handed Avyer a file. "President Bok has planned things well. Do you *know* how many people he has who would back you as president?"

"I'm not interested. Change the subject."

"You look happy." Dmitri grinned. "What are you going to do, now that you have your woman with you?"

"Keep her alive and try to not die," said Avyer.

"Top-notch plan," said Dmitri. "As I was saying, President Bok is *adamant* about your taking up the mantle."

"What happened to changing the subject?" asked Avyer. "I don't want the mantle."

"All the more reason for the people to want you to take it. A man who *wants* this position at this point in our history is either crazy or power hungry."

"Your young friend makes a valid point." Sergei's gravelly voice interrupted the conversation.

Avyer stood bolt upright and Dmitri sat up before scrambling to his feet. Both saluted as the President entered the office. "Sir."

"At ease." Sergei chuckled drily as he eased himself into the most comfortable chair in the office. "I know it was a private conversation."

"Yes, it was," said Avycr.

"However, it's not a private topic," said Sergei bluntly. "You are a *public* figure now. You *chose* to be where you are now."

"You put me here," Avyer replied. He left the thought unfinished. *You pushed me into it.*

"And here we are." Sergei spread out his hands. "You owe a lot to this planet. I'm quite aware of your personal motives that started this small revolution. I know that you aren't looking to wipe your slate clean, but the fact remains that you are a blood-stained man. You've proven your worth and penitence time and again. Put up with the people. You owe them that much."

"I'm looking beyond that," Avyer replied. "If I stay on this path, I will be stuck in politics for life."

"Would you rather a man with baser motives lead the planet?" Sergei raised an eyebrow.

"Of course not."

"Then stop complaining. Given how many people you killed, tortured and punished, you deserve much worse than you have now. After everything this planet's been through, they need a beacon of light. You along with your little wife are just what we need."

"His wife?" echoed Dmitri.

Sergei ignored Dmitri. "You and Karina unleashed a historical chain of events. Do you *know* how many people look up to you? Thousands. Are rooting for you? Millions. The ex-Loyalist Police Chief and his unconventional, anti-Loyalist wife falling madly in love and changing the course of this planet. They'll probably write operas about you two in a hundred years."

"Karina is somewhat aware of things," said Avyer. *Our story isn't half as romantic as the people are making it out to be.* "She's in denial still."

"Can't blame her," said Dmitri. "It's a lot of pressure."

"It's a burden," corrected Sergei, "but it's worth it. I have more reason to complain. I've seen over seventy winters. I left a very comfortable, sizable farm to dodge bombs and bullets all this past year and a half. I should be in a rocking chair in front of a cozy fire, coddling grandbabies but instead I'm here fighting for my grandbabies, so there will be a Gavriila. After the hell this planet has been through, if I cannot take my place when I am needed, I've failed my family."

The antique clock on Avyer's desk ticked more loudly than before.

"I can't argue that." Avyer grudgingly broke the silence.

"The price you *will* pay will be serving the people. It is inevitable," Sergei said.

CHAPTER 67
UNCLE MISHA

DESPITE THE MEDICAL attention Karina had received, it took weeks for her to heal completely. Karina started exercising as soon as the doctors had cleared her. It would not do to be out of shape. *The fight might end tomorrow . . . or in ten years.* She might need to flee. She might need to fight.

The frozen landscape thawed and the snow disappeared to reveal the dead garden beside the governor's mansion. It was warm enough for Karina to exercise outside. Avyer spent an hour every morning with her. He drilled with her and analyzed her moves.

He showed her each step in slow motion, careful to not make her twist or make any sudden moves that could reopen injuries. The first time he did that, Karina's jaw dropped.

Avyer stepped back with confusion on his face. "What?"

"Who trained you?"

"I never told you?" He raised an eyebrow. "I thought I did. It was an ex-special agent. Went by the name of Mikhail Petrov. I don't—"

Karina clapped a hand over her mouth and swayed where she stood.

"Whoa! Are you all right?" Avyer was beside her in two

strides and wrapped an arm around her, ready to catch her. Tears shone in her eyes. "You never told me your uncle's name. Was he the same . . . ?"

Karina nodded and gripped his sleeve. "What happened to him? Do you know?"

"I wish I did. He was good."

"How long did you train with him?"

"Over half my police career. Then one day nine years ago, he didn't show up. I was still rising through the ranks. I didn't look for him. You?"

"Ten years."

"I brought back some memories, huh?" His arms wrapped around Karina like a warm blanket.

"You have no idea," she replied.

"Maybe you can tell me about it sometime."

Karina nodded.

The more Karina trained with Avyer, the more she realized how much he had always held back with her. Their sparring spectacles back in Avedida? Those were nothing in comparison with what Avyer really could do. Even when Karina had her emotions under control and was focused, he always got the upper hand.

As she grew stronger, he picked up the pace. She responded accordingly. When the doctors cleared her for physical contact it was time to move on.

Karina grew frustrated, tired of losing. When she became frustrated, Avyer stopped.

"Karina." He tried to soothe her. "Calm your mind. No emotion. Breathe. Relax."

"Thanks." She grimaced. "Even sounding like my Uncle Misha."

"I love your fiery, emotional soul." Avyer put a hand on her shoulder and ran it down her arm. "But it won't save you in a fight." Now his hand cupped her cheek. "You can do this. Save the rage for later."

CHAPTER 68
ATTACK

I ALWAYS KNEW *that there would be more fighting before peace,* Avyer reflected as he strode through the control center. *I also knew Sergei should not keep coming back to plan things.* The entire city was in an uproar.

"Bentuarians are pouring in from all sides, sir." A young man breathlessly saluted Avyer.

"Secure the president," Avyer said tersely. "Send an entire squad to evacuate him. I'll take care of things here."

Dmitri kept pace with Avyer. "And Karina?"

"Phones are down. Go find her," replied Avyer. "I'm in charge while Sergei is being evacuated. I can't go look for her right now."

Dmitri mumbled something to himself. "I'll do my best."

"If she and Sasha are together, she'll be fine. They're scrappy."

"Uh-huh," Dmitri murmured. "I hope so. Are you going to blame me if she's not safe?"

"Only if you don't stop talking. Go find her." Avyer glared at his friend. "Go! I can't think about her right now." *Worrying about Karina right now would only be an unnecessary, dangerous distraction.*

Dmitri understood. He ran to the military operations center. It was crowded but the officers moved quietly and calmly, in stark contrast to the mayhem outside.

"Excuse me." Dmitri tapped an officer on the shoulder. "I know you're swamped right now, but this is a priority."

The man let out an exasperated sigh. "*What* is it?"

"Nikolai's wife is out in the city. We don't know where. It is *urgent* to locate and secure her."

"No one told her to take a tour," the man snapped.

"This hadn't started when she left." Dmitri looked at him sternly. "Alert all units. She was going to the eastern sector. I don't think it's *that* necessary to explain *why* she should be found immediately."

"Very well." The man went to the communications hub. He took the central radio to alert all military units at once. "This is Commander Arvedranov. Priority: Karina Ivanovna is missing in the eastern sector. If you locate her, transport her to a safe zone and notify us immediately. Understood?"

"Thank you," Dmitri said when the commander signed off. He nodded curtly before he ran out in search of Avyer.

Seconds stretched out into minutes, minutes into a half hour, and the half hour dragged out to hours. Despite what he had told Dmitri, Avyer was on pins and needles. *Military personnel in position. President Bok on his way out.* That was all Avyer had been waiting for.

As soon as the President had been secured, Avyer tried to contact Karina. No answer. Not even Sasha answered him on her phone. Loyalists and Gavriilans alike were blocking each other's communication, effectively canceling out all signals.

He contacted every military and police person available. Nothing.

Avyer Nikolai raced between lines of firing soldiers, one block at a time, until he had made his way to the front line. "Any news of my wife?" he called to the head officer over gunfire.

The officer shook his head before he peered around the corner to shoot again. When he ducked behind the wall, he yelled, "Both you and command have asked me the same thing. No one knows anything. If she's alive, she can't get back here. There's a strong

Bentuarian front between us and where she was last seen. She'd be blown to bits if she tried to sneak past."

"Blast it," Avyer growled to himself. "There must be something we can do," he yelled back at the officer.

The officer grunted before he peeked around the corner and fired another volley of shots. "No one in their right mind would go to that side of the city."

Someone not in their right mind . . .

Avyer's eyes brightened. "Thank you for the inspiration!" He patted the officer on the shoulder and dashed back to the secure side of Zhovkva.

The officer grunted again. "Don't know what I did." He shook his head and continued his pattern of peeking out, shooting, and hiding.

Avyer ran heedless of the gunfire. "I need a cruiser and I need it now! Send one to my current position." A soldier hailed a cruiser for him. "Get me to the IPG headquarters, wherever it is right now." Avyer hopped in.

It was a short drive. The IPG had taken up residence in a modest house several blocks from the front lines. It was far from safe, but safer than the front lines.

Avyer bounded out of the cruiser, leapt up the steps and mashed the door button. "Hello?" he called out as the door slid open.

A feminine voice with a strange accent replied. "Yes?" A head of golden-brown hair poked around the corner of a door.

A voice promptly scolded her in another language: "Nicole! *¿Qué te dije? ¡Un día de estos te van a volar la cabeza!*" *

"*Lo sé, mi amor pero reconocí la voz,*" she responded in turn. "*Es el esposo de Karina.*" † She walked into the hallway and switched to Russian. "What's going on? Make it short and sweet. We're about to evacuate."

---

* What did I tell you? One of these days they're going to blow your head off.
† I know, my love, but I recognized the voice. It's Karina's husband.

IPG personnel were running from one room to another. Some carried strong boxes, others were armed and headed on a mission, and a few looked scared to death as though they did not know what they were doing.

Nicole was armed and had a sense of purpose about her. Her eyes were fearful but she had clearly been in similar situations. "Come on, come on." She beckoned Avyer to the back.

Karura Solari's feet were on a desk. He was talking on a radio with all the calmness of an experienced soldier.

"What's going on?" Nicole asked Avyer.

"Two things," Avyer gasped in English. "First of all, I would like to request IPG air support now. I know the Special Air Forces from Pentura are here on Gavriila. Now's the time to help us. I have all of my people out here doing their best. We are winning and can overwhelm the Bentuarian forces but the IPG will ensure a swift victory."

"Listen, Nikolai," Solari objected. "The SAFs aren't my own personal air force. We can't make that call."

Avyer looked between the husband and wife.

"I don't see why not." Nicole frowned. "*Last* time we helped we did almost overthrow the Bentuarians. The SAFs are sitting a few kilometers away, rotting. Don't you know the SAFs commander? Talk to him. It can't hurt."

Solari hesitated.

"If you don't ask you won't know," said Nicole.

Solari gave her a look. "What makes you think I'll ask?"

Nicole smiled coyly. "You know I'm right."

Solari scoffed but asked to be channeled to the SAFs commander. "Yeah, Joseph? It's Solari. We've a situation here . . ."

Avyer Nikolai waited for several tense minutes.

"Ok." Solari turned to Avyer. "You'll need to communicate directly with the SAFs. They've got their own interpreter and will be on their way as soon as you send the details."

"Great! The other thing: my wife is out there, missing. If the

SAFs are out shooting up the place, they need to know whom to not shoot."

The trio rushed out to the cruiser and sped to the Gavriilan headquarters. Solari and Nicole helped Avyer contact the SAFs and relay his instructions.

More seconds. More minutes. Another half hour. Several hours more . . . the sun was dying down, casting a strong orange glow that accentuated the smoking, exploding, rubble-filled streets. The IPG had routed quite a few of the Bentuarians, and they cleared over half the city of the invasion.

"Sir!" One of the men leapt to his feet, clutching his headset. "There's a ping on Karina Ivanovna."

"Where is she?" demanded Avyer.

"On the edge of the eastern sector, near the Yitomir bridge," replied a younger man.

"That's the front line. You'd be in the line of fire," another interjected. "She's in enemy territory."

"Doesn't matter." Avyer straightened his jacket. "Give me the coordinates. General Karahnsha, you're in charge. Work *in* unison with the IPG. If there's a very urgent matter, send a messenger."

"Yes, sir. And sir?"

"What?" snapped Avyer.

"Wear this just in case." The general handed him a Strev vest. "Better be safe than sorry."

Avyer strapped on the vest and accepted a helmet another officer handed him.

CHAPTER 69

PRECIPICE

KARINA AND SASHA shivered as they huddled inside the overturned dumpster. The temperature was dropping rapidly with the setting sun.

"We shouldn't have gone out," Sasha hissed.

They had been on the run all day. Their phones were useless, but they had a radio they turned on and off in hopes of making contact with Avyer or the Gavriilans.

They had been cornered in an apartment complex alleyway since late afternoon, when a squad of Bentuarians had nearly caught up to them. Enemy footsteps tramped all around the block, and heavy gunfire echoed on every side. It would be a matter of time before they were discovered and shot. Even Karina knew better than to try to fight their way out of this one.

"Get in and get further back," Sasha shoved Karina back in the metal box, burying her under mounds of garbage.

Karina half-gagged under slimy rotting piles of unknown refuse touching her face. "This is not going to protect us against most blasts."

Sasha raised a finger to her lip. "Quiet! And if we don't get out of here, I love you." Sasha wrapped her in a strong hug.

"Love you, too." Karina squirmed under Sasha's hug.

Their radio crackled to life, more loudly than they would have liked.

Karina yanked it from her belt, turning it on. "Ivanovna here, over."

It crackled again. "Nikolai . . . confirmation . . . loca . . ."

"We're being jammed," Sasha whispered. "Turn that karking thing off."

"Just let me send our location." Karina pinged the radio before she turned it off. *Perhaps that reached Avyer. I hope so.*

They huddled in the dumpster for what felt like hours. Shouting accompanied the gunfire. It came closer and closer to their dumpster. Something large and metallic struck Sasha's side of the dumpster, leaving a considerable dent. Sasha clapped a hand over her mouth to contain a scream. Karina's eyes widened at the sound of grinding metal.

Sasha edged over to Karina and shook her head vehemently. *Don't go out. Not yet.*

When the shouts and gunfire died away Karina turned the radio on again but kept the volume at its lowest setting. "Ivanovna here, over."

Dmitri's relieved voice broke the silence. "Send your location and reinforcements will extract you. Over."

Karina pinged her coordinates.

"Received. There's a team nearby. Stay where you are. Over."

"We're hiding in trash right now." Karina coughed. "Is it safe to come out? Over."

"Copy that. One moment. Over." There was a pause. "There are no Loyalists nearby, so that should be fine. Over."

Karina sighed with relief. She clambered out of the dumpster, giving Sasha a hand to pull her out of the trash.

"That was awful." Sasha wrinkled her nose as she wiped slimy bits of paper off her arms. "Remind me to not do that again."

"Yeah." Karina scanned the area. The team had not arrived. She leaned against the dumpster.

The blasts, explosions, and gunfire in the distance seemed to be moving away from them, toward the city center.

"Where do you think they're going?" Karina wondered aloud.

"Who knows?" Sasha shrugged.

A platoon rounded the corner of the apartment building. Karina tensed at first. Her shoulders sank in relief when she saw Avyer leading them. He rushed for Karina.

"Are you ok?" He wrapped his arms around her despite the filth coating her uniform.

"Yes." Karina leaned into his hug and sank her head on his chest. His warm body thawed her frozen bones. "What's going on?"

"Stepanov and Ternovvy led a Bentuarian strike team here," Avyer said tersely. "They got wind that we're here."

"Both of us?" Karina's brow wrinkled in confusion.

"Yes. Both of us. They hate you as much as they hate me."

Karina laughed. "What?"

Sasha rolled her eyes. "Undervaluing yourself as usual."

"Did you think they were coming after you just to get to me? Sasha is right," said Avyer. "They want us dead. There's a bounty on both of our heads."

Karina's jaw dropped. "And when were you going to tell me about this?"

"Now seems like a good time. Let's go find them. I hate to disappoint," said Avyer. He cued Sasha. "Follow the plan. Get up high." He spun Karina around to face Sasha.

"Right." Sasha ripped the *Ivanovna* tag off Karina's jacket, replacing it with her own *Bondaruk* one. She took a deep breath as she slapped Karina's tag on her jacket. "This will work."

"What?" Horror dawned on Karina's face. "NO!" She lunged at Sasha, but Avyer grabbed her by the shoulder and turned her to face him. He jammed his own helmet on Karina's head, adjusting the chin strap.

"I know what I'm doing, Karina." Sasha winked when Karina looked back at her. "I'll be fine."

"Viktor will take you." Avyer pointed his thumb at a tall blond soldier.

"Yay. Let's go." Sasha followed Viktor.

"What about me?" Karina frowned.

"YOU are not going anywhere. You are staying with me until this is over." Avyer's strong fingers interlaced Karina's.

CHAPTER 70
SASHA

VIKTOR GUIDED SASHA to a tall building overlooking the Capitol building entrance. A squad trailed behind them as they entered the building. The squad dispersed between the stairs and the lift to stay behind at intervals between the ground floor and the rooftop. Viktor and Sasha took the lift all the way to the top.

"They should be here soon," said Viktor. "Get set up wherever you like. The men guarding the stairs and floors will keep us safe so you can focus on what's down there."

"Yeah, yeah, yeah." Sasha cautiously approached the rooftop edge. Her breath caught in her throat as she peered twenty floors below.

"Where do you want this?" Viktor held up a long black case he had carried up for Sasha.

"Let me see." Sasha surveyed the ground below. Avyer had instructed her to defend the area around the Capitol building, specifically to watch his back as he led Karina and their people into the Capitol. "A lot of ground," she muttered to herself. If she were on the corner of the roof she would be at the perfect angle. *I would have preferred a flat surface.* The lip of the rooftop rose at an odd angle. "On the corner over there. Spot for me when the fun begins."

Viktor placed the case in the corner. She unpacked the pieces of the sniper rifle, expertly assembling the gun and resting it on a mount. It took a few minutes to adjust the mount and stabilize it, given the protruding eave. She scanned the stairs and adjacent buildings. There were a few stragglers, but no sign of Stepanov or Ternovvy.

"Tell me if you see anything. Are we sure they're here?" She made another pass around the area.

"Nikolai is certain of it." Viktor looked through his binoculars to help her scan the area.

"Ok."

"Bondaruk." Viktor's voice was sharp. "Nine o'clock."

Sasha whirled to the left. "See them." She eyed the group through the scope. "Bentuarian." A flash of khaki and black uniforms gave away their allegiance. "Be quiet."

Sasha let her jaw drop. She exhaled and closed one eye. She squeezed the trigger of her rifle once. One of the Bentuarians fell to the ground. *Clean headshot.* The others froze in shock as they tried to understand what was happening. Sasha took advantage of their hesitation and squeezed off two more shots to leave a total of three bodies on the ground.

"Get down!" Viktor warned as he dropped to the floor.

A blast spat at the corner of the building. Sasha dropped and shielded her eyes from chips of cement pelting her and Viktor.

"Clear?"

Viktor edged his way to the corner and peered over the edge. "No sign of them. Nikolai and his team at three o'clock." He beckoned for Sasha to return to the rifle.

Sasha spared the rifle a glance before looking through the scope. It was not damaged. She made out Avyer and his men. Karina was behind him.

Muffled shots rang out, but Sasha did not see anyone actively firing weapons. It sounded like an intense firefight was nearby.

"Anyone near them?" she asked.

"On their six," Viktor replied tersely. "Coming up on them."

Sasha swiveled the rifle downward. Three Bentuarians. Avyer's team knew they had company, and they fired shots. The Bentuarians were dead.

"Good work," breathed Viktor.

"Focus!" Sasha swept all around Avyer and Karina.

"There!" Viktor pointed at a building across from them. "Sniper. Third window down, first to the left."

Sasha's scope homed in on the building. She drew a sharp breath. There was indeed a Bentuarian sniper. He sat on an overturned box, taking aim at Avyer's men. She exhaled through her open mouth, relaxing her jaw.

A shot rang out behind her, but Sasha did not flinch. She squeezed the trigger, pulling off a shot at the man about to shoot Karina. "Got you." His body splayed backwards and he did not make a reappearance.

She eyed the side of the Capitol building. Avyer and Karina had disappeared behind the building.

"How are we?" she asked Viktor. She swiveled the rifle to look to the left.

A body hit the floor with a sickening thud. As Sasha whirled around to see what had happened, a strong hand grabbed the scruff of her coat. It dragged her to edge of the building. Sasha screamed. She kicked. She squirmed.

She caught a flash of black and khaki uniform as she tried to free herself. She stopped struggling when the hand forced her to totter on the edge of the building. It was a long way down, too far down to be struggling.

Gunfire ceased. Sasha shivered at the deathly quiet. A man with an impressive quantity of badges and bars clanking on his coat stepped beside her. He smiled mockingly.

"Got you, Ivanovna." He ripped the tag from Sasha's uniform.

Sasha gaped at him in horror. Many men had come with them to guard this building. Were they all dead?

The man put a loudspeaker to his mouth. "Hey, 'Chief' Nikolai," he roared. "This is what we think of you and your government!"

Don't come back, Sasha mouthed in a silent prayer. *Don't come back.*

He forced Sasha closer to the precipice. She was suspended between her coat collar and the eave . . . As she looked below one more time, her golden eyes widened in fear and her breath caught in her throat.

Kark it.

"Don't come back!" Sasha's yell was more of a strangled scream.

Avyer reappeared. His team peered from behind the side of the building.

I told you to not come back!

The next thing Sasha knew was that she was flying down, down, down, falling to the pavement. Icy wind screamed in her ears as she fell, and everything flew past in a blur. She could not hear Avyer Nikolai roaring with fury from the Gavriilan side of the conflict. She did not hear Karina screaming in agony.

It likely hurt, striking the pavement after falling from such a height. It might have been too fast to feel anything. Only Sasha would have been able to describe how it felt, but there was no asking her. Her lifeless body lay spread out on the sidewalk.

CHAPTER 71
FINDING THE LOYALISTS

TWO OF AVYER'S men grabbed Karina by the arms, yanking her to safety. They ducked back behind the building. Karina fell to her knees and let them drag her.

Someone's screaming. She was screaming. She could not stop screaming. She knew that had been out of Avyer's control. She knew that he and Sasha had been trying to keep her safe. That did not take away the pain. Nothing could. Nothing ever would.

She would never again look into Sasha's golden eyes. She would never hear Sasha's endless sighs. They would never chat about everyday life. Their relationship would have only been one of survival. Sasha was gone. *She's gone.*

Tears streamed down Karina's cheeks. Everything in front of her blurred. She heard several soldiers say her name. One of them gently shook her shoulder, but she could not move.

Gunfire came closer from the left.

Someone shook her shoulder harder. "Ivanovna!" The voices were more urgent.

Strong hands grabbing her from behind dragged her out of the street into the Capitol building. They lifted her to her feet, and one of the hands cupped her faced gently to force her to look up. *Avyer.*

His eyes burned with rage and regret. "I'm sorry! I'm sorry! I'm so sorry." He shook his head. "We've got to go, Karina. Stepanov and Ternovvy are inside and I am going to kill them. I don't want to leave you. Are you coming?"

Karina's breath came in uneven gasps as she tried to control her sobbing. She wiped her nose and blinked away the tears. "Which . . . one . . . is yours?" She choked through the words.

There was a glint in Avyer's eyes. "Ladies first."

"Ternovvy is mine." She gnashed her teeth.

"Let's go." Avyer took her hand as he radioed a team. "Nikolai here. Have the snipers been replaced? Over."

"All snipers in position. You are clear to go. Over."

Avyer signaled his officers to take their places. Two platoons made their way up chipped white marble stairs to distract the Bentuarians guarding the front door. Two other platoons flanked the building.

"And that just leaves the back," Karina croaked to herself.

"Going through the back," said Avyer. "Follow my lead. And for the love of everything holy, do what I tell you." He eyed Karina worriedly. "Are you sure you want to take on Ternovvy?"

"Extremely." Her voice was stronger. Her eyes were shining with deadly rage and a few drying tears.

"Stay sharp," Avyer said. "And stay right behind me."

Karina kept a few paces behind Avyer. She scanned all around them. Just because she was with Avyer and a whole platoon did not mean she could drop her guard.

They made their way through the back halls and passed many office doors. Many signs pointed to the open offices having been recently evacuated. Data sheets were strewn on the carpeted floor and chairs had been hurriedly shoved aside.

They reached a grand staircase branching right and left. Avyer motioned for Dmitri to take the right with one squad, while he and Karina went up the left.

Their surroundings changed as soon as they climbed up the

stairs. Sparkling gold walls stretched from the floor to the ceiling, with ornate white molding interrupting the golden sheen.

"Whoa," Karina breathed.

"Focus," Avyer warned.

Karina stopped admiring the walls. *If we survive this I want to walk around and admire the art.* Avyer punched a code in the door panel, and the decorative door slid to the side. She followed Avyer through the doorway, uncertain what to expect. She half held her breath, but there was nothing big or important behind the door. It was another decorative hallway. She exhaled.

Avyer did not hesitate as he made turns through fancy halls, ignoring closed doors and cautiously passing open ones. He led them to a hall ending in an immense double door locked with a code panel.

"One on either side." He split his men into two groups to flank the doors before he used his radio. He pushed Karina beside the code panel, behind him. "Nikolai here. Dima, do you copy?"

The radio crackled. "I'm here, Avyer." Dmitri sounded grim. "Reinforcements are behind you. Requesting instructions. Over."

"Are they in the throne room? Over."

"Confirmed. Over."

"We go in. There's a balcony in the next room. It's a rectangular room with columns on either side. Eight hundred square meters. Pay attention to what's above and below," Avyer said. "Over." He turned to his platoon. "Everyone got that?"

The men collectively muttered and nodded their heads. A few hissed through their teeth or sighed, but everyone shouldered their weapon, ready for the conflict.

"Move out in thirty seconds. Do you copy?" Avyer spoke into his radio again. "Over."

"Copy that. Over."

Karina swallowed. She wanted to catch Avyer's eye, but he was intent on punching in the code to open the doors.

"Stay close," Avyer told Karina as the doors slid open. He ran his hand down her right arm. "Behind me."

The doors opened completely. Silence fell over Avyer and his men as they grimly stepped forward.

CHAPTER 72
THE THRONE ROOM

NO ONE EYED the white marble walls. No one appreciated the embossed images set into the walls, the golden chandeliers sparkling above, or the ornately tiled floor under their feet. Everyone's eyes flickered nervously from the massive columns lining the throne room to the narrow balcony running the length of the room up to the throne itself.

And with good reason. The balcony was full of Bentuarian soldiers. Their black and khaki uniforms threatened to overflow the balcony. Countless weapons were trained on their group as they entered. Avyer judged there were eighty Bentuarians in the room.

Avyer's men swarmed to form a human shield around Karina and Avyer. Half of them trained their weapons on the soldiers in the balcony, and the other half aimed at the Bentuarians hiding behind the columns on the ground floor. Karina was jammed behind Avyer, but she caught glimpses of the throne as they stepped forward.

"Dima, Dima, Dima," Avyer muttered. His best friend should have burst through the doors behind the throne already.

Stepanov relaxed on the gilded throne, leaning into the velvety red upholstery as though he were sitting in an armchair at home watching the news. A gloating Ternovvy stood behind him.

"Finally," Stepanov growled. His cold eyes spotted Karina hiding behind Avyer before they rested on Avyer himself. "My ex-favorite police chief. It was about time we ran into each other. We've a lot to talk about."

Ternovvy stepped from behind the throne. "Including your lovely wife." As though they had run into each other while on a stroll in the park. He gave her a saccharine smile. Karina glared at him through the space between Avyer and one of his soldiers.

"What do we have to talk about?" Karina felt goosebumps as Avyer pronounced the words. It was the exact same tone he had used with her when he had pinned her to the Vadim stable wall. "I can think of quite a few things, but you could be more specific."

"Don't waste—" Ternovvy began.

"Well, we might begin with the fact that you've left our planet in shambles." Stepanov held up a hand to silence Ternovvy. He stood from the throne. "Then there's the fact that you, my most loyal public servant—"

Two explosions rocked the room and the doors flanking the throne were blasted inside the room. Avyer threw himself over Karina, which sent her sprawling to the floor. He shoved her behind several men.

"I'm fine!" she yelled at him.

"Stay down!" He shoved her helmeted head down. "If you want to stay that way."

A wall of Bentuarians descended from the balcony, forming a barrier between Avyer and Stepanov. A blast struck Avyer in the left shoulder. He fell to his knees beside Karina. Charred, raw flesh smoked where the blast had hit him.

His men tightened their formation around Avyer and Karina, shielding them from gunfire as Dmitri's platoon came in. Half of the Gavriilans sprayed the balconies with gunfire and the other made its way around the columns to eliminate the Bentuarians hiding behind them.

Shards of glass from the chandeliers rained down on everyone on the ground floor. Karina screamed and huddled. The helmet protected her head, but the glass fragments were like tiny daggers. They raked her exposed hands and wrists and stabbed her coat. Avyer shielded his eyes with his arm until one of his men put a helmet over his head.

When all the glass had fallen, Karina shakily rose to her feet and surveyed the destruction around them. She stood in a puddle of blood pooling from Avyer's soldiers. It was blood from the men who had been shielding her. While everyone was wearing a Strev vest, there was only so much damage the vests could take. Bodies were draped over balcony railings like laundry left out to dry. Blood spattered every visible surface.

But the Bentuarians had the upper hand. Ten remaining Bentuarian soldiers surrounded Karina, Avyer, and Dmitri. The trio stood back-to-back looking death in the face. Karina groped with her left hand to clutch Avyer's sleeve. It was wet. *Please don't be blood.* She wiped her fingers on her pants and gripped her gun more tightly with both hands.

The ten Bentuarians aimed their guns at the trio.

"Stop!" Stepanov raised a hand. "Not very sporting of me, is it?"

Karina looked out of the corners of her eyes. *Ten to three. Odds hardly in our favor. That leaves three to me, three to . . .*

Dmitri and Avyer exchanged glances. Avyer imperceptibly lifted his head. Both men dove at the soldiers' legs, bowling four of them over.

Karina dropped to the ground. She shot two Bentuarians through their visors before she rolled out of the line of fire. She leapt to her feet to wrench another soldier's arm behind his back. She used him as a bulwark to shield herself from one soldier shooting at her. She shot him and let her bulwark slump to the floor.

Karina analyzed the situation in seconds. Avyer was down to one soldier. Dmitri had managed to overpower his three but lay unconscious on the ground. His chest still rose and fell, but his blood was trickling from gashes in his arms and a wound in his side, adding to the immense pool of blood that nearly covered the throne room floor.

Stepanov and Ternovvy remained standing. Stepanov had a gun pointed straight at Avyer. Avyer had just slit the last Bentuarian's throat.

Karina's hand seemed to move in slow motion. It was not fast enough. It would not be fast enough. Everyone she loved was going to die today. *You're a mediocre shot on a good day.* Avyer's words rang through her head as she raised her gun and took aim at Stepanov's head. Ternovvy ducked to the side. *Coward.*

Avyer turned. Just as he turned Stepanov fired. A spray of blood flew from the side of Avyer's head. His eyes closed and he fell to the ground.

"No!" Karina screamed as she pulled her trigger harder than necessary. Once, twice, three times, four . . . She lost count of how many shots she fired.

What she did know was that Stepanov's bullet-riddled body fell to the floor, rolled down the small staircase leading up to the throne, and slumped to the floor of bodies.

"Just you and me," Karina snarled at Ternovvy. They both had their guns aimed at each other.

Ternovvy's hair was disheveled and his face was smeared with blood and sweat. Karina would have sworn that she could smell his fear. She tried to follow his movements with her body and her eyes but her helmet had been scratched so many times that visibility was poor.

"I don't fancy dying just to kill you. I'm not like Stepanov. I'll be sporting about it." He grimaced. With his eyes still on Karina he lowered the gun muzzle and bent to drop his gun to the floor. "Just you and me. You know that's what you want."

"You have no idea." Everything Karina had been through . . . her family nearly dying, Sasha dying, Avyer on the floor . . . had been too much. Karina removed her helmet and tossed it aside. She kept her gun up as she cast about the room.

Ternovvy laughed breathlessly. "They're all dead. Or if they aren't they will be soon. Put the gun down. It's just you and me."

Karina drew a deep breath. *Don't waste your words.* She mirrored his movement and slid her gun to the floor.

"You know." Ternovvy circled her. "I'm not so sure how much I believe you took on three men in one night, including Nikolai there."

"Find out."

"Oh, I have every intention of doing so. Shame. I really liked you. I was rooting for you for a while. Who would have thought you would corrupt Nikolai? Ah, well." He raised his fists in a defensive stance. "Plenty of fish in the sea."

And you'll be a dead one.

She did not, could not think about Avyer's inert body on the floor. Any emotional thought would distract her from killing Ternovvy. Memories of training with Uncle Misha and sparring with Avyer flooded her mind. *Save the rage for later.* Thoughts tumbled around her brain. *Breathe. Relax. Focus. Kill him.*

"I never went through Saratov, either," Ternovvy said as he took a step toward her. "It wasn't quite the right career choice for me. But you . . . look at you." His eyes raked her up and down in undisguised admiration. "You would have been perfect."

Glass shards incrusted Karina's uniform and Strev vest. Blood had splattered her entire uniform and soaked her boots. An ugly gash was oozing blood from her left upper arm and tiny cuts from the chandelier glass marred her hands.

Karina went on the offensive. She slowly closed the meters between her and Ternovvy. At the last minute she broke into a run and slid on the bloody floor. She ducked under Ternovvy's fist and swept one of his legs out from under him.

He fell to the ground, the breath knocked out of him. Before Karina could pull her usual arm-wrenching maneuver on him, he struggled to his feet and shoved her away from him. He drew a knife from his belt. The blade nipped past Karina's cheek.

It's what you do with what you have . . .

She let Ternovvy edge closer with the knife before she deflected his arm to the outside. She twisted it with a snap that sent the knife flying from his hand. She gripped his wrist. He leaned in with his other hand searching for her throat. Karina gave him a feral grin. *Not falling for that one.*

She released his wrist as she dodged his other hand. She was on the outside and kicked him in the small of the back. He slipped on the wet floor.

"You little . . ." Ternovvy roared in pain.

A rifle rested beside her foot. *Can I . . . ?* She crouched to snatch the rifle.

"Yes, I'm little," she spat. She swung the rifle with fury, bringing the butt to connect with Ternovvy's head. His head whipped back and he fell with a squelch in a bloody puddle. He remained inert, unconscious. "But there's no reason to be rude about it." She slid a belt off a dead soldier and tied Ternovvy's hands behind his back with a vicious knot. "That's for Sasha."

She glanced around the room. The doors were open, and more footsteps began to echo toward the throne room. Karina froze. Dmitri's backup poured through the doors.

"You're such an idiot." A weak voice broke Karina's paralysis. "I would have just shot him."

"Avyer!" Karina scrabbled to her feet, slipping and sliding in blood. She fell to her knees when she reached him. "Why didn't you . . . ?" The bullet that had grazed Avyer had carved a small path along the side of his head. Blood trickled down his cheek and ear.

"You had it under control." He smiled weakly. "And I was too dizzy to get up. I would have gotten in the way."

CHAPTER 73
CHANGES

AVYER NIKOLAI WAS stone-faced as he accompanied the highest military and political personnel to the Great Hall. The central heating had been fried in a firefight, so a roaring fire in the majestic fireplace at one end of the room was all that alleviated the winter chill.

Those seated at the table rose when Avyer entered. As Avyer took the head of the table he favored his sore shoulder.

"Please, everyone be seated and relax. This has been a trying day for all of us," Avyer said. "Doubtless you all know that President Sergei Bok was killed in a skirmish today. We had evacuated him from the city, but he left too slowly and his escort was ambushed. His remains are in the adjoining room if you wish to pay your respects. This means that the burden of the presidential position has temporarily fallen to myself . . ."

Dmitri nodded off in the corner of the table closest to the doors. Medics had performed emergency fusion surgery to close his wounds and they had filled his veins with all the right meds. The only relief from the talks was a much-welcome scalding cup of coffee. Despite the coffee, his head limply fell to the side more than once. He jerked back awake when he realized that Avyer was making his closing remarks.

". . . and while I cannot adequately express my deep appreciation for each and every sacrifice that . . ."

Dmitri grunted. What a smooth talker. Avyer would be an excellent politician. A soft hand fell on Dmitri's shoulder. He jumped in alarm.

"I apologize, sir," a woman whispered in his ear. She ran a hand through her short, greying hair and scratched her head. "It can't wait. The president's wife is asking for him, but I can't very well interrupt."

"I'll take care of it." Dmitri stood up so eagerly that he nearly knocked his chair over. Many curious faces turned toward him and witnessed his abrupt exit.

The woman showed Dmitri to a smaller hall. Karina paced in front of a small fire as though she were warming up for a race. Bags under her eyes betrayed her state of exhaustion.

"Hello." Alarm was clear on her face. "Where's Avyer? What's going on? No one told me anything after he left me in the infirmary."

"Follow me. Things are moving fast," said Dmitri as he escorted her down the hallway. "I'm sorry. I'm tired. You're tired. Probably in shock. Your husband is president."

"What?" Karina wiped silent tears rolling down her face. "Really?" She sniffed.

"Yes, really and truly."

Officials were pouring from the Great Hall by the time Dmitri had returned with Karina.

"Where's the president?" Dmitri asked the first person he saw.

"He's in the Great Hall by the fire," said a young woman with a pen tucked behind her ear.

"Thank you."

Karina trailed behind Dmitri as he entered the room. "Avyer?" He cleared his throat.

Avyer stood at the end of the room facing the fire. "Yes? If it's more business I don't need or want any of it."

"Not at all." Dmitri motioned for Karina to move beside him.

They walked closer to Avyer. When they were only a few meters away Dmitri spoke again. "Turn around."

All traces of annoyance disappeared when Avyer turned around.

Karina swayed slightly as she looked up at him. "Let's go to our room." She took him by the arm. "There are many ears down here, and I'm tired." Tears welling up in her eyes blurred her vision.

Avyer nodded robotically. They walked upstairs hand in hand. Avyer gripped hers tightly. When Avyer dropped her hand to close and lock the door behind them Karina slid out of her coat and sat on the corner of the bed. She held her head in her hands and let her eyes drop to the floor. *So much happened today. Should I cry for Sasha or be glad that he's alive?*

His coat rustled as he draped it over a chair near the crackling fireplace. Avyer's feet stopped where her eyes met the floor.

Karina was entertaining the idea of looking him in the eyes, but Avyer scooped her up from the bed to sit down and cradled her in his arms before she could make the decision. Karina yelped in surprise.

"What?" Avyer asked. His gaze of adoration and relief was so intense that she looked away, blushing.

"I thought I'd lost you." Her eyes shuttered.

"The thought was mutual. Let's not *ever, ever, ever* do that again," Avyer hugged her tightly, cupping her face with his hand.

"Agreed," Karina said quietly. She stretched out a hand to caress his stubbled, tired face. "Never."

As he pressed his lips against hers Karina leaned into the kiss. He rolled to the side to lay Karina on the bed. They lay there admiring each other. Avyer kissed her forehead, her cheeks, and her neck.

Karina closed her eyes as his hand caressed her cheek. It made its way from her cheek to her neck until it ran down her back. It came to a sudden stop at her waist and his other hand settled into the curve of the other side of her waist.

He drew her closer to him. Karina's heart pounded against his chest. She felt every breath he took, and she felt as though she were breathing in time with him.

"I . . ." The words caught in her throat.

"What?" The warm glow of the fire only deepened the warmth of his dark brown eyes.

Karina buried her face in his shoulder. "I love you." She squeezed her eyes shut.

"I loved you first," said Avyer. She heard the smile in Avyer's voice.

CHAPTER 74
CAPITAL

KARINA STRETCHED HER ACHING BODY. She shivered as her arms abandoned the warmth of the pile of blankets Avyer had heaped on her before he left for the day. She exhaled deeply to see if it were cold enough to see her breath, but it was not quite that cold in their bedroom.

A flood of feelings threatened to drown her as yesterday's events flashed through her mind.

Karina rolled over. *Sasha. Sergei. Avyer. Presidency. Now all eyes are on us.* Karina groaned and ducked under the covers. *I don't want to get up. What time is it?*

She poked her head out from under the covers and blinked. The sun glared through half-open curtains. Karina ducked back under the blankets, rolled over again and groaned as her body moved stiffly, sore from yesterday's fights. She remained in bed for hours, drifting in and out of consciousness.

Hours later the bedroom door opened and the lock clicked shut. Karina groaned in protest from under the blankets.

Avyer's hand rubbed her shoulder. "I've made arrangements," he said softly. "Everything's ready."

"For what?" Karina squeezed her eyes to stave off tears.

"Funeral for Sasha," he said. He massaged her shoulder as Karina processed his words.

"Why did it take so long?"

"The ground was frozen solid. It took a while to find a good place. We're waiting for you. Do you want to eat before we do it?"

Karina shook her head.

"When you get up, we'll go."

Avyer's frame descended onto the bed beside her. She wrapped her arms around him, and they lay there until she sat up.

"What time is it?" Karina looked around the dark room.

"It's eight p.m."

Karina leapt to her feet. "It's late."

"Yes."

"How should I go?"

"Wear whatever you'd like," said Avyer. "It's just going to be us. I tried to find her family. No luck."

A lump formed in Karina's throat. "She did say they didn't care about her that much. Probably dead or in hiding."

Karina slipped into a black shirt and black pants. She felt around the mantelpiece until her hands met with a stiff piece of fabric. Avyer had retrieved Karina's patch from Sasha's body. Karina slipped her and Sasha's patches in her coat pocket. Avyer took her by the hand as they walked out the door.

"Is it far?" she asked.

"No."

Avyer led her to the Great Hall. A handful of people surrounded a casket on the immense wooden table. As Karina approached the casket, she saw that the body had been enveloped in white fabric. A few flowers were strewn on Sasha's body and in the casket. Karina leaned against Avyer and choked back a sob. Tears overflowed, dripping down her cheeks.

There was no smell of death, only flowers. There was no blood and no indication that Sasha's body had been cruelly mangled. Avyer had seen to that.

Karina's entire body went weak as she leaned over the table to kiss Sasha's forehead. Teardrops dripped from her cheeks onto the white fabric.

"I'm sorry," Karina whispered. She reached into her coat pocket and pulled out the two patches. Her hand hovered over Sasha's body, hesitating. She pocketed Sasha's tag but placed her own tag on Sasha's chest, next to the flowers. "Keep it."

She endured the few people offering condolences and the long walk out to a cemetery on the outskirts of Zhovkva. She watched Sasha's body lower into the ground. Karina tossed the first shovel of dirt on the body.

Avyer watched Karina with worry in his eyes. Karina had not uttered a word after placing the patch on Sasha's body, but tears streamed down her face the entire time. At the end he wrapped his arms around her, pulling her tight to his chest.

Sobs wracked Karina's body. All the pain she had been suppressing came out. It was pure grief. Avyer silently held Karina while she cried and left large damp circles on his shirt.

A few of the attendees patted Karina on the back and gave sympathetic stares as they left the grave. Dmitri tousled his curly hair and raised an eyebrow at Avyer. Avyer shook his head and tilted it in the direction of a cruiser.

"I'll wait," said Dmitri.

Avyer nodded. He stood with Karina in front of Sasha's grave until her sobbing subsided. Karina raised her head and turned to look at the filled-in grave.

"I'm sorry." Avyer's thumbs traced the path of fresh tears up her cheek, up to her eye, and wiped them away.

"It wasn't your fault," Karina said thickly. She squeezed his hand.

"We can have a memorial meal now or later."

"Later." Karina took one last look at the grave. "When we put a headstone up. I can't do it right now."

Avyer nodded in understanding.

"I'm ready."

The next day dawned as frigid as the previous day. Karina shivered as she washed her face with ice cold water and pulled back her hair. She eyed herself in the mirror, scrutinizing her red face and puffy eyes. *That will have to do.*

She glanced at her old uniform coat on the chair by the fireplace. It was in tatters. Sasha's tag rested on the mantle once more. *I had to have something from her.* She pressed her lips tightly together as tears threatened to fill her swollen eyes again.

She forced her unwilling legs to walk downstairs. *Don't cry. The president's wife can't bawl her eyes out in front of everyone.*

"Where is President Nikolai?" she asked a servant downstairs.

"He returned to the government building early this morning." The young man bobbed his head in deference. "A lot going on today."

"How are people getting the news these days?"

"There's a few news channels running: two on TV and four or five radio programs," he said.

"Thank you," said Karina. "And what time is it?"

"Half past eleven." He checked his watch. "Anything else I can do for you?"

"Food and a phone," said Karina.

"Any particular order?"

"In that order."

"Please follow me."

He guided her to a private dining room. A servant stoked a roaring fire close to her chair and soon a hot meal in a warm room thawed her out. Another servant left a phone on the table.

She was about to leave when one of the female servants stopped her. "Lady Nikolai." She bobbed her head. "It's cold outside. I'll bring you a coat."

"I don't have a coat . . ." Karina began. *I'm not wearing that old one, never again.*

"The president had some clothing brought up. It just arrived," she explained. "Please give me a moment, and I'll bring it."

"Very well." Karina settled back in front of the fire.

Minutes later the lady helped her put on a thick winter coat and tucked a long scarf around Karina's face. As soon as Karina stepped outside, the chill air bit at her cheeks and dried her damp nose.

People milling about the streets bought and sold goods. Machines thrummed with regularity. Evidence remained from the other day's conflict: rubble littered the ground and tiny streams of smoke and ashes blew from burned out buildings. Blasts and bullet holes riddled some areas, while others remained relatively unscathed.

Karina felt as though Sasha should be beside her, sighing or making snarky remarks. More than once she turned to look at Sasha and her eyes met with . . . nothing.

This city looks like my life. All of it. I've lost people, I've lost things, and somehow I'm still alive.

"Good morning, Lady Nikolai." Many passersby greeted her.

Karina replied civilly. She rambled around the outside of the government building the servant had mentioned. After a few minutes she spotted a familiar face.

"Karina!" Dmitri waved her over. "You should not be out on your own. Looking for Avyer?"

Karina nodded.

"He's in a meeting right now. If you'd like you can wait for him."

"Where could I wait for him?"

"The office would be best," said Dmitri. "I'll let you in." He led Karina inside through a heavily carved wooden door. "Have a seat. I'll lock the door behind me. I've work to do before lunch."

"Thank you." Karina sat down.

"You're welcome. Have a good afternoon."

Dmitri keyed the door code after it slid closed. The lock clicked behind him.

So different from his first office, Karina mused as she took in her surroundings. She sniffed back a few tears and forced herself to look around. The marble walls were nearly bare, except for one picture of horses and hounds. *He must have added that.* Closer inspection of the walls revealed slight holes and indentations: likely there had been portraits of Bentuarian glory there.

Karina stepped behind the heavy black marble desk. "I wonder how many of these will be kept or thrown out," Karina murmured as she read the titles lining an expansive bookcase. *Law and history books.*

After an hour of standing she sat down and stared at nothing in particular. Tears leaked from the corners of her eyes now.

The door lock pinged as someone typed in the code. Avyer appeared in the doorway. He sighed as it closed behind him. Karina wiped away her tears.

"Dima told me you were here," Avyer said as Karina followed him to his desk. He sat.

"How are things?"

"As well as can be expected." Avyer leaned on the desk, propping his head up with one hand. He drummed the fingertips of his free hand on the desk for a few seconds. "I'm not going to bore you with the details unless you just have to know."

"Is there anything I can do?" Karina's eyes flickered from his drumming fingers to the intense look on his face.

"Mmm," he grunted. "Nothing that would be appropriate in this office." He drummed for a few more seconds before raising his head. "Do you feel like you still haven't done enough?" he asked.

"Yes." Karina avoided meeting his eyes. "Everyone is busy except for me."

"Come on." Avyer scoffed. He took her hand and pulled her next to him. "Look at me," he said, tilting her chin to force her eyes to meet his. Karina blinked and swallowed hard. She bit her lip to keep the tears at bay. "You've done enough. All you need to do now is rest, stay alive and be here with me. If you're intolerably bored, stay with me all day." He wrapped his arms around her. "If that's suffocating, go riding or sparring with someone. I'll have someone accompany you. You can't wander alone again."

"What do you *want* me to do?" asked Karina.

"Whatever makes you happy."

"That's not what I asked."

"I want you with me." Avyer pulled her into his lap. "All day every day. I don't want to be separated from you ever again, wondering where you are or how you are. After all you've done no one would deny you a place at my side."

Karina caressed his cheek with her hand.

"So what do you want?"

"I want *you*, to be with you." Karina kissed him lightly on his cheek. Once . . . twice . . . thrice . . . going down to his lips.

"Good." Avyer smiled. "Good." He met her lips with his.

CHAPTER 75

THE IPG

KARINA WAS CURLED up in an armchair with a history book when someone knocked on Avyer's office door. Karina started.

"You expecting anyone?" She looked up from her book to Avyer.

"Nope." Avyer checked his watch. He tapped the camera feed to see who was outside. "Not right now. Show them in."

Karina set the book aside and partially opened the door. "Yes?"

That IPG girl, Nicole, and her husband—what was his name again? —Karura Solari. He still gives me the creeps.

"Hello," Nicole greeted in her interesting accent. "I know we don't have an appointment, but do you and President Nikolai have a moment? We're on IPG business, albeit unofficially."

"Oh." Karina glanced at Avyer. He nodded. "Come in." She slid the door open the rest of the way and waved them in. *Do they ever change clothes?* Karura Solari only wore black, while Nicole dressed in shades of gray and black.

Karura and Nicole eyed their surroundings quickly—and Karina suspected, thoroughly—before sinking in the office chairs.

Karina took a place standing beside Avyer after she had closed the door.

"To what do I owe this pleasure?" Avyer began the conversation.

As before, Nicole interpreted for Karina: "The IPG is about to pull out its troops since everything is under control. However, they want to ensure your personal well-being."

"And exactly *what* would that involve?" asked Avyer.

Karura and Nicole exchanged glances. "The IPG is offering, in an unofficial capacity, our services as bodyguards."

Avyer laughed. "After all we've been through, does the IPG really consider that necessary?"

Karura answered thoughtfully, "The IPG is quite aware of your strategic genius, not to mention how you and your wife are accomplished fighters. However, things can happen to the best of us.

"I was Lautu Loman's bodyguard for several years, and thwarted multiple assassination attempts. Nicole and I recently broke up a major crime organization on Qinir. We are up to the task. Our job would be to foresee and prevent future incidents."

"Understood," said Avyer. "I have a lot of work today. I'll give an official reply by the end of the week."

Karura and Nicole nodded in acknowledgement. "Thank you." Karina showed them out.

"Well," said Avyer after she had closed the door. "What do you think of that?"

Karina shrugged. "They're a bit . . . different." She recalled how Nicole and Karura were so comfortable together, Nicole in his lap as he was piloting.

"How different?" asked Avyer.

"They're married."

"I know that. Watch them both," said Avyer. "Just their body language, what they say and what's left unsaid. Then tell me what's different about them."

"Solari doesn't speak Russian," Karina reminded him.

"Some things transcend language barriers."

The rest of the morning was uneventful. Karina finished another book while Avyer stared hard at his computer screen. Before lunch Avyer scrolled through the schedule. He frowned.

"Yes, you'll help me with this one."

"What one? What?" asked Karina.

"Meeting with IPG reps this evening. Call that blond IPG girl with her assassin husband. She can interpret. I don't want one of the run-of-the-mill IPG interpreters. IPG can use her and I'll have Dima find someone from our side of things."

"Why them?" asked Karina.

"They may be IPG people but they're freelancers." Avyer glanced up at Karina. "They're as disinterested a party as we'll get. Solari wasn't exaggerating: they took out a major gang on Qinir on their own. He checks out. His wife, too."

"What is she, exactly?"

"She's a dead shot. Before getting married she was a university languages professor."

"In short, neither of them necessarily have a vested IPG interest." Karina rephrased Avyer's observation.

"Exactly." Avyer scrolled through his calendar. "Go find them now. Please. Hopefully they've not gone far."

Karina wandered around the building until she found Nicole in the dining hall. "Hi." She slipped into line behind Nicole. "Could you do us a huge favor?"

"Some of the soup, please," Nicole told the server. "What kind of favor?"

"Interpreting."

"Oh, kark. Yes, a slice of that bread." Nicole kept her eyes on the next server. She did not look at Karina right away. "It's for the meeting tonight, right?"

"Oh." *Of course she knows.* "Yes. My husband wants on you the IPG side."

"Of course he does," Nicole murmured. "Tea, please," she said to the last server. As the server poured her a hot cup of tea she turned to Karina. "You do know I've not had time off for months? This meeting could last for hours."

"I know," said Karina, "and I'm sorry. I wouldn't have asked if it weren't important."

"I know," said Nicole. "I'll do it, but Karura will be there with me, and we get a day off tomorrow."

"Done," said Karina.

"Ok. We'll be there," said Nicole.

———

Avyer was pleased. "That will get us to a good start."

"Can I go with you?" asked Karina.

"Of course."

It was another dull afternoon. Avyer spent the entire time holed up in the office making conferring with Gavriilan military, strategically positioning troops around the planet. By the time they had to go to the Great Hall, Karina was sleepy. *I hope the meeting isn't as long as Nicole thinks it will be.*

The meeting began as soon as everyone was seated. "Would you do us the honor of opening the meeting?" The main IPG representative deferred to Avyer.

Nicole interpreted Avyer's response.

"Of course." He walked to the display screen. "The past month we've made quite a bit of headway. Thanks to IPG reinforcements, the remaining Loyalist leaders have been detained and Loyalist troops and police forces have been routed . . ."

Karina would have fallen asleep, had she not known the importance of the meeting. As the meeting dragged on Karina blinked back sleep. The voices droned on and on.

Nicole took sips of coffee between interpreting. *She was smart. I should have asked for coffee.*

Karina observed Karura Solari and Nicole Watson throughout the meeting, searching for what Avyer had mentioned to her. *What had he seen?*

She could not quite figure out what was going on between them. Nicole's finger twitched and she gave Solari a brief glance. He barely tilted his head as he raised an eyebrow. They were communicating something.

"Have you reached an agreement regarding leadership?" asked an IPG delegate. Karina had not caught his name, but he was probably important, judging from the glinting bars on his uniform.

"Yes," said Oleksaandra. "The committee unanimously confirms Avyer Nikolai as President Interim. He will hold office for three years while we organize all provinces for an official voting system and put the planet back together."

"Very well," replied the delegate. "And when will there be an official ceremony to instate Avyer Nikolai? I assume there will be a swearing in."

"Of course." Oleksaandra gestured for a colleague to continue the explanation.

Jaromir Igoshinov of Dnipro picked up the topic. "It will be held at the end of this week," he explained.

Karina started. *So soon?* Avyer had failed to mention that there would be a ceremony.

"Myself and the entire committee will be there," Jaromir said. "The Zarvii representative, Boris Balakin, will officiate in honor of our recently fallen President Interim, Sergei Bok. We'll send invitations out tomorrow evening at the latest. We are just ironing out a few minor details." He proceeded to explain the ceremony plans.

Karina's attention wavered. *What should I wear? Will I have to do anything? Everyone will be watching me.*

"That's excellent news, indeed," Nicole interpreted for another IPG official.

Karina's thoughts about the ceremony ended when she heard the words: "In conclusion . . ." Nicole was interpreting again. "This weekend, we'll announce the details of the agreement between Gavriila and the IPG."

"That is correct." Avyer nodded.

"Very well." The main IPG representative stood. "At the end of three years we will revisit the terms." He reached out to shake Avyer's hand, then rotated around the room shaking hands with the other Gavriilan representatives. "Thank you for your time. We'll be in touch."

The IPG officials left first. Nicole yawned shamelessly as soon as the IPG and Gavriilan officials alike had exited the room.

"Thank you," said Karina.

"You're welcome." Nicole continued yawning. "If you need us, we'll be in bed. Good night!" She checked her watch. "I mean, good morning. Or whatever."

Avyer gave Karina his arm and they stepped out a back door.

"I didn't know there was going to be a ceremony at the end of this week!" Karina exploded outside. "Why didn't you tell me? I don't know what to say. I don't know what to wear . . ."

Avyer put a finger to her lips. "Shush. Don't complicate yourself. You don't have to say a *thing*. Just look pretty. And before you fret over your wardrobe." He lifted his finger from her lips. "I already took the liberty of choosing what we'll wear. You don't have to worry about a thing. I've made you worry enough the past couple of years. I will worry for you." He took her arm and they continued their stroll to the mansion.

"Ok," Karina said slowly. She watched her breath float in puffy clouds in the air. "But I'm not ready."

"For what?"

"To be the president's wife. To have everyone looking at me and watching me every day."

"Well, you renounced that right the day you picked a fight with me." Avyer laughed. "Don't worry, we'll eventually have some ridiculous scandal or something."

"What?"

"I'm just kidding. Don't be ridiculous. You're perfect as you are and everyone loves you. I'm the one who needs to be careful."

CHAPTER 76

SWEARING IN

"YOU LOOK WONDERFUL." Sofia straightened Karina's dress. "Doesn't she, Mama?"

"Yes," said Viktoriya as she surveyed her older daughter's outfit. "You said you have to take off the coat when you're in the booth?" She looked askance at a winter coat on a chair next to the full-length mirror.

"Yes," said Karina.

"Good. Otherwise, no one would see how beautiful that dress is under that heavy coat."

"I think that's one reason the committee opted for a heated booth," said Karina. "Gavriila may have been kicked down, but we still have pride and want some pomp."

Viktoriya sniffled in approval. She blinked a few times.

"Are you ok?" asked Karina.

"Just . . . proud of you." Viktoriya gathered herself. "We'll be cheering you on outside. See you soon!" She put an arm around Sofia.

"Yes, see you!" Sofia called back to Karina as Viktoriya steered her out of the dressing room.

The guards closed the doors behind Sofia and Viktoriya. Karina sighed.

"So." Nicole came out from the corner. She had been silently watching the exchange between Karina and her family. Nicole tossed her braid to one side. "This is very nearly our last hurrah here on Gavriila. How are you feeling?" She crossed her legs and leaned against the wall.

"I'm not ready." Karina said. "It's a lot to do."

Nicole laughed drily. "I may not be the president's wife, but I do know that life throws stuff at you when you're not ready and you just have to deal with it as it comes. Can't ask or expect any more of yourself than that. Period."

Karina looked herself over in the mirror. *I wish Sasha were here. She deserved to see this day.* She ran her hands down the dress's long velvety skirt, brushing off lint from the dark green bodice. "I wish you and your husband the best," she finally said as she put on the heavy overcoat. "You deserve it."

"Thanks," said Nicole. She opened the door for Karina.

Avyer stood outside waiting for her. Karina's hand slipped into his.

"Feels like old times." She took a deep breath.

Avyer squeezed her hand reassuringly. "But it's not. It's new times. I love you."

"I love you, too." Karina squeezed his hand back.

"Thank you for being here." He kissed her forehead. "With me."

A lump filled her throat and her eyes watered as they walked down the hall to the Congressional Lawn. Avyer's steady arm hid her trembling arm. Karina swallowed. *Breathe. At least I don't have to say anything.*

"Just a little longer," Avyer said under his breath as they stepped up on an elevated stage in the center of the lawn, "then we'll be alone." He focused his eyes on the huge crowd surrounding the temporary stage and podium.

"President Avyer Nikolai and the First Lady, Karina Ivanovna." A man at the microphone introduced the couple on stage.

Karina did not know where to look first. Morning sunlight

glinted and glared off many camera lenses. A swelling roar rose from the crowd, followed by thunderous applause. Karina could not even begin to guess how many Gavriilans were in attendance.

Avyer waved with his free hand. He nudged her gently with the hand he held. *Smile. Wave.*

Karina smiled and waved. More roars came from the people. The lump in Karina's throat grew tighter. She looked up at Avyer. "Good job," he mouthed, drawing her close to him in a reassuring hug.

He was right. It's ok. We're ok. Everything will be ok.

Boris Balakin rose up behind them. Karina took her place behind Avyer as Balakin officiated the ceremony. Karina's legs shook despite the warm booth. *It's a good day to wear a long dress.*

Once the swearing in was done, it was President Nikolai's turn to give a speech. The crowd clapped and cheered as Balakin gave him the podium.

Avyer stood behind the podium but did not begin his speech. He looked back at Karina and extended his hand to her. "I didn't do all this alone." The microphone caught his words and they resounded through the lawn. Cheering turned into immediate silence as the crowd hung on his every word. Everyone knew this couple's story, but waited with bated breath. Was he about to share his side of the story publicly?

Avyer took a step back to Karina. She took his hand and they stepped up to the podium as one. Karina's stomach churned as she met the sea of faces staring at them. Avyer gave her hand a squeeze.

"Gavriila"—he began in a strong, clear voice—"this is indeed a great day. I was just informed that ninety percent of the planet has been liberated of Bentuarian forces, thanks to the coordinated efforts of Gavriilan and IPG forces. I thank those of you here today, and wish to salute and remember those who fell in battle. On a personal note, I wish to remember Sasha Bondaruk and Illya Melnyk, both of whom sacrificed themselves for your current first lady. None of them died in vain nor will they ever be forgotten. Let us have a moment of silence, in their memory."

The enormous screen behind them filled with images of skirmishes and conflicts, as well as hundreds of photos of those who had died. The crowd froze, eyes glued to the screen until the last image had faded.

Only when the memorial video had finished did Avyer resume his speech. "We have an arduous task ahead of us. I call upon all Gavriilans to work in unity. Together we can achieve great things.

"I hope you can forgive my using a more personal example: it is like a marriage. There you unite two very different people with similar goals. Take my wife and I: anyone looking at us sees substantial differences between the two of us."

A ghost of a smile flitted across Karina's lips.

"I came from a long line of police and military people. In my past life I would have called Karina a commoner. However, Karina is one of the noblest people I know, and I consider myself in stark contrast, most savage. I married her so she wouldn't be sent to the Saratov Trials, because I love her. You might say that our freedom is her fault."

Karina took quick, shallow breaths. She forced herself to keep watching Avyer. She peered out of the corner of her eye at the audience. They were hanging on Avyer's every word.

Cameras panned over to Karina to project her and Avyer on the big screen behind them. When she realized that they were on the big screen, Karina's eyes flitted around nervously until she met Avyer's gaze. There was nothing but warmth in his eyes. She was trapped, bewitched with the rest of the crowd.

"We need to work together to focus on ourselves and our world. We are stronger and better together." He wrapped his hand around her waist. "This is the beginning of a new, better life. I thank you all for your devotion to our planet, and I pledge myself to you all and its restoration. Thank you." He half-bowed to the audience.

As if on cue, the Gavriilans let out a deafening roar of

approval. Karina followed Avyer from the podium. They made their way to the Congressional Hall for his first reception as President of Gavriila. Their personal Gavriilan guards went ahead, and the IPG mercenaries trailed behind. None of the media could follow them.

When they reached a narrower hall Avyer pushed Karina against a wall, not ungently pinning her wrists against the wall. Karina glared at him and fought her instinct to give him a savage kick in a weak point. "How long do you want to live?" she threatened.

"A nice long life with you." Avyer laughed. "But I wanted to tell you something." He laced his fingers through hers, leaning closer as though he were about to kiss her.

"What?"

"Thank you for causing so much trouble."

Karina twisted around and shoved him against the wall. *He's not even trying.* Karina's soft but strong arms wrapped around his neck, and her lips met his. Time slowed as she pressed her lips into his. The desire in her eyes contrasted to his startled but not displeased expression.

"You're welcome."

ABOUT THE AUTHOR

L. A. Tucker is an emerging dystopian author. This is her debut novel. She is completely bilingual in Spanish and English and has dabbled in Russian. She's an avid reader, and loves to lose herself in a good sci fi or dystopian novel, as well as stories that combine realistic and fantastic elements. She prefers to write with more than one culture in mind because our world is more than any one country or continent. In her free time she enjoys reading, art, gaming and hanging out with her dogs. She has four Chihuahuas: Niko (Nikolai), Dima (Dmitri), Agatha, and Midna. Any of those names sound familiar? Guess which one was with her as she began writing this novel.

LOMAN BLOODLINE SERIES

COMING SOON...

She has amnesia.

He's a Sentinel mob boss.

Remembering could kill them both.

Joon Ren maintains perfect control of his planet—until he acquires a valuable young woman with amnesia.

He names her Ha-Yun, and he soon realizes she's the eye of a deadly storm: militants pursue her, rival gangs begin to defy Ren, and a foreign power insists upon an alliance.

Neither enemies nor allies will wait for Ha-Yun to recover her memory, nor give her and Ren time to explore the dangerous bond they've formed to survive.

Can Ha-Yun remember her past before it catches up to her and destroys them both?